INSTEAD OF EDEN

h, with
the air.
nd the
st with
y in the
erhead,
s a vast
blue sky. Chloe knew nothing about the universe but she felt the greatness of the earth. Even in her depression, she couldn't ignore its challenge. She knew she would not kill herself, baby or no baby. And certainly not in such dank and dirty water. Not now, not ever.

Placing her hands over the firm, rounded bump in her abdomen, she set off down the towpath with new resolve. Somehow she would find something better.

For my husband, Tony

INSTEAD OF EDEN

Alice Mitchell

A STAR BOOK
published by
the Paperback Division of
W. H. Allen & Co. Plc

A Star Book
Published in 1988
by The Paperback Division of
W. H. Allen & Co. Plc
44 Hill Street, London W1X 8LB

First published in Great Britain by
W. H. Allen & Co. Plc in 1985

Printed and bound in Great Britain by
Anchor Brendon Ltd, Tiptree, Essex

ISBN 0 352 31846 5

I am not Jennifer,

Nor is Beth my mother;

Chloe Moffat did not exist,

So do not look for one another!

PART I

CHLOE

'Footfalls echo in the memory
Down the passage which we did not take
Towards the door we never opened
Into the rose-garden.'

T.S. Eliot
Burnt Norton

CHAPTER ONE

It was a hot and brilliant day in June. One of those rare jewels of a day when the trees, undisturbed by any wind, hang breathless and startlingly green in the air and the tar on the roads begins to melt and crack and run into oily trickles. The sky behind the trees was blue, shading into dusty white where it met the horizon. Chloe's house was silent and dark and she could not bear it.

The clock on the mantel measured away each hour, chiming oppressively every quarter. Everything was in its place. If she went blind tomorrow she would still find it. She had no need to straighten the antimacassars on the heavy wooden furniture nor to sweep the clean but fraying carpets. Nevertheless, there was a faint smell of must about the parlour which she could not get rid of, no matter how hard she tried. It depressed her because she knew it was the pervasive aroma of age.

In the kitchen, she washed and wiped the pots and pans from lunch with tired hands and stacked them all away. Willie had painted the kitchen for her recently. Previously it had been brown.

'Lighter and brighter, please,' Chloe had requested. 'You know, more like Beth's.'

After all this time she still longed in her heart for 'nice things.' Willie had painted the kitchen beige with a job lot of paint – all of it – ceiling, walls, woodwork and doors, all beige, and a tide of despair rose within her every time she looked at it.

On the dot of five – never any earlier and certainly no later – she would be in here again, setting out their plain white teacups. Willie's looked as if it belonged to a giant; her own was smaller but hardly dainty. She would mash the tea and butter the bread very sparingly, laying out a thin strawberry jam which wouldn't stick to the knife and just two small slices of currant cake. She would do it all as she had done it for years. Until then she wanted nothing to do with the kitchen.

Willie was working in the garden and, because it was hot, he had put up a deckchair for her in the shade. It was good of him really, Chloe thought sadly. But there was a terrible restlessness inside her today. The house was suffocating but the garden would be no better. She could not bear to watch the stubborn look on Willie's face as he patiently hoed the vegetable patch, nor to have her remarks grunted at all afternoon.

No, she had to go out. She really wanted to see Beth, because they had had a disagreement earlier in the week. But her daughter had already driven past the house this morning, pressing an elegantly heeled shoe down to the floor as she shot past in her white Spitfire. Beth was evidently not yet ready to forgive. So it would have to be Dorothy instead.

Despite the heat, she slipped a dark coat over her navy print dress in the way that old people do, whatever the weather, as if it were eternally winter in their hearts – or at least their bones. Then she pinned on her hat over the grey hair she wore coiled and netted in a tight little bun. Sighing a little, she picked up her gloves and bag and checked to make sure that her purse was inside.

Willie had rolled up his shirt-sleeves above the elbow and secured them with metal bands. His back was bent and the sun beginning to redden the top of his bald head.

'I'm off to Bradford,' said Chloe.

'Nay, not shopping agen.' Willie's back emanated disapproval though he did not look up.

'Not shopping,' agreed Chloe, pulling on her gloves. 'Just going to see Dorothy. I may not be back in time for tea.'

She turned away and he heard the garden gate click open, then shut on the little terrace house where she had cooked and washed, mended his clothes and polished his boots and served him in such utter dreariness for so many years.

He sat back on his heels, hesitating, slightly incredulous over tea. She was wearing her best hat, the navy straw one with the wide brim and the white rose and he could see it bobbing determinedly away from him up the lane. There was something in her manner that almost made him want to call her back. But he shrugged his shoulders and dug his trowel into the dry earth again.

On her way up the lane to the bus-stop Chloe had to pass the church. Beside it stood the vicarage orchard with the grey chimney-pots of the vicarage itself just visible above the trees. The blossom was tired and almost gone now. A gaggle of geese, introduced by the latest incumbent, trampled its soiled remains. The wall between orchard and graveyard had crumbled this winter so that the bolder geese were able to waddle and cackle amongst the graves themselves. Everything was overgrown and the church itself decaying. The bells hadn't been rung for eight years because they were unsafe and the parish lacked the funds to repair them. The roof was holed and, inside, Chloe knew that the plaster was peeling. The Reverend Samuel Henry Wordsworth Kaye would have found it a sorry state of affairs. It was as well he was long gone.

Chloe was only seventeen when she entered service with the Reverend Kaye in the spring of 1906. Her greatest dream was that her Aunt Elsie, recently emigrated to

America, would one day send for Chloe to go and live with her, as she had promised. Until then she must be a maid or work in the mill. She had chosen service and the local carrier put her down outside the gates of Sowerton vicarage one Friday morning towards the end of March. The ruts in the drive were full of puddles for it had been raining hard and he didn't want to risk his cart getting stuck. Up on the moors above the village, the rain was still sheeting down from a pebble-grey sky. Down here, in the lee of those hills, the rain had stopped though the dark, dank leaves of rhododendrons still dripped onto the drive. There seemed no colour anywhere in the world. Certainly not in the vicarage of Pennine stone which now loomed before her. It was the first time Chloe had ever been away from home.

To her horror the Reverend himself answered the door. He had been pacing the full length of the hall in pursuit of a sermon forming with some difficulty in his mind and was not one to tolerate jangling doorbells. He eyed her with disapproval for she was a good-looking girl and that was the last thing he desired in a maid, or in any woman come to that. Her brown eyes looked back at him out of a pale face, frightened as a doe rabbit's. But it was her auburn hair he really objected to. For although it was plaited and twisted neatly enough out of harm's way on top of her head, it hinted of a certain luxuriance.

Chloe was equally dismayed by the sight of her prospective employer frowning on the doorstep. She thought she had never seen such a physically powerful man, as he was both heavy and tall. He also sported impressive black whiskers which burgeoned about his cheeks and upper lip but spared his chin and the blackness of his parson's clothing added a final note of severity.

But he managed to smooth away the frown and shake her hand and welcome her to the parish before the housekeeper appeared, hastily wiping floury hands, and took her upstairs to Mrs Kaye's sitting-room. The house seemed very grand to Chloe with its ceilings way above her head whilst the broad and splendid staircase she climbed spoke of endless polishing; but she rather liked it all the same.

'You mustn't be afraid of my husband,' said Mrs Kaye kindly. 'So many people are. I suppose it is his manner and his bearing. But really Samuel is the gentlest of men.'

'Yes, ma'am.'

Chloe found the conversation a little strange and was not convinced. She shivered slightly. The windows of the room were wide open despite the chill in the air and a feeble spring sun, which had now broken through the clouds, flooded through, lighting brocade and mahogany, only to fade as suddenly as it had come.

Mrs Kaye was the perfect antithesis of her husband. Small and mild and as slight as Chloe, she was also severly lame in one leg and walked with a stick. She was also dressed in black and this included a frilly bonnet which covered her grey hair demurely, though these were now well out of fashion with the passing of the old Queen. Chloe thought her very elderly then, but in fact she was only in her fifties and had been a life-long invalid.

'He has his rules, of course,' she was saying. 'Every household has to have discipline. But you will not find us unnecessarily harsh. Mrs Feather here, our housekeeper and cook, will see you know what to do. I am afraid you will find us rather quiet. But it's a big house to look after and you won't have idle hands. Doubtless you may be surprised to find you are the only maid. But remember there is less fear of losing God when you are hard at work.'

Chloe felt instinctively more at home downstairs in the hot kitchen. Mrs Feather hung her wet coat to dry by the range and made her a cup of tea.

'You'll have to work hard, love,' she said, banging

away with her rolling-pin and making her fingers all floury again. 'I hope your mam's trained you proper! But they're not a bad old pair, the vicar and his wife. Oh, he rants and raves somethin' shockin' from t' pulpit. But he'd give the shirt off 'is back to a stranger. I've been with him long enough, so I should know. Of course we have to go to church twice on a Sunday, but that's only natural for decent folks, i'nt it?'

Chloe dared not mention that her family had been unusual in attending neither church nor chapel. Her father, for some unexplained reason, hated them both 'and Romans worst of the lot'. It was her mother who had arranged for her to enter a religious household, although she too was banned from churchgoing and had once had her bible burnt.

Mrs Feather nodded as she paused to line her pie-dish, fluting the edges of the pastry firmly with her red and beefy hands.

'Definitely no gallivantin' on a Sunday' she said.

'Gallivanting?' Chloe repeated shyly.

Mrs Feather chuckled. 'Not much opportunity for it round here, I 'spect you're thinking. Not compared to Bradford. Don't you believe it! You're a pretty one, Chloe and all the village boys'll be after you. Such a little tiddler too. Just be careful, that's all, and mindful of your mam . . . and I'll do my best to stand in her place whilst you're here.'

The last sounded encouraging. Surely life at Sowerton could not be too bad with Mrs Feather as her ally and mentor?

But the very first Sunday at the vicarage gave her nightmares. The Reverend Samuel Henry Wordsworth Kaye's sermon was to blame. It was a beautifully fresh Spring morning, the skies colourwashed clean after rain and the sun deceptively bright with the promise of summer to come. Encouraged by its rays, a few daffodils were nodding into flower around the stone buttresses of the church. The Reverend pointed them out with his walking-stick and claimed them for God.

'Behold! The Lord renews his promises in the golden trumpets of Spring,' he declared, warming up for what was to come. 'The Feast of his Resurrection is almost upon us.'

But the wind felt bitter as their solemn and halting procession rounded the south side of the church. It struck them in the face, catching the Reverend's cassock and making it flap like the wings of a crow, and causing the frills on Mrs Kaye's bonnet to flutter violently like a black paper windmill. Inside the church all was dark and quiet. There is something about a dimly lit church interior which hints of mystery and sanctuary even to a non-believer. Chloe knelt happily enough to pray, then watched the other villagers file and shuffle in to take their places. The bells which had seemed so loud outside the church were muffled and faint within. Then they stopped altogether and the organ took over, creaking a little at each change of key. Chloe amused herself by watching the patterns the sun made through the stained glass of the east window. She felt a little tired and the peaceful atmosphere comforted her.

Then the Reverend reappeared and the congregation rose as one man and broke into lusty song. Chloe did her best to sing up as Mrs Feather had intimated this was expected of her, though she only had a weak voice. When the time came for the vicar to take the pulpit, she settled herself back in the pew attentively, anxious to please.

The Reverend waited until all the shufflings and coughings died down. He stood stiffly to attention with lips pursed and hands folded while his eye roved around the congregation noting the precise position of any gaps for future reference. Then, gripping the stone of the pulpit, he leaned forward and glowered darkly at them all, his magnificent whiskers bristling with indignation.

'Sodom and Gomorrah!' he thundered, so loudly that Chloe jumped. He swayed back slightly on his toes, surveying his effect, then pitched forward into battle again.

'A long way from Sowerton and Braithewaite, you might think!' was the next bellow.

'But I tell you no! A thousand times no! Lent draws on to its close but we must be ever more wary, for temptation is all around us. The sins of the flesh are as well represented here in our little village and its neighbour as in Sodom and Gomorrah. What man or maid amongst you has not entertained the thought of them?'

More than one pair of male eyes, fastened inquisitively on Chloe as Mrs Feather had predicted, swivelled hastily away.

'But I tell you, as the Lord himself told us, that these very thoughts are evil as the deeds themselves! Oh yes, my brethren, we are all sinners in His eyes . . . some of us more than others.'

The Reverend Kaye looked round sharply at this point, as if about to divulge the very names of these unfortunates. A few bottoms fidgeted awkwardly on seats and a finger or two tried to ease a stiffly starched collar. Then that powerful voice reverberated around the aisles again.

'We must beware of trivialising these sins of ours, my brethren. We must not think them so very unimportant. We must be fully aware of them and repent . . . yes, I say to you *repent* – NOW – before it is too late and we feel the scorching heat of the flames of hell licking at our feet! If we do not, then Judgement Day, which comes to us all, will find us sorely ill-prepared. Then how we shall moan as our limbs are torn apart and our eyes wrenched from their sockets.'

There was a great deal more of this and Chloe listened to it all in horror. It did not occur to her that the Reverend was putting on a performance and a pretty unoriginal one at that. Deep in her heart, she couldn't really believe in such rough justice. Some of her father's healthy scepticism had tainted her. But the Reverend was an educated man, a man of breeding, a superior being. He had to be right. To question his judgement was tantamount to questioning the laws of the universe – or at any rate the laws of Edwardian England which seemed much the same thing.

By the time the Reverend had finished and the congregation rose for the offertory hymn, Chloe felt quite disturbed. If she had known that the eyes of at least one young man had returned to her face she would have been mortified. As it was she was far too nervous at the prospect of serving the Reverend Kaye with his Sunday lunch to notice.

Chloe's room sat at the very top of the vicarage, up the attic stairs. It had only a poky little window with no view for it was surrounded by trees. When the window was open, Chloe felt as if she shared the birds' nests among the boughs. At night the stirring of the leaves sent her to sleep and it seemed a safe enough haven.

One Saturday afternoon, a fortnight after her arrival at the vicarage, Chloe sat at a table in front of the open window, penning a letter to her sister. She wrote neatly and laboriously, paying rather more attention to the handwriting than the spelling or grammar.

Dear Dorothy,

'After two weeks here I am beginning to settle down very well. The work is not too bad as the house is very quiet, though there is such a lot of it I am on the go all day long. Mrs Feather the housekeeper tells me what to do but she is very kind. She does all the cooking though I help her when she asks. I also have to serve at table which gets me all worked up. The cleaning is less trouble although it's hard work. I help Mrs Kaye dress sometimes too but I don't mind that. The only thing is I get ashamed of my hands then because they feel so rough and hard from making up the fires and polishing and washing. The Reverend and Mrs Kaye have also been kind although he frightens me half to death, I must say, especially

in church when he looks so fierce and shouts something awful, really I don't know how we all stand it but of course we do . . .

Somewhere in the depths of the house a bell rang and startled Chloe, making her smudge the ink. She sat up straight and listened. Mrs Kaye was taking a nap and the Reverend was out on sick calls. But the doorbell had been rung and rung again persistently.

She hurried down the stairs, trying to tie her apron and pin on her cap as she went. The bell rang again. Couldn't they wait? It was a long way from the top of the house to the front door and she was afraid that Mrs Kaye would be disturbed in a minute or that Mrs Feather, who also had her feet up before the fire no doubt, would emerge from the kitchen. But Chloe managed to get there first, out of breath and becomingly flushed.

It was one of the bellringers – Willie Moffat, a young, good-looking lad of about twenty with fine blond hair like pale silk and grey-blue eyes. He touched his cap but did not take it off.

'Begging your pardon, miss, but could I be having the tower key?'

Chloe was uncertain. 'You're ringing this afternoon? Mrs Kaye is resting.'

'Nay, not ringing. I'm just going up to do some work on t'bells.' He indicated a bag of joiner's tools beside him. 'One of the stays got broken last Sunday . . . gave old Oliver quite a turn.'

'Oh, I see.'

Chloe went to fetch the keys from the vicar's study.

Willie took off his flat cap and twirled it in his fingers, smiling at her puzzlement.

'You've never seen a bell then?'

'No, never.'

'Why don't you come up with me and take a look?'

'Oh, I couldn't leave the house right now,' said Chloe, suddenly bashful.

Willie took the keys from her hand.

'Another time then?'

'Yes . . . I would like that.'

'When you're allowed off.'

'Yes.'

'Let me know then.'

And he carefully replaced his cap on his head and swung off down the drive. How tall he was, thought Chloe, watching him go. And how fit and healthy looking. There was a lot of confidence in the way he carried himself as if he was sure of his place in society and satisfied with it. She envied him that.

Back in her room, she dipped her pen into the ink-well again.

All in all, it isn't a bad life here. But a bit lonely. I don't really know anyone yet. I think the villagers look on me as a bit of an outsider. Still, the village is pretty enough . . . so green after Bradford and so quiet and clean. At first I thought it was bleak when I saw all the grey stone and the grey walls everywhere and the moors above the village, all of it in the wind and the rain. But now the weather is improving, I can see it can be nice.

She hesitated, then carried on, pressing the nib down more firmly:

Sowerton is quite satisfactory as a temporary measure in fact. But is there any word from Aunt Elsie yet? Sometimes I think she will forget and never write but I know she meant what she said and cannot be properly settled yet.

Here, she gazed deeply into the mass of leaves around the attic window and allowed herself to dream without restraint. America! There was never a day go by when she didn't think about it. Elsie had promised to write for her – the eldest girl in their family – to go out as a companion and help, as soon as she had enough money to send the fare. Chloe knew she must be patient.

Looking forward to seeing you on my day off at the end of the month. I hope all is well at home and Father not drinking.

Give my love to him and Mam, all the boys, especially Matt, and of course yourself and Daisy. Your ever loving sister, Chloe.

She sighed as she finished off. Supposing Aunt Elsie never made enough money to send for her? But that was unthinkable. America was the golden land of opportunity and, although Aunt Elsie's husband was no good, Aunt Elsie herself was indomitable and would make his draper's shop succeed. Chloe knew she would keep her word. There was no one on earth she admired and respected more. She wished she could have been like her but knew already she wasn't made from the same mould. Elsie would teach her things though. And America would mean a new and entirely different life . . . far away from these confining hills which tightly bound in the claustrophobic valleys.

At the end of the month, Dorothy was waiting for Chloe when she got down from the tram in Forster Square. They hugged each other enthusiastically. It was Chloe's first day off. She laughed as she looked around her at the station's grimy façade, the horse-drawn and motor traffic, the shops and the stony streets which climbed steeply up in every direction from the centre of the city.

'My . . . isn't it busy?' she said. 'I'd forgotten already!'

'Let's go and have a cup of tea,' Dorothy begged, 'and a bun. Mam said we could.'

Chloe agreed, savouring her freedom and the feeling of money in her purse, little enough though it was.

In the tea-shop she asked about home.

'Mam's not been too well, but she's all right now,' said Dorothy. This was nothing new. Their mother was a frail and tired woman who sat around the house looking bewildered, letting her daughters organise her. With hindsight Chloe realised she had been worn away into that state by the strains of poverty and too many pregnancies too quickly.

'Is Father at home?' she asked.

'He is now. He was off drinking again earlier in the month though. Matt paid the rent again.'

'How is Matt? I do miss him!'

'He's fine. Got a new girl as usual.'

'What's she like?'

'Pretty,' admitted Dorothy reluctantly. 'Thinks she's a cut above our family because her Dad's a clerk in t'mill, not just a hand. She works in Linyard's on the haberdashery. Her name's Polly.'

They drank their tea and Dorothy looked reflective.

'She said I might be able to get a job there in the Autumn.'

'Would you like that, Dot?'

'I wouldn't mind. Better than t'mill. If I could but get it. Happen she'll put in a word for me. But do you think Mam'd be all right on her own all day?'

'Well, she wouldn't be, would she? She'd still have Daisy most of time. 'Bout time she pulled her weight.'

Dorothy's face became very red. 'I've got somethin' to tell you, Chloe,' she said. 'Only I don't know how to.'

'What is it?'

'You won't like it.'

'Goodness, tell me quick.'

'Aunt Elsie's written.'

A cold finger of fear stole over Chloe.

'What's happened to her? Is something wrong?'

'No, nothing like that. She's doing quite well now and she's sent the money for . . . for Daisy to join her.'

Chloe stared at her sister's embarrassed face. 'Daisy!'

'Yes.'

'But she's only fourteen!'

'Yes.'

'She said she'd send for me.'

Dorothy nodded helplessly.

'Why should she change her mind, Dot? Why? I would be of more use to her . . . so would you, come to that! It's not right it should be Daisy. It's not fair!'

'I know it's not. I'm sorry, Chloe.' Dorothy was almost

equally distressed. 'I expect she changed her mind because she can't have children and she wanted the youngest of us after all. I don't know. Maybe she thought you were settled in service now.'

'Settled in service?' Chloe repeated emptily. 'But how could she think that? How could anyone think that?'

'Well, you did sound quite happy with it in your letter from the vicarage.'

'I did not!'

'You did too!'

'But not forever, Dorothy . . . not for all my life!'

Panic grabbed her at the prospect, now turned into ugly certainty.

'I don't understand,' she said. 'I always thought Aunt Elsie liked me. I shall never, ever understand why. It would have been easier if she hadn't sent for any of us, never mentioned it at all. She's a cruel woman.'

Dorothy said nothing but her head was bent and her cheeks were burning. She began to play nervously with the long brown hair that was still down on her shoulders like a child's. She was plumper as well as being younger than Chloe and had yet to blossom.

Chloe took out her purse quietly and emptied most of its contents on the table between them.

'My wages for Mam,' she said simply.

'But aren't you coming home to see her? You're not going back yet surely?'

'I couldn't face it now. Not today. Especially with Daisy there. Just say I wish her well. Say I wish them all well. That I didn't have much time today and I'll be over next month.'

In the street she smelt rather than saw the traffic, her eyes blurred with hot tears that stung right down into her throat. Elsie had rejected her after all and it was the first great disappointment of her life.

CHAPTER TWO

'Strange you should call today,' said Dorothy, pouring out the tea with arthritic fingers and fluttering her eyelashes in the strange way she had adopted recently. 'I've had a telegram from Daisy to say Aunt Elsie's dead.'

Chloe unpinned her hat and laid it on the table in Dorothy's flat in Manningham Lane. It was not easy to find a spare inch in the room, which was none too clean. Most of the surfaces were stacked high with books and clothes and dusty bric-a-brac for Dorothy lived in the ambience of a perpetual jumble sale. Chloe mopped her brow with a white, lacy handkerchief which smelt faintly of lavender. It was hotter than ever. Dorothy had the windows open, thank goodness, and they could hear a roar of cars and buses and motorbikes from the road . . . the traffic was more than a hundredfold the volume it used to be, the remaining trees were covered in dust, the area deteriorated. It had been respectable when Dorothy moved in. But then, so had she.

'I'm glad,' said Chloe, 'I hated to think of her in that institution with the mind of a child.' Neither of the sisters were surprised. The death was expected. Elsie's body had lasted an amazing eighty-nine years, but her reason had not.

'Daisy says there'll be some money for us,' Dorothy went on. 'Not a lot, because the nursing-home was so expensive over the years. But something. For both of us. Apparently she never forgot us even though she never came back.'

'It's too late,' said Chloe.

Dorothy shot her a suspicious glance. 'You're not still bitter about it, are you, Chloe?'

'I'm not bitter. I'm just stating a fact. We're too old now.'

Dorothy hesitated, examining a piece of fruit cake closely, as if searching for flies. She had grown very fussy about some things, though careless of others, and also very fat. Finally she came to a decision and ate the cake. The mice would be disappointed.

'You were her favourite, you know. She didn't really let you down.'

'What do you mean?'

'I mean that she did write for you to go to America after all . . . and not for Daisy. Daisy persuaded Mother to let her go instead, telling Elsie you couldn't leave service. She cried and she cajoled and begged and pleaded. Oh, you remember what she used to be like!'

Chloe's face was a study in horror.

'And they let her?'

'Yes. Mother was useless with her, as you know. And Father might have stopped her but he was in bed drunk. The boys regarded it as being between us girls. I did my best, Chloe, I really did . . . but Daisy won!'

'All these years.' Chloe's voice was full of anguish. 'All these years and you never even told me! Why, Dot?'

'There didn't seem to be any point after it was done. It would only have made you hate Daisy. You took it badly enough as it was. Anyway, Daisy made me swear not to tell . . . '

'Then why now?'

'Well, it doesn't look as if either of us'll see Daisy again now and after Aunt Elsie's death I didn't think you should go on believing she had let you down.'

Chloe nodded at the logic but her lips were drawn very pale and tight.

'Another cup of tea?'

Chloe let Dorothy refill her cup, though she didn't really want any more.

'It was a terrible thing to do,' she said and her voice was very quiet.

Dorothy nodded vigorously. 'Yes, it was. Still, things didn't turn out too badly, did they? You weren't at the vicarage for ever. There was Willie.'

'Oh, yes,' Chloe echoed. 'There was Willie, all right.'

Dorothy had never understood properly, she thought. Not then, not now, not ever.

'I can't stand to see Willie come down our stairs one more time,' she burst out, suddenly.

Dorothy was startled, not to mention uncomfortable at such talk. 'Come now,' she said, flushed and fiddling with her brooch. 'You've been married a long time. Husbands and wives get to feel like that sometimes, but they don't mean it.'

Chloe said nothing. But they do mean it, she thought. Everyone usually means everything, deep down. And it was nothing to do with the long time at all. It was the summation of all the little things, like painting the kitchen beige and turning the oven out on her Christmas cakes to save the gas; all the little harshnesses, the denials and the disappointments over that long time. But she couldn't expect Dorothy to know and wouldn't dream of telling her, for her sister had remained a perpetual spinster after her young man had been killed at the Somme, along with all those others. Sometimes, Chloe wondered if Dorothy had, after all, been better off that way. Then she felt terribly guilty at having such a horrible thought. Today she had it and didn't feel guilty.

When Chloe left Dorothy's, she didn't go straight home. Instead, she took one of the blue Corporation trolley-buses, already marked down for extinction, up towards Duckworth Lane. It switched and clacked its way up the hill, jerking and jolting her around on the torn and dirty seat until she wondered what she was doing there. But when she got down at the roundabout by the trolley shed, the feeling of impulsion returned. The pressure of the past was weighing down heavily. She crossed the road, then two more and finally turned into the end of Back Bower Street.

The corner shop was still there, not of course run by the stable Mrs Binns of her childhood, with stripy cats sleeping on the counter and a slate for 'tick', but by a Pakistani family. Basmati rice and (to her) strange spices and chutneys vied with cornflakes and baked beans in the dusty window.

The houses were still there too, standing back to back like grim and grey survivors from another age. For years they had been scheduled for clearance but somehow nothing had happened and they were still standing. Some of them had even gained a new air of respectability with fresh paint and new glass doors, plant-pots in the front windows and (no doubt) inside toilets. They seemed confident of reprieve. But number seventeen was empty and the windows boarded up. How small it looked! To think that all nine of them had been born in that upper room! For it was here that she and Dorothy had lived, long before her sister became spinsterish and arthritic and learnt to flutter her eyelids.

Chloe stood, one hand on a gate with a broken latch, and stared at the ghosts which rose from the past. Her father and Matt loomed the largest, for she had loved them both dearly. The memories filtered back across the years.

Her father: not a tall man, with a thin face that was nervous yet handsome, rather like Beth's had become; his hair the colour of a new copper coin and quite unlike Beth's; long and delicate fingers worn rough by the work at Lister's woollen mill, and such a winning smile. Coming in – calling her name – sweeping her off her feet and into his lap for a cuddle. Capacious pockets, full of surprises . . . . bits of string, an apple, a penny whistle, a new ribbon and once – a puppy. Her mother had made him take it away again when it bit Chloe's finger and made her scream. She deeply regretted the screaming afterwards but her mother was adamant. Those were the days before her decline. Her father never raised his hand or his voice to any of them and he always had time to talk. Those were the better memories anyway.

Matt was a lot like him really – the same smile, the same charm and the new-penny hair. Taller though – and more responsible. He had always looked after them all and stood up for them. Looking back, Chloe realised she had been unfair in loving her father so much more than her mother. Her father was appealing but weak and there were days on end when he wasn't there at all. When he came back he smelt of more than tobacco and slept solidly for several days. The truth was, he could only cope with his life if he managed to escape from it every now and then.

While he was away there was no money, hardly anything to eat and a harassed and sick-at-heart mother. Gradually Matt and the other boys were able to take over. They became the father and he became the son. Until that happened, Chloe's mother had to cope as best she could selling the furniture when she couldn't pay the rent and taking in washing and mending as if she hadn't enough of her own. By the time Chloe and Dorothy – born a year apart – were old enough to help her, she was almost finished. A particularly nasty miscarriage seemed to drain her of all energy and life. She had had eleven pregnancies in all, but the last four had withered and died either in or out of utero. The surviving children were Matt, Charlie and Arthur, Chloe and Dorothy, then Daisy and George.

Chloe wondered why she hadn't felt sorry for her mother before. Because such a life was common? Or because they had never been close? How could they have been with so many other claims for attention? Chloe was just the eldest girl and a good little helper. Dorothy suffered too. The older boys had a different status whilst Daisy and George remained the babies. But the girls in the middle lost out. And what was the result of all that rampant Rawlinson fertility? Only the girls had survived into old age after all.

The darker memories came. Her father had eventually been knocked down by a tram, undoubtedly while drunk. Everyone felt that was a blessing for he must have been so unhappy by then. Their mother, fading daily, had already been an easy victim for the influenza epidemic after the war. It still hurt to think about the boys though.

Only my children will go on, thought Chloe. Not of course as Rawlinsons in name, but they are the only ones. Daisy had married an American but had no issue by choice, whilst Dorothy was growing old alone.

She turned sadly away. Why had she come? Why hadn't she . . . (the thought came despite being forbidden) . . . gone to Scarborough instead and breathed the heady freedom of sea air and different memories? It would be a lovely day for Scarborough. She would have done it too if it had not been so far away. Maybe it would have lessened this new bitterness over Daisy.

Yet she could understand why Daisy had done it after all – knew the desperation which had driven her to snatch such a dishonourable escape out of Back Bower Street, even at that tender age. How could she blame her? And if not Daisy, then who? God or fate or nothing at all?

She found herself back at the bus-stop, in front of a row of decrepit-looking shops. One of them was a paint shop and it gave her an idea. She went in and asked for a small pot of gloss in red.

'What sort of red? asked the girl. 'Magenta Red, Blushing Poppy, Clear Red, Pillar-Box?'

'Bright scarlet,' said Chloe, firmly.

'We ain't got that.' The girl was chewing gum and pushed a lank curtain of hair away from one eye.

'Then which is the nearest?'

'Pillar-box, I s'pose.'

'Then I'll take that.'

'Just the one small pot?' the girl sniffed suspiciously. 'What you want it for?'

'Doorknobs,' said Chloe. 'Kitchen doorknobs. I want them bright red and I think I can just about manage that myself.

The girl stared. Funny old bird, she thought. Looks a bit flushed in the face too. Still, it is very hot. Fancy having all that clobber on on a day like this. Hat and coat and gloves. All dressed up and nowhere to go, I'll be bound.

'That'll be plenty, then,' she said. 'More than enough.' She had to fetch steps and climb them to get it and Chloe could see the top of her tights quite clearly up a mini skirt which only just covered her bottom. Inevitably she was reminded of the time when it was considered indecent to show an ankle.

She took the brown paper bag with some dignity and left the shop.

Clutching her purchase, Chloe at last headed for home.

She had made her journey much longer by the pilgrimage to Back Bower Street and now had two buses to catch back. It should be three, but the local single-decker that heaved its way up the hill to Sowerton was so irregular that the Bradford bus was bound to miss it and she would have to walk the last leg, as she had done so many times before. No chance of being home for tea-time. Just as well she had warned him!

Willie! Her fingers tightened round the paint pot. She would show him! Deep inside a still, small voice of reason told her that her gesture of defiance was pathetic . . . and her eyes clouded with tears as she gazed unseeingly out of the bus window. The agony of not going to America was back after all these years . . . and worse because of them. No good blaming Willie for her life either. Because she had loved him once. She couldn't deny it because she really had. That was the catch.

When Chloe returned to the vicarage after Dorothy's bombshell, she told no one of her disappointment at first. But every night she lay awake with wet cheeks, lonely and full of despair listening to the leaves rustling around her window. At last Mrs Feather asked what was wrong and Chloe told her. The housekeeper was full of good sense.

'It's a shame, of course,' she said. 'But who knows what God has in store for you? Maybe it's for the best. Either way, you've got to forget about it now and put it behind you.'

Chloe tried but it wasn't easy. The visit of the Reverend Kaye's sister didn't help. She was a surprisingly stylish lady, several years younger than her brother, and a wealthy widow. She arrived in a motor car no less, chauffeur driven, raising dust up to the very front door. With her were a tremendous number of boxes and bandeaux . . . and naturally her own maid. The latter thought herself a very superior creature and left Mrs Feather, and particularly Chloe, in no doubt as to their relative lowliness on the social scale.

So it was that Chloe had nothing to do with dressing the Reverend's sister or looking after her wardrobe. But she still noticed things whilst cleaning the room. There were several muslin frocks with tucked bodices to emphasise a large bosom and a tiny waist; and there were striped taffeta gowns for the afternoon. There were enormous hats, top heavy with flowers, a real French hair switch, lacy camisoles and a chemise of genuine Japanese silk. When no one was looking, Chloe touched them guiltily, stroking the silk with an especial thrill. No doubt the Reverend Kaye would not have approved of his sister's underwear, but Chloe's longing for such luxuries was too deep to care. She would have liked to try on one of the hats but didn't dare. How she wished she could at least change places with the other maid! By the time the vicar's sister left, her dissatisfaction with her own lot had been fuelled further and it left her feeling restless and vulnerable.

Summer was coming and the trees in the orchard below the vicarage were heavy with blooms. The air was growing warmer and gentler and the nights shorter and lighter. The birds woke earlier in the morning. And one day she met Willie Moffat on her way into the village on an errand.

He recognised her straightaway and raised his cap.

'Morning, miss.' Then without further ado: 'I'm going up to check the ropes again, this Sat'day. Would you like to come and watch?'

Chloe said that she would. Shyly, she tried to match his step.

'How're you liking it here, then?' asked Willie.

'Very well,' said Chloe. 'A bit quiet after Bradford.'

'Aye. My mother was a Bradford woman.'

'Was she?' eagerly now.

'Aye. From Manningham. She had a milliner's shop. Afore she was married o' course.'

'Oh. Chloe was impressed. 'And what do you do, Mr Moffat?'

'Joinering,' answered Willie. 'Me father and grandfather are gardeners . . . me father down at the big house. But I couldn't be doing with a life of a skivvy – even in t'open air. Me mother's father taught me the joinery trade instead in Bradford and now I've come back here to set up on me own. It's much better making something with your own hands that others are willing to pay for . . . ' then he added: 'meaning no disrespect, like.'

'Oh no,' said Chloe, with dignity. 'I quite understand. I'm sure I wouldn't have gone into service either, given the choice.' She was impressed with him again and suddenly snobbish because of it.

Willie left her at the village school, having arranged that she should meet him at the church tower on Saturday at three, with the keys. He had a job to do for the headmaster and the prospect of a cup of tea from his attractive daughter, if he played his cards right. That and the respectful look on the pretty vicarage maid's face was enough to keep him cheerful.

Chloe had second thoughts about her arrangement to visit the belfry for she knew in her heart that the Reverend Kaye would not think it proper. And yet he had spoken to her about the bells and urged her to take an interest. But she knew perfectly well that the meeting was nothing to do with bells. It was about seeing Willie again, alone.

At ten to three, she was waiting by the tower door, the keys clutched tightly in a rather hot hand. What was more, she was not in her uniform but had changed into a skirt of navy serge (her best) and a white frilly blouse, with the one brooch she possessed neatly pinning the throat. Her hair was also freshly washed and dressed and she was rather pleased with the result.

Willie meanwhile was late and she began to feel nervous in case the Reverend should return from his rounds and spot her dressed that way. True, it wasn't a Sunday but . . .

'Hello,' said Willie, startling her. He had appeared casually round the corner of the church. 'I'm sorry. Did I give you a fright?'

Chloe shook her head shyly.

'You've got the keys? Shall we go up, then? Watch your step, now. Some of the stairs are a bit worn.'

They were steep and narrow as well as being worn and Chloe found the climb hard going in her long skirt. Willie took her above the ringing chamber to the bells themselves, where she marvelled at their size, at the wheels and at what Willie told her happened when they were rung. He pointed out a stay and explained how the wood must be ash. Then they climbed even higher and Willie helped her out onto the tower-roof, holding her hands just a little longer than was necessary. It was a good view. Most of the village was spread out below them. The trees that surrounded the church and vicarage were newly in leaf of that lime-fresh green which is never repeated later in the summer. The roads out of the village twisted and clambered up to the moors where birds wheeled and called high overhead.

They descended again . . . into the dim, cool ringing chamber with its pendant ropes and striped sallies, surrounded by wooden tablets commemorating past successful peals. Willie tried to explain how the bells were rung, then rang one up to show her. Chloe watched shyly.

'Like to have a go?' he asked.

She felt very uncertain. 'It looks difficult.'

He smiled. 'Yes, it is . . . at first. But I won't let you do it properly. I'll catch it for you. I won't let you come to any harm. You won't feel any weight.'

He stood behind her to demonstrate where she should place her hands and his arms encircled her tiny body. Chloe wasn't sure whether she was more frightened of him or the bell. She pulled tentatively on the thick sally but nothing happened.

'Bit more,' said Willie. She pulled harder and the sally dipped down, then jerked up and away suddenly like a live creature. It stung the skin on the palms of her hands before she let go quickly, remembering Willie's instructions, stepping backward in alarm into the warmth of his body. That gave her a shock too. He calmly pulled in the backstroke, catching the sally neatly and setting it to rest again.

'Try again?'

She shook her head firmly, stepping away.

'Oh no, thank you!'

Willie laughed, though not unkindly. 'Well, at least you can say you done it once! More than most women.'

He rang the bell down again whilst Chloe wandered around the chamber and read the boards. She felt unsettled, without knowing why. Willie's name was on some of the boards. He also featured in a new photograph of the present band of ringers, which was pinned proudly to the wall, and looked very handsome in his Sunday suit and high, starched collar. She stole a look at him, steadying the sally as the rope bobbed finally into its resting position and felt the first stirrings of something new inside. Later she remembered thinking he was 'rather nice.'

'I have to check the ropes now,' he said. 'You can wait if you like. I'll only be a few minutes.'

'Er, no . . . I'd best be getting back,' said Chloe, hastily. 'The Reverend or Mrs Kaye might want me soon.'

'Please yourself.'

'Thank you very much for showing me the bells, though. It was most interesting,' and she held out her hand very stiffly. Willie squeezed rather than shook it, so that Chloe flushed deeply.

'Pleasure, I'm sure,' he said. 'I'll be seeing you in the village, I hope.'

She nodded in some confusion and escaped down the stairs. But supposing I don't see him, she thought ruefully, almost at the bottom. She dropped her handkerchief deliberately on the last of the stairs, then picked up her skirts and ran back to the vicarage, her heart beating faster with the excitement and audacity of it all.

But, if Willie saw the handkerchief, he did not take up the implicit invitation. Chloe saw him from a distance in church every Sunday and once or twice in the village, too. But, although he smiled and bade her good-day, she was disappointed to find that that was all. It surprised and bothered her but she tried to shrug it off. Obviously, he was merely being kind before. She mustn't imagine anything else. And for a while she did succeed in putting him out of her mind. She might even have forgotten about him altogether had it not been for the cricket season. That was her real downfall, for Willie in cricket whites was unforgettable.

Like most Yorkshire villages, Sowerton was intensely interested in and proud of its cricket team. The Reverend Samuel Henry Wordsworth Kaye himself considered it a wholesome and decent sport and bowled for the village with renowned and feared ferocity. But Willie Moffat was the leading light when it came to batsmen.

The coming of midsummer and the cricket season transformed the weekends for Chloe. Mrs Feather, as the vicar's housekeeper, was the main provider of the teas and of course Chloe lent a hand. It was she who helped take the hampers down to the cricket field and spread and served the refreshments in the pavilion. There was cold ham and beef and pickles, sandwiches and cake and scones and even real frothing ale (although the Reverend watched that like a hawk).

It was a treat to leave the gloomy vicarage on a hot afternoon and feel the grass of the cricket field springy under her feet and the sunlight warm on her face. It was a treat too to sit on the steps of the pavilion and watch the game, listening to the sharp crack of the bat upon a ball that took flight upwards and was echoed by the gentler patter of clapping hands. The full ephemeral glory of summer was all around, like a scene from a picture book, except that it lived and breathed as the wind stirred through the grass and the trees.

Willie scored run after run, a dazzling white figure with fair hair turned gold by the sun. He seemed more friendly too, always ready with some opening gambit of conversation over tea, his grey eyes become bluer in a tanned face. Chloe did not know that the schoolmaster's daughter was playing her own game with him, attracted by his physical charms, but not taking him seriously. Chloe merely revelled in his fresh and undisguised interest, for it had become apparent to her that Willie was popular. Most of the village girls turned up to the game each week and they applauded Willie more than anyone.

Whilst this was not unreasonable in view of his prowess, it was quite obvious that this was not the sole reason for their enthusiasm. The fact that Willie was so generally admired made him even more desirable in Chloe's eyes. She was, after all, still only seventeen. When he eventually asked her to walk out with him (the schoolmaster's daughter needing a lesson) she felt as if she would burst with pride.

The courtship was not, she supposed, looking back, very special. Willie never actually took her anywhere. But just to walk with him, along leafy lanes, beside streams, in the woods or up on the moors, seemed enough. Chloe was in love.

Gradually, the most important thing in the world came to be pleasing Willie. For he was not, she discovered, always smiling and kind but sometimes morose and laconic. She had to judge his mood then carefully and watch what she said. For she was afraid of losing him. She had, by then, heard the talk about the village schoolmaster's daughter. So, little by little, she allowed Willie 'to take liberties', as Mrs Feather would have put it, when they were 'out gallivantin'. And she discovered it was very pleasant, not only to hold Willie's hand, but to let him kiss and cuddle her, as they lay in the grass. At the back of her mind, the Reverend Kaye's dire warnings needled, but she pushed them away. Willie seemed to be the brightest and best bit of her life and she wanted to keep him.

It was August when her doom was sealed. Already there was a hint of the year growing old in the air and rowan berries tossed in the breeze. The heather was out on the moors though the woods were still green. The day had a still and peaceful quality about them and the nights were ridden by an orange harvest moon. She met Willie as usual on her day off, having stopped going to Bradford long since. They met in the meadow below Sowerton Close – the big house where Willie's father worked – and walked up the hill and over the fields known locally as the 'Hanging Banks'. Chloe loved this walk . . . it was full of steps and stiles and little gates and, at the very top of the hill, one could sit in sheltered dips and hollows beneath strange mounds and hillocks. One could sit there and be out of sight of the world, staring across the valley to the neighbouring hamlet of Braithewaite. It was a peaceful and idyllic place. But that day Willie was dispirited.

'What's the matter, Will?' Chloe asked him, solicitously.

'Nowt's the matter. Let's sit down for a bit.'

They sat in a dip amonst cow-parsley and dandelions and listened to the birds call. In the distance, towards Braithewaite, they were haymaking still in some of the fields. It had been a good summer. Willie's father had grown his biggest gooseberries ever at the Close and won the village championship. Everything was coming to fruition and the weather was holding out for the harvest.

Willie thought gloomily of his mother. She wanted him to take her cousin's daughter to the forthcoming Harvest dance. Willie had already decided to ask the schoolmaster's daughter. But he knew his mother would get her way. Her cousin's girl was plain and dull and he viewed the whole idea with distaste. It was too bad of his mother to wreck his plans. Why, he would rather take Chloe, despite her lowly status on the Sowerton social scale. At least she was pretty, and gentle and willing. Yes, he thought, he would much rather take Chloe.

Of course he knew there was no future in it. He wanted to do much better for himself. But there was something infinitely reassuring and comfortable about her presence. He felt easy with her because she didn't give him a hard time. There she sat, gazing across the valley with her hands clasped around her knees and a few stray locks of auburn hair escaping from under her sunhat. Something in her troubled expression made him reach out his hand and touch her arm.

'It's me mother,' he explained. 'She's a hard sort and

we've had a bit of an argument.'

He supposed it wasn't fair to keep her dangling on a string like this. He didn't want to hurt her after all. Perhaps he should stop seeing her soon.

'What about?' she asked.

He hesitated, then decided to adopt a slightly distorted version of the truth.

'She wants me to take her cousin's girl to the village social next month and I wanted to take you.'

Chloe took off her hat and laid it across her knees. 'You should probably do as she says then.'

'Don't you mind?' Willie was sly now.

'Yes, of course I do. But I understand why you can't take me.' Now it was her turn to be hesitant. 'Does your mother really want you to take her cousin's girl or do you think she doesn't like me?'

Willie chuckled. 'I ain't told her about you.'

'Oh, I see.'

Hastily, he made amends. 'Oh, she'd like you all right, but she'd have to meet you first. She thought it was a bit of a comedown marrying my father . . . into service like, you see . . . though lord knows it was her choice. Allus wanting us to keep away from it, she is. So she wouldn't be too keen knowing you was a maid.

Chloe's face fell. So that was it. She wasn't good enough. She had sometimes wondered why Willie had never taken her home and been careful not to meet her too near his house. For the first time she realised their romance was unlikely to last and a large tear rolled down one cheek and plopped onto Willie's hand, without her meaning it to.

'There!' said Willie awkwardly. 'Don't take on. She'd get over it if she knew you, all right.'

'But she won't, will she?' and Chloe prepared to scramble to her feet.

Willie forestalled her by putting his arms firmly around her shoulders. 'What do you mean?'

Chloe faltered. 'Nothing.' She was afraid now that if

she accused Willie of never intending to introduce her it would be the end, as if her suspicions could be summoned into reality by voicing them.

'I'm sure I don't know,' said Willie. 'You'll meet her all right . . . in time. Don't worry about that.' And he chose that moment to kiss her on the lips, more intimately than ever before, as if to quell all doubts.

Chloe was confused by his ardour. She felt her love for him rekindle as he pressed her slowly down onto the grass. Perhaps there was hope after all. Would it come right then in the end? Willie seemed determined to persuade her that it would, physically if not in words. He had moved on top of her and his hands were running through her hair, his mouth continually seeking hers. Chloe felt the fine blond hair at the back of his neck beneath her hands and was filled with a vision of cricket whites and clapping under the sun. She pulled him closer and felt new sensations stir inside – a consuming tenderness and an ache in a part of her body she never admitted to.

Willie was raising her skirts and running his hands up the inside of her thighs. He paused to fiddle with his trousers and she grew suddenly frightened at what they were doing. But something mesmerised and held her motionless on her back. She felt welded to the grass beneath and the sky above for ever, half blinded by the sun and dazzled by Willie. He was pinning her closer now and pressing down, feverishly pulling aside articles of clothing.

'I don't want you to,' she whispered shyly, though she only half knew what to expect.

But his skin already lay bare against hers and that was pleasurable enough. Then he did hurt her as he pushed right into her and she cried out with the shock and dug her finger-nails into his shoulder-blades. But he seemed not to notice, breathing heavily and rocking to and fro as he was, until quite suddenly it was finished and he moaned and drew away from her immediately.

So that was it, thought Chloe. Pleasure for him and pain for her. Wasn't that what everyone implied after all, although it could never be mentioned? It was true then.

A cow wandering close at hand gave a deep moo and Chloe sat up, startled. The world came right way up again and reverted to normal. No one was around but she guiltily adjusted her undergarments and skirt and stabbed fiercely with hairpins at the curls, that had come tumbling down. She daren't look at Willie. The significance of what had happened was too much.

Willie felt it too, raising himself shamefacedly on one elbow. It wasn't what he had intended at all. Not at all. Her slightness and her softness and all that lovely russet hair falling onto the grass had taken over. He cleared his throat, embarrassed.

'I'm sorry.'

Chloe finished pinning up her hair and plonked her hat on top of it.

'It wasn't all your fault. I should have stopped you sooner.'

'I didn't mean to take advantage . . . '

'I know.'

He helped her to her feet and they walked back to Sowerton in complete silence. Despite herself, Chloe began to feel a warm glow mingling with some of the horror inside. At the vicarage gates, Willie plucked a wild rose from the hedgerow and gave it to her. It was his only romantic gesture ever. Then he touched his cap shyly and disappeared, all without a single word. Chloe watched him go and the glow faded into sadness. Somehow she knew it could never be the same between them again.

As she passed the church, her strong sense of shame took hold and she slipped in fearfully to kneel and say a prayer of contrition as some atonement for her crime, for its magnitude appalled her.

Chloe was eighteen on the thirtieth of September. She

awoke to a misty morning with the promise of another perfect day to come and felt intolerably miserable. For it seemed as if she had frightened or shamed Willie away for good. She had not seen him alone since that cataclysmic day in August and he had made no attempt to arrange a meeting. What was more she had seen him hand in hand with the schoolmaster's daughter in the village, second cousin or no.

Slowly, Chloe swung her legs out of bed and tried to control the immediate waves of nausea that built up to make her retch feebly on an empty stomach.

'What's the matter, child?' Mrs Feather had taken to asking in the mornings. 'You look right peaky.' And only yesterday – she had added, 'Shall we get the village doctor to see you? It's not right for you to feel so tired and go off your food, like that.'

This Chloe rejected vehemently. For, deep in the recesses of her mind, lay an awful fear that kept on growing. She had never felt like this before. She didn't know much but she did know (just about) how you got a baby and she remembered what her mother was like in the early days of carrying George. She dare not see a doctor. But she must see Willie. The question was how. Unthinkable to go to his house! Impossible to waylay him in the village! She could only think of one way. Writing a note asking him to meet her the following Saturday at three in the vicarage orchard, she kept it closely hidden between the leaves of her prayer-book.

But three whole Sundays came and went before Willie took the collection in church as she had so often seen him do. Then, standing at the end of her pew and returning the plate, she feverishly pushed her note into the palm of his hand and bent crimson over her hymnbook, scared rigid in case someone had seen.

The orchard was on fire, its dying leaves a riot of colour. Chloe sat on a log under a tree in the still, sharp air, watching the occasional leaf flutter and fall to earth singly. It was one of those surprisingly warm and beautifully calm afternoons in late October. But Chloe was far from calm for in the midst of peace and serenity, she sat with clenched hands and a churning stomach.

Willie saw her as part of a picture in faded gold, brown and red, the colours of the orchard and the colours of Chloe in her old brown skirt (the navy serge could no longer be buttoned) with hair that was both golden and red in the fading sun. She met his greeting with frightened eyes.

'You wanted to see us?'

'Yes.'

Willie sat down beside her, reluctantly.

'You've been avoiding me.'

Willie shuffled. 'I thought it were best. After what happened.'

'That's what I want to talk to you about.'

'Aye?'

Chloe screwed up all of her courage. 'I think I'm going to have a child.'

The words dropped like pebbles into a silent pool. She could hear Willie swallowing hard and thought he would never speak.

'You're sure now? You've seen the doctor.'

'I've seen no doctor,' said Chloe. 'Not yet. I had to see you first. But I'm almost sure, yes.'

There was another long silence. Willie wouldn't look at her and played with his fingernails. His cheeks were burning.

'I can't marry you.' It blurted out suddenly and hung in the afternoon air.

'It's me mother,' Willie went on, embarrassed. 'She'd never allow it. I would otherwise, honest. But it's out of t'question. You understand that?'

Chloe, assimilating the shock, found it wasn't really a shock at all. She had expected it.

'What can I do then?'

'You must do what you think best.'

'But it's your baby too, Willie!'

He shook his head, confused and unable to accept the fact.

'You know you are the father, Willie! There's been no one else. I swear it!'

'Shush!' for she had raised her voice in panic and he looked round nervously, though there was no one to hear.

'Don't take on! I believe you, all right.'

They continued to sit glumly on the log, together and yet apart.

'The Reverend Kay – you reckon he'll dismiss you?' Willie knew it was daft to assume otherwise but he had to think the situation through.

Chloe shuddered. 'You know what he's like. I daren't even think about him . . .' Overwhelmed by the harshness of it all, she covered her face with her hands.

'You'll go back to your family in Bradford, then?'

'I suppose so. There's nowhere else to go.'

Willie rose to his feet and laid a tentative hand on her shoulder.

'If you do that, I'll send you some money . . . for the child. It won't be that much but enough to keep it decent. I'll promise you that providing you don't let on to no one it's mine. But I don't want to see it, y'understand?'

And with that he was off through the trees, shabbily hurrying away as if the whole affair was too much for him and he couldn't cope with the idea of it or bear to talk about it a moment longer. Chloe stared after him in disbelief. How could he be so unfeeling?

She sat on under the trees as the light began to dwindle and the air grow colder. She had no alternative but to accept Willie's offer. It would be foolish to be proud. She needed to contribute some money to her keep and that of her child's in Back Bower Street. But what a dismal prospect for them both! No husband and no father for ever. Beyond the pale of respectability, while no one would ever know what Willie had done. His life would be unchanged. She realised the money he would send would have to be a pittance, so no one should find out.

Yet she couldn't be really angry with him, knowing he was as frightened as she was. Still it hurt. It bit deep into her that he didn't love her at all. She shouldn't be so surprised. He was the blue-eyed boy of the village and she wasn't good enough. She had known that before. But the ache of rejection was hard to take. Why had he bothered with her at all then? And why, after all, did he think himself so important? It wasn't fair. He had dallied with her and didn't love her. Now she was ruined and he didn't care. And, despite everything, she continued to want him.

Not knowing what to say or how to say it, Chloe said nothing at all. She let herself drift through the days with her secret growing inside her and told no one. Physically, she began to feel better, as the sickness was almost gone. Perhaps she had been wrong after all. She began to believe it.

Then one day, in early November, she fainted whilst carrying the coals. She was only out for a moment or two but looked very pale and sweaty and Mrs Feather packed her off to bed and called for the doctor.

'Well?' asked the housekeeper anxiously as the worthy man emerged at last from Chloe's room.

The doctor coughed politely and did up his bag.

'Nothing wrong, Mrs Feather,' he said. 'Not in the true sense of the word. No, she's a fine, healthy young girl. Ahem! But she is well over three months pregnant and should not have been carrying coals.'

Mrs Feather clutched dramatically at her ample bosom, her very worst fear realised. Later that day, she sought an interview with the Reverend Kaye.

The parson listened gravely to what she had to say. 'And she positively refuses to name the father, Mrs Feather? That is most disturbing. Why shouldn't she? Is he, I ask myself, a married man? Does she, the Lord have mercy on her, really know who the man is, I wonder?'

Mrs Feather sprang to Chloe's defence. 'Oh yes, sir. I'm sure she does know. She's not really a bad girl at all. Just been led astray. I reckon it's that Willie Moffat, myself. No two ways about it. I've never seen her with anyone else.'

'Willie, eh? Well, that's not so bad. All right, Mrs Feather. Send her in and we shall see.'

Chloe was almost paralysed with fear as she entered the vicar's study, especially when Mrs Feather was dismissed and bobbed discreetly away. It seemed to her that the Day of Judgement itself, which the Reverend was so fond of preaching about, could hold no greater terror. The Reverend stood at the window, a black figure blocking out the sun. When he turned she was far too frightened to see that his face was kindly or to notice that he tried to speak (for him) softly.

'Now, Chloe. Mrs Feather tells me you are in trouble. The worst kind of trouble for a young girl.'

She lowered her eyes and nodded.

'Well, Mrs Kaye and myself will do our best to help you.'

Astonished, her eyes jerked upwards to his.

'Oh, it's not the first time it's happened in the village and I'm afraid it won't be the last. The vicar allowed himself a brief paroxysm of rage. 'On consecrated ground too, before now! 'Not, I am sure,' softening again, 'that that was the case with yourself.'

He thrust his hands behind his back, suddenly embarrassed. 'Now Chloe, Mrs Feather tells me you are unwilling to disclose the name of the father of your child. Really, that will not do. Such a fact cannot and should not be hidden. There is reparation to be made and responsibility to be faced. You must put your sin right in the eyes of God.' The Reverend paused to let this speech sink in and then went on: 'Mrs Feather believes it to be Willie Moffat. Can you look me in the eye now and tell me truthfully that she is wrong? Think carefully, Chloe! Your soul is already in peril and to lie before God is a terrible thing!'

Of course she could not deny it. Chloe's voice was almost a whisper in reply.

'No, sir. It is Willie.'

The Reverend was mightily satisfied. 'Good, good,' he said. 'Now he must be told. He has a right to know.'

'But he does know, sir. Begging your pardon.'

The Reverend was almost speechless. 'Then you will be marrying?'

'Oh no, sir. It isn't possible.'

'And why is that?'

'He won't marry me, sir.' And Chloe burst into tears though she had tried to hold them back throughout. Then out it all came. About Willie's mother and not being good enough, though really she feared Willie simply did not love her. And even about Willie's offer to send money providing she went back to Bradford and told no one.

The Reverend said nothing until Chloe had sobbed to the end. But his face began to swell and suffuse with an odd, purple colour until it grew quite grotesque. Then he let out an enormous bellow as if in pain and Chloe shrank back, alarmed.

'Won't marry you?' he shouted at the top of his very considerable voice. '*Won't* marry you! And for such a reason! We'll see about that!'

He grabbed his largest and thickest walking-stick from the corner of the room and brandished it wildly above his head, then flung the door open with a crash and burst out of the room, yelling for his hat and coat. Mrs Feather came running in a dither from the kitchen and even Mrs Kaye was seen to emerge from her upper sanctum – though not by Chloe, who had fallen into another faint and lay senseless on the floor.

CHAPTER THREE

The wedding took place two weeks later. Chloe never found out what the Reverend Kaye had said to Willie, nor even if he had really used his stick, but there was no further mention of her unsuitability as a bride and, if Rebecca Moffat muttered about it, she did so under her breath.

When Chloe first met Willie's mother, she found her courteous enough, if not kind, and resigned rather than angry. Even so, her heart sank from the moment she saw Rebecca. She was a large and strong woman with a round, doughey face and an awe-inspiring bosom. But the plumpness in no way implied softness. Her eyes were too frosty for that, her mouth too thin and hard a line in the over-large face and her clothes too stiff and smart . . . surprisingly so for a gardener's wife. Chloe concluded that, she must once have had money of her own.

Rebecca did not lag far behind Mrs Rawlinson in fecundity, though her seven pregnancies had been unsullied by failure. Every one of them had been born safely, crying lustily and weighing-in well. Until Willie's transgression, Rebecca had ruled them all with a rod of iron. There was no doubt she was a remarkable woman. To Chloe, she seemed unapproachable and unsympathetic.

Was that why she felt less than happy on her wedding morning? She couldn't understand it herself. Initially, she had been overjoyed when the Reverend told her of

Willie's change of heart. She was to be his wife, after all. It was almost too good to be true. And, if Willie was a little shy and awkward when they met again, she did not mind . . . it was hardly surprising. She was determined to prove a good wife so that he wouldn't regret his decision. She was very grateful to him and sure that one day he would love her.

They even had somewhere to live. Chloe had soon discovered that all Willie's talk of returning to Sowerton to set up on his own was something of an exaggeration. The village was not big enough for two joiners and in fact Willie spent most of his time helping out Oliver Horrocks, the established man. Together they eked out their trade by undertaking as a sideline. Even so, there were times when Oliver couldn't afford to hire Willie and he had to go into the surrounding villages or even right into Kingley – the nearest small town – looking for work. So it was not essential that he lived in Sowerton and when the Reverend Samuel Henry Wordsworth Kaye himself found a vacant cottage to let in Braithewaite, Willie had no excuse not to take it. He earned just enough to pay the rent and, being careful, had enough put by to pay in advance and start them off right with a few essential items of furniture. What they lacked they were able to beg or borrow and Rebecca gave them some things. It would be a very simple home to begin with but they would manage.

'I just wish it had been Sowerton,' Willie confided to Chloe. 'Even if it is but a walk over the fields.' He had the feeling that the Reverend had done it on purpose – as a kind of exile whilst Chloe grew bigger. In truth, the Reverend was a wise man who knew that Chloe and Willie would stand a better chance of cementing their relationship away from Sowerton in general and from Rebecca Moffat in particular.

Chloe loved their cottage. It was situated in a more sheltered nook than some of its neighbours – just off the main street – and faced the sun and the fields. Ivy softened the grey stone walls and made it picturesque. It had an outside earth closet but that was not unusual. Inside it was tiny with whitewashed walls. But it was their home and she would enjoy making it into one. She was perfectly content with it. So why then did she sit in the semi-darkness of her attic room, with the blankets of her bed huddled round her knees, and let the doubts creep in as she looked at her bridal clothes hanging ghost-like in the gloom of the dawn?

She could hear a light drizzle pricking a pattern out on the window and the bare-branched trees stirred and scratched restlessly against the glass. It was a dismal, cold day by the sound of it but she made an effort to be cheerful. What did that matter when she was marrying Will? Yet still the thought only succeeded in making her feel frightened and a little ill.

Sighing, she rose and fumbled to light the oil in the lamp. Holding it high, she inspected her bridal costume. It was a plain, blue suit but it was new (well, nearly) though not hers. Her sister Dorothy (who still ran to puppy-fat and was not as neat and trim as Chloe) had bought it on discount from Linyard's and had lent it to her for the day. It fit her reasonably well now that she was bigger and was a pretty blue. White was naturally out of the question. Not that Chloe could have afforded lace and frills, anyway. But with her one good blouse which ruffled at the neck, the suit would look smart enough. And then there was the hat.

Chloe drew it out from its striped box and at last felt a thrill take hold of her. She had bought it herself in Bradford. It was big and blue with a nest of cream flowers clinging to the crown and it would transform her whole appearance. It had swallowed up all her money but she had been determined not to look shabby in front of Rebecca. She had bought matching gloves too but couldn't afford flowers as well so would have to do without. But that was a secondary importance.

The wedding was not until three and the morning

dragged as Chloe went about her work as usual. It was odd to think that from tomorrow she would perform such tasks (lovingly) for Willie. She had told the Reverend she would work out her notice but he wouldn't hear of it.

'No,' he had said. 'The work's too heavy for a woman with child. Besides, you will need the time to sort out your own house for Willie and get ready for the babe. We shall manage to get someone else quickly enough.'

At lunchtime, Mrs Feather insisted on Chloe having an extra portion of stew.

'You don't want to be fainting away in church,' she pointed out. 'It's a long time till those few tiny sandwiches and cakes we've put out for everyone in the vicar's parlour . . . and I don't suppose you'll eat any of those anyway, what with all the excitement.'

Chloe struggled obediently with her plateful.

At a quarter to two, Matt and Dorothy arrived from Bradford in their best clothes. Chloe's mother was not well and her father steadfastly refused to set foot inside a church, even for the sake of his daughter. Chloe was disappointed because she had hoped up to the last moment that he might change his mind and come. The Reverend Kaye was deeply shocked. But there was Matt. He had come to give Chloe away instead and Dorothy was to be her witness. She was proud of the way they looked. Matt seemed especially handsome though somewhat ill at ease in his stiff collar. He was shown into the Reverend's study to wait whilst Dorothy helped Chloe dress.

In her room, Chloe found two parcels. The smaller one was wrapped in tissue-paper and contained a paste but pretty diamante brooch from Mrs Feather. The other held a white-backed prayer-book and a florid hand inside the fly-leaf identified it as the gift of the Reverend and Mrs Kaye. 'Wishing you every blessing', it said. Chloe's eyes misted over. True to his word, in loco parentis, he had done everything he could to help her. Like a battleship in full sail, with guns bristling, he had used his unquestionable authority to change their lives and would shortly be binding herself and Will together sacramentally for ever. She was still frightened of the Reverend – always would be – but she now knew he really was very kind. She let Dorothy pin the brooch on the neck of her blouse and took the prayer-book in her hand.

It was really the Reverend Kaye's day as much as it was Chloe's. He couldn't help feeling satisfied as he waited for her in his black cassock and white surplice just inside the church door, trying to avoid the blasts of rain gusted in by the wind. Such a relief that young man had come to his senses. Three souls had been saved and he was firmly convinced of the moral rectitude of the outcome. He was not a man to entertain doubt.

Matt Rawlinson was perhaps more astute. 'Are you sure about this, Sis?' he asked, fumbling with a big, black umbrella in the vicarage hallway.

'Yes,' lied Chloe, adjusting her hat. Then: 'Well no, I suppose I'm not. Not entirely.'

Matt's blue eyes were troubled. 'You could come back to Bradford with us, you know. Forget the lot of them. You don't know these people. We'd look after you, you know that.'

Chloe shook her head. 'What future would I have, Matt, with a child? I'd never have a husband or a home of my own then. And how could Mother manage another baby while I was working? The way she is? I'd have to work, for you couldn't support us all forever. What about when you wanted to marry youself?'

Matt laughed. 'I shan't get married. I'd rather have you.'

'Of course you wouldn't. You have lots of girls now but you'll change too.'

'I think not.' He was right in a way, although they didn't know it then.

'I'm sure you will. Anyway, I do *want* to marry Willie! I do. These are only wedding nerves.' She reached up and kissed her favourite brother on the cheek. 'Let's go, Matt.

We're keeping them waiting. You mustn't worry about me any more. Will isn't a monster. We'll be all right.'

Reluctantly, he took her arm and they stepped outside into the wind and the rain. He did his best to shield her from it with his body and the vicar's umbrella whilst Chloe clung on to him and her hat and the Reverend waited.

'Dearly beloved . . . '

How pretty Chloe looked, thought Dorothy enviously. How lucky to be so grown-up already, getting married – especially to someone as good-looking as Willie – and having a baby of her own. Of course, the baby should have come later but it didn't matter so much now. That suit looks better on her than it does on me. I should give it to her really, as my present, to keep. That hat and the gloves are so elegant and match so well. She looks like a real lady.

'Secondly, it was ordained for a remedy against sin.'

Willie's done well for himself, thought John Moffat, standing next to his wife Rebecca. Can't see what all the fuss was about. She's a sweet and kind-looking girl. Why Rebecca preferred that schoolmaster's daughter with her flibbertigibbet ways and modern ideas or that dreadful cousin Hilda's girl is beyond me. Willie's got the better of you this time, my dear, whether he realises it or not.

No folks on her side of the church, of course, thought Rebecca contemptuously. You could hardly count Mrs Feather. Mind you, she knew some of the villagers had crept in at the back to watch and she rather wished they hadn't. It wasn't a marriage to be proud of in her eyes. She'd be surprised if this slip of a girl managed to carry the child to the end. If it hadn't been for the Reverend Kaye poking his nose into matters that didn't concern him, Willie would have been well out of it.

'Wilt though have this woman to thy wedded wife . . .?'

The wind moaned around the church and Chloe tightened her grip on her prayer-book as Willie cleared his throat to answer 'I will.'

Then it was her turn as the Reverend Kaye joined their hands together and took them through their vows.

' . . .for better, for worse, for richer, for poorer- . . . . .and to obey . . .'

Mrs Feather blew her nose noisily.

'Those whom God hath joined together, let no man put asunder.' The Reverend's voice swelled to a menacing crescendo as he crushed their hands beneath his and Chloe winced at the pressure against her very new and very thin band of gold.

It was still raining when they emerged from the church but Chloe didn't mind getting wet now as they hurried back up the path to the vicarage. The Reverend had provided tea and sandwiches for all in the parlour.

'I hope you're not superstitious,' said Will, as they gained shelter, all breathless and blown about. 'Over the rain, I mean.'

'Oh no,' said Chloe. 'Not at all.' It was her second lie that day. Then shyly: 'You haven't kissed me yet, Willie. Quick, before the others get here.'

He pecked her dutifully on the cheek.

Chloe found that Mrs Feather was right and she couldn't eat but she drank some tea. It had been a very discreet and respectable little wedding despite its cause and now everyone hung around stiffly, not knowing what to say. Matt at least was trying to inject some jollity by joking with the other Moffat boys and Dorothy was preening herself in her second-best suit. Thank goodness they had come. Otherwise she would have had no one of her own. And what a lot of Moffats there were!

There was John the father, with his enormous beard and tiny eyes that crinkled kindly; and Rebecca, whose kiss she could still feel like ice on her cheek. John the son seemed merely a younger edition of his father. Then there was Fred, who looked very dashing in uniform and moustache and had fought in the Boer War; and Oliver, who was married to a plain girl, with two children already and another on the way. Willie came next and then the girls: Rose, as tough as Rebecca at a guess, and Amy, who seemed dreamy and quiet and perpetually out of her depth. There followed a gap of eleven years, during which Rebecca must have thought her childbearing was over. But, nonetheless, she had borne Harry in 1901 and he now sat fidgeting and restless in his sailor suit, next to the sandwiches. It was odd to think that, at the tender age of five, he was already an uncle several times over.

My family now, thought Chloe, looking round. Soon she would have to say goodbye to Matt and Dorothy and the Rawlinson part of her life would be gone forever. A hard lump formed in her throat at the thought and she felt suddenly – stupidly – quite alone.

The gloom of the November afternoon continued to deepen but at least the rain had stopped so that when they saw the carrier's cart arrive (it had been allowed up to the door as a special concession) they were reasonably sure of a dry ride to Braithewaite.

Suddenly there were lots of goodbyes, flustery and confused. Chloe, clinging tightly to Matt's warmth, hardly felt or heard them. Then they were up in the cart with its sacking thrown hastily over the floor and Willie was trying to arrange a rug around her skirt to keep out the cold. Matt and Dorothy were waving, the Moffats stood together and the Reverend Kaye looked solemn but serene, his duties discharged, with Mrs Kaye on one side and a tearful Mrs Feather on the other. But Chloe's lasting memory as the carrier flicked his whip and drove them away was of the coldness on Rebecca's face and she shivered.

'Chilly?' asked Will, laying an arm about her shoulders at last. 'Soon be in Braithewaite now.'

It was very quiet in the cottage after Willie had gone to work. Two up and two down didn't take long to clean after the vicarage, although Chloe took a pride in keeping it spotless. She soon discovered that Willie expected her to be frugal but she was used to that. After all, she was better off now than she had ever been. She didn't mind making and mending their clothes and linen or scrubbing them clean. It gave her something to do in the long process of waiting for a child. She had worked hard on the cottage but the result pleased her. She ought, she knew, to be content. But something was missing. Was it the quiet which disturbed her? Back Bower Street had been rowdy and even the vicarage had had Mrs Feather. Chloe missed her. Yes, she decided it must be the quiet. But she was really very lucky. And the child would make a difference.

Every night, Chloe looked forward eagerly to Willie's coming in. She fussed around, making sure the cottage looked warm and welcoming. Every night she tenderly removed his boots and set them aside for polishing. Then she would put the finishing touches to his meal, while he sat in his armchair by the fire, sullenly smoking the pipe he had taken to recently.

'A busy day, dear?' Chloe would ask.

'Fair,' Willie would reply. Or maybe: 'Fair to middling.'

Sometimes he would just grunt. Occasionally, he would have a newspaper and laboriously rustle each page as he turned it. Then he might read her a passage if he was in a good mood.

Often he would go out again straightaway after dinner. There was choir practice and ringing practice twice a week in Sowerton. Then he would stay on afterwards with his friends in the Sowerton Arms. Chloe would lie awake in bed waiting for him until her eyelids drooped despite herself. She was surprised to find him never drunk.

She knew he was disappointed. Disappointed in having to live at Braithewaite and disappointed in her. They shared the same bed, but only to sleep. Willie had muttered something about it not being good for the baby and Chloe had agreed . . .with some relief. Still, she would have liked him to have at least cuddled her now and then. Sometimes she worried about it, staring at his turned back and listening to his heavy breathing in the night. She knew it couldn't be right. She stretched out a hand to touch him now and again, but even in his sleep he moved away. Perhaps after the baby . . . She was very determined to be a good wife and in time to repay her debt.

Every Sunday, wet or fine, they walked over the fields to the service at St Mary's and then stayed to lunch with Willie's parents. Every Sunday, Rebecca would more or less ignore Chloe and talk to Willie about his returning to Sowerton. Willie would ask her to keep a look-out for any empty cottages they might afford to rent and Chloe's heart would sink.

One day, on the long walk back, she tackled Willie about it.

'Don't you like our little cottage, Will?' she asked. 'I'm ever so fond of it now and I have tried to make it look nice.'

'It's right enough,' said Willie absently. 'But it's a trail back here all the time and we don't know anyone in Braithewaite.'

'I'm getting to know the neighbours,' Chloe said, 'and the shopkeepers. And there's a girl down the road who's having a baby same time as me. I like her and we're getting friendly.'

'Friends is all very well,' said Willie. 'But they're not family. Our family's in Sowerton.'

Chloe did not argue. She accepted the fact that Willie's family were hers now without any difficulty.

'It's not that far, Willie, to see them. And Braithewaite is a pretty place really, smaller and quieter than Sowerton. We're going to have some lovely roses round the cottage door in summer.'

Willie stared at her, uncomprehending. 'And what about winter when we're cut off? Or walking' little ones across fields full of snow? That won't be so pretty.'

Chloe was so pleased at his reference to 'little ones' that she cheered up and acquiesced softly, 'There is that, I suppose.'

She slipped her arm through his and no more was said.

Yet she couldn't help but feel the blight of Sundays. Lunch at the Moffats was a large scale family affair. Not to attend would have been unthinkable. They all sat around the enormous dining table feeling beleaguered and exposed, constrained or merely bored. It was common for the adults to squabble. The children had to sit still and be silent until the end of the meal and, under Rebecca's martiarchal eye, they did, racing into the garden when released.

Chloe had a keen sense of not belonging, despite some small kindnesses and attentions from Willie's father. It would not have been so bad but for Rose. For some reason, Willie's closest sister had taken a dislike to Chloe and was not slow to show it.

'Don't you think, mother, that Willie's looking pale?' she would ask.

'Give over, Rose,' said John.

'I'm right enough,' came from Willie.

Rebecca, caught in the middle of serving out, would ladle and extra portion onto Willie's plate.

'Yes,' she said thoughtfully. 'Are you eating well enough?'

Chloe felt her face burn.

'Of course I am.'

'Well, maybe it's all that extra walking you have to do living at Braithewaite. I'll be glad when you're back. Goodness knows how little Chloe will be able to cope with that baby over there on her own.' It was meant to sound disparaging and it did.

'She'll manage fine,' said John. 'Leave the poor girl alone.'

Rebecca turned on her husband and squashed him with righteous indignation. 'Well, she won't have her own mother there, John – her being such an invalid. I'm only thinking of Chloe's welfare!'

'That's very kind, Mrs Moffat,' mumbled Chloe, more embarrassed than ever at Rebecca's fine motives and her own ingratitude.

At Christmas, Chloe longed for snow. Sometimes Braithewaite really was cut off. But rarely so early in the winter. Still, the wind changed a few days before and gave her hope. On Christmas morning, they awoke after all to snow though not enough of it yet.

The world lay in muffled beauty, mysteriously white. There was ice inside the window-panes and the water-butt was frozen over. Willie got up to do the fire. He was fidgety and anxious.

'You'll manage the fields?'

Chloe nodded. She was resigned. 'I expect so . . . It's not that deep, is it?'

'Nay . . . nobbut a sprinkling.'

She found she didn't mind that much after all. The baby had moved inside her for the first time and she was enthralled by the fluttering feeling . . .for all the world as if a tiny bird were trapped and trying its new wings. Christmas was really meant for families.

Willie's Christmas present had softened her too. It was a cradle for the baby and he had, of course, made it himself.

'It's beautiful,' she gasped, rocking it to and fro. 'I

couldn't have asked for anything better.' And she kissed him boldly on the cheek. Willie seemed pleased enough . . .with her as well as himself.

'Aye,' he said. 'It's a rare bit of mahogany. Had my eye on it for a while in the yard. Oliver were good to let us have it.' He was quite a craftsman when he put his mind to it.

She wore her wedding hat to church and sang up almost as loudly as the Reverend Kaye would have liked. Willie was in the choir now as they were short of tenors. So she had to sit along with the Moffats, sandwiched rather uncomfortably between Rose and Rebecca. But today she was determined to be generous. It was good to have a family at Christmas. And Rebecca's dinner would be undeniably good and the house festive enough. John would have got a Christmas tree from the Close and there would be a goose. These were rural luxuries for a girl from Back Bower Street.

'I've got a splendid surprise for Willie,' said Rebecca, as they walked back from the church. She took Chloe's arm and propelled her firmly along, although she would much rather have waited for her husband.

'How lovely,' said Chloe. 'Is it a present?'

Rebecca withered her with a dry little smile.

'Oh dear, no! We couldn't afford another present, so soon after the wedding coming so sudden. Hardly fair to the others. No. But Willie will be better pleased with this.' Her gloved hand tightened on Chloe's arm like a pincer. 'I've found you a cottage.'

'Oh! Where is it?' Chloe tried to sound bright.

'It couldn't be better, my dear. It's the end one of Croft Cottages – right across the road from us. Not very large of course but it'll do till your family starts to catch up on mine.'

Chloe felt the ground slipping from under her feet.

'They do look very tiny,' she said feebly.

'Oh, nonsense, girl! It's no smaller than that awful

place you have now. Willie will be delighted.'

And so he was. But Chloe's Christmas had been spoilt at a stroke.

It was well after dark when they returned to Braithewaite and they had to trudge painstakingly through the snow. Willie's lamp made a swinging circle of white against the blackness all around, Chloe was scared of slipping and followed exactly in his prints as he had bidden her. She was cold and miserable and tired, while Willie was ever so slightly merry.

'Won't have to do this much longer,' he said.

'No,' admitted Chloe, negotiating a stile with some difficulty. 'That's true. But Willie . . .'

'Yes?'

'I know you want to go back to Sowerton.'

'Of course!'

'But . . .'

'But what?'

'Well . . . you didn't even ask me if I wanted to or not!' She sounded timid but definitely reproachful. Willie stopped short with one leg over another stile.

'Well, really Chloe,' he said, 'I'll be blowed! Anyone can see it's better for you. Mother'll be able to help you a lot with the baby.'

That, thought Chloe, is probably what I'm afraid of. And then she felt guilty and was immediately lost. Of course, Rebecca's experience would be invaluable. And anyway, Will wanted to go back so much. He was her husband and she had sworn to please him. She simply must learn to do that without grumbling. She still owed him and always would. Moving house would make her a little sad and much more tired, but it really wouldn't be so bad.

There was nothing intrinsically wrong with Croft Row. It was a low and squat terrace built out of grey stone like its neighbours. Rebecca had made much of theirs being an end house but the winds blew more chilly around three walls because of it. They were still two up and two down with an outside earth closet and a small kitchen range and Chloe could see no great advantage. Next door lived Miss Blanche Beanland and her elderly mother. Blanche took the infant class at the village school and was a pleasant enough girl. Her mother was very deaf and for all practical purposes also dumb as she had given up speaking to anyone years ago. Even her daughter was answered in monosyllables. There was nothing to bother Chloe on that side.

She gazed miserably through the old mullioned windows. They were far too small and made the rooms dark. Through them she could see the field full of cows which separated the cottages from the village school and the playground. A charming enough scene which lost some of its appeal because the path to the road led through the field and Chloe, in her present state, felt strangely nervous of the cows. And she didn't want to think about the school.

On the other side of the path that led to school and road, lay Rebecca's house. Chloe now longed for the peace and quiet of her Braithewaite home. Here, she felt constantly overlooked. There was always a danger that the net curtains which suffocated the Moffats' windows would tweak apart and Willie's mother peer out. Five minutes later, the doorknocker would inevitably bang and on the step would stand Rebecca or Rose.

Rebecca was undeniably philanthropic. She wanted to see how Chloe was – to chat about children – or to bring Willie some of her freshly made soup. Chloe knew she was being supervised and taken over. There was nothing she could do about it. It was unthinkable to be rude. But Roses's visits drove her to it.

Rose was a strange girl. Chloe couldn't fathom her. She was not particularly attractive at close quarters due to a certain coarseness of skin and hardness of manner. But, from a distance, her rich figure and glossy brown hair were probably enough to guarantee her a future husband. Willie was undoubtedly her favourite brother and she seemed to resent Chloe taking him over. The circumstances of their marriage made matters worse. As Chloe grew bigger, Rose became more biting.

It was she who drew Chloe's attention to the fact that Willie still paid visits to the schoolhouse.

'You must have noticed he never comes home early, Chloe,' she said. 'Not even when there can't be much work about. He drops in there regular in the afternoon – when her father's teaching, that is.'

'I'm sure,' said Chloe, trembling inside, 'that if he does, he has a good reason.'

Rose laughed. 'Of course, he does! He's still sweet on her. You'd better be careful!' Rose was brutal now. 'Don't pay too much attention to that baby when it comes!'

I won't listen, thought Chloe, determinedly. Rose is just trying to cause trouble.

'And why are you telling me all this?' she asked, politely but with frost in her voice.

Rose shrugged her shoulders. 'Thought you ought to know, from the family, like, before anyone else tells you.'

'I don't suppose anyone else would.'

'There you are then!'

Chloe felt very angry. 'Yes,' she said, 'here I am – in a fine mess and lumbered with in-laws who don't like me and can't wait to see me hurt!'

Rose realised she had gone too far. 'Steady on,' she said, nervously, 'Remember your condition.'

'I'm hardly likely to forget it! Please go, Rose! I don't want to hear your tales. I don't believe them. I've done nothing to you but you take a delight in tormenting me!'

Rose was open-mouthed now.

'Go on – get out!' Chloe had flung open the door. 'Go snivelling to your mother and tell her what I said, if you like! Only go and don't come back!'

'All right,' said Rose, affronted at last. 'I might just do that, Miss High-and-Mighty! But remember – I was only trying to warn you! Most people would have considered it a service!'

When Rose had gone, Chloe bust into tears. The worst of it was she knew Rose could well be right. And she had made her into even more of an enemy than before, and alienated her mother-in-law as well, for the tale was bound to be repeated. Or was it? Maybe not, considering the subject that had raised the storm. That could hardly please Rebecca either.

Should she say anything to Willie? She couldn't. Adultery was for sweeping under the carpet . . .a male indulgence not to be talked about. After all, it was most unlikely that Willie would ever leave her – no matter how serious this affair became. They were married. She was his wife. It was obvious that she was now safe. So what did it matter? But matter if did.

Over the next few days, she could think of nothing else. Rose, of course, was a liar. But Willie did have the opportunity. And he was often home late. But then surely the schoolmaster's daughter was almost a lady, a respectable woman, much older than Will, who would be shocked at the very idea of such a dalliance? Chloe wasn't so sure. She had heard the woman held very modern views, calling herself a Fabian and supporting universal suffrage! That might make a difference.

Willie himself gave no clues. Every morning he set off nonchalantly for work, with the lunch Chloe had packed for him swinging in his joiner's bag, his fine pale hair shining in the sunlight. He reminded her of the old Willie she had fallen in love with. Coming back to Sowerton had done it. He was back in the old niche he knew and liked. Chloe was almost an irrelevance. It was not that he was unkind. But she couldn't touch him. She knew she was not that important, though he appreciated having her around. It was as if . . . Chloe caught her breath in pain at the thought . . . as if she was his servant.

The sunlight did its best to spill softly through the mullioned windows, but Chloe hid her face in her hands.

That is exactly what I am, she thought. But I never meant to be. She looked out at the cows. She was sure Rose was right. And it did matter because it hurt. It hurt almost as much as Daisy going to America in her place. It reminded her forcibly that Will hadn't wanted to marry her. And now she was being passed over again. She was only second-best. She knew she should fight it. But could she . . . here? The twitching net curtains across the way were hardly on her side.

There was the baby, of course. But she realised she was pinning too much hope on the unborn head. It worried her more and more. Her fears circled round like the motes of dust in the beam of sunlight. Then something inside her snapped and gave way to an instinct that came straight from her father.

She went upstairs and mechanically packed a small bag. Nothing much, so as not to attract attention. She considered leaving a note for Willie but that demanded too much. Instead she slipped on her hat and coat and dropped the latch, taking a last look round. Then she forced herself to walk through the cows. Chloe was running away.

CHAPTER FOUR

She had taken the rent money from its jar, though it wasn't hers, and the thought burnt into her as she left the last houses of Sowerton behind. She had no idea where she was going. Automatically, she took the downward road – towards the valley towns and away from the moors. But there were too many walkers and Chloe was afraid she would see someone she knew. Once past the Close, she came to the canal and turned left along the towpath.

The bank was muddy in places after a night of rain and Chloe, with only a month to go now, found the going hard. Her boots were soon caked in clay, ruined no doubt, her stockings wet and her dress spattered. It didn't take long before she felt tired as well. Her abdomen was so tense and uncomfortable with the baby's head pressing down so that she continually wanted to pass urine. When she came to a stretch where the bank widened out beside a rise of double locks, she sat down.

The grass was damp and the wind chilly but she didn't care. Overhead, the harsh crowing of rooks filled the air. It was the end of March and they were busy repairing their nests. Barely a year since Chloe had first arrived in Sowerton. The most eventful year of her life. It had left her full of regret and this longing to escape. A rashness she had succumbed to. But now what?

The lack of options floored her. She didn't want to go back. But what else was there? Any thought of Back

Bower Street had to be discarded. They had their own troubles and she had severed herself from them by marriage. If it hadn't been for the child she might have gone back and got work in Bradford. But then if it weren't for the child, she would still be at the vicarage. Chloe remembered her now lesser unhappiness there, lightened only by Willie. How quickly it had all changed! It seemed that ever since Aunt Elsie had sent for Daisy, there had been no hope for her. And now no way out. Other than the canal.

She looked into the dirty water of the first lock. It sucked and smacked at the brick walls on either side and leaked through the wet wood of the lock gates. Chloe tried to imagine its depth. She had seen it open once for a barge and it was much deeper than the rest of the canal. Across the top of the lock gates ran a wooden ledge – a safe enough way of crossing for someone with nimble feet. But if I climbed up there and stood in the middle, thought Chloe, if I shut my eyes and waited, I'd soon feel dizzy and fall. She couldn't swim. There was no one around. No one to stop her and no one to see. How long would it take, she wondered? Would she sink to the bottom or drift endlessly backward and forward between the gates like canal weed?

She stood up and walked to the edge. She even laid a hand on the arm of the lock gate. A kind of fascination held it there on the splintered wood. Then the most violent movement from within made her catch her breath.

It had to be a protest. She wondered what on earth she was doing and her eyes were instantly wet. Another month and the child could live without her. And anyway, she didn't really want to die. She just wanted something better. And that wasn't the same thing at all.

It was a mild and bright day for March, with more than a promise of Spring in the air. She could smell the freshness and the wetness of the earth, about to burst with new life. There was an extra urgency in the song of the nesting birds. And, overhead, ragged clouds bowled briskly across a vast blue sky. Chloe knew nothing about the universe but she felt the greatness of the earth. Even in her depression, she couldn't ignore its challenge. She knew she would not kill herself, baby or no baby. And certainly not in such dank and dirty water. Not now, not ever.

Placing her hands over the firm, rounded bump in her abdomen, she set off down the towpath with new resolve. Somehow she would find something better.

But, within four hours, the new hope was beginning to fade. She had been very tired by the time she reached the tram terminus at Stone Flatts. The tram-ride itself was a welcome rest. But then, for the last hour and a half, she had merely trailed the streets of Bradford, trying to think more clearly, conscious that night was coming and aware that she attracted curious glances. It was not really done to parade such an advanced stage of pregnancy. Feeling more desperate, she made a cup of tea and a bun in a tea shop last as long as she could.

The afternoon wore on and it grew colder. What was she to do? There was the workhouse, but she couldn't bring herself to go there. Still, even one night in a cheap hotel would cut too deeply into her remaining money. It would have to be Back Bower Street after all. She was ashamed to go back but she had little choice.

She was surprised to find the house quiet when she pushed open the door. then, 'Who's there?' An anxious voice came out of the gloom. Closing the door, Chloe moved on into the room. Her mother, an old woman at forty-seven, with rings under her eyes and a perpetually pale face, looked up from the fire. There was no one else there.

'It's me, Chloe.' She sank wearily into a chair. 'Can I sit down? I'm tired.'

Her mother leant forward to poke the fire, pushing stray wisps of untidy grey hair from her eyes as she did so.

'Where is everyone?' asked Chloe. 'It's very quiet.'

'It's allus quiet now with Daisy gone. Dot's working late at Linyard's, tonight. And the boys aren't often in before seven.'

'And father?'

Her mother shrugged her shoulders for a reply.

'We haven't seen much of you since you were wed.'

'No.' Chloe hung her head. She could hardly describe the atmosphere as welcoming. Biting her lip, she carried on: 'I've left Willie.'

Her mother was nowhere near as shocked as she had imagined.

'I wondered if I could stay here . . . just a few nights like . . . till I decide what to do.'

Her mother gave her a long, hard look. She didn't seem so bewildered any more. 'You'd better do your decidin' pretty quick,' she said. 'A wonder you're not in labour already, by the looks of you.'

Chloe was shamefaced. 'Yes, I know,' she said. She longed to ask her mother for advice but the constraint of uncommunicative years lay between them. There was a silence. Then her mother's tone softened.

'It's no good running away, Chloe. Not unless you've somewhere to go.' She sighed and stared into the fire. 'Many's the time I've wanted to. But there's nowhere to go in the end. And one like your father in the family is quite enough.'

Chloe said nothing.

'What's wrong?' asked her mother. 'It hasn't taken you long to tire of Willie.'

'I think he's seeing another woman.'

'Oh, aye?' Her mother didn't seem very impressed.

'And his family get me down. Living so close to them an' all.'

'I expect they do.'

'And he's not very . . . well, loving – I mean affectionate. I don't think he loves me at all,' and she blushed.

'Does he beat you?'

'Oh no, nothing like that!'

'Does he get drunk?'

'No, not really.'

'Or keep you short of money?'

'Oh, no. He's very regular with his earnings on the whole and particular about giving me the same amount exactly every week. I have to manage with that but it's just about enough if I'm careful.'

'That's good, then.'

Chloe bit her lip again. Her mother was making her feel guilty now, as she had known she would.

'It doesn't sound so bad, does it . . . put like that? I can't explain my feelings, Mam or make you understand. But there's so much unhappiness inside of me.'

Her mother looked at her and sighed again.

'I can see that. But Chloe – running away's no good! You've got to make the best of it, now. It could be much worse, you know. And there's the baby to think of!'

'I don't really feel that much for the baby.' Chloe's voice was very flat. It was the first time she had admitted it, even to herself.

'Not yet. But you will. When it's here. You're going to be a mother, Chloe. You know what that means?'

Chloe was silent.

'It means you're not a girl anymore . . . ever again. You're a grown-up woman. You were still a child when you got wed . . . but not now. This is no time to run away and there never will be one again.'

Chloe shut her eyes. Her mother's words held the ring of truth. She knew it. No time for me, she thought, desperately. Ever again? And not yet nineteen!

'You must go back.'

'If he came for me . . .' Chloe spoke softly now, with her eyes still shut. She tried to picture Willie with the sunlight on his hair. 'Then maybe I would.'

'Aye, but he might not.'

'No.'

'Well,' said her mother, kindly enough, 'you can have supper with us of course. And stay. For a bit. But you think on, my girl.' She herself remembered that Chloe was still her baby. (And I nearly lost you – it had become more difficult every time. A wonder you and Dot and George are here at all. Daisy was always a survivor – even in the womb.) She felt a little guilty about Daisy . . . perhaps she ought to have been more firm over America. But then Chloe had always been such a good girl. She had never visualised these problems. Surely they would be resolved when the child was born? She went on hurriedly, 'You'll have to sleep down here with Dorothy, though. Your dad and I sleep in the girls' old room now. When he's here. You know he lost his job?'

'No, I didn't!'

'Small wonder, of course! Jack lets him help out at t'greengrocer's now, but that doesn't amount to much of a wage. Still, he's the only one'll have him.'

Chloe digested the news with sorrow.

'Thank you for letting me stay, Mam. I can give you some money.

'I'll be having none of it, if it's your husband's! At least he does an honest job. Not like your father!'

Chloe went red. She hated to hear the contempt in her mother's voice for her old idol, although she knew she couldn't blame her. She hesitated and then plunged on, encouraged by the new intimacy with her mother.

'There's something else too . . . something I've got to know – . . . before the others come.'

'What's that?'

'The baby . . .'

'Yes?'

'How will it be born?'

'It should be safe enough. You're a strong, healthy girl.'

'No, I don't mean that. I mean how will it be born?' Chloe was desperate now. 'How are any of them born?

What's going to happen to me, Mam?'

Her mother stared at her. 'Don't you know? You silly girl!'

Chloe's embarrassment was complete.

'I never saw you, Mam,' she pleaded. 'I never actually saw it happen.' It was true. She hadn't.

'Well, you know how you got it, I suppose?' Her mother was impatient now and tired.

'Yes.' Chloe's voice sunk lower.

'Well it comes out the same way.'

'But how can it? It must hurt so!'

Chloe's mother was unhelpful. It was beyond her to explain that physiological changes took place and that it was not so terrible as it sounded.

'Nobody said it wouldn't hurt,' she replied, testily.

Chloe lay awake for a long time, worrying and watching the patterns cast on the wall by the dying fire. She listened to Dorothy's breathing and watched her humped back instead of Willie's.

Her mother had frightened her, but also made her face the truth. There was no way out. Her labour was inevitable, no matter how much she disliked the idea. So was the child. And so was living in Willie's house sharing Willie's life. She could only consider leaving him if the baby died. Somehow she knew it wouldn't. Just as she felt sure it was going to be a boy. Willie's boy. But also hers. Maybe it would make life bearable after all. Whether or not, tomorrow she must go back. When the child grew up she would get away.

Strangely enough, she slept well at last, having come to a decision. In one of her dreams, she confronted the village schoolmaster and his daughter with new-found confidence and maturity. But then, towards morning, she became aware of a persistent backache through her blanket of sleep and in the end it woke her up. She sat up and the bed was suddenly wet. A strange, clear fluid was coming from her – leaking every time she moved – and she didn't know what it was or what to do.

Dorothy woke too and asked what was wrong. But Chloe merely bunched the bedclothes more tightly around her knees to hide her shame, and shook her head. The backache was bad though . . . she could scarcely think of anything else. Dorothy interpreted the scared look on her face correctly and dashed upstairs to ask if babies could come early.

So Chloe brought her first-born into life in Back Bower Street, of all places, after all. Right in the front room in the bed she had shared with her sister, before the warmth of the fire her brothers had relit before going out shyly to work. Her mother – animated again, on familiar ground – held her hand and wiped her face with a silent empathy. There was Dorothy too, hovering in the background with enormous, frightened eyes in a pale face, terrified but determined to stay. And there was the midwife who had worked these streets for years – the same one who had delivered Chloe and Dorothy and most of the others as well.

Nurse Flanagan. Her hands old and worn and cool. Her face as cracked and rutted as a road that needed mending. Her voice very Irish and her eyes dark but kind. Chloe surrendered to the voice and the eyes and did as she was told. Flanagan was old and not so good when labours went wrong, but with a wealth of experience to stop the normal ones getting into trouble. Chloe could have had a lot worse. And Nurse Flanagan told her she was coming along fine . . . champion for a first timer. Oddly enough, she knew it was true. It hurt right enough, but not at all in the way she had imagined. And all the time, her pain was accelerating her on.

Then, at last, there was the head – dark and wet – and then Nurse Flanagan holding up the slippery, bloodied little boy that was hers. Not screaming as she had thought. But squirming and whimpering just enough to show that he was most definitely alive and intended to remain so. Chloe would always remember the sight of him against the firelight. When they had both been washed and wrapped and she was holding him warm at last in her arms, she was relieved to find that she did feel something after all, even if it was mainly a stunned wonder.

It was then that the door was flung open with a crash and they all looked up startled. The boys had been banished from the house, even though their work would be over now, and the three women were alone, with the midwife packing up her bag ready to leave. In the doorway stood Chloe's father, back from a binge, bottle in hand, his handsome face now flushed and bloated and his new-penny hair unkempt. His eyes took in the scene slowly, absorbing the fact that Chloe was there and holding a baby. Some forgotten instinct from the past made him cross himself quickly. His florid face changed and the tears streamed down it so that none of them could be cross with him. That too, Chloe would always remember.

Willie came to fetch her home three weeks later. Matt had been to see him in the interim to explain. He stood, shy for once and very serious, in the Rawlinson's front room where his son had been born.

'I'm right glad it's a boy,' he managed when he was shown the child. Chloe knew he meant it because his throat was husky.

'I thought we'd call him John William,' she said. 'After you and your pa. And maybe Jack for short.'

She spoke quietly and calmly and Willie fingered his collar. She realised he was a little afraid of her, nervous of what she might say or do.

'It's a good name,' he said. 'Aye. We'll call him that.'

For once she was in charge. 'He was a good weight you know, despite being early.'

'Aye. You did well, I hear.'

Chloe continued to unfold the fresh clothes he had brought her. 'I was very unhappy, Will,' she said. 'I'll not deny it. I think you know why. I didn't want to come back.'

He dropped his head. 'Matt said.'

'I thought he might.' Matt had always been her champion. She carried on with the well rehearsed speech. 'But now I have responsibilities, I'll not shirk them. I am your wife and Jack's mother and I'll not go again.'

Willie cleared his throat, somewhat relieved. He didn't say so but he had missed her. He had also got an earful from his mother once she had ferreted out the facts.

'I'm glad, Chloe,' he said. 'You'll find things different, I promise.'

Their eyes met for the first time.

'Will I?'

'Oh yes. Right different. I know what upset you and it won't 'appen again. There were never much in it anyway.'

'I'm glad, too,' said Chloe.

'That's that then?'

'That's that then.'

Looking back, Chloe realised the years that followed were her best. With little Jack – and Sam who followed within eighteen months – and then Ted four years later. All boys.

She leaned on the canal bridge and mopped her brow again with the lace hanky. Such a hot day. The bridge wasn't the old stubby arch of her youth with a hump in the middle, but a new and complicated swing affair – light enough for a boathand to move with relative ease, but still wide enough for the local bus to get across. Chloe distrusted it. It seemed to shiver every time a car passed over and the bus really made it shake. The road was quiet today though and she wanted to look down the canal – towards the bend which hid the locks from view. The path was overgrown with weeds now and weeping willows choked the water's edge, while the canal itself lay largely undisturbed.

She thought about the day she had run away. She had

achieved something after all, for Willie was almost certainly faithful to her thereafter. Not that that wrought a transformation in their lives. But she did feel more secure, though the fear of being unloved still lingered. But Will had taken to her again in bed. She couldn't claim to enjoy it but understood and accepted that as the normal way for a woman to feel.

There was no doubt that Willie was proud of his boys – all of whom were healthy and strong. He became very conscious of his position as head of the family and it made him even more careful with money. Chloe continued to run a well-ordered home, working ceaselessly that it should be so. There were far more clothes to 'scrub and tub' and further to stretch the food but she didn't complain. Willie continued in his old routines. Choir practice and ringing, followed by the pub, while summer evenings were devoted to cricket. Chloe's life very soon became the boys' – though again she didn't see anything unnatural in that. But she did find it difficult to have any conversation with Willie. As the years started to slip by, he grew increasingly laconic and she left him alone. The response was hardly worth digging for. But she never neglected his needs. The boys had to wait while their father was served and attended to first. He never lacked respect in the house. When he had gone out again, the boys might reclaim and vie for Chloe's attention.

While they were little, she would have counted herself happy, had it not been for Rebecca, whose interference was hard to ignore. She always meant well in those days, but that was hardly the point. By the time Ted was born, Chloe was tired of her mother-in-law's regular advice, hating much of it instinctively anyway. She was then twenty-four and Ted was her third child. But Rebecca still referred to her publicly as 'little Chloe'. She had never forgiven her for 'catching' Willie and despised her heartily for running away, even though she had been almost as cross with her son when she discovered the reason. She was determined to keep them both under her wing now. There were other grand-children of course, whom she forever compared favourably to Chloe's boys. But only Jack, Sam and Ted she could see every day.

The situation depressed Chloe. It was an uphill struggle bringing up the boys her way instead of Rebecca's for she couldn't argue. Rebecca was easily offended and she had to take care. Anyway, she hated the idea of a direct confrontation. It was not in her nature. So she drifted her way along, steamrollered through life. One day, she thought . . . one day it will all change. When the boys have grown, I shall get away.

Still, the boys had been fun. Chloe smiled at the memory, forgetting the hard work now, as older women are apt to do. It didn't seem that long ago since they had been chubby and blue-eyed and waddling about. They had always loved and needed her then. *Her*. Not Rebecca, not Aunt Rose, not even (to the same extent) Willie. She alone had been their mother, though Rebecca had done her best to intervene. And she had enjoyed it. Not just because they had given her a sense of purpose and importance. But there was no doubt that it was wonderful to love and be loved unquestioningly in return.

Of course they had grown up. Terribly quickly. They had all left the village school at twelve as village boys did in those days, despite the new rules. Jack followed his father's trade, Sam his grandfather's and Ted, who was good with his letters, became a clerk in an office in Kingley. When the Second World War came, Ted had joined up straightaway to everyone's surprise and his mother's horror. He read the papers carefully every day and tried to explain to her his reasons. Dimly, through a paralysing mist of fear, she recognised them as being different to the average young boy's. But it didn't help. She could only think of the first war. Sam wore glasses and was accepted only for the Military Police, whilst Jack went to work for an armaments firm. Chloe agonised over Sam and Ted every day they were away. She grew so frightened she could hardly eat or sleep and her weight dropped to five and a half stone. In the end, the inevitable happened and Ted was badly wounded. But he didn't die, though his chest and right leg would be weak forever afterwards. Sam too was spared. Chloe could hardly believe it. She had buried them many times over in her mind and mourned herself into a shadow.

And now all her sons were middle-aged and married, with children of their own, all living up and down the Aire valley. She still worried about Ted's chest because he had developed some heart trouble in later years and had to take tablets now to stop his legs swelling. And he never seemed to have any money. They had all thought a white-collar job meant such a lot. But now Sam was better off, while Jack, still in Sowerton, running his father's business with a foresight Will had never had, was doing best of all.

She didn't feel she knew them very well any more. And she didn't see that much of them. She knew they found coming to the house a bore now and she didn't really blame them. Willie, for his part, was loath to go to them.

Chloe closed her eyes on the bridge. Yes, those were the best days – when they were little. You could hardly count Scarborough. That belonged to another life, not really hers at all. Even Beth had always been so complicated. And the boys had grown up before the Great War, when life was only slowly changing, so that they were hardly aware of it. She had still been young and strong then.

Opening her eyes, she sighed at the prospect of the hill ahead. It climbed from the banks of the canal steeply past the 'Hanging Banks' and Sowerton Close, into the village itself. It hadn't seemed so steep in the old days, but today it seemed like a mountain. No good putting it off though. She must get started. Will would be waiting for his tea, despite her warning.

Some things had changed for the better after the Great War of course. Like women's rights. Not that it had affected Chloe much, even though she had been entitled to vote straightaway, being over thirty. Will always told her how to vote anyway and she never once thought of disobeying him. She was too numb to care much at the time anyway.

Her boys of course had been all right, because Jack was only seven when War broke out. She remembered how it hadn't seemed to touch them at first. Only Willie's brother Fred was involved early and he had always been the soldiering type. Nobody thought it would last long anyway, if they thought about it at all. And then, in the December of 1914, the Germans shelled Scarborough from the sea. Suddenly, the whole of Yorkshire seemed to be falling over themselves to join up. The threat was real and awful now. Matt, Charlie and Arthur – Chloe's three eldest brothers – all went and were accepted. Willie went too. But he was told he was of greater use practising his trade at home. For the first time ever, aeroplanes were being used to fight. And joiners were needed to make the struts. So Willie was sent off to a factory in Brough in the East Riding, instead of France.

Chloe was ashamed to find she didn't miss him so much at first. Of course she was glad he was not in danger. But she felt freer without him. Suddenly she could light the lamps in an evening without having to ask Willie first and she found she rather liked it. The village was shorn of men. Apart from the doctor and the vicar and the schoolmaster, only the very young, the old and the disabled remained. A few waited for conscription and were generally scorned. Even some of the women had gone – to nurse or fill other jobs. Rose and Amy had both started work at a munitions factory in Kingley. Chloe was tethered by her children and, apart from Willie's long absence, the War hardly seemed to affect her at all.

Until the Somme, that is. It started on July 1, 1916, when Chloe was two months short of twenty-eight. She remembered every detail of the afternoon Dot came to see her, about a week later. She had just returned home from seeing Mrs Kaye. The Reverend had literally dropped dead two years before, bursting a blood vessel during one of his choleric sermons. His widow now lived in a cottage near the school and seemed entirely alone. Chloe called frequently, with shopping or washing, or just to read aloud as Mrs Kaye's sight was failing her now. She did it out of a certain respect and gratitude for her former employer and the ailing woman was gradually becoming more dependent upon her, although she had her own maid. Chloe was part of the old days and she liked her.

That particular afternoon was a perfect summer's day and, affected by the sun, Chloe felt unaccountably happy. It was warm enough to sit out in the garden patch when she got home. From there, she could keep an eye on Ted who went back into the field with his ball, impatient for his older brothers to return home from school. She sat in the sun and sewed and wondered how she would feel when Ted went to school too. By then Willie would surely be back home. Plenty of work of course in the home. But she would miss having a child follow her round, tugging at her skirts.

No more though. Willie was right when he said they couldn't afford it. Three was enough. She didn't want to lose her health like her own mother had. Still, she would have liked a little girl. Then she shook her head and laughed at herself crossly. That was purely selfish. Everyone knew life was better for a boy.

It was then that she saw her sister approaching over the field. Even at a distance, there was something in the set of her shoulders that jarred with the sparkling sunlight on the ripening corn. Chloe was surprised to see her, though not immediately uneasy. But she did know there had been a big offensive in France. Mrs Kaye's newspaper was full of it. She laid down her scissors and wondered about Dorothy's young man. The King's Own Yorkshire Light Infantry had been involved in the first wave of the attack. Could he have been killed? That would be dreadful. At twenty-six, it was high time Dot was married. She would have been already, but for the war.

Chloe felt certain she was right as she watched Dorothy's figure grow nearer. There was a kind of blankness upon her face as if someone had wiped all the life off with a duster, leaving a clean, blank slate underneath. She scarcely seemed to notice Ted, though he ran after her for a while shouting, then gave up and returned to his ball.

'Hello,' Chloe said, nervously, as her sister reached the gate. She got up. 'This is a surprise. Shall I make some tea?'

'Yes,' said Dorothy. 'You'd better make some tea.' She followed her into the kitchen and sat down, still lifeless, in the first available chair.

'What is it, Dot? Is it Joe?' Chloe's heart was beating faster at the unpleasantness of the situation but she had to broach the subject.

Dot nodded and Chloe sat down, leaning across the table and putting a hand out to her sister's arm.

'Oh, Dot! I'm so sorry. At this Somme river?'

Dorothy cleared her throat rather carefully.

'They say he's missing. Just that. His mother had a telegram from the War Office . . . and then a letter from his commanding officer.'

'Then there is some hope?'

'No, I don't think so.' Dorothy shook her head. 'Not from the letter. The officer was extremely kind but he explained that it's not always possible to account for everyone . . . afterwards. There were so many of them you see – and such terrible injuries.'

Her calmness faltered and she put her head in her hands. Chloe tried to busy herself with the tea things and wondered what was the best thing to say. It was so unfair. A vision of Dorothy's future life suddenly flashed upon her inner eye with appalling clarity. Dorothy wasn't the type to find anyone else. What a terrible waste!

The sunlight dappled the blue check tablecloth in the silence between them, while Chloe thanked God for the safety of her own family and the children. She found she couldn't sit still watching Dot's bowed head and got up again to refill the pot, although they hadn't touched it. She felt very inadequate.

Dorothy raised her head at the clatter of kettle and pot.

'Sit down,' she said dully. 'I haven't finished yet.' She looked suddenly tired and much older than her sister. 'There's more.'

'What do you mean?' Chloe was frightened now because she knew. She knew why Dorothy had bothered trailing all the way here from Bradford. It was nothing to do with Joe. Dorothy didn't want to talk about that.

'Matt?' she whispered. 'It's Matt too, isn't it? That's what you've come to tell me.' And the tears which hadn't come for Joe, sad and shocked though she had been, sprang immediately into her eyes.

Dorothy nodded again, like an unwilling executioner. She took a deep breath and looked desperately at the ceiling for help. But none came.

'Not just Matt. Matt and Charlie and Arthur. Mother had a telegram too. Rather more definite, I'm afraid. All three of them. All gone . . . all killed in action – and probably my Joe as well. Though they never found him.'

Chloe had sunk slowly back into her chair. Her fingers dithered and trembled over lips that had drained completely white.

'That's not possible,' she stammered. 'That just can't be.'

'Oh, but it is. They were all in the same regiment and

the same battle. You see, thousands died that day. Thousands upon thousands. I know. A girl at Linyard's got a letter from a boy who was there. She showed it to us. It was horrible.'

'But they said it was a victory. The papers! The papers – they said it was.'

'They got some land.'

Chloe stared at her sister. 'You're so calm!'

'I know.' Dorothy looked away. 'I can't cry. I don't know why. I just can't.'

She rose abruptly and started pulling on her gloves.

'But you can't just go! Wait a while with me.'

'There's mother to think of.'

'Oh yes, of course. I'm sorry! How is she?'

Dorothy sighed deeply. 'The whole house is silent and I mean silent, Chloe. Can you imagine?'

'And father?'

'Very good. Very sober and very quiet. Tears almost always in his eyes. He sits and holds Mam's hand most of the time he's not at work. She doesn't notice though. She doesn't notice anything. It's hard for him. I wish he'd go away and drink but he won't. Mother won't speak. She just sits and looks into the fire, holding that rag doll we all had on her knee. I tried to take if from her once but she wouldn't let me. I think she's gone . . . you know . . . not mad, but soft in the head.'

Miserable tears coursed down Chloe's cheeks. She couldn't bear the scene that Dorothy had created for her.

'It's horrible for you,' she sobbed. 'Worse than anybody . . . and you've got to look after Mam and Father too.' She couldn't believe the boys were dead but she could see with her own eyes the change in Dorothy. Dorothy gave her her handkerchief. It was perfectly dry.

'I'm glad you're crying,' she said. 'I'm sure it's best. I wish I could.' She knelt down beside her sister and Chloe put her arms around her shoulders, drawing her head close against her own knee. For a long time they stayed like that. The teapot grew cold in the sunlight. They could hear Ted laughing and shouting in the field. His brothers had joined him on the way home from school and they were running and playing together. But the world had turned sour. The noises they made reminded Chloe of Matt, Charlie and Arthur when she too was just a child. I'll never let them go to any war, she thought. I'll make sure of that. They'll have to kill me first.

Dot raised her head. 'I must go, Chloe.'

'I'll come back with you. Rebecca'll look after the boys tonight.'

'Oh no, you mustn't!'

'I want to help you and to see . . . them.'

'Honestly, Chloe, there's no point. Maybe later. Mother looks at me and George as if she's not sure what to call us. You would think . . . wouldn't you . . .her only surviving son, that he would bring something back into her eyes? But he doesn't. Not yet.'

'Poor George!'

'Yes.' Dorothy hesitated. 'He could be drafted soon.'

'But he's too young!'

'You're forgetting he's twenty-one.'

'Yes, I know, but he still seems young . . . ' George was the baby . . . *her* baby brother.

'Anyway, they'll probably send him the East Coast and not France. He should be all right. I do hope so. The others went off all jolly and brave. But how can he do that? Now he knows.'

Dorothy smoothed out the fingers of her gloves. It was strange but she was beginning to find such repetitious movements a comfort.

'I will come later then . . . as soon as I can,' said Chloe.

Dorothy picked up her hat and placed it precisely on her head.

'It really doesn't matter.'

Suddenly, Chloe realised Dorothy didn't want her help with their parents. They're all she's got, she thought. I have my own family but Dorothy only has them and George.

'I'll wait a while then,' she said, 'and bring the children Just for the afternoon.'

Dorothy nodded. 'Yes. Leave it a while. I would.'

Chloe kissed her and started crying again.

'I'm sorry. I can't help it and I've still got your hanky.'

'Keep it. I doesn't matter.'

When Dorothy had gone and the children were in bed, Chloe tidied the cottage and lit the lamps. She ached with tiredness. Rebecca had been over to see why Dorothy had visited and had returned home subdued. Chloe knew that her mother-in-law genuinely felt for her for the first time ever. Fred was still in France and now Rebecca worried too for she hadn't had a letter for some days.

Chloe decided to write to Will. But once she had laid pen and paper out on the kitchen table, she found she couldn't concentrate. Willie's last letter from Brough had been full of how bored he was in the factory and how poor the food was at his boarding house. Reading it over now, it hardly seemed appropriate.

He should be grateful, thought Chloe, in tears again. He really should – to be alive at all – and not to be in France. It was Matt's loss which hurt the most. She mustn't think about Matt. Not yet. It was too painful. The air tonight seemed oppressive. She left the house and went out into the garden.

It was a clear, warm night and the sky was full of stars. The scent of the honeysuckle that old John had planted for her after Jack was born, and trained carefully up the side of the house, was overpowering. She leaned on the gatepost and looked out at the field where her own boys had played that day, unaware of their uncles' fate. Poor boys! Poor big, little boys. She savagely stripped some of the leaves from the hedge which divided their patch from the field and her vindictiveness increased with the pain of her memories. She couldn't bear to think about her mother. But gradually the night sky in its vastness and the cooler air calmed her a little.

I will get over it, she thought. In time. Though the sadness must always be there. But Mother and Dorothy won't: ever. The realisation brought her back to her eternal guilt. Here she was somewhat cross with Willie for being safe. When all the while she was the lucky one.

Across the fields, the shadow of the church tower was just visible through the dark. She bowed her head and thought about the Reverend Kaye, although he was no longer the incumbent. She was sorry he was dead and gone, albeit a little relieved. He had always kept an eye on her after her marriage, nodding with approval when she shepherded the boys up to the communion rail. If he really knew the truth, he would not be so pleased with her now.

For Chloe was aware that her love for Willie had gone, dissipated, she knew not where or why. Their children had replaced him in her heart. His absence had made her realise that she had been content enough not to have seen him for months, to have him safely quartered in Brough, sending her money. She shivered at her own wickedness. Perhaps God was teaching her a lesson in taking her brothers. The gospel according to Reverend Kaye was still imprinted on her mind. The new and awful possibility made her cry again. It was true that she didn't cherish Willie in her heart as she ought, despite his rectitude. And her brothers were gone. The two facts became inescapably linked in her impressionable and superstitious mind and the idea took root.

I'll make it up, she promised the sky. Really I will. If you can just save George for Mother and Dorothy. Only leave him alone and I'll make it up to Willie.

The war dragged wearily on and George was drafted, though only to Bridlington at first. In a frenzy, Chloe wrote longer and ever more dutiful letters to Willie. Her vow sat heavily on her now. She began to see Willie again in cricket whites in her mind's eye and persuaded herself that she really did miss him after all. The separation was over-long.

In 1917, the indomitable Fred Moffat had both his legs blown off, but miraculously survived – no one understood how. Eventually he was sent home, in a wheelchair for life. Rebecca was justifiably proud, and oddly relieved rather than bitter. Her war was over now and it had done its worst. Old John was too old to be conscripted and Harry too young. Young John had a heart murmur and was medically disqualified, while Willie and Oliver both worked in protected trades. But no one could say Fred had not done his bit.

Chloe was shocked when she saw Fred's deformity. But Rebecca seemed to be more resilient – she acted as if he had given the Moffat family kudos, and the sacrifice was worth it. However, Fred was not to live with them. Instead, he went to a home for ex-Servicemen which John and Rebecca visited every month. He was defiantly cheerful on his departure but whether or not he remained so Chloe was unable to say, as she never saw him again.

In the end, George had to go to France too. Chloe prayed fervently every night for his safe return but it did no good. In the closing weeks of the war he was badly wounded. By the time he died, an armistice had been signed but there was no way to halt the sepsis marching through his body, for his wounds had festered. Three days later, Chloe learnt that Willie was coming home.

CHAPTER FIVE

Even Willie could see a change in Chloe when he returned home. She felt as if the world could never be the same again. Hardship and disappointment were no strangers to her, but these sudden and awful visitations of tragedy were different. George's death was a great blow. It showed her once again that her kind were not immune from disaster, that she personally was powerless to help and that a greater fate or divinity than she had ever imagined was out and about seeking retribution from them all. Or so it seemed to her.

She could not shake off what the war had done. It left her with a dreadful sense of pessimism, and sadness sat upon her like a mantle. She was resigned to it now and doggedly carried on with her household duties, in a tired kind of way. But when they were done and the children were in bed, she sat hopelessly in front of the fire, staring into the flames with her hands folded in her lap, waiting for sleep to come. She didn't cry, nor did she complain. But the realities of life failed to touch her any more. Even the death of her mother from influenza and her father's fatal accident with the tram left her totally unsurprised and almost unmoved. She was concerned for Dorothy, left alone in the world now, with her footsteps firmly planted on the path of eccentric spinsterhood, but knew she could do nothing. She continued to feed and clothe and listen to the boys but her mind was only halfway there.

Willie, to do him credit, was really worried. Uneasily,

he saw in Chloe the spectre of her mother. Of course he understood about her brothers. He too had felt the shock waves. He had experienced a nasty spasm in the pit of his stomach when he had realised it could have been him. Then again he might have drawn Fred's card. He felt sure that was worse. Either way he knew he'd been lucky – damned lucky. Chloe had certainly had a rough time. But the grieving had to stop. It had already obliterated the sweet young girl with auburn hair and a ready smile that he had married. That was natural enough, he supposed. But now he could see the gentle mother (and the only woman he had ever really felt comfortable with) on her way out too. He couldn't see why she was so depressed when she still had him and the boys. But he knew he had to get her back somehow.

'We're in for a good time now the war's over, lass,' he told her. 'There's talk of a big building boom and that's just grand for us joiners.'

She smiled and nodded but he saw he had left her unmoved and continued to ponder the problem. Perhaps the house was a wee bit small now the lads were getting bigger. If the building trade really did take off – and he was sure that it would – they might manage something a little better – in Sowerton, naturally, but not so close to Rebecca. Even Willie occasionally resented her all-seeing eye. Yes, that was it. No point in raising Chloe's hopes just yet of course. But he had good reason to feel confident . . . .

Oliver Horrocks was leaving the village to set up a small firm in Kingley. Indeed he had offered to make Willie a partner. But Willie had turned him down, sensing an element of risk and being more tempted by the surety of his status as the only Sowerton joiner, with Oliver gone. It was, of course, a mistake. Horrocks Joinery grew into a national concern and Oliver made a million, while Willie remained the village joiner for the rest of his life, with a steadily dwindling clientele until Jack took over. When Chloe discovered what he had done, she suffered fresh pangs of discontent and frustration. But, since Willie never bothered to discuss it with her, it was many years before she found out.

And at first Willie did appear to prosper. Money was no longer so tight, though Chloe scarcely noticed with Willie continuing to be as careful as ever. She knew it was a habit with him now. It gave her a new sense of despair. The boys were growing up fast. She was no longer as important to them as she had been and she began to see the future alone with Will – a Will whom daily became more set in his ways and chained to Sowerton and his mother.

In truth, the acute pain of Chloe's bereavement was lessening now. But her feeling of being trapped in a time-warp with Will grew. He had slipped easily back into his old routines since coming home. She knew he was glad to be home although, being Will, he hadn't actually said so. She even knew he was worried about her, had sensed her unhappiness and wanted to help. But she couldn't seem to reach out and help him help her. And there was no way that Willie could manage it alone.

As her old numbness wore off, Chloe became more desperate. I'll never get away, she thought. We're here for good now with Oliver gone. Together. She couldn't understand where their fleeting passion had gone – nor even remember it now. She was only aware that she longed for more than Willie could give. She was hard on herself too, feeling that she wronged her husband and this restlessness was wicked. The more it plagued her, the more she strove to please him. He, for his part, would have been content but for a vague realisation that something was still wrong with Chloe. So they both drifted through the days, scarcely speaking and not really saying anything when they did, their emotions crystallising into ice-forms.

And then, not surprisingly, Chloe fell ill. It started innocently enough with a troublesome cough but, within twenty-four hours, she was laid low with a fever, shaking and shivering as if unable to bear the cold, though her skin was burning hot. Her breathing was rapid and shallow and Willie feared the worst when the doctor came downstairs and confirmed pneumonia. There was very little he could do. It was the spring of 1922 and the great revolution wrought by antibiotics had yet to come. He could only offer advice and talk about a crisis. When he had gone, Willie had to wait for Chloe's body to fight its own battle.

Rebecca took care of the boys and nursed Chloe during the day while Willie sat with her at night. He knew she was very ill and he grew afraid. The doctor had stressed her underlying youth and strength but Willie had seen his face and knew it was no guarantee of survival. Anyway, he remembered Charlie Driver, a boy barely out of his own class at school, who had caught pneumonia. Willie had helped make his coffin and carried it.

The only way he could cope was by imagining Chloe well again and planning how to cheer her up. He was no longer sure moving away from Rebecca was such a good idea, for he had to admit she had been indispensable in this crisis. Anyway, although there was talk now of houses built by the council coming to the village, they had yet to materialise.

It was the doctor who gave him the idea of a holiday. Despite an obvious unwillingness to be drawn into discussing Chloe's recovery, he agreed that a period of convalescence would be necessary.

'Sea air's the thing,' he declared, 'if you can't have a Swiss mountain. Sea air and perhaps a little spa water and plenty of rest. Why not take her to Scarborough? It has everything. At least a week mind and preferably two.'

Willie wasn't sure he could spare two. They could leave the boys with Rebecca, but what about the yard? Jack had been his mate since leaving school but could hardly be expected to cope alone and he had no intention of paying another. A week might be all right. Then he looked at Chloe's flushed face and her long hair wet from the sweating and remembered she might die as he watched her laboured breathing moving the ribs up and down in her chest. She had become so thin and he felt ashamed.

Chloe reached her crisis after a week and Willie was terrified that she would die, while Rebecca was convinced of it. But something vital within her refused to succumb and, when the fever left her quite suddenly, although she was still very weak, it was plain that she would survive.

Chloe was bursting with excitement when the train from Leeds steamed into Scarborough station. The North Eastern line entered the town through a deep cutting, flanked by rather dreary boarding-houses of brown brick, with iron fire-escapes and black window-frames. But the clean stone of the station with its gold-painted clock spire promised better things to come.

Chloe had inspected her fellow-travellers minutely since their departure from Bradford that morning and was relieved to see that she was not too unfashionable after all. This had been a matter of some concern to her as, although Scarborough's former glories were already fading, she knew it was still considered quite elegant. She had taken her wedding-suit out of its moth-balls and in the end had removed all of the white flowers that made her wedding hat so topheavy. She had wound a long, white scarf around the crown instead, leaving the ends free to tie under her chin and pull down the brim slightly. A very old fox-fur belonging to Rebecca draped her shoulders and she considered herself fortunate to borrow it. But her greatest daring had been in shortening the hem of her blue suit until it showed four inches of leg above each ankle. She still remembered the look on Willie's face when she had visited the joiner's yard in the village to show him what she had done. She had expected him to be pleased with her thriftiness and ingenuity. But, as she had picked her way daintily amongst the curly wood-shavings that strewed the floor, he had looked up from his lathe, at first non-plussed by her finery and then horrified.

'Don't you like it?' she had said. 'Nobody wears their skirts on the floor anymore.'

Willie grunted.

'Not much. And why have you spoilt your hat?'

Chloe was at a loss to explain, though she understood her reasons very well. Willie turned back to his work unimpressed. She realised it was going to be a coffin and shuddered automatically. Of course that was silly because someone had to do it. She just wished it wasn't Will.

'Don't go cutting your hair, that's all.'

'Lots of women are now.'

'Aye . . . factory workers.'

'No, not just them. Ladies too.'

'Well, I like it long.'

'Yes, I know, Will. I wouldn't really think of cutting it.' For some time now, she had worn her hair in a neat bun at the nape of her neck. It was easier and more practical than piling it up high as she had done in the old days. She liked to think it still retained a vestige of elegance and would never change it now.

She was glad she had altered her clothes though. Especially now, standing next to Will who was pulling their case down from the luggage-rack of the train. For he had new tweeds and a cap and still cut quite a dash with his silky blond hair.

Scarborough was a revelation to Chloe. Though their back-street boarding-house (of the brown brick and black-windowed variety) was modest enough – at 2/6d a week with a cupboard for your own food – the grandeur of the front took her breath away. The sense of space and the sight of the sea rolling in over seemingly endless miles of sands intoxicated her.

'It is good air, Will,' she exclaimed. 'Lovely and fresh.' The air was in fact borne in by a stiff sea-breeze and it was distinctly chilly for the middle of June. But Chloe didn't mind that. She thought it was marvellous. Down on the sands some hardy souls had used the rows of brightly-painted changing-huts and were bathing in the water.

'Oh look, Will! Imagine – how nice.'

'Must be freezing!'

At the north end of the bay, only noisy seagulls roosted on the cliffs under the castle and the sea came crashing in. But, at the south side, the Spa stood proudly on the foreshore, gracefully epitomising pre-war days. The two ends of the bay were divided by a rocky headland which carried the ruins of the castle and jutted out to sea. Around its point clustered the harbours and the remains of the lighthouse the Germans had shelled. Chloe liked to stand by the harbour wall and look across the sweep of the South Bay at the classy hotels on the Esplanade above the Spa and the magnificent Grand, whose façade dominated the entire shore. Indeed, at first she was perfectly content to walk up and down the Marine Parade all day, with her arm linked through Willie's drinking in all the new sights and sounds.

But, by the third day, she was eager to try something new. The cliff lifts were a source of particular fascination to her.

'Shall we try one, Will?' she asked, watching the ascending and descending cars cross over on St Nicholas' Cliff, for at least the hundredth time.

'What? Pay good money to be carried a couple of hundred feet on a toothcomb?' Will was incensed. 'We can walk up as quick while they're waiting for passengers, I'll be bound.'

Chloe's cheeks burnt with a mixture of shame and anger. Why did he have to make her feel like that?

'I felt a little tired,' she faltered.

'Oh, I see. Happen we ought to go back to the lodgings, then.'

'Oh no, Willie! I don't want to go back just yet. I do want to walk up and see the Grand. Let's just have a sit down here for a while first.'

They sat and gazed across the yellow sands to the sea. It was, by then, a fine day with little wind to ruffle the ocean and really very warm for once.

'Weather's settling down a bit now,' observed Willie, taking out his handkerchief and wiping his neck carefully, running the square of well-pressed linen under his collar. 'Should be champion the rest of this week.'

'We're staying the full ten days, though?'

'Oh aye, of course.'

They fell silent. Chloe knew Willie was ready to go back now. She watched a bathing-party – 'bright, young things' – making their way to the sea. They were all laughing and talking with animation and, in their midst, walked a beautiful girl in a black bathing costume. She tossed and shook her short black hair so that it bounced up and down and gleamed in the sunlight. When she neared the waves, she broke into a run, bare-toed through the sand, then splashed straightaway into the water, shrieking and protesting at the cold. I wonder what it feels like, thought Chloe.

Closer at hand a family were modestly picnicking on the beach and the little boy and girl were building sandcastles. There was a man walking his dog along towards the Spa, repeatedly throwing a stick for the animal to retrieve. Out at sea were sailing boats with people in them. Chloe was aware of a procession of life before her in which she took no part. These were people with things to do and places to go, intent on enjoying themselves and she was nothing but an eternal spectator. She was utterly miserable and a few tears stung her eyes.

'Ready then?' asked Will. 'Feeling rested?'

She gave him what he was later to classify as 'one of her odd looks', but nodded and stood up.

They toiled up the hill and paused to admire the Grand Hotel with its balconies overlooking the sea, its pillared windows and its crowned cupolas. Solid and unashamedly baroque, it really was rather splendid. Afternoon tea would be being served now, thought Chloe wistfully. No good asking Willie to go in, though she was sure they could have afforded it just once. She knew what he would say. Something about 'expensive places for the toffs' and having 'plenty of tea back at the boarding-house'. She sighed and tried to tuck her desires away as they admired the view.

That evening, Willie was sick. They had had fish for supper and he blamed that, saying that it couldn't possibly have been fresh. Chloe was upset because she had bought it and cooked it herself, not to mention having eaten it too and remaining unaffected. The next day Willie stayed in bed, excepting frequent trips to the bathroom, and refused all food. Chloe settled down in a chair with some embroidery she had brought with her and prepared for a boring day.

'You must go out,' said Will, 'and have a walk. Don't stay in on my account. We came here to get you better with plenty of fresh air and that's what you should have.'

So Chloe dressed up in her blue suit and hat and her fox-fur and went out. Willie had been wrong about the weather. It was still very unsettled. The morning had dawned into the middle of a sea-fret and it was ominously cloudy and cool. She wandered about, trying not to feel disconsolate, along the Esplanade and past some of the other hotels she had admired from a distance, down the paths and the steps and through the gardens to the grey-glassed Spa. There weren't many people about. The wind came belting in from the North Sea, bringing immense breakers with it. A few black figures with dogs moved about on the wet sand. Chloe stood for a while and watched them against the backdrop of the thundering waves. In the distance, the sea spumed and sprayed against the harbour walls and the white ruin of the lighthouse. It was so different from the previous day. No bathers now.

She shivered and drew Rebecca's fur more closely around her shoulders. Then she came to a decision and stepped down onto the sand itself for the first time. It scrunched under her feet and she found it difficult to walk at all at first. But then she reached a firmer patch where her shoes made more transient prints, glowing briefly then vanishing as soon as she lifted her foot, and she made better progress. She would ruin her shoes of course and Willie would be very annoyed. But what did it matter?

Leaving the Spa behind, she struggled on in front of the receding tide. The wet sand shone like a mirror before her. The clouds gathered about the headland and the castle were a darker grey now and spitting some rain. But she didn't mind. In a way it was exhilarating and good to be alone.

Then her hat blew off. She watched in horror as the strong gust that had ripped it off her head bowled and spun it along like a child's hoop across the glass-like sand. Then a man she hadn't seen till now came sprinting past her from behind and, after several attempts, managed to catch it.

He was dignified enough when he brought it back, though Chloe could see that his cheeks were flushed from the effort of running and there was more than a hint of humour in his eyes.

'A little wet, I'm afraid,' he said ruefully, as if it was all his fault. 'And sandy.' He held the hat out to her, brushing it off with his hands.

'Thank you, sir. You're very kind,' and Chloe blushed.

He couldn't imagine what she was doing there. She was so small and slight it seemed the gusty wind must blow her over any moment. Indeed, even as he hesitated, she swayed forward a little and he had to put out his arm to steady her. Hatless, her auburn hair did its utmost to escape from the neat little bun nestling on her neck. Thin tendrils of it were whipped forward by the wind and played around her pale face. There were the beginnings of lines around her eyes and more than a few grey hairs amongst the auburn, but he could tell that she was still quite young – mid-thirties at a guess. How vulnerable she looked and how hopelessly old-fashioned. He felt almost instantly responsible for her.

'My name is Maurice Sinclair,' he said, holding out his hand more formally. 'How do you do?' Chloe immediately recognised a gentleman.

'How do you do, sir.' She shook his hand timidly and almost bobbed her knees.

'It's a rough morning for you to be walking the beach.'

'Yes,' Chloe sighed as she looked at her feet. 'I didn't realise how wet the sand was.'

He escorted her back to the promenade and in the meantime ascertained that she was on holiday.

'My husband . . . Mr Moffatt . . . is indisposed,' Chloe explained, 'and resting back at the boarding-house. But he was anxious for me to come out and take some fresh air, as I'm convalescing.'

Although she felt it was rather bold to strike up a conversation with a total stranger, she was glad of his arm, for the blasts of wind were leaving her slightly breathless. And he really wasn't at all menacing. She was surprised how small he was, scarcely more than her own height. He was very dapper, with dark curly hair cut close to his head, revealing ears which seemed too large for a small face, and a thin moustache. His eyes seemed kindly and were startlingly blue under such dark brows. The small bones in his face were especially prominent and somehow she sensed that he wasn't very strong himself.

'It's going to rain more heavily,' he said. 'Have you far to go?'

She told him where.

'Then you must take my umbrella.'

She started to protest.

'No, really. You must. You'll be drenched otherwise.'

'But what about you?'

'I'm only staying at the Grand. I can easily nip up there in a tick. Though really I think I should escort you back to you lodgings.'

'Oh, no – you mustn't do that!'

'Then you must take the umbrella.'

'But how will I give it back to you?'

He smiled.

'I'm here for a little while. You'll probably see me again. And if you don't, not to worry. I have several umbrellas.'

Willie was worse rather than better when she got back and, although he slept well enough, the following day found him still unable to eat.

'Shall we go home?' said Chloe, sadly. 'It isn't very nice for you here. And it can't just be the fish. You are really ill.'

'I couldn't face the train ride,' Willie moaned. 'No, I'm right enough here – as long as I'm left quiet and don't have to eat.'

'I'll stay in with you, today.'

'You won't!'

'But Willie . . .'

'I only want to sleep, anyway. But we paid good money for this holiday. You must go out and get the air. All day. Otherwise it's been wasted. Go on, now. You needn't come back early on my account like yesterday.'

'I'll need some money if I'm to be out all day, Will.'

'Then tek some from me purse.' He was anxious for her to be gone.

'Shall I bring you anything back today?'

'No, not yet. Mebbe tomorrow.' He pulled the sheets around himself fussily and settled down. 'You can get me some fresh water an' that's all.'

Chloe took the umbrella with her when she went out. She hadn't mentioned it to Willie for some reason but had left it in the stand in the hall of their lodgings. She wouldn't need to use it today. The clouds had rolled off out to sea and the weather was fine and warm again. But she might be able to return it to its owner.

She decided to repeat her walk of yesterday. Then, this afternoon, she might visit the castle. It would be a long day on her own but Willie was right. She shouldn't waste it. He didn't seem to want her to look after him and she felt a little hurt. Should she have insisted? She didn't see why she should. She was sorry of course that Will was poorly but couldn't help feeling more than a little exasperated with him as well. It was their holiday . . . their first ever. It was so tiresome that he should be ill and so ignominiously at that.

When she reached the cliff-top, she forgot about him as the view of the bay took her breath away. Everything was fresh after the rain. The trees on the hillside nodded and waved new lime leaves. The gardens were in full flower and the beach and promenade were already sprinkled with gaily dressed figures, while the sunlight struck a thousand diamonds off the gently rolling blue sea.

She walked right along the beach towards the harbour but Maurice Sinclair was nowhere to be seen. Then, still clutching the tightly-rolled umbrella, she made her way into the town and did a little shopping. At lunchtime, she ate her jam and bread sandwiches in St Nicholas' Gardens, around the corner from the Grand. She even stood and watched the cars roll up to the doors for a little while from the square. But still she did not see the man with several umbrellas.

After lunch, she found her way through the streets and up the hill to the castle ruins. From here she could survey the sweep of both great bays and became convinced she would never find him again. It was unthinkable to keep his umbrella, of course. She must leave it with the hall porter in the Grand. But the idea of walking through those imposing doors intimidated her. She would have felt happier at finding a servants' entrance. So tired though she was, her feet were drawn back along the foreshore to the South Cliff Gardens, there to consider the problem further.

She found him almost at once, sitting in a quiet recess of the gardens, beyond the Spa, facing the sea. Although she had been looking for him all day, she felt suddenly nervous and unsure of her ground. He was dressed in flannels and a striped blazer and wore a boater on his head, which was bent intently over a book.

Chloe hovered and coughed politely. He looked up, taking an instant or two to recognise her, and then sprang to his feet with a smile. She wore a summer dress today, of a green floral print, and a wide straw hat and generally looked so much better that she had surprised him. The exercise and the air were beginning to put colour back into her cheeks.

'Mrs Moffat,' he said, bowing slightly over her hand. 'How delightful. Do sit down.'

'I've brought your umbrella.' She laid it with dignity on the seat. He noted her seriousness and smiled. 'That's very good of you. You needn't have bothered today.'

'It was kind of you to lend it to me.'

'And how is Mr Moffat today?'

'No better, I'm afraid.'

'I'm sorry to hear it. What on earth have you been doing with yourself?'

'Oh, I've been visiting the castle.'

His eyes wandered across the bay to the headland.

'Did you find it interesting?'

'Yes, very.'

'It has quite a history, hasn't it? Right from the days of King Henry II. And there was a settlement and some kind of fortress there long before that.'

'I didn't know that.'

He studied her face. 'Have you walked all the way there and back this afternoon?'

She nodded.

'You must be tired.'

'I am . . . a little. I think I'll sit down a while – if you're sure I won't disturb you.'

'Oh, no – not at all.'

'But you were studying . . . ' He looked blank and she indicated his book.

'Oh no, not studying really. Just reading . . . '

'Then I'm interrupting your story . . . '

'No, it isn't a story. It's a poem. Look.' And he passed the green-bound volume across to her. Chloe took it from his hand with shy curiosity, looked at the open page and read:

Strange Meeting

It seemed that out of battle I escaped
Down some profound dull tunnel, long since scooped
Through granites which titanic wars had groined . . .

It was quite a long poem and written in a way which was totally unfamiliar to her. She didn't understand all of it and read with considerable difficulty – but she felt its meaning clearly enough and when she had finished it there were tears in her eyes. He noticed her reaction too late and took the book away.

'Mrs Moffat . . . I'm so terribly sorry. You're upset and I'm a blithering idiot not to have guessed you might be. Please forgive me.'

Chloe brushed away the tears from her cheeks and fumbled for her handkerchief but couldn't find it.

'Allow me.' He pressed his freshly laundered one into her hand and Chloe felt she ought to be embarrassed but laughed instead through her tears.

'You're always lending me things, Mr Sinclair.'

'I do seem to be, don't I? Perhaps you should call me Maurice, then? I'm so sorry for having wounded you.'

'Oh, but you haven't really. I'm glad I read it. Its just that all of my brothers were killed in the war, you see – every one of them – and, well . . .'

'Yes, I do see. Really I do. I should have known.' His voice was very low.

'Oh, but's that silly – how could you have known?'

'I should have guessed you must have lost someone –

so many did.' There was a darkness on his face now and he fell silent.

'I've never read a poem like that before.' Chloe was perfectly calm now and anxious to talk. 'It's very good, isn't it?' Maurice's face relaxed in a brief smile.

'Yes, I think so,' he said. 'So do a lot of people . . . and many more will in time. It was written by a man called Wilfred Owen.'

'Was he a soldier?'

'Yes.'

'And what happened to him?'

'He was killed in 1918 . . . a week before the armistice was signed.' Chloe digested this, silently.

'Did he write any other poems?'

'Oh, yes. This book is full of his poetry.'

'I should like to read it.' Chloe was amazed at her own audacity. Yet it seemed the most natural thing in the world to say and she meant it. He wasn't at all shocked but looked at her and smiled.

'I'm not sure I should let you. They're mostly rather grim.'

They sat for a while in a comfortable silence and then Chloe said: 'Were you – you know – involved . . . in the war, I mean?'

'I was at the Front for a short while. I may as well tell you I didn't volunteer – I was conscripted. And I spent most of the time in a hospital for nervous diseases. You would have been ashamed of me if I had been your brother, I'm afraid.'

'Oh no, I wouldn't have,' Chloe assured him.

'Well, my own family were, you see and I really don't blame them.' His voice cracked slightly. 'Most of the time I was very ashamed of myself.'

'Why do you read about it?' asked Chloe, gently, 'when it upsets you so much? I'm sorry – I shouldn't ask.'

Maurice recovered himself.

'Not at all. It's a very good question – I don't think I

can answer it! But I can't just forget it, you see, and sometimes I feel as if everyone else has already, and I don't think they should.'

'Yes, I see.'

He rubbed a hand over his moustache and shook himself slightly, sighing.

'Tell me, what is your name?'

Chloe stared. 'Mrs Moffat.'

'Ah, yes.' Maurice frowned and smiled at the same time. 'I know that. But I meant what's your *real* name? I can't go on calling you Mrs Moffat, after a conversation like that. It is a rather comical name anyway, you know!'

Chloe went pink. 'My Christian name is Chloe.'

'Chloe . . . "a young green shoot". Yes, that's much better. Are you hungry, Chloe?'

'Well . . .'.

'Of course you are, after your walk. Let's go and find some tea.' He consulted his watch. 'It's nearly four o'clock.'

Standing up, he offered her his arm.

'Oh, I'm not sure . . .'

'But I insist!'

They strolled together past the Spa.

'Er, where are we going?' asked Chloe.

'Back to the Grand.'

'Oh, but I couldn't!' She withdrew her arm in alarm.

'We'll take the cliff lift in case you're tired.'

'Oh, no, you misunderstand me, Mr Sinclair.'

'Maurice! Would you rather go somewhere else?'

'No, but . . . it's just that . . . I'm not really dressed, not smart enough, you know.'

'Oh, that!' Maurice laughed. 'What nonsense! You look fine to me. Anyway, it's not that special, you know.'

But, although she said nothing, he became aware of a great excitement rising inside her as they stood together in the lift. When the car jerked before setting off, she grasped his arm and then her eyes widened with incredulity as they moved smoothly upwards. When they walked through the revolving doors of the Grand Hotel and stood for a moment in the foyer, looking up at the ornate dome of the roof and the vast, winding staircase, he thought for a moment she might faint and was relieved when she only gasped with pleasure. Her innocence began to intrigue him.

He steered her towards a table in the lounge and Chloe, (whose legs were wobbling) sat down gratefully. She thanked heaven she had her gloves with her to hide her work-worn hands and nails. She couldn't really believe all this was happening to her, for they were in an elegant room with a high ceiling and a chandelier. Swathed drapes curtained the windows, various potted ferns of an enormous size stood in the corners and the deep pile of a Persian carpet muffled footfalls on the floor. The waiters bustled to and fro with cakes and tea on silver trays and the general murmur of other people's conversation, with the chinkle of their cutlery and bone china, threatened to drown the desultory playing of a formally-dressed pianist at the baby grand. Chloe sat motionless and breathless and drank it all in.

'You must tell me about yourself,' said Maurice, when they had ordered.

She did try but was continually distracted. At one point, her eyes almost popped out of her head when a carefully made-up lady, with extremely short hair and a very plunging neckline, sat down at the table opposite and proceeded to light a cigarette in a long black holder. The dress made her blush. Of course, ballgowns could always be a little risqué she had heard. But in the afternoon!

'What are you looking at?' asked Maurice. Chloe blushed more deeply and indicated the lady with her eyes.

'Don't you think?' she asked with a whisper, 'that she's terribly smart?'

Maurice, sitting with his back to the opposite table, snatched a discreet look.

'I suppose,' he said, 'she has a certain brittle charm. But, frankly, I much prefer you.'

Chloe was rather pleased.

'Another cake?'

'Shall I?'

'Yes, you must. I don't think I would forgive you if you didn't.'

'Oh,' Chloe sounded quite serious. 'Then I will, of course.' She watched him raise his finger a fraction and marvelled that the waiter saw and came.

'So you live in a small village called Sowerton and your husband is the joiner,' Maurice prompted. But he only half-listened in the end because he realised she was only giving him the barest of details and missing out all the important things he would have liked to know. But still he found her unbearably touching. Although she was behaving impeccably, she could not disguise the fact that she was totally unused to her surroundings, to his manner of speech and to his whole, rather effete, way of life.

'Tell me, Chloe,' he said finally, 'have you any plans for tomorrow?'

'Well, of course that rather depends on Will, my husband.'

'And if he remains unwell?'

'I really don't know.'

'Would you do me the honour of letting me show you around the town?'

'That's very kind of you, but I couldn't possible presume . . . . '

'Why not? I would enjoy your company. I'm here on my own too, remember, and it does become rather boring at times. I would be delighted to have you with me.'

'Well, perhaps, if Will isn't fit to go out . . . '

They arranged to meet in the gardens at ten.

Afterwards, Chloe's memories of the next two days

rolled into one exciting blur. They did so much and the weather stayed so fine. Each day they picnicked on the beach, though she discovered that Maurice's idea of a picnic was smoked salmon, followed by strawberries washed down with champagne. He continually shocked and then delighted her. She declined a visit to the Seawater Baths in horror of the unknown and he did not press her. But they did take a boat trip out into the bay. There were quieter moments too, like listening to the orchestra play in the Spa rooms and their visit to the mediaeval parish church and some of the old houses in Sandside. She thought he must be a well-educated man for he seemed to know so much about the history of the place. Nor did he neglect more vulgar delights like the Underground People's Palace of Amusements and the Grand Pavilion Pictures. From champagne to cinema, it was all new to Chloe. She sat spellbound in the dark, watching jerky people move like clockwork across a flickering screen. Maurice seemed very close in the next seat and, for the first time, she wondered if he expected anything in return for his largesse. In her heart she knew she should have been more circumspect. Will knew nothing of how she was spending her days. But she wanted the enchantment to go on. And anyway, Maurice had behaved most honourably . . . even here in the cosy gloom of the picture-house.

She forced herself to admit that he was an odd character. To the casual passer-by, he might seem almost a caricature of the well-to-do, young English gent of the day. But his solitude, his brooding over the war and his slightly foreign name and darkness set a jarring note. She gathered that he was passionately interested in the arts. He seemed full of life to her and audacious in his disregard for convention. And yet he was not raucous or pushy. She was not in the least bit frightened of him. Overall, despite his obvious material advantages, there was an air of disappointment, of sensitivity and shyness about him which struck a chord of recognition in Chloe and she warmed to that. And it was not just that he entertained her so well, nor that he was such a contrast to Willie. It was the way he set up some pleasure for her and then sat back quietly, watching her reaction, seeking and smiling at her approval.

Two days out of a lifetime. Hardly long enough to know anyone. And yet two days well spent in the constant company of another can be most revealing. So important that it was Chloe in the end who, though timid and trembling, reached out to lay a hand on his in the half-light of the Pavilion. He curled his fingers gently round hers, then raised them briefly to his lips.

Outside, she voiced her fears. 'I'm afraid I may not be able to come out with you tomorrow.'

'He is better?'

Chloe nodded and lowered her head.

'Much. He says he is still very weak but I feel sure he will be up and about tomorrow.'

'And out?'

'I don't know. Perhaps.'

'If you can, will you meet me for lunch in the Grand?'

'I will try, but I'm not sure. I wanted to say thank you, you see – in case I can't.'

'But it really was a pleasure.'

She avoided his eye. 'I must go now . . . I promised to be back early today.'

'Of course you must. But please don't forget about tomorrow.'

'I shan't forget,' said Chloe. 'I shan't forget any of it.'

He told himself that she wouldn't come. The husband waiting in the shadows would be hale and hearty today. Or maybe she had just taken fright. He wouldn't be surprised. He knew what she must be thinking. Girls nowadays had everything weighed up so carefully. Then he reminded himself that a girl who gasped at the Grand Hotel, Scarborough, was not a woman of the world. That was what had attracted him in the first place. He stared gloomily over acres of white linen tablecloth and knew she would not come. Maybe if he had arranged to meet her outside . . .

And then there she was! Looking extremely bashful, in the hands of a waiter guiding her stumbling footsteps over to his table. He leapt to his feet and beamed.

'My dear Chloe!' That made her blush terribly. She was wearing the blue suit – but without a hat – and the colour of her hair in the sunshine was wonderful. Despite the warm weather, the awful fur was wrapped round her neck and he thought she was quite enchanting.

'Can you stay?'

She nodded and her eyes sparkled. 'Will and I went for a long walk this morning and he is quite tired out. He's going to rest all afternoon.'

'That's splendid.'

Her look reproached him. 'But this will be the last time we can meet. I haven't told Will, you see. I know that's very wrong but I didn't think he'd understand.'

'I'm sure you're right.'

Chloe lowered her eyes. 'I don't feel very happy about it now, to tell you the truth. I don't think I've done right.'

'But Chloe! Such an innocent few days.' She was not then as unworldly as he had supposed. Maurice came to her rescue. 'You do know, Chloe, don't you, that I expect nothing in return?'

Chloe kept her eyes down and reddened to her forehead. 'I wasn't quite sure.'

'Well, I don't and you mustn't spoil what I hope was an enjoyable day or two by feeling awkward or guilty in any way. It was a pleasant time, wasn't it?'

'Oh, yes . . . it was wonderful!' Chloe looked at him again and then smiled.

'Then let us finish in style. We must have some champagne opened right away! What am I thinking of?'

Chloe sat a little bemused while the waiters ministered to their needs. In truth, she felt more comfortable with Maurice alone than in such a public venue. But he was so anxious that she should be pleased; she could not deny him it. And it was a lovely lunch. When it was all over, she felt very strange. She had suddenly realised it was all at an end. But the worst thing of all would be saying goodbye to Maurice.

'Would you like a walk?' he asked for he too had fallen very silent. Chloe shook her head.

'No, thank you,' she said. 'I feel rather tired.' Then she heard her voice carry on through a haze . . . as if it belonged to another woman and certainly not to Chloe Moffat at all. 'I should like to rest a while . . . in your room.'

If he was surprised, he did not show it. She remembered him escorting her up the vast staircase like something out of a dream. She admired his room, turning delicately away from the bed, saying that it was four times the size of theirs at the boarding-house, remarking on the furnishings and the immensity of the bathroom, just visible through an adjoining door. Maurice stood with his back to her at the window and lit a cigarette.

Suddenly, she slumped down in a chair and started to sob. In alarm, Maurice moved to her side.

'I've made you very unhappy,' he said in a low voice. 'I'm sorry.'

She held her head in her hands but shook it, violently. He wasn't sure what to do next and laid a hand tentatively on her shoulder.

'Do you want to go back to your lodgings?'

'No . . . that's just it! I don't! I don't want to go back.' She raised a tear-stained face. 'This is very difficult for me. But it isn't just the champagne. I want to say what I feel. But I'm afraid of what you'll think of me.'

Maurice was bewildered. 'But I won't judge you or think ill of you, whatever you say. Why, what can it be?'

'I want to stay.' She looked into his eyes and implored him to see her real meaning. He took her in his arms.

'You mean this?'

'Yes. And now you'll think I'm cheap and common. But I'm not, you know. It's just that I'll never see you again and I did want something more to remember after all.' Maurice smiled sadly.

'It's not so terrible a thing,' he said and put out a hand to touch her hair, drawing her to him.

'You don't have to go back,' he said, after kissing her, 'ever again. Why do you have to? If you stay with me, you know I'd try to be good to you. I could show you so much . . . much more than in these paltry two days. Say you won't go back ever.'

Chloe closed her eyes, frightened at last.

'No,' she said. 'I can't. There's the boys.'

'But you told me they were growing. You said they didn't need you any more.'

'I can't leave them and I can't ever leave Will.'

'Why not? He doesn't deserve you. I can tell that. It stands out a mile.'

'I owe him.'

'But you don't love him.'

'No . . . not any more.'

'Why do you owe him?'

'I just do.' She shook her head. 'You mustn't ask.'

He made love to her then. They lay on the bed, with the window slightly open and the curtains stirred and fluttered in the breeze. The sound of the sea and the voices from the shore came floating up from the beach.

When it was over, Chloe's resolve was shaken for she

had been truly aroused for the first time. He had been very tender, allaying all her fear and doubt. A phrase she had thought of when she first met him came into her mind: Entirely without menace. And she had responded to his gentleness. What she had really viewed as some sort of sacrificial offering, because of her finer feelings for him, had turned into something very different. She lay in his arms for a long time and let him quietly stroke her hair. But he didn't ask her if she would change her mind and she was grateful.

At last she said: 'What time is it?'

He reached over her for the large fob watch on top of his pile of clothes. 'Ten to four.'

She caught her breath. 'I must go. It's nearly tea-time!'

'Will I see you again?'

Chloe struggled hopelessly with hooks and eyes.

'No – I don't know! Perhaps I could try.' Then she stopped what she was doing and looked at him with wet eyes.

'No, Maurice. I really don't think so.' She ran most of the way home and arrived at the end of their street in a lather. Forcing herself to walk and breathe slowly, she covered the last few yards with more dignity, though her hairpins, thrust in too hastily, were almost all falling out.

To her horror, Will was not only up and dressed again but in obvious good spirits and sitting at the tea-table.

'You're late,' he said. 'Did you walk too far again? – You're flushed enough. Shouldn't have hurried on my account. Still it suits you – nice to see the colour back in your cheeks.'

Much later that night, Chloe lay wide awake, staring at the ceiling, with hot rivulets of tears running silently down each cheek into pools on the pillow. Willie was fast asleep and snoring. He was most definitely better and had been amorous in his usual clumsy way. Chloe had lain still, hating it. But, most of all, she had hated herself. The fact that Willie had been inside her too brought home the full force of her transgression. What kind of a woman was she? What would he say if he knew? To think that she had got up from the bed of another man and come straight to his in this manner! And she had once rebuked Will, albeit silently, for what had probably been a much lesser dalliance!

And what about Maurice? Her mind, unbidden, kept returning to him. She could love him so . . . she already did. He would understand her so much better than Will, he would try to make everything all right. But could he? Useless to think in such a way. It was over now. But she wished it hadn't finished like this. She had her memory – the beautiful memory she had wanted – but Willie had made it bitter-sweet now.

Only two days remained of their holiday and Willie did his best to make sure that Chloe enjoyed them. She was painfully aware that his best was not enough. On the last day, she saw Maurice in the distance and was aware that he followed them, without any sign of recognition. But, when Willie was taken short and had to disappear into the public conveniences, he made his move and was beside her in a moment.

'Chloe!'

'Hello.'

'How are you?'

'Very well now. We're going home tomorrow.'

'I see. Well, I leave soon too.' He hesitated and looked out to sea, not daring to face her eyes. 'You could come with me.' Chloe was silent. 'You know where I am.' She shook her head sadly.

'It's not possible. Our train leaves at eleven.'

'It is possible not to be on it. Please think about it, Chloe. Don't throw your life away on Willie.'

At this point, Willie himself re-emerged and, tipping his hat formally and bidding her good-day, Maurice strolled on.

'Who's that?' said Willie.

'Just a man. Chatting about the weather.'

'Cheeky blighter! These toffs are all the same.'

Chloe passed another sleepless night, plagued by temptation. Maurice was the answer to her dreams! Her last chance of escape. Her only hope of gaiety and luxury. She wanted him very badly. But she knew that, if she went with him, she would be beyond the pale. Cut off from respectable society; damned forever in the eyes of the Reverend Kaye. And loaded with guilt over Will and the boys. It was a burden she couldn't carry. But she still craved it, imagined herself with him and wavered. The door would not be finally closed until her train drew out of the station. Then it would be too late, for she did not know Maurice's home address, nor he hers.

It was a drab dawn. As they breakfasted and packed, Chloe wondered if Maurice would come to the station. It seemed unlikely and yet she couldn't believe they had already said goodbye. They made their way there on foot, with Willie carrying their case. He wouldn't relinquish it to any porter in a hurry. She had never found him more annoying as he fussed and faffed over tickets and money and train times. They were too early, of course, and would have quite a wait. Chloe felt nervy and couldn't keep still. The steamy smell of the station with its noise and bustle went to her head. She began to wander up and down the platform and Willie went to buy a newspaper. Left alone, Chloe felt the outside world pull. It wouldn't take long to run through the barrier onto the street. And this time she would have somewhere to go.

Then a little boy tugged at her skirt. She looked down, half expecting Ted, but it was an unfamiliar face that thrust a small package into her hands, pointed a finger up the platform, grinned and ran off.

He was there – sitting on a bench a hundred yards away. He rose to his feet when she looked in his direction and took off his hat, then he stood and waited. She panicked and turned away. When she next looked, he had gone. Even then, it wasn't too late. But she knew in her heart that the moment of refusal had come and gone.

Twenty minutes later they were on the train, clacking and rocking over the points onto the main line and the door into the garden had clanged shut forever. Chloe watched the steam billow and eddy past the window with hopeless eyes. Willie was asleep, his jaw fallen open and his newspaper on his lap. She drew out Maurice's package from her pocket and unwrapped it gingerly. It was the volume of poems by Wilfred Owen. Inside, he had written:

'A strange present for a lover to give and a woman to receive. But it did ease our way to friendship. You were right of course when you said you should read it. I know now you will not come to me. I do not blame you, but I grieve for us both. I hope this book will be a tangible memory of our brief but halcyon days together, in love, M.S.'

She wasn't sure what halcyon meant. But it sounded beautiful.

CHAPTER SIX

The baby was due in the middle of March and Chloe was horrified at her own fertility, though glad of it too, while Willie congratulated himself on his sagacity. That little holiday in Scarborough last year had done the trick all right. At first, when they had found out Chloe was expecting again, he wasn't sure if she would be pleased after such a long gap. But he needn't have worried. The maternal instinct was still there. Perked her up good and proper it had. Wonder he hadn't thought of it before. He whistled as he followed his elder son down the path from Croft Row on their way to work and waved at his mother in her window. Nothing like a baby to keep the women happy. Champion if it were another boy!

Chloe watched him go, noting the wave to Rebecca. There was none for her and she sighed. But it didn't really matter any more. The baby thumped and kicked inside her and she had to sit down for a moment. It had been a harder pregnancy than her others. Perhaps it was only because she was older, yet she couldn't rid herself of the feeling that everything about it was different. Because it would be a girl and because Maurice was the father. She would never be able to be entirely sure of course. Willie had unwittingly made certain of that. Just as well! Although she longed for the child to belong to Maurice, she felt rather scared in case a complete absence of family resemblance should be commented upon.

She was looking forward to the baby's arrival. There hadn't been much time to devote to the boys individually, with them coming so close together. But this one would be different – and it would really be the last. A shame it was due in March. March was the month she had first come to Sowerton and the month in which she had run away. She was convinced it was an unlucky time of year for her. True, Jack had been born safely in March. But he was a boy and that was different. If she was to bear a girl, she didn't want her daughter to start out under the cloud of her own misfortunes.

She rose to clear the dishes. Somehow this morning she must find time to slip in and see old Mrs Kaye, for she would have to go to bed in the afternoon. Already her ankles were swelling and the doctor had tut-tutted and warned her to rest. It had come as a shock because she had borne the others so easily. But she did try to obey him, in the afternoons at least. She would lie on her bed feeling indulgent, knowing that the house was quiet but there were still jobs to be done. It might have been an occasion for brooding. But, although it was true that she often daydreamed about Maurice, she now had something else to occupy her thoughts. He had opened up a new world to her without knowing it and the fact that the Premier Bus Company now ran a regular service between Sowerton and Kingley made this world accessible. For when she had finished secretly reading Wilfred Owen's poems, she had taken the bus to Kingley and visited the Public Lending Library.

At first, she found the place intimidating. The rows of shelves seemed endless, the wooden gates that let you in and out most alarming and the overall hush, heightened by rustlings and coughings, was fearful. Then there was the way the young man who stamped her books looked sternly over his glasses. But, gradually, she became used to the routine, found her way around and realised the young man merely had a nervous habit. Then the library became her greatest treat. At first she read anything, but novels rapidly became her main solace. Jane Austen, the Brontës and Mrs Henry Wood were firm favourites and, after reading Louisa May Alcott, she determined to call her hoped-for daughter Beth.

In her final month, she grew so tired that she took to reading most of the day. The house still looked neat and the meals were made, but she knew that dust was settling in the corners. She was amazed to find that no one seemed to notice. For years she had been terribly houseproud and now she realised that no one – not even Willie – really noticed. She couldn't understand it. Even Rebecca didn't criticise for she had her own sadness to deal with. John Moffat – her elder by eight years – had died suddenly at the beginning of March. He hadn't been ill but had collapsed in the garden as he would have wished to and it was all over in a few moments. Chloe missed him. John alone among the Moffats had always been sweet to her. She wished he could have seen the new baby at least once. But it wasn't to be. Rebecca coped well as she did with everything, a little grimly but with steadfast determination. Only her mouth pursed into a more pessimistic line as she grew older and stouter.

The middle of March came and went and Chloe was overdue. She was glad because, although she was anxious to have her labour over and see the child, the importance of not delivering it into the world in March had grown large in her superstitious mind. She wouldn't even leave the house now for fear of bringing her labour on and Willie was exasperated. He couldn't remember her being so careful before. She must be getting older. This baby should definitely be the last. True, she was happier and more restful, but he vaguely sensed some further withdrawal from him at the back of it all.

It was Rebecca's birthday on the 31st and Chloe had had irregular pains all week. That morning they settled into a more definite rhythm and everyone was sure the baby would be born before sundown and said how nice that would be. But it was painfully slow in coming, as if it sensed its mother's reluctance. Midnight passed and Chloe relaxed into the morning of the first of April with her baby still unborn. But the womb was stubborn now and she had lost control.

At six o'clock in the greyness of dawn, when Chloe lay exhausted in a sweaty miasma of never-ending pain, no longer caring about the day or the date, the village doctor put on the forceps and hauled out her only half-alive daughter. Chloe tried unsuccessfully to focus on the crumpled and slippery little body. Before she could even begin to feel afraid, and against all the rules, she heard the indignant cry of her newborn. She raised herself on one elbow with her head swimming. It really was a girl! Only about six pounds after all that trouble, and with hair as black as night.

Beth's baby eyes remained blue but her hair lightened hardly at all. She was a pretty baby, though difficult from the start. She neither slept nor fed well and was irritable even at the breast. When she was ill, she was always iller than any of the others had been. Chloe loved her dearly, but was baffled and perplexed. The toddler stage was exhausting, for Beth was very determined and not easily distracted. Chloe found herself wondering if her own daughter would turn out as spoilt as her sister Daisy. But then, at last, when she had almost given up hope, Beth began to settle down into a charming little girl. Only Chloe knew the power for good or evil which still raged not very far beneath. She was like no one else in the family. She was not even, despite the tell-tale dark curls, like Maurice. Chloe felt she would always be a mystery.

When Beth was three, they moved into one of the eagerly awaited council houses and Chloe thought it was heaven. It was an end terrace in the lane past the church, with a fine view from the back down the valley to the Aire and the hills beyond. It had an inside toilet and a proper bathroom, three bedrooms (although one was rather small) and a much larger living-room than Croft Row, with the kitchen completely separate. The lighting was by gas, though Willie thought they would probably be converted in a year or two to electricity, and Chloe was delighted with her new gas cooker, even though it didn't have a Regulo dial. Outside, there was a garden at front and back, fenced all the way round, and Willie put in roses facing the road and had a vegetable patch and some grass at the back. He made a swing for Beth there, knotting it round one of the branches of an old apple tree the builders had left standing. A young family moved in next door with a four-year old girl for Beth to play with and Chloe knew that it was all perfect.

She had given up grieving over her lost opportunities, just as she had given up over Will. Somewhere, in the years since Beth's birth, she had come to terms with herself and her life. Often, when she looked at Beth, she thought of Maurice and her secret gave her a thrill. But she didn't allow herself any empty longings. She still retreated into her books every night when Beth was in bed but now she recognised that the people she read about were different from herself, without envying them so strongly. Occasionally she would read a passage aloud to Will – much as he had once read the paper to her, without expecting her to understand – with a 'fancy that' or 'just listen to this'. Her daytime hours were absorbed by Beth but her evenings, in this way, remained her own. She even had a night out occasionally, for Willie had let her join the W.I. and the Mother's Union. After twenty years in the village, she was still remembered by Rebecca's peers as 'the girl from Bradford who was the maid at the vicarage that Willie Moffat had to marry'. But at least she was tolerated.

Her relations with Will were settled. Beth had her own bedroom now and they slept alone again. But they had fallen out of the habit of sex with having the child sleep in their room so long and Willie didn't resume it. It didn't bother Chloe any more and they never discussed it. She assumed his disinclination to have further children was the cause, but it didn't seem to bother him either. Although he was only forty, he was beginning to lose his hair on top and she could see his figure stiffening into middle age. He still rang bells and sang in the choir, but his days of notching up an effortless century on the cricket field were gone. Still, she had come to accept him as he was. If anything, she was more obedient and deferential than ever. Not only did she remain grateful but she now had a transgression to hide. The struggle was over and she had capitulated. She was still captivated by 'nice things', but thought of them as being entirely meant for others. She knew she wasn't intended for anything better now.

What she didn't know was that she had one more sacrifice to make. It was barely six months after they had moved into their new home and she was wandering round the back garden, blessedly not overlooked, looking at the vegetables. It was a breezy summer's day and the washing flapped gaily like bunting on the line. She felt very happy. Beth was swinging under the tree, shouting to be pushed higher all the time, for she hadn't learnt to work it with her body yet. The house was straight and clean and tidy and she was pleased with the way it was looking now. It was time to think about shopping for their dinner tonight, but it was so pleasant in the garden that she would let Beth play on a bit longer. All the boys were out at work now – even Ted who had just started as a clerk for the Gas Board in Kingley and went off on the bus every day with his sandwiches.

Then she heard a shout and turned to see Jack running down the road. He was nineteen now and a handsome lad and she watched him fondly. She couldn't deny he looked like the young Willie, but there was a hint of Matt there too. What on earth was he doing running home at this hour? He was quite out of breath.

'Mam!' he shouted, still on the other side of the road. 'Dad says come quick – up to the Croft. Gran'ma's had a stroke!'

Chloe dropped the peg-basket she had been holding and the wooden pegs with their round heads scattered all over the path. Not Rebecca, surely! She was indomitable and still only sixty-six. Jack reached her side and grabbed her arm, repeating his message and panting hard.

'Where's your father?'

'Up in the house with her. The doctor sent for him.'

Chloe thought quickly.

'You'll have to look after Beth. I'll get my coat and go up straightaway.'

'I've got to get back to the joinery.'

'Then take her with you . . . only mind she comes to no harm.'

Rebecca was still conscious but unable to speak, though she moaned continually and tried her best. Her face had slipped down one side and her tongue protruded slightly while her left arm and leg hung useless. They had laid her on the sofa in the parlour and Chloe wondered however they had managed it for she must have fallen to the floor and was a good fourteen stone. The doctor was still there, attemtping to calm down an agitated Willie and the room was full of neighbours. Chloe recognised Blanche Beanland and remembered that the school was on holiday.

The doctor was saying that there was nothing he could do to help her now. It was a matter of slow recovery and good nursing care. No, he couldn't get her into hospital. It was true that the prospects were not good but she was a strong woman. Will power was very important. Of course she would need constant attention. What had happened to the family? What indeed? Chloe swallowed hard and her heart sank.

Will found his way to her side through the well-meaning throng.

'We'll have to take her, Chloe. For the time being, till something can be worked out.'

'I know. She can't be left here.'

The truth was that the family had drifted apart since John Moffat's death, despite Rebecca's wishes. Only young John, a bachelor of forty-six, still lived in the house. He could hardly be expected to cope. It was woman's work.

'She'll get better, of course,' said Willie later as they walked home. 'Mother always does. It's her spirit.' They had left Rebecca plucking distractedly at the bed clothes. The doctor had said it was better that she wasn't moved for a day or two and so John had been called home from the gardens of the Close, although plans had been made for Chloe and Willie to take over as soon as possible.

'It's true she's determined,' admitted Chloe. 'That's good.'

'She'll be walking again soon, you'll see. I don't think t'old doctor knows much these days, you know. He's getting on.'

'Yes.' Chloe was doubtful now. 'I like him though. He's always been good to me.'

'Oh, aye, he's nice enough. But he is gettin' old. He was in his prime when you were having Jack.'

'I suppose so. Do you think John will manage tonight? We'd better pop up after tea.'

'We'll hear soon enough if he doesn't. Any road, doctor says we can move her in a day or two.'

'Where are we going to put her, Will?'

'Beth's room? Next t'bathroom?'

'I can't put the child in with her!'

'Then Beth can sleep with us again.'

'She'll get too old for that.'

'It's only for a little bit.'

Chloe thought again. 'I don't think that's such a good idea, anyway. How will we get her up and down stairs? She's awful heavy, you know. Perhaps we ought to put a bed in the living-room and she could have a commode. You could make her one, couldn't you? Then Beth could stay where she is. Her room's tiny, anyway.'

'Aye . . . 'appen you're right. We'll do that to start off with then.'

So Rebecca, plus her bed, was duly installed. There

wasn't a great deal of improvement. She could speak but her words were indistinct and rarely made sense.

'At least she know us,' said Will.

'She called me "girl" today,' said Chloe.

'Aye, but she still knows you,' Will insisted.

'If she doesn't get better . . . '

'Oh, she will!'

'*If* she doesn't, mind, what then? John can't manage her. But it's not going to be very easy like this, is it?'

'Don't you want to look after her? She *is* me mother.'

'Oh, I know, Willie, I know! It isn't that. But I'm not sure she's that happy with me. She's never really liked me, you know. Maybe Rose or Amy would be better. And it isn't easy in our house, is it?'

'I'll have a word with t'others,' Willie promised.

Will was as good as his word, but with little success. He concentrated mainly on Rose. While the other members of Will's family lived alone or in houses as crowded as his own, Rose now lived in a place he considered a mansion, up Summer Garden Lane at the better end of Kingley, and she had a maid. She had achieved this by marrying the manager of the engineering firm in Kingley where she had worked on munitions during the war. It had been a great surprise to them all for he had been a widower with three almost-grown children then and thirty years her senior if he was a day. But then somehow Rose had been born old. What he saw in her remained a mystery, unless it was a comfortable shape. Rose – in an era shorn of young men – smelled security and was not wrong. She hardly ever came back to Sowerton now, but promised to visit her stricken mother.

In the week before Rose came, Rebecca was especially trying. It was, by now, obvious that her stroke had been a bad one. No power seemed to have returned to her affected limbs and she certainly couldn't walk, nor even feed herself without difficulty. It was true that she could speak more clearly. But, although she could force the words out, the process of selecting the right ones remained very difficult. She would sit slumped in her armchair, furiously thinking, until she grew red in the face and banged her useless stick on the floor in growing frustration. Often, there were tears of rage in her eyes. Chloe saw her distress and grieved for her. But Rebecca didn't want that. When the words wouldn't come, she vented her spleen on Chloe, never speaking her name, but shouting endlessly for her 'girl'.

Chloe grew to know most of her desires without being told. But it was still very difficult. One bone of contention was the chair. The doctor had warned them that on no account must Rebecca be allowed to lie in bed all day or she would worsen and die. So, every morning, Will and the boys would haul her into the chair. It was really the commode which they had made for her, padded with cushions, so that during the day Chloe could remove these and lift the seat when required. That was enough of a struggle as it was. So Rebecca was supposed to stay in the chair, at least until after lunch, when one of the boys might drop in to put her to bed for a nap or move her into the garden if it was fine. But, no sooner had the men gone, than Rebecca started to wail for her bed.

'I'm tired, girl! I'm tired. Where are you? Put me back! Put me back. I'm tired, girl, I'm tired!'

One day, Chloe, pitying her and wearied half to death, struggled alone and actually got her back into bed. She had meant to get her up again after an hour or so, but had wrenched her back so that it pained her too much to even try. So there Rebecca had had to stay, triumphant and quite unrepentant.

Will was angry when he got home and instructed Chloe not to give in again on any account.

'She'll die,' he said, accusingly. 'Doctor said so. You must keep her up, I don't care what she says. Ignore her.'

So then Chloe would attempt to reason with Rebecca. But in the end she had to stick it out and ignore her. It was exhausting.

The day that Rose came, Chloe got out the best china. She made a delicate afternoon tea, cutting the crusts off the bread and arranging the cakes on paper doileys. Ever since her days of working at the vicarage, she had known how to do things properly. Then she left mother and daughter alone to talk and went and sat in the garden.

After about a quarter of an hour, Rose came out. Chloe stood up and Rose took her deckchair. Beth was playing in a corner of the garden with some old tin cups and saucers.

'She's growing into a pretty child,' said Rose. 'Like a little gipsy with all that curly black hair. Not a bit like Will!'

Chloe followed her gaze. 'She reminds me of my brother, George.' It was perfectly untrue, but she had learnt early that it paid to be devious with Rose.

'What do you think of her, Rose? Mother, I mean.'

Rose sighed. 'Not so good, is she? It's awfully hot out here, Chloe. Could I have a glass of water?'

'Of course.'

Chloe trotted obediently into the kitchen. She filled a tumbler with cold water from the tap and wiped her hands on the pinafore she always wore now. Underneath it was her favourite summer frock – the green floral one she had worn at Scarborough – though it was faded and well-washed now. It was loose on her too for she had lost more weight since having Beth. She seemed to be visibly shrinking and her face was very lean and pointed like an elf's. Rose looked well, she thought. Filling out and stiffening up. But exceedingly smart. She held her handsome figure like a ram-rod in the deckchair and looked very much like her mother in her earlier days, though her clothes were obviously far more expensive. Rebecca must be proud of you, thought Chloe.

She handed the water and Rose took it without a word.

'You do see, don't you?' she said, 'that it's quite out of the question for me to have mother?'

Chloe was silent.

'If I only had myself to consider, it would be different. But I have to think about Ronald and his position in the town . . . and then there's his children. I'm afraid it's just impossible.'

Chloe cleared her throat. 'We had hoped . . .with you having more room . . . and a servant and that. It's so cramped here, you see, and she has to stay downstairs.'

'Mercy me, I don't think she minds that! It's really rather nice for her being amongst the family, I think. And I'm sure she'd rather stay in Sowerton than move away. Will was always such a good son to her. Why, I only ever knew him cause her pain once . . . ' Rose's hard and rather small eyes bored into Chloe who dropped her own before the challenge. 'I knew you would understand.' Rose began to gather her gloves together. She dropped one and Chloe stooped to pick it up.

'Could she come and visit you sometimes – so she doesn't get so bored? It's very frustrating for her being inactive all the time, I'm sure. Perhaps if you could send the car and then the boys would help Ronald get her in.'

'Dearie me, I don't think Mother's ever been in a car, before. Don't you think the excitement might harm her? It doesn't sound like a good idea at all, to me. Very unsettling and frightening for her.'

'I suppose so.'

Ronald was waiting at the garden gate and he got out of his car to wind the starting handle as soon as he saw Rose appear.

'Of course, I shall visit when I can,' said Rose, settling back into her seat. 'But I'm sure she's well looked after where she is and everything's for the best.'

They drove off with a couple of bangs, scattering shale and white dust from the rollered limestone road that had replaced the old sand-track of the village.

We shan't see much of them again, thought Chloe sadly.

Inside the house, the afternoon tea had not been touched which surprised Chloe for Rebecca had an alarmingly healthy appetite. Then it occurred to her that Rose had probably not realised she had to feed her mother.

'Here you are, Ma,' she sighed, putting some sandwiches on a plate and placing it in her lap. Rebecca pushed them all in at once with her good hand, rather like a baby, and Chloe had to rescue the bits which dropped down. Then she made urgent noises through a mouthful of bread and butter and pointed to the teapot. Chloe nodded and, pouring a cup, held it to her lips with a hanky ready to catch the dribbles. She tried not to feel disgusted when the old woman slurped and spat it out.

'Is it cold, Ma? I expect it must be. I'll make you some more.'

It was not, after all, Rebecca's fault. Chloe was close to tears as she filled the kettle and they were not all for herself. Rebecca had been so strong. Now she was a wreck and no one wanted her. It was clear to Chloe that she had to stay.

Beth came sidling round her skirts, asking for a biscuit.

'Granny going to live with Aunt Rose?' she asked. 'Is she?'

Chloe gave her the biscuit and said brightly, 'No, she isn't. Granny's going to live with us.'

'What? Forever and ever?' Chloe had been striving to teach her the Lord's Prayer.

'Until she's better,' she said, firmly.

Willie asked the same question when he got home and Chloe told him about Rose's visit quietly, in the kitchen. Will snorted his reply.

'Too high and mighty for her own mother now, is she?'

'I can understand it,' said Chloe. 'There's Ronald to consider. She's looking very well these days, I must say.'

'She might have offered to pay summat towards her keep.'

'Well, she didn't.'

'You'll be wanting me to give you extra housekeeping then?'

'Just a little. I could stretch it more easily but she eats nearly as much as the boys.'

'Aye. She's a big woman.' Willie considered. 'Looks like we're landed then.'

'Yes.'

'Is she to stay downstairs?'

'I can't put her in Beth's boxroom, can I?'

'No. She mun stay downstairs then.'

Chloe carried on slicing vegetables for dinner and Willie darted her a suspicious glance.

'She is me mother, you know.'

'I know that.'

'And she did help look after you when you was ill.'

'I know that, too. Though it was rather different. But I'm grateful.'

'Well then.'

'I never said anything about it, Will.' Chloe was impatient. She knew she had taken the news calmly enough. 'She'll be well looked after by me, if that's what you're meaning.'

'I know, I know. It's just that you've never liked her.'

'No, Will – she never liked me. Still doesn't, come to that. She won't call me by my name, you know – only 'girl'.'

''Appen she's forgotten it.'

'Maybe, but I don't think so. Still, it'll make no difference. Not now.'

Willie nodded and was satisfied. He knew it was hard on her. To be honest, he couldn't get over how well she had taken it. Deep inside, he knew that all those years ago the Reverend Kaye had done him a great service.

'You're a good lass,' he said and went to sit in the front room with his mother till dinner was ready. He would have liked to have patted her bony, little shoulder but somehow he could tell she didn't really want him to any more.

There then began a long, hard trial for Chloe. Rebecca

never did walk again. Her by now immense weight put her at a grave disadvantage and there was no real recovery from the paralysis. She was practically immobile and disliked being left alone. But she could still tap her stick and did so in an endless summons for Chloe. Even in the garden – hanging out the washing or trying to play with Beth – Chloe could still hear it, drumming on the floor. Sometimes she fell asleep with it in her ears and even her dreams were never totally free of it. If she didn't go, Rebecca would start to holler. Always for 'girl'. Doggedly, she refused to acknowledge the hand that fed and clothed and cared for her without complaint.

It was easier when the boys and Will were home in the evening. At least Rebecca tried to talk to them. In fact it became very difficult to stop her butting in on every conversation. Even when the old gas brackets were taken out and they got electric lights and the wireless, they couldn't listen with wholehearted enjoyment as Rebecca would burst into cackles at an inappropriate moment or merely keep on talking throughout the programme. If Chloe wanted to read, she had to creep up into the cold of her bedroom to get some peace now. Ted brought her library books and although he did his best, he sometimes forgot what Chloe had read before, or brought her home new ones she didn't really like. Still, it was better than having none at all. But she couldn't read very often because Will and the boys naturally liked to get out. She couldn't blame them when Rebecca and her bed dominated the living-room.

There came a time when everyone began to realise that Rebecca was deteriorating rather than improving. She began to wet the bed not long after Beth became reliably dry, so there were still endless sheets to wash. Her eating habits had become truly dreadful and, worst of all, she was really uncooperative about being washed and dressed. If she was in the least bit thwarted, she would cry like a child. One day, the old doctor came round to call. He was really saying goodbye for, at last, he was going to retire and Chloe was touched. She decided to ask him about Rebecca and managed to get him into the kitchen while she made tea.

'Mrs Kaye was never like this, doctor,' she said. 'She was lame for years and then had a stroke before she died, but I don't ever remember her going like this.

'No, well it isn't just the stroke now, Chloe, I'm afraid.' He always called her by her Christian name and Chloe liked it. She seemed to have known him such a long time now, since that day he had come to examine her in the vicarage. She reckoned he had saved her life over Beth, no matter what Willie said and she would miss him now he was going.

'Rebecca has dementia, I am sure.'

Chloe looked alarmed.

'You mean she's going mad? I can't have her in the same house as Beth if she is.'

'No, no,' said the doctor, kindly. 'Not mad as you understand it. It's just a medical term which means she's ageing rapidly and her mind is failing her first . . . becoming senile, so that her judgement and her memory are impaired. She may become quite confused.

'I see. But she's not that old really, doctor. I grant you we all think she is now, after the stroke. But she's not really. I think – I'm not sure exactly – she's about sixty-seven or eight.'

'Yes, but in this condition people may age before their time. That's what's happening to Rebecca. The stroke doesn't help but it wasn't the cause alone. She may have become like this anyway. And sixty-eight, Chloe. Remember the three score years and ten? It's still a good rule and there's many don't make that even, though that will change, but not in my lifetime, I fear.'

'She used to be so strong,' said Chloe, sadly. She knew quite well that the old doctor was more than three score years and ten himself but didn't mention it.

'I know. I remember her very well. It is sad . . . but perhaps most of all for you.'

'Will she get worse?'

'I fear so.'

'And, begging your pardon, doctor – when do you think she might . . . die?' Chloe knew it wasn't a very discreet question and lowered her eyes, her cheeks reddening. But the doctor was not at all embarrassed or surprised.

'Hard to say, Chloe,' he said. 'I'm sorry, but I fear that her heart belongs to a bulldog and will go on beating a good while yet, even though it isn't perfusing the brain tissue very well.'

Chloe didn't really understand the answer but thanked him all the same. 'I'm sorry to ask, doctor.'

'Not at all. It's hard on you, isn't it? Especially with a little one as well.'

'Beth'll be off to school soon. It's not too bad.'

'You could do with a break, though.'

'There's no one else can have her.'

'Or will, you mean! There are homes you know – just for a while – I could put you in touch with a reputable one.'

'We couldn't pay, doctor.'

'I would have thought Willie was doing nicely now.'

'There's not that much trade, doctor. Willie says its the recession and times are bad.'

'Oh yes, I know all about that, Chloe. But Willie still has his trade and some orders. Steady but sure. And he's always been such a careful lad. I cannot believe he hasn't got a bit put by, you know, after all these years.'

Chloe shook her head, doubtfully.

'I really don't know, doctor.' She didn't. The thought had never occurred to her. She was so used to being poor, she accepted it as a way of life. The way Willie acted had never encouraged her to believe any different.

'Well, you ask him,' said the doctor. 'Tell him I advised it. Mind you don't forget now.'

Chloe did think about it after he had gone. It had been a particularly trying week, to tell the truth. What heaven it would be to have a break! They might take Beth to the seaside. Not Scarborough. That would hurt too much. But Morecambe perhaps. You could get the train direct from Kingley now. She tackled Willie about it after dinner. In her heart she knew it wasn't a good time because Willie was sitting at the kitchen table polishing his boots ready to go out. It was ringing night. But she couldn't wait any longer. She was washing up, as usual, alone. Beth was in bed and the boys were getting ready to go out too. She could hear them laughing and talking and tramping about upstairs.

'Doctor called today.'

'Oh aye?'

'Came to pay his respects, really. The new man comes next week.'

'Oh aye?'

'I asked him about mother.'

'What did he say?'

She told him.

'She's not going mad! Just a bit confused. T'doctor's retiring none before time, if you ask me.'

'He didn't say she was mad, Will.' Chloe urged herself to stay calm, although she could feel the rising tide of despair inside. 'He just said she won't get better but worse. Like a child. Demented, they calls it, but they don't mean mad. She'll get worse though, till she dies.'

'Oh aye and when will that be?' Willie spat on his boots.

'I don't think he knew,' Chloe said.

'There you are then. He dunno much at all.'

'But she is getting worse, Will!'

'Oh aye, we can all see that. Don't take a medical degree to see that.'

Chloe took a deep breath and plunged her hands into the soapy water again.

'He said it would be hard going, maybe for some time, and he suggested – no, he advised – a break for us.'

Willie looked amazed. 'A break. How does he mean, a break?'

'Well, a holiday I suppose. Or just some time without her.'

'Well, we would if we could. You know that. I'd tek you to t'seaside again if you wanted. But how can we?'

'He said he could get Rebecca into a home.'

Willie stopped brushing his boots, his hand poised in mid-air.

'Just for a week, like.'

'You know what that sort of thing costs?'

'It would be nice though, wouldn't it?' Chloe was speaking very quickly now, unwilling for her fantasy to be shattered. 'We could take Beth with us to the seaside. She's never seen it.'

'I can tek her for t'day, sometime, if you like.'

'But I'd like us all to go, Will. I'd like to go too. With Beth. And you.' An image from the past in Scarborough was strong before her eyes. It was the family she had seen picnicking and making sandcastles on the beach.

'I really want to go.' She gripped a plate in the sink very tightly, so tightly she thought it would break, longed for it to crack, in fact, but it didn't and she could hardly bear the suspense.

'We can't afford it. You know how things are at the yard.'

'Haven't you got – a bit put by?'

Will became very uncomfortable. 'A bit.'

'Well?'

'That's for emergencies.'

'Well, then?'

'If we spend it, we won't have anything left for a real emergency, will we?' He started brushing his boots again, fussily morose. He knew it was hard for her and that Rose and the others hadn't pulled their weight but that wasn't his fault. He hated it when she made him feel that it was.

'What happens if trade don't pick up?' he continued to justify himself.

Chloe started washing up again. The tension had gone. She knew the fight was over and that she had lost.

'You said it were bound to.'

'I could be wrong. What if it don't, Chloe? We got four children.'

'I know. I had them.' For once, she couldn't help being tart.

'What about them then?'

'The boys are working. They're doing all right.'

'And Beth?'

'Yes,' said Chloe, softening at last. 'There is Beth. And she's not going in to service, Will. I won't have it.'

'We've agreed about that. Anyway, girls don't go into service now. Not when they can get other jobs.'

Chloe hadn't told Will, but she had started saving some money for Beth. A very little from the housekeeping each week. She kept it in a tin under the bed and, when there was enough, she would put it in the bank . . . or maybe the insurance was better. Of course, Will was right really and she said so.

'There you are, then.' Will finished his boots and put them on. They were interrupted by the steady beating of Rebecca's stick through the wall.

'It's me mother.'

'I know it!'

'Well, then?'

'You go, Will. You go.'

'I'm off out!'

Irritated beyond all, Chloe flung the wet tea-towel across the table at him and it flapped ineffectually onto his face. He was most surprised. She left the room with clenched fists but inside her daring was making her tremble and worse – much worse – it was already making her feel ashamed.

I haven't changed, thought Chloe, as her fingers closed around the pot of red paint in her pocket. I really haven't changed at all in thirty-eight years. I feel now just as I did then, when I threw that tea-towel at Willie. I thought then it was a last gesture of defiance, but here I am, a silly old lady of seventy-seven, who should know better, planning to paint the doorknobs red in my very beige kitchen. And all the time I know it will do no good. It will even make me suffer more. How absurd these impulses are! And how unlike me to give in to them.

For she had buckled down again after the incident with the wet tea-towel. There had been no holiday, of course. No rest at all until Rebecca died. And she had taken another four years to do it . . . longer even than the old doctor would have estimated, if nailed down. It was true that, in the last year, she had stopped speaking altogether and no longer tapped the stick but she remained a heavy physical burden. She wore me out, thought Chloe. I never really felt well again afterwards, just chronically tired. My days of being a young woman had gone. After Rebecca died, everyone began to talk about war again and I grew so frightened for the boys I could hardly eat. She certainly hadn't been interested in travel any more, though she still read her books. But really the children were her only other solace.

Children! They were hardly that any more, of course. The boys had all got married and were having children of their own, so that Chloe now was Granny Moffat. Beth was soon sixteen and poised on the brink of womanhood and Chloe worried constantly over her. With the boys, she only ever worried about the war. But her fears for Beth were less specific. She still recognised a certain waywardness in her daughter that she couldn't understand. They had always been good friends. But, now she was sixteen, that had gone and Beth no longer discussed her problems with her mother if she could avoid it. Chloe was hurt, especially as she knew there was a quiet determination inside her daughter which was steadily growing, fuelled by something she couldn't even identify. It hadn't helped when Willie had insisted she leave school. Chloe and Beth had been equally heartbroken over that. The schoolmaster had even been down to see Willie to try and make sure that he realised his daughter was bright. But Willie was adamant. He refused to let Beth go to the grammar school, scholarship or no, there was no way the likes of them could afford everything that entailed – or so he said. It was time for Beth to start earning as the boys had done.

So Beth started work as an assistant in a shoe-shop in Kingley and Chloe's heart bled for her, for she knew her daughter was desperately unhappy. At the back of her mind, she kept thinking about Maurice. If only she had known she was going to have his baby! She would never have let Beth sink into obscurity in this way then, despite the scandal. She would have been prepared to barter her soul for a better life for her daughter. Willie knew he had alienated them both and tried to win Chloe over to his side.

'What's the point,' he said, 'in educatin' a woman when she's only going to marry and raise children? Mark my words, Chloe, it'd do her nothin' but harm. Look at the fancy types she would meet at t'grammar school. They'd onny lead her astray. Now if young Ted had got t'chance . . . well, mebbe.' But Chloe was not impressed. She only remembered the way the village schoolmaster had shaken his head in despair and slammed the garden gate on his way out and knew it was grossly unfair. Willie had done Beth a great wrong.

But her daughter was more resilient than she supposed. After a while, she appeared to settle down at the shoe-shop and got on well. The manageress soon put her trust in Beth when she couldn't be there. Meanwhile, her prettiness was growing and the boys began to call. Beth treated them all with disdain but let them take her dancing all the same, while Chloe winced and worried and Willie was forever laying down the law over her behaviour. But it only seemed to increase Beth's wilfulness for she certainly took no notice. She dutifully handed her wages over every week but, what she was allowed to keep, she spent on clothes and make-up and cigarettes. Chloe was glad when rationing came in. She tried to interest her daughter in keeping up her schooling by getting educational books from the library. But it was too late. Beth's template for life had become the movies. When the war did break, she planned to run away to join the WAAFS and lie about her age, but Jack found her out before it was too late and brought her back. Chloe remembered yet another family scene. All the time, Beth's insurance money was growing but Chloe never told her about it. Will knew now, because Chloe had used it to try and bribe him over the grammar school, without success; but Beth didn't know.

Then she took up with an officer who came in to the shop one day when she had been there a year and, within six months, they were asking to be married. Will was all for it, but Chloe felt that, at eighteen, Beth was far too young. In the course of the ensuing argument, Chloe told Beth the story of her own marriage, something she had never done before. Beth listened quietly and sympathetically. But she was not to be deterred.

'That was quite different, Mum,' she said. 'I don't *have* to get married, but I do want to. There's a war on and Ken could be killed and we might never see one another again and I couldn't bear that. And you do like him, don't you?' Chloe did. She thought Kenneth Sugden a splendid young man – not much to look at, but kind and considerate, and from a very good family who would keep Beth most comfortably. His father had a modest haulage business in Kingley which was going well and Kenneth, as the eldest son, would inherit – if he survived.

'There's a war on.' Everyone was saying it. It was the excuse for lots of things and Chloe gave in. Out came the insurance money for the wedding, for she knew Will wouldn't pay for any frippery. It all went but it was worth it so that the Moffats could hold their heads up high opposite the Sugdens. In church, it was the sight of Beth, all in white, with the most enormous bridal bouquet ever, which gave Chloe especial satisfaction. Large bouquets were then in vogue and Beth's was one of the best. Somehow, it made up a little for Chloe's own lack of flowers on a dismal, drizzly day in the November of 1906. Beth's weather wasn't much better but at least the wedding itself was very different. Ken had to go back after two days, so Beth returned from her honeymoon in the Lakes to stay at her mother's for the time being. Chloe had Kenneth's safety to worry over then as well. But he was a survivor. And a very good husband. They had been blessed with wonderful children. Especially Jennifer. Sometimes, Chloe could see herself in Jennifer. But not very often.

Chloe stopped again to mop her brow and wondered why on earth her daughter wasn't happy. Beth denied it, but Chloe knew that it was true. It was what they had been arguing over the other day . . . and they still hadn't made up. Beth was offended. She had driven straight past the house and that was unlike her. Chloe sighed. Perhaps tomorrow she would come. Perhaps her unhappiness would heal. But she still couldn't understand why it was there in the first place.

Nearly up the hill now. She felt very weary. It must be the hottest day of the year so far. So promising for the summer ahead. The trees and the hedgerows were decked out in their full glory. The coming night would be warm and heavy with the scents of summer – a summer which was so brief. Before they knew it, the rowan berries would be out, with August tending to September. That was a time of year Chloe always found full of pathos. It was the time of year she and Willie had conceived Jack and the time of year that war always seemed to break out. The harvest always seemed bitter-sweet to Chloe.

She didn't know why she should think of it today with the countryside so resplendent. She had passed the canal and the Close long since and was coming to the crest of the hill now. Two more bends in the road and she would be home. She found herself out of breath and she knew she was really old. The heat made her sweat and feel dizzy. Far better to have stayed in the garden after all. But she had had to go, had to visit her old haunts and relive everything in her mind, though she didn't know why. It hadn't really helped.

Miss Hartley, one of her equally elderly neighbours, was swilling the step as she passed. She was a neat and precise soul who pecked about her house and garden like a bird. All her work was done by eight in the morning. But this hot weather made the path so dusty. She would have to redden the edge of the step again. Mrs Moffat, she noted, did not look well. Very nice in her best clothes and hat. But not at all well. Such a high colour.

'Are you all right?' she called. 'Stop and have a cup of tea.'

But Chloe smiled and shook her head. 'I'm fine,' she said. 'Just hot. And I should be back to get Willie's tea.' Already she felt guilty at being so late and the woman she had become was back in charge, instead of her real self. No point in dwelling on the past. Some day soon she must read Maurice's book of poems again and then burn it. She had, after all, had one adventure in life. God had never meant her to have more. She wished he had, but it wasn't to be.

Willie was leaning on the garden gate, chatting to a fellow village crony. He stood aside to let her pass and gave her a cursory nod as she went into the house. It was still cool and dark, seeming more so after all that brilliance outside, and this time she received it gratefully, for she was tremendously tired. Unpinning her hat, she laid it carefully with her gloves and her purse on the sideboard. She removed the tin of paint from her pocket too and laid it down, thoughtfully. Would Willie notice? And, if he did, would she still do it? She wasn't sure any more and no longer really cared.

Slowly, she climbed up the steep, little stairs to wash and change. At the top, a pain hit the back of her head like a sledge-hammer. For a moment, she really thought she had been struck. But it was only for a very little moment as she stumbled into her bedroom. Then came the dark.

It was some time later when Willie, nonplussed, found her. Then he ran across to the Hartleys in a panic to 'phone for the doctor, with the world fragmented and tumbling round his ears.

'She's snoring heavy,' he said in answer to the young doctor's question. 'And I can't wake her. I can't wake her at all.'

The doctor realised she was as good as gone as soon as he saw her. Together, he and Willie laid her on the bed and she slumped wherever she was put, despite her lightness. Her neck was quite stiff and rigid.

'Can she hear us, doctor?' whispered Willie.

'No, Mr Moffat. I am sure she cannot.'

Inside, the blood forced along for so long, under pressure, had burst its banks and was still spewing and seeping through the brain tissue. Wherever Chloe was, she was certainly not a part of the scene in the bedroom, which centred around her alone for the next forty-eight hours. She never knew how long a particularly tormented Beth sat beside her. And then she was gone for good.

PART II

BETH

'I should see the garden far better,' said Alice to herself, 'if I could get to the top of that hill: and here's a path that leads straight to it – at least, no, it doesn't do that – ' (after going a few yards along the path, and turning several sharp corners), 'but I suppose it will at last.'

Through The Looking Glass
LEWIS CARROLL

CHAPTER ONE

Beth jerked suddenly awake and found herself sweating. The nightmare had returned. She kicked off the bedclothes and prayed that it might be near morning. But the clock that glowed in the dark said ten past two and the bedroom was swathed in shadow. Ken lay asleep beside her and she knew she could not wake him again. Nor could she lie still and think about the dream. It was always the same. There she was, endlessly driving the car up the hill to her mother's. She could see that face, all hopeful and pleased, at the window. But she still drove on by, though the act of passing the house took a lifetime.

She got up and went into the bathroom. Obviously, she should have had that second valium after all. It was silly to try and do without. After all, Dr Jones had reassured her that losing one's mother was one of life's major stressful events. He had said it as if Beth might have mislaid her down at the supermarket and she had thought how ridiculous the phrase was. Chloe had died and had done so, to all intents and purposes, on the day when Beth had driven past her door. The dream was not even subtle. But she must not feel guilty. She had, on the whole, been rather good to her mother. It was merely an unfortunate coincidence and any other week would have been different.

Beth sat on the lid of her peach-coloured toilet seat, swallowed her tablet, stared at her peach-coloured, fitted bath with its gold chrome taps and soap-dish, and cried. Good she might have been but it wasn't enough. Then she rose and splashed her face with cold water at the sink, drying it carefully on a fluffy towel, trying to pat the delicate skin around the eyes rather than rub at it. She wondered wearily how long it would take for the valium to work. Don't let it get you down, said Ken. There's nothing you can do about it now. It's all in the past. Fine, sensible words. But Chloe wasn't his mother and she wasn't his past. The events of the final week were a minor sadness. But if I live to be a hundred, thought Beth, I shall never be rid of all those other memories.

She left the bathroom and tiptoed across the galleried landing in search of cigarettes. There was a big, bright moon and its soft light stole through the leaded panes of the windows to make criss-cross patterns on the floor. She went downstairs and stood in the hallway in the half light. It was July now and the central heating wasn't on, so that she shivered slightly in her nylon negligee, though it wasn't really cold.

In the kitchen, the fluorescent tubes flicked everything into harsh relief. A packet of filter-tipped cigarettes lay on the beige plastic table. She lit one and filled the kettle, then plugged it in. Its sibilance joined the hum of the refrigerator, as she waited for it to boil and examined her blue tiles and geometric wallpaper – much admired by Chloe. Already, she was tired of them – they seemed too clinical after all – and anxious to redesign the whole kitchen as a result. Normally, she would have thrown herself into the project with vigour. But, since her mother had died, a gap had appeared in her life. It was really nothing to do with Chloe's absence, but seemed rather as if a hole had been waiting here all along and she had suddenly fallen into it in her middle years. She had arrived at a time of stocktaking and everything totted up fine. Yet the mood which prevailed was one of uneasiness. Beth didn't understand it. She wasn't normally given to self-analysis. Her mind ran along everyday tracks between strictly parallel lines. But it was impossible not to question, today, for it had been the most extraordinary of days.

Three weeks had passed since Chloe's funeral and Beth had promised Willie that she would go and sort out her mother's clothes. On her way through Sowerton, she had stopped at the joinery for a coffee with Jack. There was nothing unusual in that. She didn't get on with his wife and it was a good opportunity to see him alone. Jack ran 'Moffat & Son, Joiners & Undertakers', now, although his father remained a partner, despite being retired for years. Jack had been trying to put Willie's affairs in order too and his chief bugbear was that the old man refused to invest his capital. He sounded off to Beth about it, but it wasn't until he told her exactly how much Willie was allowing to stagnate in his current bank account, that she really sat up and took notice.

'Do you mean to tell me,' she said, 'that the old bugger saved all that and never used it? When he kept mother in abject poverty and never took her anywhere or bought her anything nice?'

'He wouldn't touch it,' said Jack, 'and still won't. Many's the time I've tried to get him to buy a nice bungalow for them both, with proper heating. Took him to see some. Said I'd fix it all up and they wouldn't have to worry about a thing. But he wouldn't have it. Preferred to stay where he was! That house freezes in winter, as you and I both know. Mam was only allowed to put so much coal on the fire. But he reckoned that owning property, instead of renting it, was too much of a risk. I ask you! These days! Well, I suppose he's had to hang on all his working life, through wars and recessions and slumps. He can't adapt his ways to good times.'

But Beth was less charitable. 'He's just a mean old sod,' she said. 'It makes my blood boil.'

By the time she arrived at Willie's house, she had worked herself up into a real rage and intended to tell him exactly what she thought of him. He wasn't in the garden for once, although it was another fine day. Not as hot as the day on which Chloe had died, but still very summery and pleasant. The house seemed just as stuffy and gloomy in contrast. Beth entered through the back door, noting with contempt that Willie's breakfast things lay unwashed in the sink.

'Dad,' she called out. 'Are you there?' Her heels click-clacked angrily across the linoleum and through the kitchen door into the parlour.

Willie sat alone, bending over his newspaper with a magnifying glass in one hand and his spectacles in the other. Beth was surprised because she didn't know he was having trouble reading. The clock on the mantel chimed the quarter so noisily that she couldn't speak. In the seconds of grace it gave her, she noticed two other things. The first was that the old man looked pathetic and utterly lost and the second was that Chloe's hat and gloves and purse and even the tin of red paint (which had mystified them all) still lay on the sideboard, just as she had placed them on her last day of consciousness. When the tones of the clock had echoed away, Beth's anger had ebbed too and all she said was:

'I've come to tidy up. How are you?' and then, when his lips trembled and she thought he might be going to tell her, 'Will you come to lunch on Sunday?'

'Aye, I 'spect so . . . after church. Thank you.'

They had never been easy with one another and now it was too late to start. Beth moved briskly over to the sideboard.

'Well, I'll take these things upstairs then.'

'No, don't do that!' He was at her side, all agitated, in a moment and Beth felt embarrassed.

'I'll leave the paint-pot, of course, and the purse. But shouldn't that hat and gloves go with the rest?'

'No, I'll not 'ave them touched. They remind me of the way she looked. She looked real pretty that day . . .afore it happened, I mean.' She had never heard him speak like that before.

'But, Dad,' gently now, though trying to instil reason, 'It's nearly a month. They've got to be moved sometime.'

'They'll not be touched.'

He had really loved her then. The idea confounded Beth. Despite all evidence to the contrary, he really had loved Chloe and still did. It didn't fit Beth's conception of him at all. Had he only now found out, or did he love her in his way all along? She hated what that implied. Her judgement of them both was quite wrong and she longed for air and light.

'Well, if that's the way you want it, of course I won't touch them. I just don't think it's . . . well, good for you, to keep them there like that.' But then why shouldn't he have his shrine? He deserved to suffer a little, after all. 'I'll be going upstairs, then. Do you want to come with me?'

'Nay, I don't. The rest of her stuff can go. That doesn't bother me, so long as I don't see it go.' That was a relief then.

'A cup of tea would be nice,' said Beth, pointedly.

'Oh aye, of course. I'll mek you one.'

For a moment, she had wondered if he was even capable of that by himself and was relieved to see him shamble off to fill the kettle, rather laboriously it was true, at the cold tap.

Upstairs, she passed her own bedroom first. It was only a box. How small everything looked when one had grown up and left it all behind! Next to it was the boys' room, and that was just a junk-room now. Finally, she stepped, almost shyly, into her parents' domain and immediately opened the window to let in some fresh air.

The room was furnished sparsely. She looked at the dumpy, double bed with its faded green, candlewick cover. It was strange, for her, to think of Chloe and Will lying there together. Had they really . . . ? But then, they must have done – at least sometimes – to have had four children! Above the bed, hung one of those old-fashioned pictures, heavily framed, with an obviously haloed Jesus sending forth blond children dressed in shining armour. Next to it was an embroidered sampler of the 'Bless this House' variety.

Beth opened the wardrobe first. It was far too large for the room. Solid wood of course, Victorian and perfectly hideous. Inside, it was divided into halves, with a unifying shelf over the hanging space. She had inadvertently opened Willie's side first and shut the door quickly again on the row of dark-coloured suits and tweeds, feeling like an intruder. There wasn't that much hanging in Chloe's half, despite her mother's capacity for hoarding. She took out a bagged blue suit and, immediately, the smell of moth-balls filled the room. Goodness, this must be old, though Chloe had obviously taken great care of it and probably not worn it that often. There were a few simple dresses, including one Beth remembered particularly well from her childhood. It had once been a pretty shade of green and had a floral print. But now it was faded and dropping to bits. Fancy keeping it all this time!

There was a heavy winter coat and a lighter summer one, both in navy blue. Some blouses and skirts and rather a lot of hand-knitted cardigans. Jumble sale stuff, really, all of it. Beth opened the large carrier bags she had brought with her and pitched it all in. She paused momentarily at the blue suit. It was in such good condition that the material must be quality. But who would want a style like that now or could even be bothered to alter it? Into the bag it went with the rest.

On the floor of the wardrobe were some size three and a half shoes. Beth had equally small feet. But she wouldn't be seen dead in any of these. They joined the clothes in the carrier. The shelf above was full of hats and Beth felt the hot sting of tears in her eyes. How Chloe had loved her hats! They were all lovingly wrapped in tissue paper. Beth had bought her most of them . . . for Christmases and birthdays and such like. Not that Chloe had had much opportunity to wear them. Only in church. Beth was interrupted by a knock at the door.

'Cup of tea,' called Will.

'Leave it outside,' she shouted. She was determined he should not see her cry and waited until his footsteps had gone away, before blowing her nose and opening the door. It was a good cup of tea after all and it revived her. Because she had bought most of them herself, the hats were rather good ones and she packed them away carefully into a different carrier bag and labelled it 'High Class Jumble'. There was a larger, flatter box at the very back of the shelf. Beth pulled something moth-eaten and brown out of it. Heavens, what on earth was it? Ugh! One of those horrible fox-furs with claws and noses and everything that used to be so fashionable. She had never seen her mother wear that and was glad of it. (Beth had a far from mean selection of fur coats and jackets herself and her repugnance had nothing at all to do with conservation or animal welfare.) She put the fox-fur in a third carrier and labelled it firmly 'Rubbish'.

At last the wardrobe was empty and she attacked the chest of drawers on the adjacent wall. A linen cloth lay on the top. She recognised it, incredulously, as her own work, for some rather juvenile embroidery had fashioned blue-petalled flowers with yellow stamens around the edges. A dish with a dog on it anchored it to the chest. Chloe's work-basket was tucked away tidily beneath it, along with a pile of library books. O dear, no doubt they should have been back long since . . . the fines would be enormous! Still, perhaps under the circumstances . . .

A discreet rummaging through the drawers revealed Chloe's night-clothes and underwear. What a lot of that old ladies wore! Beth stuffed several pink and white woollen or cotton vests and bloomers into the carrier marked 'Rubbish'. Best burn those. And stays! Three pairs – as if Chloe had had anything to hold in! Another old-fashioned habit, she supposed. There were some thick stockings and armoured brassieres too. Plus petti-coats. She found a few scarves and handbags with pairs of gloves inside them but there was really nothing worth keeping. Endless pinafores.

Willie had laid out Chloe's wedding-ring on top of the dressing-table, whose mirrors blocked most of the light from the window. 'She wanted you to have that,' he had already told her several times. Beth picked it up, sadly, and turned the thin, gold band over in her fingers. Her own rings seemed like knuckle-dusters in comparison. She caught her reflection in the mirrors and was startled to see, as always, that her face had begun to look old. Well, she would give the ring to Jennifer. It would please the girl's developing sentimentality to have her grandmother's ring, she was sure of that. And Chloe would have liked it too, for Jennifer was her favourite.

'She's cleverer that the rest of them put together,' she had often said to Beth in private. 'She'll get on, mark my words.' Well yes, she was and she would. Beth would see to that. They would both be proud of her. Beth put the ring away in her pocket with her hopes for the future.

Jennifer would inherit Chloe's money as well . . . the belated legacy from America. Of course, Chloe had made no will, but Aunt Elsie had stipulated that, in the event of her niece failing to outlive her, her share should go to her daughter. Beth had no need of it and had already decided to put it in trust for Jennifer. The boys had done rather better out of Grandpa Sugden, when Jenny was still a baby. Anyway, it seemed extraordinarily fitting that the female line should inherit in this case. Beth felt triumphant that the money wasn't going to be allowed to stagnate in Willie Moffat's bank account.

The larger and lower drawer on Chloe's side of the dressing-table was full of photographs and Beth groaned inwardly. There were hundreds of them. Babies in sailor-suits, babies in christening robes and, more latterly, babies in rompers and diapers or nothing at all, beyond the odd sunhat. There were also more formal portraits of stiff, Victorian ladies and gentlemen with starched wing collars and stern faces . . . Several vintage ones of Sowerton cricket-team, not to mention bellringers anonymous. I can't go through all of them thought Beth in desperation. That's something for Dad to do himself. She removed the whole drawer and planted it by his bedside table, though she suspected he would just put it back again. There didn't seem to be many photographs of Chloe herself, but she did see one she particularly liked. It was a classically old-fashioned mother and baby pose – oozing with sentiment. Impossible to tell now whether it was Jack or Sam who was dandled on Chloe's knee. Probably not Ted, because he had come later and this was a very early, faded photograph. Chloe looked terribly young and very pretty in a white blouse with a high, ruffled neck. Her hair was beautifully dressed. Beth slipped it into her pocket, meaning to ask Willie about it later.

Only one drawer left now, the upper one, and she knelt down to it on the worn, red carpet square for it was crammed full. There was a little jewellery – again nothing valuable – and the empty box for her wedding-ring. Lots of hatpins in a little dish. A yellow christening shoe which had once been white and some icing and a horseshoe from Beth's own wedding-cake. Four envelopes containing four locks of baby hair: the first three were indistinguishable shades of reddish gold. But there was no doubt whom the fourth lock belonged to: Baa baa, black sheep! Beth grimaced.

There were also three books, which explained why the small drawer seemed so packed. The first was a bible and the second a prayer-book and both were well-thumbed. The fly-leaf of the prayer-book was inscribed: 'Wishing you every blessing, the Rev and Mrs S.H.W. Kaye.' Beth grimaced again, recalling her mother's embarrassed story about her wedding. The third book was an old volume of poems by Wilfred Owen and Beth opened it with curiosity. She wouldn't have thought them to her mother's taste. Of course, there were the brothers . . . She flicked through the pages, reading a line or two here and there. She knew of the fate of her uncles in the war. It was almost the only thing she did know about the Rawlinsons. Not that Chloe had spoken of it often. But she had been even more reticent about her parents and her sisters. Mysterious even, as if ashamed, or at least unwilling to remember. She had at least been proud of her brothers, though bitter. How awful! To think that four of them could have gone from one family! And the worst of it was that it wasn't so unusual. A whole generation had been wasted. At least in her own war, as she thought of it, they had been fighting for an identifiable cause. That had been awful, too, of course. All that austerity and rationing and the raids and the fear . . . The fear that Ken or Ted or Sam wouldn't be back. (For she hadn't realised, until afterwards, how afraid she should have been of Hitler and defeat.) She had just been starting out, then. Still a teenager at the beginning . . . Her thoughts were suddenly arrested. The fly-leaf of this book was inscribed too and, astonished, she read:

'A strange present for a lover to give and a woman to receive. But it did ease the way to our friendship. You were right of course when you said you should read it. I know now that you will not come to me. I do not blame you, but I grieve for us both. I hope this book will be a tangible memory of our brief but halcyon days together, in love, M.S.'

Underneath, Chloe had inscribed something even more damning, something which made Beth's mouth feel suddenly dry and a pulse start pounding in her ears:

'But you gave me so much more than this, my dear Maurice, because I am sure you gave me Beth.'

Beth rocked back on her heels. She picked up the four envelopes of baby hair again and stared at their contents. There was no doubt about it. That old skinflint downstairs, shuffling about in his carpet slippers, was not and never had been her father! She closed the book with a snap and held it very tightly between her fingers.

Then she gazed in wonder round the room. It was emptied of Chloe now. Everything personal – apart from those photographs – had been purged and lay in three carrier bags. Beth had chosen to keep very little. There hadn't been very much for a lifetime. And yet how loaded with significance it all was!

She felt sobered as she considered Chloe's secret. Of course she knew about the holiday in Scarborough and had long ago, with adolescent arithmetic, worked out that that was when *she* had been made. Brief but halcyon days? How on earth had Chloe managed it? What exactly had happened? And did Will know or not? Unthinkable to even try and find out! The secret must continue to be kept. For the moment, she hid the book of poems in one of the carrier bags, intending to reclaim it later. She also checked the pages of the bible and the prayer-book more carefully, before placing them on Willie's bedside table – just in case of further shocks. But there was nothing. She collected everything up, removing a hairbrush set and a box of hairnets and pins from the dresser top and took the library books too which would have to be returned. The workbasket could stay . . . Willie might have need of needle and thread, though she doubted if he would know how to use it.

On her way downstairs, she paused at the bathroom. But there was nothing intrinsically feminine in there. Two toothbrushes still stood in the rack, but it was up to Willie to decide when one should be thrown out. She met him again warily, noticing how he looked, as if it was the first time they had met. He was old and stooped with a bullish sort of head – bald on top, with a small amount of bristly grey hair at each temple and some longer, silky strands at the occiput. His eyes were a faded grey too and contained several opacities. Since Chloe's death, they often looked wistful or watery. He was in the habit of wearing stringy, grey pullovers or cardigans, which didn't improve his appearance at all and always the same striped shirts which still had detachable collars. His sleeves were permanently rolled up.

'I think that's the lot, dad.' The word came out easily enough. 'There's nothing of hers in the spare rooms?' He shook his head. 'Well, I'll get rid of all this, then. I've left some photographs upstairs for you to sort out. There are some mementoes too . . . baby shoes and hair and the like. I didn't know whether you'd want to keep them or not, so I've left them all. Oh yes, but I would like to take this photograph of her myself, if I may?'

'Oh aye, of course.'

'Do you know if it's Jack or Sam on her knee?' He wasn't sure, though he was visibly moved. 'Well, it's a nice picture, anyway. I thought I might have it framed, but let me know if you change your mind and want it back. There aren't that many of her in the old days. Are you all right then, now? Anything else I can do for you?' He said he was fine. 'We'll be seeing you on Sunday, then.'

She escaped with relief to put the bags in the car. But, before she started the engine, she smoothed down the skirt of her jersey dress. It was a bright emerald colour and showed the dust she had collected from kneeling on the bedroom floor. They would have to find the old man a cleaner. She turned the key in the ignition, then paused to light a cigarette. To her surprise, she found that her hand was shaking. It was strange but she didn't really know how she felt about her shattering discovery. It was hardly the sort of thing one advertised, though in her heart she was glad that Willie was not her father. But what a plague of questions then arose! Who was Maurice and what was he like? The only facts she could safely assume were that he had curly black hair and wasn't a giant. But that was all. It seemed that he had wanted Chloe and she him, although she had refused him in the end. But she would never really know. Could he be traced? It seemed unlikely. Perhaps an advertisement- . . . something on the lines of: 'Maurice S., last seen in Scarborough, in the June of 1922, is requested to get in touch with . . . ' But then she remembered she would be looking for an old man who might be dead. The time lapse was a greater handicap than the lack of a surname. No, it was useless. Better to let it rest anyway, perhaps. She reversed the car in the road, turned round and roared off.

When she showed the book of poems and its inscription to Ken later, he thought it all quite a joke.

'Well, you never liked the old bugger,' he said. 'I should think it's a great relief, isn't it?' She was rather peeved at his levity and made him swear not to tell anyone. It shouldn't come out. Everyone knew Jack had been on the way before Chloe and Will had married, but this was totally different. If the old man ever found out, he might cut her – and, more importantly, the children – out of his will.

Beth stirred her tea, reflectively, in the kitchen. The noise of the spoon in the cup sounded very loud in the middle of the night. Yes, it had been an extraordinary day! But it didn't really make any difference. Willie had, effectively, been her father and brought her up. She had had to accept the rules of his house. She felt sure Maurice S. would have let her go to the grammar school – probably somewhere better – and that thought sickened her. For a moment, she was struck very forcibly by the far-reaching influence of chance happenings and minor accidents of time and place. Her life could have been so very different! Then, of course, she wouldn't have met Ken, which would have been a shame. But she might not have needed to. The idea was tantalising, though she shouldn't really allow it breathing-space. It was useless to ponder. If the Reverend Kaye hadn't taken a stick to Willie in 1906, no one in the family but Jack would have existed anyway. No Sam or Ted, no woman that was anything like herself, and no boys or Jennifer.

She examined her fingernails and tried to clear her mind. The shocking revelation meant nothing, nothing at all, except that she had a surprise bundle of genes in her body, which did not come from Willie. Nothing else had changed. She could hardly cast Willie off now, like it or not. He had, however grudgingly, fed her and clothed her until she married. He had also ruined her chances of improvement and she couldn't forgive him for that. Someone else might have shrugged it off, but not Beth. There was a deep well of insecurity inside her because of it. But Willie was the only father she knew, real or otherwise, even though she despised him.

Still, the memories of her mother insisted on crowding back. Beth promised herself she would give up smoking again next week and lit another cigarette. Of course she knew why Chloe hadn't run off with Maurice. As long as she could remember, her mother had waited on the boys and Willie. Only a few months ago, when Jennifer had had the mumps, Chloe had not visited her for fear of catching it. But it wasn't her own health she was worried about. Beth could still remember her actual words:

'If I should get it, who'd look after Willie?'

It had always been the same. Beth's childhood was synonymous with the latter years of Grandma Moffat. In fact, her earliest memory, around the age of three, was of swinging under the apple-tree on a glorious day. She wondered if she could touch the clouds if she swung high enough. Her beloved mother was pegging washing on the line. She might even have been wearing the green, floral frock but Beth couldn't be certain of that now. What she did remember was that Chloe had drawn faces for her, on some of the old wooden clothes-pegs, and dressed them in scraps of material. Then her big brother, Jack, had come running down the lane and into the garden, shouting. Chloe had dropped her basket and the pegs had scattered and clattered all over the path. Beth had cried because she was frightened and everything was spoilt. After that, Granny Moffat came to live with them in a big bed downstairs and nothing was ever quite the same again. Mummy was much too busy to play with pegs.

Another figure that had deeply etched itself into Beth's childhood was that of Aunt Rose. Her visits were infrequent but attended by a great deal of prior preparation and fuss. Instinctively, Beth felt her malevolence but could see her mother scraping up to her too. The seeds of resentment began to grow. She especially remembered the way Grandma Moffat made the living-room smell. She took it all in as she grew, watching her mother worn away into a shadow, trotting hither and thither, forever in attendance. She didn't understand any of the reasons but saw all too clearly the results. The boys of course were not expected to help much, but Beth was. Chloe trained her to be a good little housewife too. Except that inside she rebelled.

Beth ground her cigarette fiercely into ash at the vision of Chloe's thin and eternally pinafored body. If that was what love did to you, she wanted none of it. She remembered thinking that at fourteen. Then came the disappointment over the grammar school and the substitution of the boring old shoe-shop, with its pittance of a wage. The only good thing about that was that it was in Kingley, which meant she could meet boys who didn't live in the village. For, at sixteen, she was making determined plans. She would never lead a life like her mother's.

At last, the valium was beginning to work and sleepiness was blunting the edges of the old venom. Beth sighed at her own bitterness. It wore her out when it surfaced like this. Most of the time, it was well tucked away in an old carrier bag. She rinsed her cup under the tap, emptied the ashtray and climbed the stairs, as the hall clock struck three. On her way across the landing, she looked in on Jennifer who lay asleep, diagonally across her bed, with one arm out-flung. On the adjacent wall, above the bed, was a poster of the Beatles. It was there on sufferance for Beth did not approve. She didn't approve of anything which might pose a threat, however vague, to the path she intended her daughter to follow.

There could be no diversions until the goal was reached. Now that Jennifer was fourteen, she sensed difficulties ahead. But she was on her guard and prepared for them. Gently, she brushed the fringe away from her daughter's forehead and covered her up.

Ken was still asleep when she slipped in quietly beside him. He was a good sleeper. No doubt he had plenty of problems with the business, but he never had bad dreams about his mother. Beth sometimes felt awkward about Ken. He loved her and she was fond of him. She was aware occasionally that it wasn't enough. In a way, it had been the basis of her last quarrel with her mother. How stupid that had been! It had started innocently enough, more to do with the time of the month than anything, for her varicose veins had been aching and she was cross and tired.

'Whatever's the matter with you, today?' Chloe had asked and, instead of shrugging it off, Beth had said, unwisely: 'We've all got our problems, you know.'

'Problems! What do you mean? You haven't got any problems.'

'Oh really, mother, how would you know?'

Chloe was offended. 'Well, you shouldn't have,' she said. 'You've got everything you could possibly want.'

Beth could see her mother now, perched awkwardly on the edge of the settee, entirely out of place in the sea of the green lounge, which overflowed around her with too much affluence. She could even feel her own exasperation rising.

'Oh, don't be naïve, mother! Just because I live in a big house and have nice clothes, doesn't mean I must be happy every minute of every day, you know.' Chloe's old, little face looked troubled.

'You're unhappy then, after all? I shouldn't like to think that.'

'I'm not unhappy, for God's sake.'

'You said you were.'

'I didn't – I didn't at all! I just meant that, some days,

things get on top of any one, that's all.'

But there was no stopping Chloe now.

'You've got a good husband,' she said. That was a red rag. Beth knew she had a good husband. She knew that everyone knew she had a good husband. She did not want to hear it again and said as much.

'I don't understand you,' said Chloe, quietly, 'and I'm not sure that I want to. I only hope you deserve him, that's all.' Beth really went out of control, then.

'Well, they can't all have a free servant for a wife, can they?' she snapped. She should never have said it. Never in a million years. Even now, the words made her cringe inside. But she couldn't say sorry. Her mother had taken it very well, considering. She had merely begun to gather up her things, as if ready to go, and said:

'Well, we're not all as fortunate in our husbands. That's exactly my point.' It was the nearest to criticism of Will that Beth had ever heard her come. 'I'm sorry you're unhappy, Beth, but I really can't see why.' (It never occurred to her that her attitude was similar to that of her own mother, many, many years ago.)

'For the last time, Mum, I am not unhappy.'

'Oh, but you are,' Chloe had answered her sharply, at last. 'Perhaps you don't even know it, but you really are. It shows in your face. You look nervous and restless all of the time, just like my father did. Only you didn't use to.'

This was so close to the truth that it hurt. Beth would not have called it unhappiness. But there was a dissatisfaction within her which kept on growing. She couldn't put her finger on it. But it continued to hound her, although she did lots of things to hide it and disguise it.

'Well,' said Chloe, 'I'll be off now. I have to get Will his dinner and you should be thinking about Ken's.'

'He has a business appointment tonight.' (Sourly spoken).

'Well, give him my regards anyway.'

Those were the last words they ever exchanged and

they were laden with coolness. Beth writhed under the blankets and the valium. Why couldn't her mother understand her better? Why did she have to be so unbearably sanctimonious? Above all, why did she have to go out the very same day Beth had driven past her house in a huff, trail round Bradford in the hottest of weathers, all dressed up, and then collapse on the way home?

This was hopeless. Beth tried to lie still and relax. She began to run through her body, the way the teacher at her yoga class had instructed them. But it never worked for her. Her mind was too busy. She had had great hopes of it, just as she did of every new diet she went on, but it was no good at all. Ken turned over in his sleep and blew in her face, which didn't help. He was a big man who managed to pinch most of the bedclothes. Silly to feel bad about Ken, she wasn't that bad a wife. She was indefatigable in her efforts 'to stay nice' and not 'let herself go', which was more than she could say for him. But she had never let an instant's infidelity threaten their marriage, although there were plenty who would have been willing. But Beth still didn't trust love. It frightened her far too much. But she was, in fact, a very good wife. On and on, her mind span into the night in an endless circle of self-justification, like some nervous, over-strung violin, forever playing the same chords, until she fell asleep.

CHAPTER TWO

For once, she dreamt about Ken. It was all very like the first time they had met, when he came into the shop for a pair of black, evening shoes. She could not claim to be instantly attracted. Even then, he was rather overweight and had sandy hair, which stuck out wildly in various directions, despite his attempts to plaster it down. But his eyes were disarming because they twinkled with an irrepressible humour. He was also in uniform, so that she knew straight away he was an officer. He took size twelves and, of course, the shoes were out of stock, though Beth promised to see what she could do. He would have come back anyway, for he had been startled by her riveting combination of black hair and blue eyes and felt peculiarly weak when he looked at her. In the meantime, Muriel, who also worked in the shop, was able to supply the necessary gossip.

'That's Kenneth Sugden,' she said. 'His dad owns Sugden's Haulage Company. Now't special he weren't, but made a pile of brass. Pity Ken's not a looker, isn't it? He's a nice guy, really, but you wouldn't want to go out with someone looking like that, would you? I ask you!'

But Beth found Muriel's information distinctly interesting and was not so proud. She let him take her to the pictures and merely lifted her nose several inches higher when the other girls giggled and sniggered behind their hands and behind her back. There were compensations. She was always collected by car, duly chocolated somehow despite the rations and sat in the best seats for Ken was amazingly efficient. He was also trying hard with the Brylcreem and had gone on a diet. She had to steel herself the first time he kissed her. And yet . . . maybe Ken wasn't Ronald Colman, but he did have something. He was certainly fun to be with. He was also entirely reliable and those are rare combinations. He wasn't a fool either and that gave him the confidence he might have lacked if he had had to rely on his physical appearance alone. He was older than most of the boys Beth had been out with before and seemed to know more about the world. He was remarkably shrewd, despite his joking, and Beth was sure he would do well back in his father's firm, once the war was over.

But the war wasn't over and Ken had to go back to the training camp at Catterick. Beth certainly did not sit at home while he was away, although she did write as she had promised. But there was no real competition. Lots of handsome faces. But Beth was well fortified against those. She wanted a little more. Her girlfriends were beginning to wed right, left and centre because of the war and the way it was going. She was more circumspect. To be truthful, the very idea still filled her with horror. The only snag was that she had no wish to work in the shoe-shop for the rest of her life and could see no other way out. Little by little, the idea of Ken as a husband began to germinate in her mind.

He took her to tea with his parents, one weekend leave, and she liked them. No one could describe the senior Sugdens as anything but 'nouveau riche', but they had an honesty and warm-heartedness about them which Beth found delightful after the repressive atmosphere of her own home. In later years, she was to regard them as an embarrassment but, at that time, she hadn't learnt to be so fastidious. She thought they lived in unparalleled comfort and luxury. Ken was the only son and she began to see how things could be. From then on, she was careful not to put a foot wrong. But she still felt afraid and wavered, wondering if Ken would always dote on her as he did now.

The war was going very badly when Ken proposed and he knew he had to go into active service. He could quite see that she might want to wait. But he couldn't help himself. Beth took a deep breath and plunged into the water. It was no good fooling herself. She would never get another chance so good. Why, even if he died . . . Between them, they persuaded their parents, including Chloe who was fearfully worried because Beth was still only eighteen and they hadn't really known one another long.

The wedding took place in a romantic rush while Ken was still on leave and they had two days honeymoon in the Lakes. Beth enjoyed it because they stayed in a classy hotel and made love in the dark. Ken was very sweet to her anyway and she was used to him now. Then he was gone and she returned to live with her parents, for the sake of convenience, until his return.

She worried about him a lot. By the sound of his letters, he wasn't actually doing anything really dangerous or heroic, but you never knew. She gave up the shop and went to work in the gauge-room of the engineering works in Kingley – once again turned into a munitions factory – with her hair tied up in an unbecoming scarf. The war began to depress her terribly. It seemed to have been going on for ever. She hated the atmosphere of austerity. It instilled a permanent caution and fine sensibility of values, material and otherwise, into most of her peers. Some of them never felt able to splash out and enjoy themselves again. Everything had to be carefully calculated. But, true to form, Beth reacted in quite the opposite way. Never again would she do without, never eat margarine instead of butter or make a cake without an egg. She was not going to scrimp and save. She had had enough of that way of life with her father, now intensified by the war, and she had had a brief taste of the alternative with Ken. More than ever, she was determined to have, rather than to have not.

Even in her sleep, she stirred and sighed. No, she had no regrets about Ken. True, he had put on lots of weight and nobody, but nobody, ever gave him the eye. But she led a comfortable life and was much envied. They even got along rather well together. She still couldn't claim to love him. But she had seen dozens of marriages, apparently based on love, founder. Surely the thing didn't exist anyway! She had done very well without it. The only trouble was that it seemed to exist for other people. Willie, for instance, who wouldn't move Chloe's hat and gloves off the sideboard. Not that one would ever have guessed, the way he had treated the poor woman. It must have stolen up on him unawares, over the years. And Chloe herself, who had once loved Willie, and then Maurice, and then maybe Willie again – although she must have hated him at times as well. Yes, it was really Chloe who had the capacity to make her feel guilty over Ken. Only Chloe, now dead and gone, and maybe Ken himself, sometimes. For love existed for him too. He loved her truly, despite all her diamond hardness. In the end, she found that a burden for, way underneath the well-groomed exterior which tic-tacked about so elegantly, lurked an extremely active conscience.

Beth believed she must have only just dropped off when the alarm rang, vibrating and buzzing away like mad. Her two sons were both away now, but there was still Jennifer to send off to school and Ken's breakfast to cook.

He came in from the bathroom, knotting his tie over a gross and wobbling stomach and grinning sympathetically as Beth stirred and groaned and threw the alarm clock on the floor. He bent down to pick it up and switch it off.

'Another bad night?'

'Terrible!'

'Not the same dream?'

'Yes.'

'Those tablets don't seem to be doing much good. Why don't you go and see Dr Jones again?'

'Because he thinks I'm neurotic,' said Beth, sourly.

'Oh, nonsense! It's just your mum and the change.'

Beth did not like to be reminded of her premature hormonal dysfunctions and her mouth hardened.

'Look, why don't you stay in bed? I'll bring you a cup of tea. I can see to myself and Jennifer.'

'You have to drag her out of bed.'

'Well, I'll do that.'

'And make sure she doesn't spend half an hour in the bathroom.'

'That too.'

'And see she eats a proper breakfast and remind her she's got piano tonight, after school.'

'Don't you worry. I'll see to everything. We'll manage fine.'

Beth dozed on for a while, letting her tea grow cold, vaguely aware of hurried steps on the stairs and clattering and cheerful voices from the kitchen. Jennifer got on well with her father. Beth was glad of it and yet resented it at the same time. Someone had to be strict. She knew that Ken wouldn't make her eat her egg or see that her hair was tidy.

'Your mother's not well,' he would say.

'What, again?' from Jennifer.

Then the front door banged, the car backed out of the double garage and drove away and the house was empty. The sunlight poured in through closed curtains as Beth sat up and lit her first cigarette of the day. The morning rush had been successfully completed in her absence. She envied them their sense of purpose in going out. She had only a coffee morning and wasn't in the least bit interested in going. The hound of restlessness had returned to pursue her again.

She got up slowly and pulled back the curtains which matched her bedspread. It was warm again . . . almost too warm, and sultry as if the weather was about to break. Their house, 'Lorelei', a large detached, with pebble-dashed grey walls and a red-gabled roof – quite the nicest amongst its neighbours – commanded a fine view across the valley, over the railway line, and up to the green stone-walled hills. The house was raised above the main road in the floor of the valley, but screened from it by a bank of trees, which cut out all the noise and the bustle of the trunk road into town. It was one of the reasons why this secluded cul-de-sac on the outskirts of Kingley was one of the most desirable areas in town. The treetops strained gently in the breeze like green weed in a pond. But the view gave her no solace today and she turned away from it to run her bath.

While it was still filling, she slipped downstairs and poured herself a generous nip of sherry from the heavily ormolu'd cocktail cabinet in the lounge. She often found it perked her up enough to go out. It was not of course that she had a problem. She drank very sparingly in company. But a glass beforehand calmed her down and yet gave her the sparkle she needed. Better not have any more valium as well. She just managed to escape back into the bathroom in time, calling out a hasty 'good-morning', as she heard her daily, Mrs O'Neill, enter the kitchen through the back door.

By the time she arrived at the coffee party, Beth had the right face on. Her skin, though becoming a little taut and drawn at the edges, looked healthy and glowing enough. Her hair was a smart black cap, which had been ruthlessly straightened from its natural curl, and her make-up had been applied skilfully, although perhaps the lipstick was just a mite too glossy and red. On the whole, the bone structure which had once made Maurice Sinclair appear rather frail and delicate, had endowed Beth with a remarkable beauty. But it would not allow her to soften into middle age. She was determined to remain petite anyway, no matter how lined or how much her face might collapse inwards, just as she was determined never to go grey.

'Oh, Beth, how nice you look,' said a friend. 'What a lovely suit.' Beth's hands strayed self-consciously to her hand-crocheted, black Dior suit.

'Do you think so? I've had it for simply ages . . . picked it up in Paris. It's really terribly old.' She moved on, greeting several familiar faces. Her diamond rings sparkled and she dispensed largesse with a smile. 'You really must have the next NSPCC do at "Lorelei", you know. I'm sure it must be my turn and we have so much more room.'

The truth was that she did not feel at ease. They had met in the grammar school headmaster's house and everyone seemed to be vaguely connected with education, or else part of a set that, although far less well-heeled these days, regarded her kind, she felt, with a certain contempt. The trouble about living in Kingley was that everyone knew about your lowly origins . . .

She was descended upon by the headmaster's wife, Mrs Brown, bearing raffle-tickets. As far as Beth was concerned, Mrs Brown might well have come from a different planet. For starters, she looked as if she possibly took in washing for a living. She was comfortingly shapeless with pepper and salt hair, gone fuzzy after too many unsuccessful perms, and she wore spectacles which entirely hid her kind eyes. She was always to be seen in sagging cardigans and tweed skirts or even, horror of horrors, considering the breadth of her bottom, in stretch slacks. She was very motherly and the girls all loved her, wishing that she was their Senior Mistress, instead of the academically excellent and extremely proper Miss McIntyre, who saw to it that they were segregated from the boys, as much as was humanly possible in a co-ed school. Mr Brown, happily, was of a similar ilk to his wife and, although his staff (especially Miss McIntyre) lived in fear of him developing another progressive idea (and parents and governors alike despaired of his never-ending waffle) it had to be said that, in those days, he ran a happy and well-adjusted school.

Beth ran her eye around Mrs Brown's living-room. The word was well-chosen. It was frankly shabby. Mountains of books and magazines co-existed cheerfully with faded chintz covers which were wearing thin over the arms, and a flea-ridden spaniel gnawed its half-chewed bones on the rug. Goodness, you would have thought the woman could have tidied up a bit this morning! It was such a nice house really. A charming window-seat looked out to the grey brick and green tiles of the school, way across the playing-fields, where boys plastered themselves with mud playing rugby, and girls in green shorts and striped socks fought each other with hockey-sticks. Jennifer would be amongst them. Mrs Brown echoed her thoughts.

'Jennifer is really excelling herself this term,' she said, tearing out tickets from the book and writing on the stub. 'Such a bright girl. We have great hopes for her, John and I.' Beth handed over her money and smiled.

'Yes, she does seem to be getting on well. I'm sure her brains must come from Ken, for I never had any.'

'Nonsense,' said Mrs Brown. (She was, very definitely, a no-nonsense sort of person.) 'Tell the truth, now. We never had the chance, did we? Our generation, I mean. Except for the privileged few. It's different now, thank God. These boys and girls have got wonderful futures ahead, if they work hard.' Beth was left feeling slightly uncomfortable and her smile was brittle. She accepted a cup of coffee and moved away to sit in the window.

'Have you been away yet?' asked the woman next to her.

'We're having two weeks in Corfu at the end of the month,' Beth said absently. 'Have to wait until school breaks up still – unfortunately. It's the same hotel every year, I'm afraid, but we do find it very good. Ken and I like Tenerife too but we save that for the autumn, when Jenny's back at school.' Her companion was effectively silenced, but Beth did not notice. She had forgotten that their holiday was so close and the thought cheered her up considerably. In a way, it was almost what she lived for every year – and certainly what she looked forward to most. She loved lying in the sun next to a pool, being served drinks, for they only went to the best hotels. It reassured her that they had made it. The packing of her wardrobe would occupy her very well for the next few weeks.

She left the coffee-party at twelve and drove back into town. There was a snarl-up at the lights and she had to crawl along behind one of Sugden's lumbering lorries. Really, the main street became more impossible every day. It was high time that the by-pass was built, despite the public protest. She had to stop again by the library and remembered that she still hadn't taken Chloe's books back. The early sunshine hadn't lasted and the sky was gloomy now and heavy. As she inched forwards, the rain began to patter down in huge, isolated drops and she turned on the windscreen wipers. The fumes from the lorry in front somehow got into the car and irritated her. Still, she could hardly complain when it was Ken's livelihood. They ground to a halt again after a promising start and she lit a cigarette in exasperation.

The rain was coming down hard now, bouncing off the concrete pavements and battering the dahlias in the Town Hall Square. She noticed a grammar school boy and girl in their green uniforms on one of the council seats, sharing an umbrella and a sandwich lunch. The girl was very like Jennifer but it was not, thank goodness, her. These two were all over each other. Jennifer stayed to school lunch and took part in dinner-time societies and discussion groups. Beth saw to that.

At last she was through the lights and the lorry turned off. Now she had to find a parking place, there was some shopping to do. The rain came down in sheets from the hills, making everything dirty and cold and miserable and Beth shivered. Roll on Corfu! Perhaps because she had been thinking about her holiday, the canoodling couple from the grammar school suddenly reminded her of another couple of young lovers. It was last year, when they had been staying in the north-east of the island where the green mountains, with their sentinel cypresses and silvery olive groves, tumbled into the sea. Albania lay across the narrow strait of blue water, misty and indistinct. White-pebbled inlets and terracotta fishing-villages, bordered by golden gorse on the hills above, hugged the shore. It was a peaceful place and the high rise pile of luxury, tucked into the hillside, where they were staying, was the only blemish upon it.

Beth had been strolling in the gardens of the hotel that evening. She was secretly rather bored, though relaxed enough. She had dressed for dinner and was waiting for Ken to join her for a cocktail. The couple came over the shingle which seemed, in the fading half-light, to be like a collection of small pearls, just as the rippling sea water was becoming opalescent. Their sandals made crunching noises on the beach. They were young and American – probably students – and travelling the hard way with rucksacks on their backs. Both of them wore old jeans and tee-shirts. She guessed they would be hitching. Ken had strong views about hitchhikers, regarding them as parasites on society, but she didn't really see it. If they were prepared for the attendant discomforts and could get away with it, why not? They were obviously sleeping rough . . . no doubt in the same sleeping bag.

The girl was not exactly beautiful, but there was a certain gold-freckled freshness about her which was appealing. The boy was a mass of dark hair – long, tousled curls, newly-grown beard and strong fuzzy arms. He lifted her up to look over the wall which divided the hotel beach from the rest and Beth could see her obviously unfettered breasts dent and strain the grubby tee-shirt. They looked across the wall at the neatly laid out hotel grounds with the artificial beach and the straw-fringed umbrellas. They looked too at Beth in her three inch heels, with her gold bangles and silk cocktail dress. They looked at the gleaming white, five-star, concrete behind her. And then they laughed. They slid down their side of the wall again, and made their way back over the shingle to the rocks, his hairy arm coiled around her waist.

Beth felt wounded at the laugh. Of course, it probably wasn't personal. They were merely revelling in their own dis-advantages, in a perversely youthful manner. But it affected her and, for a few crazy moments, she envied them. She often toyed with the pipe-dream of a simpler life. No doubt this couple were in love. She continued to watch as they sat down on the stones near the water's edge and took food from their rucksacks. He opened a cheap bottle of local wine and she tore apart some bread and cheese with her hands. Beth felt certain that, when their supper was over and darkness fell, they would strip off their clothes and swim naked in the sea, before making love to each other on the beach and the idea excited her mildly in a voyeuristic way.

Then Ken came out and they went in to dinner. But Beth remained subdued. In one rare flash of insight, she had suddenly felt captive. She had realised that, in her way, she was no freer than Chloe, despite her obvious material advantages. She had chained herself to a wheel she could not get off. In her youth, she too would have looked over that wall, though with a far greater reverence and longing. Like a moth against a lamp, she would have battered herself against it. But, now that she was inside, she had looked out and wondered. Perhaps which side of the wall one viewed from was not that important, after all. It was the act of looking over which implied discontent.

Of course, she had recovered soon enough from her mood. She had forgotten all about it in fact. She had returned home to the same round of coffee-mornings and church bazaars and PTA meetings. She had revelled in her compensations and hadn't given the couple and what they had done to her another thought. But now they returned to nag, along with all the other irritations of the last few days, beneath her fine veneer.

Disconsolate, she parked the car. It was high time to concentrate on the never-ending problem of the weekend meals. Willie was coming to Sunday lunch and she decided against soup to start with. (He always slurped from his spoon and reminded her of Rebecca.) They could have pâté instead. She didn't suppose Willie would like that very much, but never mind. She wondered, irreverently, how long he would last without Chloe and decided she wouldn't rate his chances very highly beyond a year or two. Would she be so cut up when Ken went? She doubted it, somehow.

Concentrate! She really must concentrate on what she was doing, instead of staring vacantly at the cheese counter . . . the assistant was giving her a funny look. She pulled herself together with an effort. My goodness, she needed her holiday this year! She decided to come out again this afternoon and look at some beachwear. Spending money always helped when she was bored and unhappy. That ridiculous word again!

She was not unhappy. She would not change her life one iota. She had done the best she could, under the circumstances. She couldn't help it if it wasn't very honourable or elevating. Those sort of things were reserved for Jennifer now. She would get it all right. Like Alice, she would be able to enter the little door into the garden. She would be clever and educated, well-off and respected, loved and liked and finally content. Through her, Beth would gain vicarious perfection. The boys would marry and drift away. So would Jennifer, but, because she was her daughter, they would maintain a closer relationship. Jennifer would still need her in lots of ways.

Back in the car, the rain continued to stream down the

windows. Beth's nylons were spotted with mud. She would have to change when she got home. If the wet weather continued, she might pick Jennifer up in the car tonight. Her daughter wouldn't appreciate it, but surely if it was raining this hard . . . ? Beth knew how she would look. Her socks would be coming down and her beret slipping off. Her eyes would hold a wealth of seriousness. Beth knew she was impatient with her most of the time, but couldn't help it. Jennifer was altogether too soft and sensitive and took everything to heart. But she would grow out of that. And she wasn't going to be entirely unattractive. She had too much of Ken in her to ever be really pretty of course, but her hair was as good as Chloe's, though a browner and darker auburn, and her face was at least interesting, or would be when it outgrew its teenage spots. Beth was intensely hopeful, for she was sure that Jennifer could be the substrate of perfection, given herself as catalyst.

PART III

. . . AND JENNIFER

'Beyond this place of wrath and tears
Looms but the Horror of the shade
and yet the menace of the years
Finds, and shall find, me unafraid.

It matters not how strait the gate,
How charged with punishments the scroll,
I am the master of my fate:,
I am the captain of my soul.'

WILLIAM ERNEST HENLEY

CHAPTER ONE

'When I was just a little girl with pigtails,' said Jennifer sadly, 'there was hardly room for me on the seat some days on my way to school. Hockey-bag, ballet shoes, violin-case. As well as my satchel full of books. You name it and I did it. My mother was so keen I should not miss out. Of course I am grateful in a way. But I couldn't just *do* all those things: I had to excell.' She pronounced her words very slowly, though not very clearly. Her tongue needed spurring into action and her mouth was still intolerably dry so that, when the former did move, it was in danger of sticking to her palate. But it didn't really matter what she said any more. She had crossed the great divide. Purely because she was here, everything (she felt) could be taken with a pinch of salt. She was permanently discredited. That was what happened if you allowed yourself to let go. Yet the only emotion she could conjure up was one of relief. She was also very tired, despite hour upon hour of sleep. Perhaps it was only the drugs.

Inert in her chair, she gazed listlessly at the pitted face of the eau-de-nil wall behind her companion. There was one area of blebbed paint which looked amazingly human. If you shut one eye and stared at it long enough, another eye swam up towards you behind the hooked nose and pock-marked chin.

'Mrs Warrender!'

'Yes?'

'I said I didn't quite understand . . . what that has to do with your refusal to see your mother.'

Jennifer opened both eyes and thought about it.

'Don't you?' she said. 'It is connected. Somehow.'

The girl wasn't wearing a white coat. It was a ruse of course to try and make you forget she was a doctor. Just an old school chum having a chat. Except that Jennifer was now a good deal older.

'You mean you're ashamed to see her . . . because you're here?'

'I suppose so. If you put it like that. Nice and simplified. But really, I just can't stand the idea.'

The house officer tried again. 'She's very anxious about you, you know.'

Jennifer smiled wearily, without humour. 'Oh no, she isn't. Not in the way that you or I would be. You'll see! She'd come tripping in with her twin-set and pearls, looking like something from Vogue magazine. The ward would horrify her. She'd ask you for a private room straightaway.'

'Is that how you feel about it? Horrified?'

'No . . . of course, it isn't pleasant. Too green and dingy and overcrowded. And some of my neighbours are very strange. But I can't say I have any desire to be anywhere else.'

Dr Jowett sighed. 'Yes . . . well, we may transfer you to the new wing on Monday, if you're feeling better. I think it's too early to go home. But you can't avoid your mother forever, you know. Or the rest of the world.'

Jennifer made no comment.

'Would you see your father if he came?'

'He died of a heart attack last year.'

'Oh, I'm terribly sorry.' Dr Jowett flushed and momentarily lost ground. Her hand strayed involuntarily to Jennifer's case-notes on the desk, which was not exactly between them. 'Stupid of me. I should have known that. It must be in here somewhere.'

Jennifer shrugged. 'It's all right,' she said. 'Why should you remember everything?'

'Er . . . yes. Well, if you're really quite sure you can't

see your mother today . . . '

'Quite sure.'

' . . . then I'll tell her so. But I can't put her off much longer. Do think about it.' She picked up the telephone and buzzed for a nurse to shepherd Jennifer back to the ward. When she left the room, she took with her the distinct impression that the interview had not gone exactly as planned.

Mrs Sugden was waiting in the room provided for relatives. It was otherwise empty, for the afternoon tide of visitors had already been allowed in, bearing their flowers and their grapes and clean nighties, and surged up the ward to lap dutifully round almost every bed. The woman who rose to meet her was small and dark and extremely smart. She was not actually wearing a twin-set or pearls but Dr Jowett could see at once what Jennifer meant. It was more than seventeen years since Chloe had died, but Beth was little changed. Older and harder. She would soon arrive at her sixtieth birthday, though decline to celebrate it. Her brown face had become very lined, like a mask of well-worn leather. But her figure remained that of a young woman and her hair was as black as ever. She had found widowhood disconcerting, though not a mortal blow. But this business with Jennifer . . . that had rocked her small and limited world. It was the worst thing Jennifer had ever done to her. And that was saying something . . .

'Mrs Sugden? I'm Dr Jowett, the senior house officer responsible for this ward this weekend. I shall be continuing to look after Jennifer, in fact, because Dr Mahler, my consultant, was admitting this week.'

'Yes, yes. Can I see my daughter now?'

'I'm afraid not. She feels she can't see you today.'

'Why not? Is she too ill?'

'Physically, no. She's making an uneventful recovery. But . . . well . . . she is, perhaps, still a little disturbed and really doesn't want to see anyone.'

'But I'm her mother!'

'She doesn't actually want to see *you*.'

Beth gripped her handbag very tightly and, for a moment, Dr Jowett thought she was going to scream. Her face had drained of colour beneath its tan. It had been embarrassing to have to spell it out but the message had got through all right. Beth was white with rage.

'I've travelled all the way down from Yorkshire,' she said. 'Two trains. Two trains and a change of station in London. And now the madam says she won't see me! Surely I have a right?'

'Er . . . well no, not really. I'm very sorry, Mrs Sugden. Not against Jennifer's wishes.'

'It's ludicrous. Quite absurd! Why should she say such a wicked thing?'

Tactfully, Dr Jowett sat down, thereby forcing Beth to do the same.

'You have to remember she's been through a difficult time. She's still very depressed and I think she feels she's let you down.'

'Well, yes, she has!' Beth nodded indignantly and got out her handkerchief to dab at her eyes and blow her nose. 'She has let us down. If only you knew how much!'

'Us?'

'The family. Oh well, me I suppose, now her daddy's gone. Thank goodness he never knew about this! And her husband.'

'But I understood that Mr Warrender left the family home some time ago and Jennifer was suing for divorce?'

'Yes, that's true. And I don't condone what he's done,' Beth sniffed. 'How could I? But there's always two sides, isn't there? Jennifer provoked him. She's had every advantage, you know, doctor. Everything she could possibly want. I'm not just talking about material things now. But she seems to have this tendency to self-destruct.'

'I rather think she feels that way too.'

'Then can't you make her see me?'

'I'm afraid not. It wouldn't be right. And not at all

advisable.' A phrase of Dr Mahler's came into her mind . . . 'smother love' . . . and she remembered what Jennifer had said earlier. Of course it couldn't be as simple as that. But it seemed to fit together. The over-protective element. The unreasonable expectations. No wonder Jennifer had ducked the interview.

'I'd like to see your consultant . . . what's his name?'

'Mahler. Like the composer.' Dr Jowett deftly fielded the hostility but Beth looked blank. It was exactly the sort of allusion she hated. 'I'll make you an appointment for tomorrow.'

'Can't I see him before then?'

'Well, no . . . not unless it's an emergency. He isn't here. Anyway, it will be much better if he sees you tomorrow afternoon, after he's assessed Jennifer in the morning.'

'You mean he hasn't actually seen her yet?'

'Well, no. It is the weekend.'

'Then who told her she had to come here?'

'Mrs Sugden,' the house officer felt a note of coldness creep into her voice, quite unintentionally, 'your daughter is a voluntary patient. That means she is here entirely of her own free will . . . '

'But it's such a stigma . . . '

Dr Jowett was in danger of losing her cool now. Any minute now, she thought furiously, she's going to mention the word 'asylum'. Or worse.

'She was well enough to leave the medical ward. But not fit enough to go home.'

'Well, couldn't she have stayed there? That would have been so much nicer. Everyone will get to know she's been in a psychiatric ward.'

'They were very busy, Mrs Sugden. With people who needed to be there.'

'Oh. Well, what am I supposed to do about her till tomorrow?'

'Go home, Mrs Sugden. Or at least find somewhere to stay. Leave her alone for the time being. She needs to think things over by herself. It's all for the best, you know.'

Platitudes, she thought grimly, on her way back to the ward. That's what we deal with and dish out in the end. But they do seem to smooth things over. She entered the office and slapped the case-sheets down on the desk with disgust.

'Afternoon, Annabelle,' said the charge nurse, Bill Wright. 'Seen off Mrs S then?'

'For the moment.'

He laughed. 'She'll be on to Mahler like a shot. Good job it's him.'

'Oh, she's just upset. Anyone would be in her shoes. You can't actually say the patient's being reasonable, either.' Dr Jowett didn't like to admit it, but she didn't really like Bill Wright very much. He was a good nurse. He was excellent at handling what you might call the rougher element, or even the criminal fraternity, which is inevitably a part of any psychiatric ward. But his private opinion of patients like Jennifer bordered on the derisory. He also had the knack of making Annabelle herself feel inadequate.

'Can't think why she was sent over here,' he said now. 'It's not the right place for her. She should have gone home like most attempted suicides, after they've slept it off.'

'She wanted to come.'

'It's not a rest home!'

Annabelle was annoyed but chose her words carefully. She knew that Bill Wright was perfectly well aware that she had assessed Jennifer on the medical ward herself.

'I think she was a failed suicide. Her attempt was pretty determined. She would probably have made it, if she hadn't been found.'

Wright gave her a sidelong glance. 'Doesn't mean a thing. As you and I both know,' he said.

'Perhaps not. But she knew what she was doing. She's not the manipulative type. Far more quietly depressed and ridden with guilt. And – as you and I both know – it's often the quiet ones who end up doing it.' She let her pen lazily cover the drug sheet he had thrust in front of her, in order to sanction some night medication, but did not fail to notice his sulkiness out of the corner of her eye.

'Well, you know best of course.' The remark was tinged with sarcasm and followed by his trump card. 'Mahler won't like it, though. Hates having his acute beds cluttered up with neurotics over the weekend.'

'Oh, he won't mind,' Annabelle replied, smugly. 'He can always discharge her. Which I couldn't have done yesterday, without dragging him out to see her.'

'True, true.' The charge nurse mellowed at this sign of pragmatism. He had Annabelle branded as an idealist. 'Reckon he must have had a bad enough Saturday as it was, sending in Red Hot Kate on a section.'

'How is she?'

'Still high as a kite.'

'Causing trouble?'

'No, not really. Not as aggressive. The night staff had a lively time though. Had to put her down the corridor. Otherwise nobody'd have got a wink of sleep.'

The same evening, Jennifer had a visitor who walked straight in, unannounced. She didn't see him until it was too late to hide because she was lying on her bed pretending to read a magazine. His sudden appearance felt like the shock of standing under a shower which has unexpectedly run cold.

'Mike! You've no business to be here.'

'Oh, really? And why not? I rather thought that might be the object of the exercise.'

Bastard, she thought! Of course he would imagine that! So would everyone else. The anger and shame flooded up to the roots of her hair. She tried to get a grip on her feelings, but inside could only shake at the stress of confrontation. Her estranged husband took the chair by the bed with an apparent air of confidence. But when he looked at her, she saw that he avoided her eyes and she knew straightaway that he was actually nervous.

'Well, isn't there some basis to my premise?'

'You're not in court now.'

'Am I right then?'

'No.'

He studied an area ten inches above her head with intense interest. 'Maeve wanted me to come, you know. She thought it could make a difference.'

'How could it?'

'To me and you.'

'There is no me and you, Mike. There never really was. It was all so insubstantial and we should have realised that a long time ago, instead of keeping up appearances.'

'You say that now. But you acted pretty damn hurt at the time.'

'Of course I did. I was hurt. That's something else. It doesn't actually mean I loved you, even. It was just hurt.'

'I am sorry about that, you know.' He sounded awkward and embarrassed. He had never admitted it before and she knew that he really was. But to understand would become too complicated. The wounds were still fresh and she needed them to defend herself with. So she resorted to spite instead: 'Big deal.'

But her churlishness gave him new confidence. She had not changed. And her attitude and actions let him off the hook. He tipped his chair back on its heels, a habit which she had always found irritating and thrust his hands deep into his jacket pockets. He looked as if he might be going to whistle, although in fact he only frowned. She noticed that he looked very well. Still excessively handsome. No wonder really that Maeve had fallen for him. It was a pity he had no soul.

'The fact remains, Jennifer, that you committed a highly abnormal act.'

'Must you be so pompous . . . ?'

'But you did!'

'And do I have to listen to this?'

'Yes, of course you do. Don't pretend to be stupid, Jennifer. There is our daughter to consider.'

Afterwards, she reflected that what she should have said was: 'Isn't that a little late?' or 'You didn't consider her before.' But, under pressure and on the spot, in the quick hot desire to wound, she said: 'Which one?'

His face altered immediately. 'You really can be very nasty, can't you? When it comes down to it? Bringing that up! Perhaps your mind really is twisted.'

'Yes, I believe it is.'

'You know perfectly well I'm talking about Sarah. I've always said I'd be willing to give things another go for her sake.'

'But didn't really mean it.' His silence corroborated her. Jenny continued: 'Look Mike, I do not want us back together, even for Sarah's sake. That is not why I took those pills. I realise it may seem like that but it wasn't. Please believe that and go away.'

'But why did you take them? Will you try it again? Are you fit to look after a two-year-old? That's the point.'

Jennifer turned her face away. 'I accept your criticism,' she said dully. 'I shan't do it again.'

'Then why did you . . . '

'You wouldn't understand. It was a temporary imbalance. Just like they say.'

'But you knew Sarah was away for the night with my mother!'

'Yes. But it wasn't planned. Really it wasn't. I drank too much . . . that's all. Far, far too much. It fuelled an overwhelming sense of failure in the end . . . that's all.'

'Didn't you think about Sarah?'

'Oh yes. Especially Sarah, if you only knew.'

'Well then?'

'I decided I wasn't that good a mother.'

'I see.'

'I doubt if you do. Anyway, I thought someone else would do a better job of bringing her up. That's it in a nutshell.' Jennifer swallowed hard for the memory was painful. 'Anyway, it was temporary, like I said. Now I realise she does need me, imperfect as I am. And I certainly shan't let you and Maeve bring her up, if that's what you're thinking.' The idea riveted her with fear. She knew she had been crazy and irresponsible. If only she could reclaim that drunken evening and relive it like an action replay, despite the pain, but this time omitting the tablets and merely falling into bed. Mike would have a good case now for taking Sarah away. She saw it now and saw equally clearly that that would be the end for she needed Sarah to rely on her. But she need not have worried. Mike and Maeve were not fond of young children around the house when it came down to it. Not as a permanent arrangement. Not even their own.

Mike seemed satisfied with the explanation, for he suddenly changed the subject: 'Beth came to see me this afternoon,' he said.

'Whatever for?'

'She was terribly upset because you wouldn't see her.'

'Oh, that.'

'Yes, I must say I thought it was a bit thick.'

'You always did get on well.'

'I told her to take no nonsense and walk straight in next time.'

'You've got a bloody cheek. It's nothing to do with you.'

'You were grossly unfair.'

'Oh, I was, was I? Really? You think about it. Oh well, never mind, I know you've never understood what I've felt about her. But maybe it'll make her think for a change. Realise everything is not always just as she sees it.'

'Well, as you say, it's not really my business.'

A bell rang to signal the end of visiting-time and Mike rose to his feet, brushing off his jacket. Jennifer realised he had intentionally delayed his entrance until the final ten minutes.

'Well, you're much better than I thought you'd be,' he

said. 'You're not really that depressed. You're fighting back which is a good sign. I know you won't believe me, but actually I'm very glad you're not dead.'

'I believe you,' said Jennifer shortly.

'You want to get yourself out of here though.' He looked around him with distaste. 'Quick as you can . . . before you get like the rest of them. If it was me, I'd sign myself out. I don't know how you can bear it.'

When he had gone, Jennifer lapsed into misery. It was true that, during their conversation, she had really felt a spark of indignation and determination returning. But now it had gone out again like a damp squib and left her bereft. Confidence which came in fits and starts wasn't much good. Not when the path ahead looked rough for her and Sarah. How would they manage? Other people did, of course. Plenty of them. But Jennifer didn't think she had ever been like 'other people'.

She took her toilet-bag from her locker and rummaged amongst its contents for a clean tissue. Everything was in a jumble. The lady next door had kindly brought it in, along with some clean clothes, but Jennifer hadn't bothered to sort it out yet.

'Woz that yer 'usband?' Helen, her new neighbour, asked. She was a coarse-looking, incredibly immature girl in her mid-twenties with very short, spiky, striped orange hair. She spoke with some longing in her voice.

'Yes.'

'E's nice-lookin'.'

'We're getting a divorce.'

'Was 'e rotten to you?'

'Well . . . only once or twice. We just didn't get on.'

Helen assimilated this fact with difficulty. She had seen lots of broken marriages. But most of them involved a great deal of physical knocking about. She understood that sort of violence. Her own forearms were heavily scarred and she was in and out of the ward constantly as a result – her own fury being vented upon herself.

'Can I be your friend?' she asked, wheedling.

'Of course. If you like.'

'Leave her alone, Helen! Can't you see she's a bit upset? Stands to reason when her husband's been in.' This most sensible remark came from an extremely sensible-looking lady on the bed opposite. It was not at all obvious why she was there. She certainly looked cheerful enough and kept herself occupied all day by busily knitting. Jennifer was astonished at the torrent of vitriolic abuse which her remark produced. But Helen sidled off all the same.

'I'm gonna ask Mr Wright for a fag,' she said. 'Don't take no notice of 'er. She's *real* barmy. Ses 'er 'usband's tryin' to kill 'er all the time and the neighbours are 'elpin 'im.' The sensible lady did not deny it. Indeed, after Helen had gone, she added confidentially:

'It's in the drains, you see. They're always putting chemicals in the drains. And he,' in a lowered, triumphant voice, 'leaves the gas on. I can smell it.' She sniffed hard, as if she might even be able to detect it now, if she tried hard enough, nodded her neat head as if satisfied and went on knitting and purling and knitting two together, without even dropping a stitch.

Jennifer turned over to face the wall in despair. Mike's right, she thought. I shouldn't be here. I'm not like these other people. And yet . . . and yet . . .

At last the tea trolley came round with the bedtime drinks. Everyone brightened up, apart from the severest depressives. The day was drawing to a close. But it was more than that, for that really only meant another night to come after all. It was an important mark of stability, like every bit of routine in the day. Another negation of responsibility and a safety valve too, in the life of the ward. How quickly and easily one could slip into that routine! Even the tall woman with the very red hair, who had come in yesterday and kicked up such a rumpus in the night, was helping hand out the cups. True, her eyes were still a bit wild. But she seemed a lot better, although she was over-anxious to help everyone and slopped all the Milo into the saucers. Jennifer only got half a cup and no sugar. But she wasn't a complainer. When she had drunk it, she went into the washroom and cleaned her teeth. Sensible, reassuring, little actions. The very stuff of life. She hoped she would be allowed a sleeping pill tonight. There was always so much noise in the ward.

Helen was still in the television room, glued to the set. It was on very loud, as if all the inmates might be deaf. Some sort of American comedy programme, with shrieks of manufactured laughter at the end of every line. It spilled over and out into the darkened ward, but no one bothered to go and ask for it to be turned down. Each changing shot threw coloured shadows across the floor. Jennifer retreated to her own bed. The sensible lady was already fast asleep and snoring, dreaming about chemicals down the drains no doubt, or maybe it was just a difficult knitting pattern. Jennifer kicked off her slippers and climbed into bed.

Through the window of the sister's office, she could see Dr Jowett paying an evening call. Mr Wright had gone home now and his place had been taken by a kindly staff nurse with a figure like a barrel and an acne-scarred face. Annabelle looked rather tired but was smiling, sharing some joke. Jennifer watched them secretly. They looked authoritative and sure of themselves. And Annabelle was so young. Jennifer experienced a succession of envy and longing, sadness and shame, before she cut the scene by lying down on her back.

The unescapable event of the day – Mike's visit – returned to plague her. He must have felt guilty. But that wasn't what she had intended at all. Had she convinced him of that? Convinced him, too, that she would not attempt suicide again? Did she really mean it when she said she wouldn't? Oh yes. Now at least she meant it. The important thing was not to drink so much alone. That was the crucial factor. The alcohol had sent her already pervasive sense of failure rocketing out of all proportion, growing monstrously and opening out great blowsy, black petals of the darkest despair. They had engulfed her entirely. She didn't like to remember that feeling. It had seemed completely logical to take all those anti-depressants. There was nothing left for her but Sarah and, because of that, she could be no good for Sarah. Everything she had ever done had been a mistake and a failure. She had wasted her life and her personal relationships were lousy. And it was all her fault. Nothingness beckoned kindly. An end to all that pain. Eternal peace. She supposed it would be dark. But then it wouldn't matter, so long as there was nothing in the dark. No awareness anyway. Just a perpetual, dreamless sleep. It had to be like sleep without an awakening. Oh yes, she had wanted to die all right. No matter how much she wished she could deny it now.

But the lady from the Sally Army had called round. It still wasn't that late, for Jennifer had found the evening interminable and got drunk quickly. The good lady had apparently been promised a bag of old clothes last week. It sounded as if the radio was on, so she persisted and went round the back. There, through a gap where the curtains had never quite met (because Jennifer had got the measurements wrong) she saw and wondered and worried and called the police.

Jennifer was already flat out. And, at first, she only remembered waking up briefly in a strange, white bed. Then there was the acute embarrassment of realising she had not had a cardiac arrest after all. Almost immediately, came a contrary but huge relief. Gradually, she realised she was wired up to a monitor and the tubing of a drip was strapped to her arm, making it feel awkward and heavy. The green spikes on the glowing screen turned away from her must have been going fast, at least some of the time, for she felt rather breathless and there was a kind of anxiety in her chest and her throat which was extremely unpleasant. Then someone came and injected something into the drip and, after a while, she felt better and wondered if the spiking had really slowed down or not. There was a tube coming out as well as going in and she realised, with a shock, that she had been catheterised. Of course it was obvious that they would have done that, but it still felt like an indignity. Hazy memories of her transit through casualty came filtering back and they were all hot and nightmarishly unpleasant. That she could have ever put herself in that position, having seen it all before!

Then she slept again; slept for days it seemed. Her neighbour brought in her things, so she didn't feel so much like a pauper. Then one of her brothers turned up. Beth was too upset to make the journey just yet, he said. But she would come when Jenny was feeling better. Tell her not to bother, she said. I'm all right, really. Nothing much happened. But it had. You couldn't pretend it was unimportant; that decision to die. You couldn't turn the clock back inside. Peter couldn't talk about it. She saw that and felt relieved, although she knew he would never think about her in the same way again.

As the animal feelings receded, her sense of shame grew stronger. The staff (she felt) were far too kind, when all the time she knew what they really must be thinking about these interminably stupid people, who ended up in their beds so unnecessarily. She was a perfect patient except that she could hardly bring herself to speak to anyone and, when she did, her eyes instantly filled up with silent tears. In the end, when they had taken the monitor down and the tubes out, they asked Annabelle Jowett to see her, for it was the weekend. She was grateful not to be booted out. Grateful for the awful sanctuary of the psychiatric block. Relieved beyond measure they hadn't allowed Beth in. But of course it couldn't go on. The dark depthless sea had thrown her back – pretty contemptuously at that. She was stranded on the beach and had to claw her way back to the hinterland. She hadn't envisaged such an outcome and didn't really know how to do it. But after all, it did, at least, seem preferable to be alive.

Some miles away, Beth was finishing a solitary though public dinner in the restaurant of a riverside hotel. She had been unable to find anything to her liking in the environs of the hospital so the taxi-driver had taken her south-west, crossing the motorway and heading further out through London's vast suburbia. It was too far really. She would only have to go all the way back tomorrow.

She had eaten late in the hope that some appetite would return, but now regretted ordering dinner at all. The only bit she really wanted was the coffee and she had already decided to miss out on that, in case it kept her awake. She needed to be fresh and alert tomorrow- . . . for Jennifer and this consultant. The firelight flickered round the room, reflecting in the inevitable horse-brasses and dark, polished wood. It was still winter outside, even down here, though there were some signs of spring on the way. The room was warm and comfortable but Beth was neither warmed nor comforted, even though a good hotel was her natural habitat. Mike had suggested she stay at his mother's with Sarah, but of course it wouldn't have done.

She had wanted to stay in Jennifer's house but no one seemed to know anything about keys, for Jennifer had had all the locks changed recently. Oh dear, perhaps she had been going funny then! It seemed such an odd thing to do when the house was up for sale anyway and she had to find somewhere else to live. Mike had really been very sympathetic today. What on earth did Jennifer mean when she said they had nothing in common? He should have been the ideal husband.

For the first time in years, Beth thought about Dominic and felt uneasy. She recalled the coolness of his eyes as they had met hers critically and something she remembered as the sexual arrogance of his body. Well, he had challenged her and lost. She had reclaimed her daughter ready for someone like Mike. And now that marriage was ending in divorce. But it was nothing to do with Dominic. It was ridiculous to think about him now. That had all happened years ago. Though in her bones she knew he had been the start of the rot. Jennifer had been all right until then. Nothing could ever convince her otherwise.

CHAPTER TWO

The light from the sister's office made a little shining pool in the ward, like a glow-worm in the night. Jennifer dozed fitfully and woke to a rising and falling sea of muttering, stirring and breathing all around. They had not given her a pill. As usual, she had to think hard where she was. Her sleep had been full of dreams again and they were all weird – peopled with characters who might have walked straight out of Tolkien or worse. It had been like this the last few nights. She sat up in bed with the blankets hunched around her knees, wide awake in the certain knowledge she could not sleep again for hours. Didn't even want to, because of the dreams.

There had been some attempt to partition off the old-fashioned ward, but it still retained the character of a large dormitory or hostel. Down and out on our mental luck, thought Jennifer. Or maybe just children still learning. She had never been away to school. Dominic had, always. Would she have been able to escape Beth's influence if she had?

There must have been a time when she had not felt even slightly afraid of her mother. Days and even years when that chubby baby face in gingham knickers, the longed-for, late little girl who grinned toothlessly out of photograph albums, had toddled and tripped unwarily, completely without shame, into her mother's arms. But she couldn't remember that. Presumably Beth must have had to change lots of horrible nappies, pinning down with difficulty a tiny, writhing bottom, just as she did with Sarah. But there was no image left of Beth on her knees, covered with talcum powder. The newly forming thoughts behind that baby face (much adorned with unsuitable frills and lace) which beamed at the world so naïvely from its large and bouncy Silver Cross pram, had been lost and were gone forever.

She couldn't even remember Beth collecting her from school in the early days, although she must have done, because even the infants' school was a fair walk from 'Lorelei', whose garden she did remember so well. Those first school days were not a total blank, however. She still remembered with startling clarity the anguish of wetting her pants in the playground when frightened. (She wasn't really used to mixing with other children for Beth had always avoided that.) Then there was the shame (as she saw it then) of being moved up into the next class early because she was bright. She had been told terrifying stories about her new teacher, which were only partially unfounded. Then there was the liberty bodice: an odd garment much beloved by over-protective mums, which caused great derision when the time came to undress for PE. One day she couldn't unknot the laces of her navy blue pumps which had become inexplicably tied together. She couldn't bear to own up and hid, shivering in white vest and navy blue knickers behind the peg-bags in the cloakroom, the tears running down her cheeks, whilst her hard-hearted class-mates bounded into the hall. Then there were the railings in the playground which she had to climb. After a while, she became better at those but it was terrifying in the beginning. Beth didn't know about them and couldn't understand how easily her daughter's clothes got torn and dirty. She immediately sent her to ballet classes to have grace and poise instilled.

But, by the time Jennifer was selected for the grammar school, she was swimming towards the surface. She wasn't pretty and she wasn't a leader. She was bookish and not much good at games. But she was a thoughtful, pleasant child and people (including other children) liked her. Because of that she could survive. The school, although larger, was a gentler sort of school anyway. There were lots of other little girls who liked reading and drawing and doing French. Beth was over the moon of course that her daughter had followed the boys to the grammar school. But, because it wasn't such a big thing these days, she was already thinking about the future. Jennifer's worries were more immediate.

For instance, her breasts were the first in the class to start growing and she seemed to be shooting up in height. She suffered agonies of modesty in the showers. Then 'it' started which was rather useful because it let you off games altogether that week, if you had a note to say it was painful, which it actually was. Soon, other girls started to sit out too and Jennifer was relieved to note, as her class-mates began to catch up, that she was only going to be an average size and shape after all. Bigger than Beth (and Chloe before her) but not a monster. That left only the spots and greasy hair to worry about. Terrible days. She daren't ask Beth anything for fear of being called silly (which she often was) and Beth always assumed she knew. There was just one frightfully embarrassing session of instruction. Beth had never cultivated an atmosphere of frankness. But of course she knew it was important to talk about sex these days. So she did her best. But it all came out rather stiff and starchy. In her heart, she wanted to protect Jennifer from all of it. Inevitably, she tended to dwell on menstruation, pregnancy and childbirth (with all their hardships) and skipped quickly over the interesting bit. Jennifer was not deceived.

It must have been about this time that she became aware of a polarisation which had occurred between home and school, with the alignment of herself and her parents into different camps. Her real life was lived at school. All the genuine discussion went on there, amongst her girlfriends. As soon as she got home, Beth would ask her about her day – indeed it was almost an interrogation – and Jenny did her best to respond. But she found herself leaving certain things out. Over a long, slow period of time, she had come to realise that there was a cloud of free-floating disapproval emanating from her mother. Beth was quick to criticise. She also tended to assume wrong where none existed.

As Jennifer grew older and the sixties advanced, Beth kept a tighter instead of a looser hold upon the rein. It was not exactly that she reprimanded Jennifer or forbade her downright from doing anything. But the disapproval was always there. It was a case of: 'Of course, you'll have too much work to do, to go, won't you?' or 'Of course Angela and Susan and Valerie *would* be going but, frankly, darling, their parents couldn't care less.' The ultimate deterrent ran along the lines of: 'You're so lucky, I wish I'd been allowed to go to your school, I'd have worked so hard.' But I *do* work hard, thought Jennifer indignantly. I really do. A more brazen child might have given up altogether. But Jennifer strove even harder for the approval which always seemed to be almost in reach, but was never quite attained. Beth did not however, want her to be a blue stocking, and she encouraged dozens of extra activities. But the pressure was always there.

Her father was entirely different. He loved her uncritically, no matter what. But, although he was a more balanced individual, he usually ended up bowing to Beth.

'You'll have to ask your mother about that,' he would say.

Of course Jennifer hardly knew how desperate she became to please her mother. It wasn't a conscious thing at all. But she gradually began to hide all her initial ideas, in case they should be contemptuously brushed aside; she waited until she had formulated them into something more acceptable. She had no sense that she was meant to fulfil her mother's thwarted dreams. But she was aware of great expectations and longed to live up to them. For

Beth was an idol. She was so much smarter and more beautiful than anyone else's mum. And Jennifer loved her really. The truth was far less palatable.

Even before 'O' levels, the thorny subject of a career had raised its head. Jennifer was lucky enough to be a good all-rounder, so that more than one teacher was anxious to keep her in the class. Her favourite subjects were English, History and Art. She had a natural flair for painting and wrote poems, although she hardly ever dared show them to anybody.

'You do realise, don't you?' asked Beth, in a deprecating manner 'that no one actually writes or paints for a living? It's just a hobby. You have to teach or do something else.'

'I wouldn't want to teach,' said Jennifer.

'Everybody says that,' said Ken, agreeing for once, 'but lots of them end up doing it.'

'Mr Pollock says you can do a course in Art and Design if you want to be more practical.'

'Oh, Mr Pollock!' Beth compressed her lips and managed to make the name sound like a serious complaint. 'He would.' Jennifer coloured and bent over her soup, for the conversation was taking place over the dinner table. At the time, she was suffering that most awful of obsessions – a teenage crush – on the art master.

'Art college is way beneath her capabilities. Don't you think so, Ken? Mr Pollocks's been getting at her.'

'Well, she does have artistic talent,' said Ken. 'You can't really blame him for that.'

'But there are much better subjects.'

'Depends what you mean by better. You mean more academic, I suspect.' Ken winked at his daughter. 'Well, Jenny Jane, what do you say? Seems you're good at most things. You can do what you like.'

'I don't really know.'

'Of course you don't. It's far too early. You've plenty of

time to decide.'

'No, she doesn't,' said Beth. 'We have to do something about these,' she indicated the forms Jennifer had brought home with her from school. It was the month after Chloe had died. 'Choosing subjects for 'O' level.'

'I like painting,' said Jennifer. 'It's probably what I enjoy doing best. But I think Mummy's right when she says I'd have to do something else as well . . . and I really wouldn't want to teach.' A vision of Mr Pollock's classes filled her with horror, although they were the highlight of her week. Mr Pollock was not a good disciplinarian and the boys on the back row, who would rather be on the rugby field, played on him mercilessly. She hated them for it and suffered with him. How could anyone face that every day?

'Art college is for girls who can't do much else,' Beth insisted. 'Whatever Mr Pollock says. You can do better than that. And you should see the sights, Ken, that come out of it! My God, Bohemian isn't in it! No, it's out of the question.' She continued to peruse the papers, a frown knitting her brow.

'Don't you have a careers' master at school?' asked Ken.

'Not really. Just Mr Bennett.'

Ken nodded. He could see that meant no. A pity. No idea of personnel. He felt that was very wrong. Meanwhile, Jennifer was sadly discarding a favourite daydream. (She was in a garret painting. Artists always painted in garrets, although the lighting must be poor. Her hair flowed to her waist and she wore a black and white kaftan . . . very dramatic. Despite being an attic, the room was fetchingly furnished in modern style, with lots of wild flowers strewn about in vases. Mr Pollock had just dropped in to admire her work and encourage his old protege . . . His arm was stealing round her waist.)

'Actually, I don't think an arts degree at all is much use if Jennifer doesn't want to teach,' said Beth.

'Oh, I don't know,' said Ken. 'There must be some

good jobs with languages. Opportunity to travel too.'

'Oh yes ending up as a glorified "au pair", I suppose?'

'No, no . . . secretarial work, diplomatic service . . . that sort of thing.'

'Secretarial work?' Beth looked down her nose. 'I don't think so. Anyway, aren't the sciences supposed to be all the rage, these days.'

'Well, industry certainly needs bright science graduates . . . began Ken.

'Oh, industry!' Beth dismissed it with a wave of her hand. 'You can't think about anything other than business.'

'Somebody has to make the money to pay the bills,' said Ken in a huff. He knew perfectly well that, since their marriage, his standing in Beth's eyes had followed the line of an exponential curve . . . downwards. That which had once thrilled and delighted her was now old hat. Her in-laws were embarrassing, Sugden's Haulage Company slightly disgraceful. She had ridden a long way on his lorries, metaphorically of course, but it had only made her covet a cleaner, more respectable form of transport.

'Now, what Jennifer really ought to be thinking about is a solid profession . . . something worthwhile like medicine.'

'Isn't that rather hard for a girl to get into?'

'Well, she's bright, isn't she? Don't go putting her down because she's a girl! You know what I think about that! We ought to give her every encouragement. Times are changing. She might not want to get married you know – even if she does, she could still go on working.'

'I agree with you,' said Ken, though he had never envisaged Jennifer as a career girl. 'You know I do. I'm not sure about medicine though. Aren't you talking about a bit of vocation now?'

They looked at her, like a specimen under glass. Ken saw his little girl, who was growing up too fast, but recognised her all the same as an arty, quiet, rather sensitive and private woman. She had cried for days when the dog had died. Beth saw only her great hope. Jennifer, who had remained silent during all of this, knew she was expected to say something. Vocation. It was odd because she had heard the word quite recently. She wished she did have a vocation.

'I like biology,' she said.

'She's not squeamish,' said Beth, 'if that's what you're thinking of. About blood and that . . .'

'I wasn't actually. Though I'm quite surprised to hear it.'

'I thought about nursing once,' said Jennifer.

'You see?' said Beth bitterly. 'How indoctrinated we women are, even today?' And, to her daughter: 'Jenny, darling, if you want to do something like that, you go ahead and be a doctor – not a nurse – and we'll back you all the way.'

'Of course we will,' said Ken. 'But does she really want to do it?'

Then Jennifer said something surprising. She said yes. Beth beamed all over her face.

'Well, that makes the decision about subjects easier,' she said, picking up the paper again. She hovered with the pen poised. 'You must continue all the sciences. Right? English and Maths are compulsory of course. I suppose you want to continue languages for the moment?'

'I wouldn't mind dropping Latin,' said Jennifer hopefully. 'All that Virgil's a bit of a bore.'

'Oh, but don't you need that for medicine, darling?'

'Do you? I don't know.'

'Better not drop it, just in case. You can take Art as your recreational subject if you must. I wouldn't give it any more time. You'll have to drop History though.'

'Must I?'

'According to this timetable, it clashes completely with Biology. I can't see any way round it.'

'What about Geography?' said Ken.

'They take that early at the end of next year, along with English Language. Don't you ever pay attention, Ken?'

'Well, I suppose it's still a fair mixture of Arts and Sciences.'

'Of course it is,' said Beth. 'It'll do fine.'

'And did you fall or were you pushed?' asked the old man with the crooked staff and the long beard, in her dream. Jennifer tried hard to seek the correct answer, for she knew he wouldn't let her pass if she lied.

'Undoubtedly, I was pushed,' she said, 'but not so hard I couldn't have resisted. In the end, I suppose I jumped in, with both of my two feet.' He nodded as if satisfied.

'Join the others,' he said.

But when she looked along the road, she could only see a vast procession of hares and tortoises ahead. No real people at all. And it wasn't true what they said. All the hares were winning in the end.

Beth had planted the seed but there were others growing too, which began to point in the same direction. Father Bartram, for instance, was responsible for a bit of watering – quite unwittingly. It so happened that Beth had decided Jennifer ought to be confirmed. Not that she held any firm convictions herself, but Willie and Chloe had taken her to church every Sunday, as a child, and now she viewed the Church of England as a respectable institution. She attended at Christmas and Easter and Harvest Festival . . . holidays and holy days as the last vicar had been rather too fond of saying . . . with the odd ordinary Sunday scattered in between. The boys had been in the choir and were duly 'done' as a matter of course. But Jennifer seemed to have slipped through the net so far. Beth was sure she'd better send her. After all, you couldn't be a godparent if you weren't confirmed . . . and that was another respectable institution.

Jennifer hadn't been too keen at first. She had a lot of

homework now her 'O' levels were closer. She also had the feeling it was a sissy sort of thing to do. But Father Bartram changed her mind. Because she was so much older than the choristers and the Girls' Brigade bunch, she was allowed to join an adult class where Fr Bartram could give his eloquence full rein. It was rather fun to be treated as an equal and certainly more stimulating.

Fr Bartram was a bit of an oddity in Kingley. He was not a professional cleric dispensing absent minded blandness. Nor was he an earnest evangelical with rope sandals and a penchant for the trendy. He was a bit of an academic and undeniably 'High' Church . . . too 'High' for the Parish Council, it was rumoured in a whisper. No bells or incense or anything like that. He would have been out on his ear. But there were those who felt that his preference for being called 'Father' was rather embarrassing and that his bowing and scraping – quickly passed on to the altar boys – was a bit excessive. He was also unmarried, although not yet past the age when this would have been considered unalterable. Another black mark and another hint of Rome. The congregation were divided in their allegiances, but Jennifer quickly joined the pro camp. She was at an impressionable age and ready to devote herself to something. In short, she entered a religious phase.

The Great Day of Confirmation itself arrived. She couldn't bear to admit to disappointment when the pure white wafer which dissolved on her tongue left no illuminating flash of oneness with God. She didn't feel much different at all, so she obviously had a long way to go before achieving such a state of grace. She toyed with the idea of becoming a nun. Perhaps that was a mite drastic, though appealingly sacrificial. But the idea of vocation and service gathered weight. A medical missionary would fit the bill. Preferably somewhere like Vietnam or Cambodia. Of course, she would then run the risk of being shot or napalmed, and having 'lived' through her funeral once or twice – rather beautifully, of course – she gave up that idea. But medicine continued to beckon.

Mr Pollock still figured large in her life, however. She had begun to feel guilty about that. At least she had moved on from fancying the sports mistress. But, unquestionably, her daydreams in that direction could be classed as impure thoughts. He was a married man with three children (she had seen them all one school Open Day and been alternately, if not simultaneously, delighted and horrified). The unattainable has its own attraction. It was another two years before she finally threw him off. In fact, after all that time it ended quite suddenly and it happened, ironically enough, after an idyllic lesson.

The last double period on a Friday afternoon for the fifth form was Double Art – hardly a kindness on the part of the timetable planners towards Mr Pollock, but still, there it was. At least most of the boys were now out on the rugby field, or hammering away at stools and egg-racks, so the class was now much smaller and most them wanted to be there. After making numerous detours down this particular corridor all week, in the hope of seeing Ben Pollock, however briefly, Jennifer was now frighteningly assured of his proximity for the next one and a half hours. She had only recently discovered that his name was Ben, having devoted much time and effort to a consideration of his initials: B.P. ('Bloody Pillock', the awful boys called him.)

They were painting daffodils in a blue bowl, the last of the season; a book, a pair of apples. Still life. The afternoon sun glowed through the windows and the classroom was full of honeyed gold. Outside, muddy playing-fields stretched away to a bordering line of trees newly in leaf. It was May and two weeks, four days to the French oral. Beneath the trees, the ground plunged sharply down a strictly out-of-bounds bank of ferns to the river. Then it rose again steeply up the hillside which bound in the narrow valley. There was an outcrop of boulders and flat-topped rocks forming a crag at the summit. In the near distance, the tennis courts were closed in by green netting and waterlogged after recent, heavy rain. The grey bricks and green slate of the classrooms opposite formed the shorter leg of the L-shaped block. Although the sun was shining, it was far warmer in than out and Jennifer would have felt sleepy but for Ben Pollock.

'Very good,' he said, pausing behind her shoulder, 'Fine. I think perhaps the apples though . . . they could be a little larger than life, don't you think? More rounded and glossy and shining in the light?' His right hand covered hers for a moment, guiding the brush. She felt a thrill of terror and ecstasy run through her and noticed there were small, ginger hairs on the back of his hands. Then he had moved on and the moment was gone . . . another one to be slipped into the secret store of memories and relived endlessly at leisure. Jennifer rounded and enlarged her apples.

She noticed with a quick, stinging jealousy that he bent low over Andrea Lightfoot too. Andrea couldn't paint, couldn't do anything much, but had long legs and swinging black hair and was generally considered the sexiest girl in school. She seemed to have grown up a long time ago. Mr Pollock didn't criticise her work. But Jenny reminded herself he only did that if he thought you were worth the effort.

She continued to watch him out of the corner of her eye. On the face of it, he was an unlikely candidate for adoration. His features were entirely unremarkable and he was very small – tiny in comparison to Fr Bartram, whose body seemed to shoot awkwardly out of its enveloping black cassock. He was grey and gangling and ascetic. Ben Pollock wore glasses and a thin pointed beard which had turned out more ginger than the thinning hair on top of his head. But there was something indefinable there. Nice eyes. A certain manner of moving or speaking. Or perhaps attraction is really only animal and chemical after all.

The second bell rang and everyone rushed to clean their brushes with indecent haste. Jennifer lingered as long as she dared, but at length she had to go too. There was a general stampede for lockers and desks and cloakrooms and the building rapidly emptied. But Jennifer didn't go straight home. In the girls' toilets, she took a bottle of shampoo from her satchel and began to wash her hair in one of the sinks. She had started her period yesterday and Beth, weighed down still by some old-fashioned notions from Chloe, refused to let her wash it while menstruating. Jenny could see no reason for this, especially as her hair was even greasier at this time than normal. But Beth insisted. So she did it secretly at school. Of course she had really wanted to do it at lunch-time, before the art class, but she had had a violin lesson and there had been no time. But if she walked home now, instead of catching the bus, the wind would dry it before she reached 'Lorelei' and Beth would never know.

It wasn't until she was wrapping her wet towel away in the poly bag reserved for that purpose, that she realised with a shock that her watch had gone. Of course she would have taken it off to wash her hair, but it wasn't on the shelf above the row of white enamel basins. She couldn't have had it when she came into the toilets at all. It must be in the art room. The idea of returning there with wet hair was daunting. But she had to get her watch.

The long corridors were deserted now and her feet echoed alone. Row upon row of desks and chairs stood empty in each classroom waiting for Monday morning. Blackboards had been cleaned cursorily and were still chalky. A few miscreants sat in the detention room penning lines. The permanent smell of stewed cabbage wafted up the steps from the dining-hall. She turned left at the noticeboards with mounting excitement. Perhaps the wet hair didn't really matter. It could hardly look worse than before. Ben Pollock would probably be on his way home already. If he wasn't, it had to be fate.

The door to the art room was firmly closed. It had no windows which gave onto the corridor. She took a deep breath and walked straight in. Mr Pollock was sitting in the corner. He had Andrea Lightfoot on his knee. She was giggling and his arm was round her. Jennifer stared. It made no difference that this kind of scene was the stuff of her day dreams. It couldn't really happen! Their turned faces were full of guilt. Jennifer saw that immediately. It was far more compromising than what they were doing.

Andrea was the first to recover. She jumped to her feet with a smothered giggle, said: 'Bye, then,' and was off through the door in a flash, leaving him to pick up the pieces. He stood up slowly, his face as red and embarrassed as Jennifer's.

'I left my watch,' she said, stiffly. It sounded like an accusation. She turned her back on him and went to the sink. The watch was there, waiting, and she put it on with shaking fingers and growing disgust, no longer caring that her hair was wet.

Ben Pollock felt he had to say something: 'Jennifer, I do hope you won't misunderstand . . . ' his voice tailed off lamely. There was no excuse, no alternative explanation and he knew it.

'I won't tell anyone, if that's what you mean.' Her voice was savage and he thought he heard a sob. Dimly, he realised what he had done. But he could only nod sheepishly and sit down again.

'I suppose it is. I wish I could explain. It's not as bad as you think . . . ' She didn't want to hear and ran out of the room. Her sensible shoes slapped along the corridor and clattered down the steps, then were gone.

She didn't stop running until she was at the bottom of the long, steep drive which led to the school. Then she pulled up short on the pavement, catching her breath which came in painful gasps. Her throat felt hot and raw. All the time she was running, the same phrase had repeated itself over and over again: 'dirty old man, dirty old man'. It was hackneyed and childish. It was adult and true. She burst into tears and started walking along the pavement, away from the school, clutching her satchel to her sore chest, ignoring the cars zipping by. It would have to be Andrea Lightfoot! But she wouldn't tell, despite the awesome power. No one would believe her anyway. And Andrea would say she was only jealous. But she wasn't any more.

When the exams were over, she developed a sudden interest in tennis on a Friday afternoon. When she finally entered the sixth form, she dropped Art without a qualm and didn't paint again for years.

This time the dream was depressingly familiar. She had had it many times before. The moon face of the clock with its Roman numerals was omnipotent, omnipresent. It ticked so loudly and you could see the heavy black hand jump if you dared look. Rows and rows of regimented desks and bent backs stretched and strained out in front and behind and at either side. They all seemed to be beavering away. There were the inevitable coughings and shufflings and rustlings, of course. The turn of the page. The tread of the invigilator's feet. The odd fly crawling around to distract the mind. The occasional sucking of sweets. But the sheet of paper burned white and blank and enormous on the desk. It had to be filled. She had to start. And she hadn't revised. She hadn't done any work. The questions were all the wrong ones. 'Compare and contrast', 'Examine the influence of' and, worst of all, just: 'Discuss'. She woke in cold and clammy fear.

CHAPTER THREE

During the long, hot interim of waiting for results, Willie died, scarcely two years after Chloe had gone. He had nothing to live for without her. Officially he also died from a cerebral haemorrhage.

Jennifer had not been particularly fond of her grandfather. She saw him as a dry old man, full of grumbles, who came to lunch every Sunday and lay an additional constraint upon them all. Beth was always in a bad humour that morning. Ken did his best to be amiable but ended up retiring behind the Sunday newspapers with a gin. The boys weren't often there for David was twenty-five, engaged and teaching 'down South' when Chloe died, while Peter, who was twenty-one and had entered the family business when his course had finished at the 'tec, lived in a flat outside Kingley. Jenny hardly knew her brothers at all. The gap had always been large and her twenties seemed a lifetime away. She had once asked Peter about his flat.

'I couldn't live at home now,' he had grinned. 'Just wait till you get to university or college, little Sis, and then you'll see what I mean.'

He did, however, come home to get his laundry done and have a good meal. But Sundays were not his usual day, as he went to his girlfriend's instead. Jenny envied her brothers' freedom. They had always been one or two jumps ahead. She was the late baby, the afterthought. Not a mistake, as Beth had once assured her, for they had always wanted a little girl.

So Jennifer was left alone to talk to her grandfather on Sundays. She felt sorry for him, of course. Beth would always pester him so, saying he ought to move out of his draughty house into a bungalow, have Meals on Wheels and get his hair cut more often. She always fussed round him too much as soon as he was through the door, asking if he was well and trying to make him have a drink or eat seconds at lunch, when he didn't really want to. It was strange because anyone could see she couldn't stand him really.

Jennifer did her best to chat but their conversation ran on monotonous lines. Her grandfather had also become very deaf. First he would ask about school and she would tell him what she was doing. Then he would ask her what she wanted to do next and she would explain. (Beth usually appeared in the doorway, smiling smugly at that point.) After that they were stuck.

Jennifer's memories of her grandmother were vividly different. She had been a proper granny with white hair pinned back tightly in a bun. She wore navy blue flowered dresses with long skirts and thick stockings and 'Granny' shoes too. She had dispensed orange twists of barley sugar from a bottomless drawer in her room full of antimacassars and the sound of the clock ticking. She was incredibly old and small, although, when she sneezed, it came out as a surprisingly violent 'bah'. She had very kind eyes and tiny cracked hands and always smelt of lavender. She was not of course a real person at all. Beth had always hinted darkly that she had had a hard life through 'having to marry' Will. (Why did you have to marry anybody, Jennifer had wondered innocently at the time?) But it was all very hard to believe then.

Now Jennifer stood at her grandparents' graveside and twiddled Chloe's ring on the chain round her neck – for Beth would not allow her to wear it on her finger. She supposed she ought to feel more sad. But no one did really. You could tell when you looked round, though Beth had a strange harsh and bitter look on her face. It was the first funeral that Jennifer had ever been to, for she had been ill the day they had buried Chloe and not been allowed to go. Willie and Beth had both cried at that funeral.

It had been raining all morning and, although it had stopped now, the sky was a mass of darkening cloud. Drops of water still dripped from rampant greenery and the wind felt cool for July. The graveyard was muddy. It was not in Sowerton as it should have been. The churchyard there, pregnant with age and quietly overgrown, had filled up long since. Willie had had to move out of his village at last and join Chloe in the new cemetery which bordered the busy main road between Kingley and Stone Flatts. This was a vast place, severely laid out in straight lines, so that rows of headstones leant this way or that, on either side of grassed but lumpy aisles. The flowers, if there were any, stood in small black pots provided for that purpose, at the foot of the slabs, with their stems poking awkwardly through the holes of a wire grill.

Jenny read the inscription on her grandmother's grave with some fascination:

'Here lieth Chloe Moffat, beloved wife of William Moffat and mother of John, Samuel, Edward and Elizabeth.' How very odd those formal names sounded, bearing no relation whatsoever to their owners now! '1888-1965. She has gone to her eternal rest.' Had she, wondered Jennifer? And if so, what was it like? She remembered, after Grandma Sugden had died, seeing her father put flowers on the grave. The black pot had already been full, so he had stuck a jam-jar into the soft, wet earth and filled that instead. Jenny, still quite small, had been horrified.

'But Daddy, won't you hurt Granny doing that?' Ken had tried to explain that, while Granny's body was indeed there, although some way down, she couldn't feel anything and something called her soul was somewhere else. But where? And how did he know?

Jennifer was old enough now to laugh. But the explanation was hardly any clearer. Father Bartram, of course, would say that Chloe was happier now than she had ever been. She hoped he was right. Not least because one day she would also have to die.

They were lowering Willie's coffin into the ground now. The wreaths had been taken off, leaving the casket bare. Willie had made a lot of coffins in his time but this was someone else's work. It settled with a thump and an elderly female relative, whom Jennifer had not seen before, began to sob and cry hysterically. *Somebody* was upset, then. It was in fact 'that dreadful cousin Hilda's girl', always slightly soft in the head and now in her dotage. Beth looked affronted as the wails rose in volume and the uncles were obviously embarrassed.

Afterwards at 'Lorelei', 'cousin Hilda's girl' told everyone she met 'she could have jumped in with him'. It was something of a conversation stopper. Jennifer handed the sandwiches and was allowed one glass of sherry. She hovered awkwardly in a dress of green velvet which Beth had specially chosen to complement her colouring.

'Why, Jennifer!' said all the aunts and uncles. 'How you've grown! 'A' levels next, eh? And I hear you're going to apply for medicine. Your mother must be so proud.'

'If my 'O's are good enough,' muttered Jennifer modestly. But they were and she entered the sixth form as a scientist. There had been one more incident which had convinced her. She had seen an accident . . . walked past it, more truthfully, on the way to school. An old man lay in the road like a floppy clown – just a heap of old clothes really. She thought he had been knocked down. He was unconscious and his face was very white. There were several people bending over him, waiting for the ambulance. She didn't know if they knew what to do, but she certainly didn't. She felt frightened. There was no blood. But he looked as if he might be dying. The image stayed with her all the way to school and so did the fear. But, if she did medicine, she would know what to do – always. The panic would be taken away. It seemed the right answer at the time. That Sunday, the sermon was based on the parable of the Good Samaritan and Fr Bartram waxed eloquent. Jennifer enrolled at first aid classes.

Another two years passed, the final ones at school and in the main, Jennifer was very happy. There was a certain satisfaction in having come to a decision about her future and taken some steps towards it, without any possibility of imminent fruition. She had to struggle a little with the physics but managed to get by. Her position in school was secure. She had lots of friends and felt confident and mature.

Beth's cup ranneth over. She saw her daughter flower physically as well. She was still only reasonably attractive, but that was to be expected. (Jennifer always thought she was ugly in comparison with her mother but she wasn't exactly that either.) The gangliness had gone and her skin had settled down. She was allowed to grow her hair and the fringe disappeared.

'Of course, you'll have to put it up on the wards,' Beth said, wishing Jennifer had more idea of elegance, 'and in theatre. A pity your grandmother's not alive to show you how. She had beautiful hair.'

'But I won't be on the wards at first, mother,' Jenny explained for the umpteenth time. 'Or in theatre. Nowhere near patients at all, in fact. It's just hard slog at books and in the lab.' She had become aware that her mother's vision of a medical student's life was highly romanticised and that she was buoyed up by the academic and social snob value of it all. Still, it didn't matter. As long as *she* was doing it for the right reasons. She had been examining those reasons in preparation for the interview and decided she was fascinated by finding out how the human body worked, which was true, and went down well. She also said she badly wanted a job in which she could work with (and help) people – which she had no way of knowing the truth of. That seemed to be standard and fairly acceptable.

Beth was rather peeved at her choice of universities. Warned in advance about the scales of popularity, Jennifer was sticking to the Northern 'redbricks'. Her mother wasn't sure they packed as much clout as London or Edinburgh. But, if it was going to be a redbrick, what was wrong with Leeds? Nothing, said Jennifer. Except that it was too near home. (She added hastily that the staff at school had advised her to strike out farther afield.)

She was, at last, anxious to get away. Peter's arrangement would not work for her. She wanted David's sort of freedom and some days she could hardly wait. There must be other places and more exciting lives! She had had enough of the tight little valleys and the parochial mill-towns. In the end it was Liverpool which accepted her and she was glad, for she had liked the feel and the vibrant beat of the city. (Those were the days before they put grilles up on all the shopfronts or talked much about inner city areas.) Of course, she would miss all her friends. But they were all going too, to different places. They had promised endless reunions of course, like every year's students before them, but it would really come to nothing in the wake of their departure.

All summer long she shampooed endless heads of hair in a salon and stood holding rollers at the ready or checked the driers. It was hard work and didn't pay very well. She had been surprised when Beth had given her permission. But her mother wanted to demonstrate for real the difference between a job and a vocation. Beth was bubbling over with confidence anyway. She had heard someone say that once you got into medical school, you were bound to get through in the end, unless you were really bad. Being accepted in the first place was the real hurdle. Her daughter was actually going to be a doctor. She was bursting with pride.

'I was right, you see,' she kept on telling Ken. 'Bloody

Ben Pollock's art school indeed! We all know what he had in mind.' For the scandal was all over Kingley. Andrea Lightfoot hadn't taken her Art or Domestic Science 'A' levels after all, because she was having a baby and had had to leave. And, while nothing was definitely known or could be in any way proven, Ben Pollock had been asked to resign. Beth had tackled Jennifer about it and been stunned by the reply.

'Oh, those two! Yes, they've been carrying on for years. Everyone knows about it. Andrea's been very silly. She was supposed to be on the Pill. And as for him . . . well, honestly, a married man with three children! And you know, Mummy he must be at least forty!'

Beth had her breath taken clean away. But it came to her then – in her moment of triumph – that she had really trained her daughter very well.

CHAPTER FOUR

Dr Jowett was relieved to see that Dr Mahler was in a surprisingly good mood for a Monday morning. He settled himself into the armchair behind the desk, fitting his stomach between the two with some difficulty, running a hand through his curly, clownish hair and readjusting his bow-tie and his glasses. Then he spread his arms expansively over the table and winked at her and she knew she was in for a session of leg-pulling.

'I see our worthy registrar is off in London re-taking his exams again. So it's me and thee alone to face the world, Annabelle-on-a-bike!'

She nodded, unperturbed, used to him; resigned and almost enjoying it.

'Was it a horrid weekend?'

'Very quiet. Boring actually.'

'Your thirst for knowledge does you credit, my dear. You mean you don't want to watch the rugby? No, I suppose you don't. Ah, well, coffee first.'

'It's on its way,' said Bill Wright, shuffling papers and case-sheets in the doorway.

'Tell me about the new ones.'

'Just three. Of course you know about Kate. She's settling. Then I took one from the medical ward and one from a GP.'

'Who's that?'

'Dr Smith's Mrs Thomas again.'

'Don't remember her.'

'Paraphrenia. A nice sensible lady with one obsession. Convinced her husband and neighbours are trying to do her in. To be frank, as Dr Smith pointed out, it's really to give the husband a break. He can't cope. And she keeps having the Public Health Department out to inspect the drains.'

'Of course, I know her now,' said Dr Mahler. 'Knits as furiously as those women did around the guillotine. She came in voluntarily then?'

'Oh yes, quite cheerfully too. Feels safer in here she says – away from *him*.

Dr Mahler sighed: 'Well yes, she would, wouldn't she? Wouldn't you?'

'She's getting to like it,' interposed Bill Wright. 'Rather fancies herself as the ward matriarch.' (The head of the ward Mafiosi,' he had said to Annabelle, who had laughed.) 'We've had a few fireworks between her and Helen.'

'Oh yet, I forgot about Helen,' said Annabelle, guiltily. 'She sort of admitted herself.'

This time Dr Mahler groaned audibly. 'Let's stick to Mrs Thomas for the moment, shall we?' he said. 'I seem to remember we had her on depot injections now, with limited success. Or is that just another delusion?'

'No, sir, we did, but there's no record of her attendance at clinic for several weeks.'

'That's the answer then, isn't it? Get the social worker on to it, Annabelle, would you? Tell her I'm very sorry, but she'll have to bring the woman in to clinic herself every time. There's no other way.'

'Yes sir.' Annabelle made a note.

'Do you want to see her now? said Bill Wright.

'I suppose so.'

'Only we can't find her just at the moment.'

Dr Mahler looked as if he might be going to explode. 'What is this place? A holiday camp?'

'What I mean, sir,' said Bill, hastily, 'is that I think

she's gone to occupational therapy.'

'Well, get her back again'. Dr Mahler drank some coffee. 'Later will do,' he added. 'How's Kate?'

'Considerably improved. Much calmer, although her thinking isn't too clear when you pin her down. She deteriorates during the conversation,' said Annabelle.

'I suppose she's down at OT too?'

'I can have her back in a jiffy. And I've got the forms here to convert her section into a 28.' Bill Wright disappeared.

'For Christ's sake,' Dr Mahler complained to his junior. 'Is Monday morning the day I do my round here, or not?' Annabelle shuffled her feet uncomfortably and tried to placate.

'Kate certainly was here five minutes ago. I saw her myself. And I'm afraid Mrs Thomas is so used to the ward routine she's a law unto herself. She won't miss anything except a ward round.' She could see his initial bonhomie leaking away and went on, a little doubtfully, 'The third patient is entirely new.'

'Thank God for that. Though I presume she must be an OD if she comes from the medical ward.'

'Well, yes. She's thirty-one and she's called Jennifer Warrender. She was admitted after a hefty overdose of tricyclics, laced with more than a little alcohol. The medical staff say she nearly died. No previous history. I had her transferred because she still seems very depressed.'

'Quite right. Although I fear your heart is softer than mine.'

'Yes sir.'

'She impressed you, did she?'

'Yes sir.'

'And these are your notes?'

'Yes sir.'

He thumbed through them.

'Usual tale, eh? In the middle of a divorce. Lost and

lonely. Regular sympotomatic drinking, by the sound of it.'

'She dropped out of medical school just before her final year.'

'Yes . . . that is quite interesting. Her intent must have been serious. Wonder why she didn't stick to aspirin or paracetamol? Spur of the moment, I suppose. Someone obviously thought she was pretty depressed before, to prescribe tricyclics. Now why did she drop out of medicine? We used to say you had to be mad or bad, you know. The wastage rate is not that high. Any ideas?'

'She's not too keen on discussing it so far. But I'm sure it is important to her. The divorce is secondary, I feel. She sees herself as a failure and hasn't reconciled herself to it. The mother's extremely dominant. She has an appointment with you this afternoon, by the way.'

'Well, if she's not weaving a basket or plaiting raffia, do you think we might possibly see her?'

Luckily, Bill Wright turned up with Jennifer at that very moment, plus the news that Mrs Thomas was on her way back from OT, but there was no sign of Red Hot Kate anywhere and he rather feared she'd done a bunk, shouldn't he get in touch with the police? Dr Mahler looked black, nodded and drank some more coffee.

'Would you like a cup?' he asked Jennifer. She smiled briefly, but shook her head rather shyly. 'My name is Dr Mahler and I'm supposed to be looking after you. Dr Jowett and Mr Wright you've already met. Why is this lady still in her dressing-gown? The question was addressed to Annabelle who winced. He knew perfectly well it was to deter the patient from wondering off outside and cutting her wrists or something similar. But it was all part of his technique.

'I'm sure you'd feel better with your own clothes on,

wouldn't you? Bit of make-up, perhaps? Come to that, you'd probably feel better away from here altogether. What do you think?'

Jennifer shook her head. 'I don't know.'

'You've got a few problems, I see.'

'Only myself.'

'Why is that?'

'Well, I seem to have made a mess of everything I've ever done.'

'Of course you have. Most of us do. So what? Is that any reason to try and pull off a cardiac arrest? Surely nothing could be that bad?'

'It felt as if it was . . . at the time.'

Dr Mahler nodded, approvingly.

'But not now. Which makes it even more important to avoid getting into such a state again. Why did you, do you think? Apart from the booze, which we'll discuss later.'

'I don't know. It's just the way I'm made.'

Dr Mahler shook his head. 'Not good enough. I know you're too intelligent not to be able to figure it out and put things right.'

Annabelle sat back and admired his straightforward, no-nonsense approach. But Jenny shook her head too and tried to pull the shutters down. Mahler eyed her quizzically. She was not an unattractive girl. Strong, rather irregular features; fine hair and interesting eyes. Tortured depths though. He looked down again at Annabelle's notes. Thirty-one. No longer a child. That of course was probably the trouble. It takes so much longer to grow up than any of us suppose. He was reminded by Annabelle's heavy underlining of the phrase 'failed medic', that they had both attached some significance to that.

'Why did you leave medicine?' he asked.

'Oh, I couldn't cope . . . I couldn't bear it. All the responsibility and the sadness and frustrations. It really didn't suit my personality.'

'A very honest answer. But of course we all feel like that sometimes . . . '

'I felt like that all of the time.'

'What did you do afterwards?'

'I became a secretary.' She avoided his eye.

'Quite a reversal. Was that appropriate?' Jennifer was silent, so he continued. 'You know, there's only one way medicine could be said to resemble heaven. It has many mansions. I certainly couldn't face going into an operating theatre twice a week and I daresay my surgical colleagues aren't keen on the idea of chatting to psychopaths. Weren't there lots of other things you could have done – even if you didn't want to meet the patients?'

Jennifer looked embarrassed and miserable now. 'I wanted to join the microbiology course,' she said. 'Either that or biochemistry. Perhaps do some research eventually.'

'Sounds sensible enough. Why didn't you?'

'My mother wouldn't allow it. It was a matter of pride with her, you see. It had to be medicine or nothing at all.' Dr Mahler raised his eyebrows.

'How old were you . . . twenty-one or two? Hardly a child, surely?'

'Still financially dependent. I got the minimum grant. My parents said they would no longer contribute if I left medicine. I had some money of my own in trust, but that was blocked too.'

'Amazing,' said Dr Mahler, 'the things people will do.' It sounded a very odd tale. The interview with the mother should be revealing.

'There were – other things – going on too. It all came to a head at once. I left in a hurry in the end. I know I didn't behave at all well.'

'Did you have a breakdown?'

'I suppose I did in a way. I never saw anyone, you understand. I just went home and it was all hushed up. I'm not a schizophrenic, if that's what you mean.'

'Of course you aren't.' Dr Mahler resettled his glasses on his nose. He could see Annabelle watching and waiting for a decision. Abruptly he changed tack and ran through the usual questions about sleep and appetite and weight and bodily functions. He made a few notes himself. She had nice legs he noted, under the table. In the end, he said: 'Well, I think we'll transfer you to our new unit on Ward 5 and I'll see you again on Friday.'

When she had gone, he said to Annabelle: 'Worthy of a little care and attention, I think. You can give her clothes back though.'

'Any medication?'

'Oh, no. There's nothing wrong with her really, you know. She's as sane as you or I – probably more. But you can probe the relationship with the mother a little, I suspect, and find out about the 'other things.' You ought to be able to relate to her well in your position. But all she really needs is a little breathing space to sort herself out. Hardly any help from us. I'll probably discharge her on Friday, before she starts thinking she's really abnormal.

At first, Annabelle wasn't sure if Dr Mahler was right. The move to the lighter and brighter ward seemed to set Jennifer Warrender back somehow. Despite its cheery, clean atmosphere and its intentionally optimistic decor with daffodil-patterned curtains round each bed, she spent the first two days in perpetual tears. They were quiet, self-contained tears, but constant nevertheless. Perhaps it was something to do with the bleached and barren landscape now visible out of higher and broader windows of specially toughened glass. The hospital looked out over a pleasant park, but the trees were still bare, with buds screwed up tightly like fists, the sky was vast and lifeless and the earth sodden underfoot. Everything was devoid of colour. Annabelle had often thought the end of winter must be a difficult time for depressives.

'Hello,' she said, at the end of her rounds. 'Why aren't

you dressed? You can have your clothes now, you know.'

'I couldn't be bothered.'

Annabelle sat down. 'If you got dressed, you could go to OT or take a walk round the grounds.'

'I don't really want to.'

'Well, you won't get better just sitting here crying.'

'I can't get better. I'm not even worthy of treatment. Merely inadequate. That's what Dr Mahler thinks.' Was there a hint of resentment there? Unfortunately not. Jennifer seemed to agree entirely. He's got her wrong, thought Annabelle. She's riddled with guilt and totally depressive. If he doesn't put her on drugs or give her ECT she'll go out and do it again. I must pluck up the courage to tell him that.

'Your mother saw Dr Mahler yesterday,' said Annabelle. 'She's still asking to see you.'

'What did he say?'

'He said it was up to you.'

'He's a sharp cookie, isn't he?'

Annabelle was surprised. 'He's quite astute,' she agreed.

Jennifer sighed. 'Oh, all right. I'll see my mother this afternoon. Only can you restrict her time or something? Otherwise I can't bear it.'

'Of course,' Annabelle nodded vigorously. 'I'll tell her only ten minutes the first time. Doctor's orders. Can you manage that?'

'I'll try.'

Sister Sparling drifted up the almost deserted ward. Everyone else was out doing something. She was young and business-like, pert and pretty with dyed blonde hair and her skirts crackled with efficiency.

'Your coffee's ready, doctor.'

'Can I have it down here?'

'You don't have to, you know,' said Jennifer. 'Make a special effort, I mean. It's very good of you and all that. But I must be your most boring patient, after all.'

'Oh, I can't be bothered traipsing down to the office,'

said Annabelle airily. 'The 'phone rings all the time there anyway.' Then she said, coming clean: 'You've forgotten Dr Mahler will expect me to know all about you by Friday.'

Jennifer smiled and there was a glimmer of rapport between them. 'Do you like working for him?'

'Yes, I do really. He's good. Cultivates his eccentricities like mad of course! And I was frightfully intimidated the first week. But he's very fair and . . . well, human really, I suppose.'

'And will you stay in Psychiatry?'

'Oh, I don't know about that. I'm on a GP training course really, you know. I don't think I'd have chosen this job otherwise. Though I have to admit I'm enjoying it. It's a very different world. Weird sometimes, of course. But I like the relaxed atmosphere. I don't think I can specialise though. I'm engaged to be married next year. The thought of all those endless exams turns me off. And I'm sick of hospital life too.'

'I know what you mean. Don't do it though.'

'What? Get married?'

'Perhaps. Depends on the man of course.'

'That's what Mahler says. He reckons I'll be pegging nappies on the line in between surgeries in no time and of course I will. But then I know he'd like another recruit in his department and I flatter myself he likes me. Awfully difficult, isn't it? Deciding what to do for the best. I know we're so lucky having the choice now but – well – it only makes you want it all. The best of both worlds. And that's not really possible.'

'At least you survived.'

They were silent for a while. Then Annabelle said, a little timidly 'We do understand about your mother. She hasn't made it easy. Between you and me, I suspect Mahler gave her a hard time. He can be pretty brutal when he wants to be.

'It wouldn't get through.'

'But you've got to start standing up to her.'

'It's too late.'

'No, it isn't, Jennifer.' Annabelle became more insistent. 'You've got the whole of your life before you.'

'Only once you've buggered up the first thirty years, you've had it.'

'Oh no, that isn't true!'

'Think about it,' Jennifer ran a distracted hand through her hair. She hadn't combed it properly and it was tangled and wild and not unlike Red Hot Kate's. 'That's exactly what I did. With my mother's help. I know it wasn't all her fault – it was mine too – but there are some things I can't forgive.' They were back to the mother again then. 'And now she makes me feel so useless. Over the divorce, I suppose. It's no use telling her it happens to one in three, you know. She regards it as a social stigma. And it didn't happen to the boys . . . ,my brothers, so why should it happen to me? If I had merely dropped out of medicine, but managed to marry the boss and 'do well for myself', as she thinks of it, she might have brought herself to forgive me in time. But now I've messed that up too.'

'Tell me about the other things,' said Annabelle. 'You said there were 'other things' going on around the time you gave up medicine.'

'Oh, but I couldn't,' said Jennifer. 'It would take too long to explain properly. You must have something else to do.'

'Why don't you try? You can always start writing it down, for me to read later, if it really does take too long.'

Jennifer thought about it. 'I don't know,' she said, 'how important it is now.'

'Then perhaps you'll find out.'

'It was about Dominic really.'

Sister Sparling was hovering because it was time for Jennifer to go to the day-room with the others to have her lunch. But Annabelle made urgent eyes for her to go away again and she did, floating off, leaving the ward door to fall softly shut behind her. It was unusually quiet.

Outside, some of the clouds, the smaller and fleecier grey patches, had separated from each other to allow through a weak and watery sun. It came cautiously through the ward windows, as if unsure of its welcome, to switch on a tentative light and warmth.

'I suspect I can remember everything about Dominic if I really try.' Jennifer already sounded vacant. The dream was long forbidden. 'From the way that he looked and the car that he drove to the records he played. Even the way that he buttoned up his shirts. But I don't suppose you want to know any of that. You can take it that I loved him. We were happy together, too. Once, I thought I just needed love and approval from some man – any reasonable specimen would do – and it just happened to be Dominic at that time. Beth encouraged that point of view. She always thought he was trying to get me out of medicine, you see. Anyway, the conclusion was that there are lots more fish in the sea. And so there are, of course. Lots of the wrong ones. But very few even remotely right. I never met anyone like him again. I believe now that Dominic was right for me. I believe, although of course I shall never know, that I would have been able to maintain my love for him always. Instead of which, like a fool, I threw it all away.'

After Annabelle had gone, she found herself wondering if she really could remember everything, just as it was, or had she idealised it all in her mind now that time had passed? Take a simple thing like the way he looked . . . could she really be sure? He had had yellow hair – really yellow, there was no doubt about that – and it had been longish then and flopped forward onto his forehead. That had been broad like his face. And his eyes were blue – not an intense, electrifying blue like her mother's – she struggled for the exact shade . . . a much quieter and paler variety, anyhow. How awful to forget! She remembered his nose was perfectly straight though, because she had always envied him that. His lips and his chin had a chiselled look about them. Yes, she could describe each individual feature tolerably well. It was only the physical whole, the sensation conveyed only by his actual presence which was missing. She could remember the colour of his hair and his car and the fact that he liked Leonard Cohen and Dylan, Family, Jethro Tull and the Moody Blues. But she couldn't conjure that wholeness up. The pain of his absence was no longer sharp and unbearable. It had been dulled, like his image, by the years. And yet the sadness remained. The regret was as poignant and real and pulled at her as much as ever.

CHAPTER FIVE

From my window, I could see the car-park in front of the hall and I watched my parents drive away with a small and rather hollow feeling inside. I can remember that room so well. It was small and spartan and very hot. The windows were the type you pushed outwards to open, but it didn't seem to make any difference, especially on a sunny autumn day. There was an exceptionally narrow single bed, which looked and felt very hard, and was covered with a grey and brown striped spread. A unit of shelves above the bedhead separated it from a washbasin with a mirror. Next to that was the door and, opposite it, a small wardrobe. Back inside the room was an armchair and then a space, now entirely occupied by my trunk. Then there was the window with its desk and chair and lamp before it. Then you were back at the bed again. The furniture was modern, wood veneer; the colours deliberately functional and neutral. A notice on the door listed fire-drill, meal-times and made a half-hearted request for one not to pin or sellotape posters to the walls. I didn't have any then, though that soon changed and I ignored the rule like everyone else. Whilst I was unpacking, a note was slipped under the door: sherry at six o'clock with the floor tutor for all freshers. Feeling more cheerful, I tried to stow away my things.

The skeleton was a bit of a problem. His name was Joe and he came in a box, one foot by two foot six, being entirely disarticulate. I had bought him second-hand from a student my biology mistress knew in Leeds. I would have liked to sit the skull, with its mouth open like Yoric, on the desk, but wondered if that might be too pretentious. Better not. It might get knocked off anyway. And its previous owner had stressed what a good skull it was, with none of the important little bits missing. I pushed him carefully under the desk. I also had a copy of Gray's Anatomy and a very new Faculty of Medicine scarf. That was all, to start off with. Doubtless there would be a lot more books in the trunk by the end of the term.

I put away my clothes, which mainly consisted of sweaters and jeans. Plus a couple of white lab coats. And a heavy grey duffel with toggles, for the winter.

'I'm sure a medical student ought to look smarter,' Beth had said disapprovingly. 'Aren't you going to take any dresses?' I put some in, under sufferance, but didn't expect to wear them much. Not the first two years. I had however brought some make-up, some plastic beads and a rinse for my hair. The need for such props was desperate, for I had to look more grown-up somehow.

The hall of residence was a hive of activity. All around me, the individual cells were filling up. The corridors were full of harassed fathers heaving trunks and anxious mothers fussing daughters, who were all trying to look as if these parents didn't really belong to them. I had already met one girl in the communal kitchen-cum-laundry, shared by each 'side' of a floor. She had been startlingly articulate and busy deploring the drag of 'Freshers Week'. On discovering my identity, her reaction was: 'God! Not another medic. The place is crawling with them!' Whilst this sounded encouraging in its way, I was suitably chastened and retired to my room. Then I didn't really know what to do next, so I went for a walk.

It was hard to believe we were in the middle of Liverpool. Mossley Hill is a leafy oasis. The russet leaves were collecting then in the tree-covered lanes. I couldn't bear to leave the campus for long, however, in case something happened, and soon back-tracked to hall, walking through the lobby past the telephone-booths and out, through the back, into the grounds. I followed the path to the refectory building with its common-room, shared by an identical men's hall. Between the two, lay a green field surrounded by trees, fiery and splendid now in their shedding. Across them, in the far distance, you could see the tower of the Old Cathedral. It was on the field that I first met Pauline Parker.

'Hello,' she squeaked nervously. 'Forgive me for butting in.' She was small and dark and extremely plain, with her hair scraped back behind her ears. She stuck out an awkward hand and I shook it, a little surprised at such formality.

'I saw your name in our corridor. According to the list, you're another medic and so am I.' She thrust her chin inwards as she said this and walked on briskly with a bowed head bobbing to and fro. So briskly that I had to struggle to keep up. My goodness, I had forgotten about Pauline! She always reminded me of something stranded out of water, with those odd head movements and her rolling sort of walk. Perhaps, if she had lived in a tank, she would have been beautiful and graceful too.

'Looking forward to the DR?' she said.

'Well, not really, no. I mean . . . it's a little worrying, isn't it? Just at first.'

Pauline stopped suddenly and flashed me a smile, pushing her glasses – for of course she had to wear glasses – sharply up her nose.

'Feel just the same myself,' she semaphored with her chin. 'Ghastly, isn't it? Expect everyone's the same. Better when we've got it over with.'

At least she agrees, I thought with some relief. Even if she does express it in telegram speech. She really was a strange girl. Were they all going to be like this?

'Sherrying at six?' I continued to be disconcerted but nodded. 'Good. So am I. See you then. Anything you want, give me a knock. I'm just round the corner. Fairly well supplied.'

'Er . . . thank you, Pauline. That's very kind.' I retreated once more to my room. Well, at least it was progress of a sort.

There were six of us crowded into the tutor's room and three of us were medics.

'Quite an influx,' smiled the young woman filling our glasses. 'That's a lot for one floor. Considering there'll only be about twenty-five of you in the whole year. They usually split you up more. Don't know why they've done it really. You medics do tend to clan together at the best of times, you know. I hope you won't take it amiss when I say you really shouldn't . . . not in your pre-clinical years. It's your only chance to mix with the others.'

I could not imagine ever wanting to clan together with Pauline Parker, whom I was now squeezed next to on the floor. She looked different somehow . . .

'Contact lenses,' she hissed apologetically, bobbing her head in and out urgently.

'I'm terribly sorry, Pauline. I didn't mean to stare.'

'Quite all right. Do the same thing myself.' She lowered her chin and sipped her sherry noisily. What was it she reminded me of so irresistibly – could it be a pterodoctyl? – no, that couldn't be right. Something extinct anyway. The tutor was making introductions.

'I'm Dr Petty – Hilary to you – and a reader in the History department.'

'PhD.' mouthed Pauline in my ear.

'Yes, I know,' I whispered back.

'Then we have . . . Jenny Sugden, medic, Pauline Parker, medic, Susan Smith, history, Maggie Turner, social studies, Eileen Newall, medic –' she looked normal enough at any rate '– and Jocasta, oh dear, I'm sorry but I'm going to have to ask you again . . .'

The remaining girl in the group said something which

sounded like 'scissorskijinski' except that it wasn't exactly that.

'Yes, thank you . . . and you're English, aren't you – department, I mean?' We all had a titter at that, but Jocasta didn't seem to mind. I stared at her in fascination, for she was so different from anyone else. The rest of us were all obviously fresh out of school. We had put skirts on to meet our tutor. We were all trying depressingly hard to appear grown-up and pretend we always had sherry at six. Jocasta probably did. She wore a skirt too, though it was rather an apology for one. She was, without any doubt, the ugliest girl I have ever seen. Far worse than Pauline. And yet she was also devastatingly attractive. Magnetic even. She was tall and rather gangling and she was wearing this very short, green skirt with long, grey high-heeled boots. Her legs between the two seemed to go on forever. She also wore a black blouse with a very frilly collar and a cheap metal necklace, heavy enough to weigh anyone down – it consisted of three rows of gigantic green obelisks – I can see it now. Then there were her black hoop earrings. It all sounds perfectly awful, but somehow she had the verve to carry it off.

Later on, I found out that even she had dressed herself up a bit. She normally wore pink woolly cardigans. But the boots and earrings never varied. And I never once saw her in trousers. Her hair (for I can see I've painted rather an alluring picture and that is quite wrong) was a dull, ordinary light brown and she always wore it pulled back into a – chignon sounds far too sophisticated – pinned down pony-tail was nearer the truth. Her face was broad and Slavonic, her eyes prominent and heavy-lidded, her nose broad and flat, her mouth too big, her skin coarse. She spoke with an East European accent and could be every bit as imperious as she sometimes appeared. I should mention that she was at least three years older than the rest of us and appreciated her university education more as a result. She had approached it via a chequered career. Her parents were in Czechoslovakia – or was it Hungary? – I never knew much about her background, in the careless indifference of youth. I would pay far more attention now. Anyway, she lived with an aunt in London and that is all I ever found out.

In every way, she seemed more slick, sophisticated and worldly than us. And yet she was full of chuckles too, which creased up her face and, when she laughed, her shoulders shook and she wheezed a bit. She reminded me of a mischievous kitten, although Eileen, who became my other friend, likened her to a mother hen because she liked to know everyone's business and clucked over the 'floor'. Well, there was something in that. In the end we agreed to differ. Eileen could not convert me, for I had known lots of Eileens, but never anyone like Jocasta. She was my breath of fresh air.

But I thought this story was about Dominic, I can hear you saying. Well, yes it is: I had completely forgotten about Jocasta till I started it. But now she's come elbowing her way in. How strange! I have no idea where she is now. No matter, because her memory makes me feel more cheerful. And I suppose, Dr Jowett, that is your intention in the end. To make me see that it wasn't all bad and won't be again. And, actually, she was important. We discussed everything together, at one time. Naturally, she introduced me to Dominic. I might not have met him otherwise. He was never in hall and he didn't know any other medics. He did English, like Jocasta.

She didn't bring us together straightaway, however. It's funny now to think that Dominic must have been a fresher that day as well, that his lovely parents took him to West Derby with a considerably more well-travelled trunk than mine, that he ate the first of his landlady's awful food and was about to meet Jocasta. And all that time I never knew him.

'Oh Jennifer, I'm sorry to bother you . . . (I learnt later that Jocasta always began like this when she wanted something.)

'Not at all. Come in.'

'I wondered if I could borrow some coffee – I've run out.' How did you run out in the first week?

'Of course. In fact, why don't you stay and have a cup with me?' She was my first guest. Everyone else seemed to be popping in and out of each other's rooms like yo-yos and I was anxious to enter into the general swing of things.

'But you're working?'

'Not really. Just trying to read through the next section of Zuckerman in advance. In the hope I might recognise something.'

'You've started lectures then?'

'This is Dissection. But yes . . . we have started lectures.'

'We don't have any till next week.'

'I know. It's grossly unfair! Though I must admit, I couldn't stand much more of this 'Freshers' stuff.' I spooned the coffee into the mugs and went into the kitchen to boil the water.

'Would you like a cigarette?' said Jocasta, when I returned.

'Thanks.'

'I thought medics didn't smoke?'

'I don't really. Just pinch the odd one or two from my mother . . . when she's not looking, of course.'

'So how was your day?'

'Well . . . a bit harrowing, really. First time in the DR. The old medical school is ancient and the common-room's falling to bits. There are loads of people in our year. I met some second-years too, full of advice, a bit patronising, but I think they meant well. Then I bought some books and was horrified at the hole it made in my money.'

'What is this DR?'

'The dissecting-room.'

'You mean with rats?'

'Oh no, human bodies.'

'My God, Jennifer, that's bloody awful you know.' She wasn't really as alarmed as she sounded. It was just her way of speaking. 'And how did you feel?'

'A bit nervous,' I admitted. 'When I first walked in and saw all those tables covered with draped bumps. But they're not that real somehow. Not like I imagined. They remind me of dried up mummies. I suppose that's exactly what they are. The skin's all grey and tough like an elephant's. And the smell of formalin is over everything – it makes your eyes water – that's the worst part really.'

'And you have to chop these bodies up, bit by bit, following this Zuckerman book?'

'Yes, that's the idea. For two terms . . . with a viva to pass every week.'

'My God! I couldn't do it, Jennifer.'

'I don't think it's as bad as it sounds. I was worried, I can tell you. But it does get interesting. And you don't work on your own . . . there are three other students as well on the same body. Just as well because ours is enormous – we've christened him Boris because he reminds us of Boris Karloff.'

'That's disgusting, you know. He could be somebody's daddy.' But Jocasta went off into one of her convulsive chuckles and made me laugh too. 'My God, I really couldn't do it! Are you with Eileen and Pauline?'

'No, three other girls. They've divided us alphabetically this time.'

'Pauline is very nervous, I think.'

'I think so, too. She'll probably settle down.'

'And Eileen is very clever.'

'Do you think so? It's hard to tell at present. Everyone must have been reasonably good to get in.'

Jocasta changed tack and pouted. 'Well, my day was bloody awful too,' she said. 'I can't find out where I should be and when I get there, nothing's going on. My tutor obviously disapproves of me and there only seem to be two men in the whole of the English Department and they're both pefftas.'

'They're what?'

'Pefftas.'

'I think you mean "Pufftas".'

'Yes, that's what I said. Pefftas.'

'How do you know?'

'Oh Jennifer, you can tell! Straightaway. At least you're outnumbered.'

'I thought you came here to work.'

'Hell, that's right!' Jocasta narrowed her eyes. 'And I really will, you know. I'm really going to work! You've got to get a First, you know.' Eileen always poured scorn on Jocasta's noble intentions, but I could see that she really meant it, even though she convulsed wheezily afterwards.

'Jenny, why don't you wear a better brassiere?' This rather took the wind out of my sails, seeing as I'd only known her a little over forty-eight hours.

'I beg your pardon?'

'You have a nice figure, but then you flatten the bust down so and wear big sweaters. It's a shame to hide the form.'

'Goodness, you sound like my mother! I've never really thought about it.'

'You should, you know.'

'Do you want another coffee?'

'No. I am going to leave you to your Zucker man . . . ugh, how disgusting, and find someone else to inflict myself on. Do you think Hilary's in? My taps are stiff and I can't turn them on properly. How can I wash under that piddling drip-drop?'

'Use the showers,' I suggested.

'But what about my teeth? My teeth are very important.'

'I think you're supposed to complain about that sort of thing to the Domestic Bursar.' She brightened up.

'How clever you are, Jennifer! But where does she live?' I pointed her in the general direction and she went. I also implied I didn't mind if she 'inflicted' herself upon me again. Any time in fact. ('That's typical of you, Jenny,' Eileen would say, when I got to know her better. 'You should be more careful and less impulsive. That girl's a leech. You'll never get rid of her.' But I didn't want to get rid of her. I can see now I am depicting Eileen as a bit of a stuffed shirt. She wasn't at all really. She was just a nice, ordinary girl from Lancashire who covered up a kind heart with a thickish layer of reserve.)

The term slowly settled itself down. We were duly initiated. For the medics, this meant being flourbagged and squirted with foam at the faculty's society meeting. It all sounds rather juvenile now but I suppose it was fun at the time. I bought yet more books, started attending lectures and settled down to dissection. It was going to be all right and I heaved a vast sigh of relief. It didn't bother me after all and I could cope. The first Saturday afternoon, I went down Brownlow Hill and bought two 'better brassieres' and a pair of kinky boots in Lewis's (with its own fine example of male anatomy, incidentally, in the form of a statue) at the bottom of the hill.

Of course there were some false starts. I didn't seem to get on that well with my dissecting partners. Then there was a boy whom I thought was going to be fantastic, who took me out a couple of times, but ultimately proved disappointing. But in time I settled too, into my own niche, like everyone else. My particular circle of friends consisted of Eileen and another girl called Ruth, Jeremy from Leeds and Philip from the Wirral and Bonnie and Clyde, whose real names escape me now. They were a rather homely couple who had palled up from the start. Eventually we formed a clinical firm. Then there was Pauline Parker. We more or less adopted her. Poor Pauline! She was so gawky and intense. She always said the wrong thing, but she couldn't keep her mouth shut. She was that strange mixture of supreme confidence against all odds, coupled with extreme nervousness. Every year has one unfortunate, I suppose, who is made fun of and secretly despised and, for us, it was Pauline. I felt sorry for her, although she maddened me too. Because she was on our floor, in hall, Eileen and I felt some measure of responsibility and invited her onto our firm. But she was not endearing, even to us, though she tagged along willingly enough. I remember once that Jocasta tried to take her in hand and transform her physical appearance. I told her she was on a losing wicket but she wouldn't listen. In the end she had to admit defeat however and return her attentions to me. I was far more malleable. For my appearance had begun to change. Jocasta had not confined her criticisms to my underwear. I gave up rinsing my hair (after a comment similar to the one about brassieres) but grew it longer instead. My skirts shot up – and later down – with alarming rapidity. I went in for coloured tights and beads, boots and eyeliner in a big way, though practicality retained the university scarf and duffel coat.

One afternoon, towards the Christmas break, I stood outside the Students' Union, on the top of Brownlow Hill, waiting for the bus back to hall, and felt homesick. For the first time I needed to be close to someone other than Jocasta. In short, I felt lonely. It was extremely cold. The sun was setting early and the clouds were salmon-coloured. They looked like great, bellying pink sails, suddenly gone stiff as ice in a frozen sky. Winter was well on its way. The trees on Mossley Hill were bare, black thickets of twigs now and the pavements shin-deep in swishy, wet leaves. Up here, the scene was more barren and bleak, although the last rays of the sun made the old red brick of the Victoria building suddenly splendid: it seemed to be made up of amethyst arches and colonnades, with a sprinkling of black wrought iron here and there, and the clock face was suffused with pink. Over the road, the steel and concrete struts of the new Metropolitan Cathedral soared hopefully to heaven and the sun caught a last cathedral light from the lantern glass below the crown of thorns. It glowed like a whorl of claret blood.

I reminded myself I had not been to church once since the first couple of weeks, despite good intentions. Not that the Metropolitan Cathedral was 'mine.' I belonged to the vast, unfinished tomb dwarfing the decadent Georgian houses at the other end of Hope Street. And, as far as I was concerned, despite its architectural merit, it failed to grasp its elusive king. I had been a few times, as I say, and visited the Anglican chaplaincy for coffee, but suddenly all that serious fellowship had begun to seem bland, inadequate and remote. For me, the cathedral was becoming a mausoleum without any answers. I had begun to doubt and Father Bartram was losing his grip.

The depressive turn of my thoughts continued. I had seemed to make a good start. But had I really? What was I doing here at all? What in the world? I didn't know a soul in the bus queue. Doubts continued to plague me as I stamped my feet to keep warm. Ah well, it would soon be Christmas! The holidays took on a rosy glow with the realities of home, distanced as it was, only half recalled. I would have liked to invite Jocasta for part of the break, as I knew she didn't have a proper family over here. But I also knew she wouldn't go down well with Beth and I wasn't going to let her spoil my new friend for me.

I went home (as I thought) a changed person, on the train from Lime Street, with a small case full of washing. ('Good grief!' said a startled Beth, at the ticket-barrier at Leeds. 'Where ever did you get those awful earrings?')

It wasn't long however before the novelty of home wore off and I was dying to get back. Kingley seemed so dull! So boring and quiet after the city with its hectic pavements and its big black taxis, spinning and squealing over wet streets which smelt affectionately of beer. There was no sense of the sea in Kingley. No boom of foghorns on a dark, frosty evening. No throb and pulse of life with the tide. And, worst of all, there was no one to talk to. I missed Jocasta and her irreverence. I missed Eileen and all the others. I even missed Pauline Parker.

My mother, inevitably, didn't think I could be working hard enough. I attended the School Speech Day to collect the Biology Prize and defied her by wearing a black leather mini-skirt and dangly earrings. My old friends all seemed vaguely different too. Mr Pollock, of course, was no longer there, but I am sure I would have been shocked to even imagine ever liking him, in the first place, if he had. My brothers treated me in a slightly more civilised fashion.

We had a quiet family Christmas of sorts and my present was a microscope (although I had already explained several times we didn't need to buy one of our own). When it was time to go back, I was bursting to do just that. Why on earth am I telling you all this? Goodness knows, but you asked me to write it all down, everything that came into my head. I suppose what I really wanted to say was that I was fairly happy in those two pre-clinical years. I am not exactly squeamish in the physical sense of the word, you see. And I did work hard. It was OK. I was awakening and changing, but not yet faced with a crisis.

CHAPTER SIX

I didn't meet Dominic until my second year. By then, I was really settled in. I had stayed in hall although I had moved to a better room. So had Jocasta (who couldn't bear the thought of boiling herself an egg) and Pauline, though Eileen had moved out into a flat with Bonnie and Ruth. I was to join them later, if only in name, but, for now, I preferred Jocasta's proximity. I had passed my first year exams fairly respectably and was now working towards 2nd MB. It was late autumn and Jocasta was feeling restless, which meant I had to be too. (We were now into the new midi-skirts, unbuttoned to the knee, and Jocasta had a fake fur coat.)

'Come in,' I called a little crossly, when I heard her knock. I happened to be struggling with a chapter on the control of the autonomic nervous system which was inducing a definite desire to nod off. I had already been plagued by Pauline Parker. I had the beginnings of a sore throat and I was not anxious for company.

'Are you working, Jenny?'

'Not now.'

'There's a party in Carnatic tonight.'

'Yes, I know. I don't really feel like going. Do you?' This was rather mean because I could see that she did. She was back in her mini-skirt and the beads were janglier and the blouse more dressy than usual. She was also wearing a lot of eye make-up. I looked up in time to catch the merest instant of disappointment flit across her broad, Slavonic face, which I no longer thought of as ugly.

'Well, I don't really feel like going either.' She sat down and pouted. 'But it's so bloody boring in my room.'

I softened: 'Have you finished your essay?'

'Yes.'

'Well, I haven't finished reading this yet. If you make me a coffee and give me a cigarette while I'm doing that, I'll come along with you afterwards. But I don't want to stay long because I'm tired.'

'You've been working too hard.'

'Well, I don't know that I have. It's not been going in.'

'Then you need a break anyway.'

'An early night, more like.'

Jocasta didn't think much of this. 'What you need is a lover.'

'Jocasta!'

'Well, you haven't been out for ages.'

'Not true.'

'You don't know any men.'

'Don't be ridiculous.'

'You know what I mean. And you're looking very peaky.'

'I'm starting a cold.'

Jocasta was prepared to ignore this. 'Now, who do I know who could hammer a chunk of light between your books and bodies?'

Despite myself, I had to laugh. 'Chink of light. Not chunk. And we don't perform on the bodies this year, as you well know.'

She was undeterred. 'Maybe someone in the English department . . . that would be good for you, you know. Someone who wasn't a medic.'

'I thought men were at a premium on your side of the university. You also said the ones in the English department were pufftas, if you remember!'

'Did I?' Jocasta relented. 'Well, not all of them. Dominic is not a puffta, for instance. He would be very good for you.'

'It's a pretty fancy name.'

'Do you think so?' (I suppose if your name is Jocasta other people's names seem very ordinary.) 'Not really. It's very Catholic you know.'

'Aha!' I pounced on that, for Jocasta was also a Catholic. 'So you met him at Mass. You're hoping to convert me.'

'Don't be silly, Jennifer,' she said. 'I met him in the department. Dominic doesn't go to Mass. He is not a very good Catholic boy at all.'

'But good for me?'

'Oh, yes! He'd bring you out of yourself, I'm sure. Falling in love is very stimulating, anyway.'

I laughed again, with the quick, easy cynicism of youth. 'Hey, steady on! What does he look like anyway?'

'His hair is like a cornfield.'

'You mean it's fair.'

'No, I don't. I mean it's like a cornfield. Dominic is actually rather beautiful in his way. Either you won't like him at all or you will fall in love. I think you will, you know.' She nodded, very pleased with herself, now her mind was made up.

'What rubbish, Jocasta! I must say he sounds exactly like a puffta from that description.'

'Well, he isn't. Don't be vulgar, Jenny!' But she giggled all the same. 'Perhaps you could find out?'

'Thanks, but no thanks. Is he going to this party?'

'Oh, I shouldn't think so. I don't know. I'll have to invite you to meet him 'specially, I think.'

'Don't bother. I hate set-ups.'

'Oh, well . . . let's forget it then and just go to the party.'

She gave in far too easily but I assumed she was being clever.

'All right. Give me that ciggy and go and make the coffee.'

She scuttled off and I lit up, flicking through the last

remaining pages of the chapter, guiltily. I never did master the control of the autonomic nervous system entirely. But I was more worried about the smoking. I had sworn to give up after the Path lectures. It shouldn't be so difficult after a couple of years, surely? But now I would have to buy another packet of my own to pay Jocasta back for all the ones I had borrowed recently, while trying to do without. Damn it all!

When she returned, I was a bit sarky. 'It might save time if you could look in my wardrobe and tell me what to wear.'

'Really, Jenny, you're very ascerbic tonight. Just like Eileen. Have you been eating lemons?'

'I'm sorry,' I sighed and shut my book. 'Perhaps you're right. I do need a break.'

'This is nice,' she said, taking out a skinny-rib sweater dress in a rather startling scarlet. 'I haven't seen it before.'

'I bought it in the holidays in a mad moment. It doesn't really go with my hair. My mother thinks it's awful.'

'Oh, I don't know! Hitched up a bit – well, a lot actually – with a big belt and a scarf. I'll lend you those. It'll get you noticed.'

'Jocasta . . . you're the one who wants to go to this party. Why don't you just leave me to look dull and plain and then you'll probably get the best man?' But that wasn't in her scheme of things at all.

Across the way, the big bar in the common-room was almost in darkness, illuminated regularly by pulses of coloured light. For some unaccountable reason, I thought of my dead grandfather Moffat and how he would have said that was so you couldn't see your change.

'What are you smiling at?'

'Nothing.' I lived in a changed world. The floor was covered with gyrating bodies, although most people were still clustered around the bar. One of the latest Moody Blues LP's was belting into everybody's ear-drums. I began to relax.

'OK. What do you want to drink?' I yelled at Jocasta.

She told me and went to find a space to sit. She was remarkably prudish about going to the bar, so I always got the drinks, although she paid her turn. I fought my way in and eventually ordered her a fruit juice. She never drank beer and anything else was a bit expensive on a student's grant. I was the one who knocked it back (already? I can hear you saying) and ordered a pint of lager in two half-pint glasses (a shy concession to femininity) to save going back.

While I was waiting, I noticed someone further down the queue with remarkable hair. It looked weirdly white in that light, but I could well imagine that, in the sun, you might say it was like a cornfield. It flopped over his forehead and curled down onto his collar. For he was undoubtedly male, although you could have been forgiven for wondering from the back, in view of that hair. He looked across at me looking at him and I hastily looked away, then kicked myself for not smiling, for he was definitely worth a second look.

I paid for the drinks and struggled back to Jocasta. She was already on the makeshift floor, jerking about rather convulsively with a tall, hairy male. She excused herself primly as soon as she could.

'You needn't have done that,' I said. 'I don't mind sitting out. But you should enjoy yourself, seeing as you wanted to come.'

'Oh, that's all right. He was bloody awful, you know.'

I laughed. 'Thanks! I thought you said the ugly ones were sexier and far more interesting! Anyway, I mean it. I don't mind being a wallflower tonight.'

'Oh, Jenny! You're getting as bad as Pauline.'

'Compliments again?'

Jocasta sipped her fruit juice and I attacked my lager. The track had changed:-

'If only you knew what's inside of me now,
You wouldn't want to know me somehow.
But you will haunt me tonight,

We know we'll be all right,
In the end!

It was better to listen to it than dance, though there were still plenty of people swaying about in a dream on the floor. I thought about the yellow-haired person at the bar.

'Jocasta.'

'Yes?'

'There's an amazing blond at the bar who happens to be a man.'

'Is there?'

'Yes. It's Dominic, isn't it? You knew he was going to be here.'

'No, really I didn't. I had no idea . . . where is he?' She turned round too obviously to look, though really it hardly mattered with the place packed so tight. 'Oh yes . . . so it is! Hey, Nic! Hello! Over here.' She stood up and waved both hands and beamed.

'Sit down,' I hissed, nearly spilling my drink. 'He'll see you.' She sat down again. 'But that's the idea. It's all right . . . he doesn't know anything about you.'

'I don't believe you. Is he coming over?'

'Yes, I think so.'

He was but, owing to the crush, it took him a minute or two to reach us. Despite my former intentions, I smiled sweetly at the next spotty man with specs, who had just intervened and asked me to dance, and joined him on the floor. Jocasta looked a bit put out. But I wasn't going to fall in with her schemes so easily. I kept an eye on her though and noticed that she gave Dominic a convincing welcome. They even kissed each other on the cheek in a brotherly and sisterly fashion, which amazed me. They must be thick as thieves then. Doubtless he knew all about me, to the last little detail, despite Jocasta's protestations. But then why was he here? He didn't look like the sort of man in desperate need of an introduction to someone like me. Horrors! Perhaps she had exaggerated my finer points. If so, he was going to be terribly disappointed.

I made my escape from the spotty youth with specs, who looked a bit crestfallen. It was no good feeling sorry for him though. Even I knew that was no way to start a relationship. Everyone's looking for someone. Jocasta and Dominic were engaged in the kind of conversation which doesn't sound in the least bit awkward or forced, which confirmed my suspicions about their friendship.

'Oh, Nic,' Jocasta waved a casual, heavy-ringed hand in my direction. 'This is Jenny, my friend from hall.' He stood up while I sat down, which struck me as being very odd and quaint, though rather kind.

'Hello,' he said, in an accentless voice, which I can only describe as cultured. 'I've heard a lot about you.' Jocasta avoided my eye.

'Hi.' I was determined not to like him. He was not so perfect close up anyway. There was a certain Jocasta-like quality about him in that he was not really handsome at all, though he came far closer to it than she did. It was probably that which saved him from effeminacy in view of the thick cornfield. But his nose was very straight and his lips were right while his eyes and broad smile were delightful. Well, suffice it to say I already knew I had a problem.

'Jenny, we've decided this do is awful. It's so hot and crowded and noisy. I've invited Dominic back for coffee, so let's go.'

I opened my mouth to complain, but the sound which came out was a feeble croak, for my throat was getting worse. If Jocasta had been a fly on the wall, she might well have gone 'splat' at that moment. If I had been a dragon, I would have breathed pure fire and flames upon her head. As it was, I could only inwardly fume.

Justin Hayward's haunting voice and music followed us out into the sharp night air. Someone had put the same track on again:

Give just a little bit more
Take a little bit less
From each other tonight
Admit what you're feeling
And see what's in front of you,
It's never out of your sight
You know it's true,
We all know that it's true.'

We walked in silence past the fish-pond, scene of much drunken revelry after the exams, and followed the path across the field. It was a clean, cold night, pricked with stars as if someone had thrown a handful of quartz crystals across a black velvet cloth. We waded through fallen leaves and empty conker shells and I felt the influence of something external calming me down.

By the time we reached hall, I was resigned enough to offer my coffee when Jocasta suddenly remembered she had run out. I made her stick to her own room though. I was not going to be exhibited like something horrible in a jar and I also intended to take my leave whenever I wanted.

On the way for the coffee, I met Pauline Parker looking desolate and, with less than noble intentions, invited her along too. This proved to be a mistake however for it stopped the cosy discussion centring round the English department. Jocasta became fanatically interested in probing Pauline's recent doings and I was forced to talk to Dominic.

After that, I'd had it. I couldn't stop looking at him. He is still the most charming man I have ever met. That sounds sickeningly sweet and awful, I know. But I'm talking about real charm now. It's difficult to put a finger on it. He talked a great deal, though not too much. He is one of those people who uses your Christian name rather excessively. He also used the opportunity of touching someone to make a point or convey a meaning. Occasionally, I mean. Not a conventional sort of thing to do, but it seemed to work for him. Perhaps, if he hadn't been like that, I could have kept my love at a more formal distance for longer. He was another smoker, which was a black mark against him for, if I started going out with him, I would find it even more difficult to give up. For Jocasta was maddeningly right, of course. I did fall head over heels. Hook, line and sinker. Maybe more deeply than she had ever intended. I didn't put him on a pedestal, like Mr Pollock. He was too straightforward and honest for that. His views at the time were pretty radical. Dominic was real, like all the other boys I had ever been out with. But he was alone in engendering that old excitement.

It did not happen all at once of course. Well, not quite. I didn't even see him again for another week. Then Jocasta asked me to another party . . . in the flat of a friend of hers. This time I could hardly wait to go, having ascertained that Dominic would be there. I paid a great deal of attention to my appearance, though Jocasta worried me by saying mournfully that Dominic was the kind of man more interested in a woman's mind. As if anyone could make that sort of distinction! It's always the whole which counts. But, at the time, I probably swallowed it. He did seem to like me anyway.

The party was at a ramshackle house in Lark Lane, at the back of Seffy Park. Faded red curtains sagged at the windows. The room was dimly lit and reeked of joss-sticks and something else which smelled a good deal sweeter and more suspicious. It was the sort of party at which people sat 'spaced out' and cross-legged on the floor, listening to interminable songs of intense though doubtful significance, and very little tune. I was going to say, you know what I mean, but I have just realised you probably don't. It was a very seventies sort of party . . . early seventies. I mean. I didn't know anyone except Jocasta and Dominic and Jocasta immediately drifted off somewhere on her own.

Dominic saw me, looking nervous I suppose, and came

over straight away to take my arm and get me a drink. He put his arm around me in what seemed to be a proprietorial way – or perhaps he was just being kind. For he was that too, as well as being splendid. Endearingly useless of course, in a way I never objected to. For he was absent-minded and impractical and drove all his friends mad. Charm has its limitations. I knew several people who couldn't stand him. But I thought he was incredibly self-possessed and mature and marvellous. And so he was. Not a bad advertisement for his Catholic boarding school. Mind you, he seemed to have rebelled against all of that by then. He was defiantly atheist and 'anti-establishment'. But he never became cruel in his private revolution. He kept his faith with his parents and even an old schoolfriend who was training for the priesthood in that Church he now decried with such vigour. Giles, he said, had been nabbed by the 'Js'. But they were still friends. I liked that.

Of course, I know we would have grown up together and changed. He would probably have exasperated me too, at times, in a marriage. But I did love his character, as well as his charm and his body. It was the whole of him which counted.

The result of the party and its red-lit gloom was that he asked me to go to a concert with him, at the Phil. His tastes, like mine, were pretty catholic with a small 'c'. Anyway, we had a lovely evening. Tchaikovsky's first piano concerto. We fought for a drink in the bar of the other Phil – the Victorian pub across the road – in the interval. Then we caught the bus back to Aigburth and ate fish and chips from a paper for supper. He walked me back to hall through a litter of leaves in the park. There was a bright, full moon like a big silver penny and the autumn gales swept tattered rags of cloud, like smoke, across it.

'You know Jocasta looks like the cat that got the cream,' I said. 'Or at least she did when I told her where I was going. You must have known she would.'

'I didn't know. But I can imagine.'

'She thought you would do me good. Liven me up.'

'And do I?'

'Yes, I rather think you do.'

Other evenings followed in rapid succession. We often went to the cinema in Aigburth and then for a walk down at Otterspool Prom.

Otterspool Prom! Yes, there were innumerable evenings when we just went to walk there. Before the light goes, the smoky cinders from Eastham power station, across the wide, pearly water, stream triumphant to the setting sun. Then the sun dips down over the distant Welsh hills and the globed lamps come on. No otters. Just channel buoys bobbing up and down and seagulls wheeling and crying and the occasional tanker passing down to Eastham, with its cargo for the refineries at Stanlow. And the slurp and slop of the muddy, Mersey water on the concrete walls which contain it. But, when darkness comes and the lights spring trembling out on spiky cranes and gantries and cooling towers, the whole scene is transformed into an industrial fairyland. The river is broad and the sea beckons. We used to sit or lie on the dune-like grassy banks, when it was warm enough, and watch it all, without speaking. Other nights we might talk a lot. I could always talk to him about anything. They've landscaped it all now for posterity – for after all, it really used to be a rubbish dump. I wonder if the tramps still sleep out on their benches, wrapped in newspapers? Plenty of courting couples still, I suppose.

It was when we had been down there one evening that I asked Dominic in for coffee and he said no.

'Is something wrong?' My heart contracted painfully.

'Far from it. But if I do come in I shall want to stay. The night, I mean.'

In a matter of seconds, my world turned upside down, inside out, shook all its contents crazily and then resettled them, though not necessarily in the same order. My predominant emotion was one of joy and expectation.

'Then why don't you?'

'No,' he kissed me to soften the blow. 'Not yet. You'll resent me if I do. And you might get thrown out of hall.'

'I shouldn't resent you. And there are lots of people who get away with it in hall.'

'Nevertheless, I think my bedsitter would be better. And later on.'

'Yes, of course.' I blushed slightly, though it wasn't supposed to be such a crime then. Perhaps we weren't as free as we thought. Even Dominic had used the old: 'I happen to have these concert tickets', gambit when he had first asked me out.

'Don't be embarrassed,' he said. 'You haven't got it wrong. It'll happen inevitably. When the time's right. I want you to think about it first, that's all.'

I nodded and laughed. 'We're not that modern after all then?'

'Of course not.'

'Well, you probably are – but I'm not.'

'What do you mean?'

'Well, sometimes I can't see why you like me at all, you know.'

Dominic was genuinely surprised. 'You have a marked tendency to run yourself down, you know,' he said. 'You really don't have to. It's not funny. It's alarming.'

I felt uncomfortable at that, but brushed it off. 'Goodness, you remind me of Jocasta!'

At that moment, a window above us flew open and someone leaned out. (I have forgotten to mention we were entwined against the wall of hall itself, and the entrance was nearby.)

'For God's sake, will you two stop wittering and either get on with it or go home? Some of us are trying to sleep!' The window slammed shut and we slunk away round the corner, doubled up with hysterics.

'I hope it wasn't someone I know,' I said, when I had recovered slightly, drying my eyes and then going off into gales of laughter again.

'I see! You're ashamed of me then.'

I collapsed on his shoulder. 'Idiot! You know I'm not. I didn't think we were talking that loud, did you?'

'We weren't. She must have wanted to listen.'

'Mind you, when these windows are open . . . '

'When can I see you again?'

'I don't know. I've got a lot of work. I'll let you know.'

But I did think about what he'd said and, in the end, I decided what he'd meant by it. I paid a visit to the Brook Clinic, shrine of family planning, on Gambier Terrace opposite the Old Cathedral. I am ashamed to admit I had to screw up my courage to go in. Supposing they refused? But it was all very official and business-like and the waiting room was crammed with students. I had a long wait although my medical details, blood pressure, wee and weight were attended to fairly quickly. The woman doctor didn't seem at all surprised at my needs. She certainly asked no intimate questions. In due course, my packs of pills were doled out by a sweet, middle-aged lady who would have looked more at home in the WI. Outside, the river glittered in the winter sunshine and a vast recessed arch in the redbrick of the Cathedral seemed to yawn. I heaved a sigh of relief, though I continued to worry and crept away for my bus with something of a nagging conscience. Supposing that hadn't been what Dominic had meant at all? After all, he had been a Catholic once. But now he was more responsible. I didn't think much about my parents, though obviously this secret would have to remain hidden. They were too far away.

Dominic gave me a couple of weeks grace. Then he took me back to his room. It was after another party. All I can remember of that is the glow of companionable faces in the dark and dramatic, drumbeat music. Deep Purple, I think. Jocasta was there but I hardly noticed. I was living and breathing Dominic. He played 'Lay, Lady, lay' on his stereo when we got back and, if you know the song at all, you will realise it is rather appropriate.

There wasn't much doubt that he wanted me anyway and I was not slow to respond. His bedsit was way up in an attic (shades of a daydream though rather more spartan) and we snuggled down together in his narrow bed. The rain was pattering on the roof and streaming in splodges and rivers down the window. It was all around us like a silver, shining curtain. A gentle, watery, tintinnabulation. Inside, the gas-fire made the room warm and glowing red. We weren't in the least bit nervous or inhibited. Well, I suppose I was a bit, but it didn't last long. Dominic didn't appear to be. It all became very exciting. Then we slept in each other's arms and woke later and did it all again. Several times. As you do at the beginning of such a relationship. But the best thing of all was waking up in his arms in the morning, no longer alone but with the one person in all the world I wanted to be with. We shared a cigarette. I cooked his breakfast on the one tiny ring and made the coffee. I would have jumped out of the window if he had asked me to then.

At first, I thought I'd better prepare myself for the idea that it really couldn't last. But it did. Summer came after a late, long drawn-out Spring, just when you've given up hope, like it always does in the North (not that I was concerned that year) and there was no sign, no possibility even of a split. Summer shows the city up for what it really is. The trees collect dust and the buildings look more sordid. Dingy exteriors can't disguise their peeling plaster in the light of the sun and the awful flats, festooned with washing in the concrete jungle, look fire blackened. Everything is rotting.

But we escaped into the feather-green park . . . went rowing on the lake, walked under the trees and lay together on the newly-mown grass. The tower blocks and decaying streets are distanced there. We didn't miss the daffodils and narcissi, the forsythia and rhododendron flowers. Nor the apple-blossom, the lilac or the candles on the horse-chestnut trees. I had better add, in case your mind tends the same way as my mother's, that we worked together quite a bit too. I don't remember ever quarreling . . . and that isn't entirely retrospective idealisation. I suppose you could say it wasn't a real situation. University life is only a microcosm anyway. We were just playing at being lovers. Beth said something of the sort later and I allowed myself to feel afraid it was true. (I shall have to call her Beth from now on for I wish to sever the umbilical cord for good.) Well, it must have been easy to criticise. Even Jocasta occasionally poked fun. She called us 'the great lovers'. Inevitably, in our commitment, we lost other people along the way. Jocasta was one of them for me, although Dominic seemed able to remain friendly.

And we were committed. Not by rings or papers or even what we said or did behind those curtains or in between those sheets. But by the way we actually felt. I missed him so much during that long summer break. Something inside me always quickened whenever I saw him again – even after the trivial absence of a mere day. I came to think of it as my heart 'flipping over'. I yearned to be physically close . . . nothing really to do with sex . . . more of a desire to get under his skin. His company was the only stimulation I needed. In other words, I loved him entirely and thought myself overpowered by this love.

Of course, I cannot really say if it was the same for him. He was probably always more self-sufficient. But he needed me too, in his way . . . though I didn't understand how or why . . . to feel complete. He was often anxious about me. Did he sense, even then, I was not as grown-up as I appeared? Maybe. And I, for my part, was always determined to be so good to him. Dominic would always come first. But then, in the end, I went and betrayed him just the same.

CHAPTER SEVEN

It was the following year when things began to go wrong. By then I had moved out of hall and was ostensibly sharing a flat with Eileen and the others. But, though my name was on the rent book, I was hardly ever there. I lived with Dominic in his new flat. We were still happy together. The trouble was that I had now become a clinical student. The first term wasn't too bad but the second was dreadful. So many things I had never even thought about suddenly hit me with a sledgehammer.

On the day of Dominic's birthday, in the middle of February, I managed to leave the hospital early and do some shopping on the way home. I didn't normally cook for Dominic in the evening – he ate in the Union or the pub and I in the hospital canteen – but today was special. I bought some steaks and a bottle of wine and some expensive, forced spring flowers and rather wished he hadn't been born in the middle of winter. It was an awful day – drab and dark and bitterly cold, with hardly a dawn at all between morning and night. The land of the midnight sun. Except that meant no sun at all. Every now and then, a blacker cloud than the others would darken the sky and there would be a flurry of wet snow which melted as soon as it hit the grimy, wet pavement. It never settled here, unlike home where we often had drifts, for there was too much salt in the air and the wind blew from the west all day. I can only ever remember real snow on the ground once, in my first year when the hall buses were stuck, and even that had been churned to a dirt-stained slush, in the city, within hours.

I climbed to the top deck of the bus and tried to feel more cheerful. But my head ached as I pressed it against the window-pane. It was already almost dark though it wasn't yet four and the street-lamps were on, dissipating their yellow sodium through the gloom. We stopped and started monotonously and the taxis and lorries and cars which overtook, sprayed us with dirty water. Row after row of terraced red-brick houses, some of them three-storied and elegant once, jerked and jolted by in their death throes. We turned down Princes Avenue and the bare, black trees scratched at the windows like pencils. A twisted, tortured metal Christ leapt from the wall of a church with straining innards. I had noticed it many times before and it never failed to affect me, even though I now believed, like Dominic, it was all a myth. Today it reminded me of something I was trying to forget.

I got down at the roundabout by Princes Park and turned into Croxteth Park Road to walk along and down towards Ullet Road. Flatland really, this, right the way over to Sefton and Allerton on one side and Aigburth on the other. There couldn't be many of the shambling Victorian houses which hadn't been ruthlessly divided and quartered for tenants. Some of them had mushrooms under the wallpaper and even the best of them had a damp patch somewhere, inadequate heating, plumbing which clanked and a family of mice. Yet I still regard the whole area with great affection.

I let myself into 'our' gargantuan house of discoloured yellow brick, which fronted the drive that runs round the park, and climbed the communal stairs, having first collected Dominic's post. He was not back yet then. Good. I paused at the shared bathroom where the loo-handle had to be jerked twice, short and sharp with the seat down, and then did a passable impression of the Niagara Falls while the pipes burbled and groaned at the strain of having to fill up again. Then I let myself into

Dominic's bedsit with its tiny kitchen, off-left as they say on the stage. I lit the gas-fire with a match and checked we had enough candles, in case there was a power-cut later, for the miners were on strike. Then I changed into the scarlet sweater dress he especially liked, because I had been wearing it when we first met, and brushed my hair. I was a more natural Jennifer by then, though muted tones of Jocasta's influence were still there. But I had developed my own style. The dress was a hangover.

I laid the small round table with a blue checked cloth and put my costly daffs and anemones in the middle, along with the bottle of wine. If it had been summer, I could have loaded it with white lilac. Still, it looked cheerful enough. We had done our best with the room. The wallpaper was liable to give anyone nightmares, for it was largely a purple mesh of writhing curlicues. Left to ourselves, we would have stripped it instantly to leave white walls (and probably got into a dreadful mess) but of course we couldn't. However, it's amazing what you can overlook when you're happy. I thought that room was wonderful. The furniture was archaic without being in the least bit attractive or worth preserving. But we hardly noticed that either, except for the bed and the table. We had stuck lots of posters up to hide as much wallpaper as possible – Toulouse-Lautrec, French Impressionists, La Belle Epoque – that sort of thing, and the room was full of books and records. The bed was covered with a patchwork quilt, made by Dominic's mother.

I collected up the usual coffee-mugs and ash-trays and went to wash them in the sink in the scullery. You couldn't see out of the tiny window in there because the glass was frosted, but the main room had a bay window which looked out over the park, so green in summer, so deserted now. That, along with the size of the room, had been our main reason for choosing this flat. A shared bathroom was of secondary importance, despite cold nights and mornings. The place was our home and peace normally descended on me as soon as I entered the door. But today was different.

I made a cup of tea and began to peel the potatoes. I had left the landing door slightly ajar for Dominic and the resident ginger tom weaved his way in, tail erect and bristling, cockily expectant of a saucer of milk at the very least. He had followed me upstairs and come to rub affectionately against my legs.

'Hello Victor,' I said. 'How are you? Caught any mice today?' He started to purr and I poured him his milk, then donated the remains of a tin of sardines. No wonder he kept coming to us. He wasn't anybody's cat really. He belonged to the house and was an inveterate scrounger. He made the stairs smell disgusting and laid the odd dead mouse across everyone's doorway, as proof of his usefulness, no doubt. He polished off the sardines in seconds, then proceeded to spruce up his whiskers. I seasoned the steaks, laid them on the grill and went to set the table, then hastily returned to move them to a safer spot. Victor could not be trusted, as I had once found out to my cost.

It was still early for Dominic. I emptied my case on the sagging brown sofa and had a look through that morning's lecture notes. Victor came and had a look too, then sat on them until I moved him. Well, they were reasonably legible for once. I wasn't going to write them out again. The rest of the day had been less successful. I had been on the surgical wards and in theatre. It would have been all right but for Malcolm Smith's laparotomy. I must stop thinking about that. I got up and moved over to the window, just as Dominic's car drew in to the side of the road. Good, he was early! He parked the yellow Beetle by the pavement. He had bought it second-hand last term, with a loan from his father which he was rather ashamed about. Pragmatism had won in the end however, because the benefits were enormous. He got out and my heart flipped over as usual. Then I listened for his step on the stair. One, two, then a bigger gap as he took two at once. Then the door was open and he was there, throwing down his books and his car keys, pulling off his jacket and scarf and startling Victor, who shot through his legs and was gone.

'Hello!' He ran a hand through his blond hair, which immediately flopped straight back over his forehead, and smiled.

'Happy birthday, again.'

'Thanks.'

We kissed and stood together for a moment in the window. I drew myself closer and laid my head on his shoulder. 'Hold me tight.'

He hugged me and he was warm and alive and whole and well.

'Anything up?'

'No . . . no, of course not. I do love you, Dommy.'

'And I love you. So when are you going to let me meet your parents?'

'Oh,' I shoved him away playfully. 'Easter. Definitely Easter.'

'That's what you said at Christmas, if you see what I mean. They ought to know about us. Otherwise it will all come as a great shock.' He was right of course. I had visited his parents several times. (His father was a GP in Southport and an equally charming man. His mother was the arty type. And I loved them both. Dominic had three sisters I hadn't met, but was the only boy.)

'It will anyway! But I will arrange something, I promise. Only don't be so damned candid like you were with yours. You don't have to come straight out with it and tell them we're sleeping together, like you did with them, you know! I nearly died.'

'They took it very well.'

'They didn't really approve.'

'But they know me and they accepted it.'

'Yes . . . well my parents aren't a bit like that. Promise me you won't tell them, Dommy.'

'If you insist.' I threw a cushion at him, which he caught easily. 'Say it then.' He was not to be trusted, like Victor, on certain matters.

'I promise. I say – you're convinced they won't like me, aren't you?'

'No, of course not.'

'Jenny!'

'Well, I'm sure Dad will. It's just my mother.'

'Is it my . . . background?' He pulled a face and struck a pose.

'Hardly. More your reaction against it, actually.'

'I see.' He picked up the record I had given him that morning and slipped it out of its sleeve. He liked to have music on all the time, except when he was working. 'I'm sure she won't be as hostile as you think.' I'm sure she will, I thought desperately. But I didn't want to spoil his day.

'Have you had a nice time?' I asked him.

'Mm. Yes. We went to the pub at lunchtime. Jocasta gave me a present.'

'What is it?'

He eyed me uncertainly. 'It's meant to be a joke.'

'Well, show me then!'

He fished around in his briefcase and eventually produced a pair of tiny lemon bootees.

I laughed. 'She doesn't change.

'No. Actually, she said she was going to give me a rosary as well, just to hammer the point home, but knew that would be unused whereas these . . . '

'Oh yes? I think you'd better open your wine.' I indicated the bottle. 'And don't push the cork through like you usually end up doing. It's slightly better than the usual plonk.'

'I can see that.' He still had to struggle with the corkscrew and I retired into the kitchen, to avoid putting him off. Jocasta's joke was pretty pointed. Dominic believed that marriage was outdated unless you wanted to have children. And he wasn't at all sure whether it was right to bring more of those into the present world. No wonder he never went to church, long before me and the Pill. In those days, I took every word he uttered as gospel although, if I had stopped to think about it, I would have realised his behaviour was entirely at odds with his fine theories. He was touchingly faithful to me, and I to him. We thought it was because we were 'free', but now I wonder. I am sure that, at that moment, we both visualised going on together forever.

At last Dominic came into the kitchen with two full wine glasses.

'Here you are then.'

'Thank you.' I toasted him. 'Happy birthday, Dominic. Why didn't I buy you a better corkscrew? There's cork in it! But I love you anyway.'

But the things I didn't want to think about began to intrude as we ate our meal. In the end, Dominic filled up my glass and said: 'What's wrong?'

'It's nothing really.'

'Would you rather have gone out?'

'No, of course not.'

'But you haven't finished your steak.'

'No, I'm not very hungry.' I looked down at the untouched meat which was too red in the middle, though I normally liked it that way. Thank God it hadn't been liver.

'Please tell me what's wrong, Jenny.'

'It's nothing . . . nothing at all.'

'Look.' Dominic ran a hand through his hair in desperation. 'It really isn't that relevant you know, that twenty years ago my mother happened to give birth. It's only a convention to celebrate the fact. I'd far rather know what's eating you.' To my horror, I found there were tears in my eyes and they were threatening to start out over the lids and course down my cheeks. 'What is it? Is it me? Do you want to finish with me and don't know how to say it? Is that it?'

'How can you think such a thing? God, no! It's nothing

to do with us. It's just . . . my work. Something which happened today. That's all.'

He leant back, relieved and yet still worried. 'This year's hard going for you, isn't it?

'Yes. How did you know?'

'Oh Jenny, I can tell.'

Suddenly, the lights went out and the record on the stereo wowed to a halt. Dominic leapt up to rescue it, but blundered about in the dark.

'Have you got those candles?'

'Yes.' I fumbled too but struck the match.

'It's not supposed to be our area tonight, is it?'

'I don't know. I'm not sure. Perhaps it won't be off long.'

We got the candles lit and knelt down on the rug in front of the gas-fire, with the last of the wine. We were lucky having the fire.

'Tell me about it, anyway.'

'I don't want to spoil your day.'

'You can't do that as long as I know you love me.'

So I told him, in the dark, relieved only by the hiss of the gas and its warm glow and the light from the guttering candles.

'I've been in theatre today . . . and there was this man – Malcolm Smith – I shouldn't really tell you his name, but you'll never meet him. I clerked him yesterday when he came in, he's one of 'my' patients. He was down for a laparotomy – that's an exploratory operation on the abdomen.'

'Yes, I know.' He must have known almost as much as I did, after hours of testing me for vivas and exams.

'Well, he's only about forty. Obviously ill. Yellow all over. Obstructive jaundice. But no pain. Oh, definitely not, doctor. He said it so confidently in the way people do when they don't realise that makes the diagnosis more likely to be sinister. And he'd lost a lot of weight. And you could feel a mass. God knows it was obvious enough he had cancer. But he was so nice. Kept on showing me all the photos of his children. He must have married late because they're still only tiny. They mostly are nice to us – the patients – you know. I mean, they know we're not qualified and they're so anxious to help. I think they open up to us more as well sometimes, because they know we're not exactly official. Anyway, I knew he'd had it. But I thought they'd be able to do something – a bypass maybe – just temporarily, of course.

'Then today I was allowed to scrub for his op and assist. They opened him up and there it was. Carcinoma of the head of the pancreas. Way advanced. Everything stuck down to everything else. Secondaries in the liver. And fluid all over the peritoneal cavity . . . every millilitre of it full of malignant cells, no doubt. So they just sewed him back up again. Without doing a thing.

'I'll have to take his post-op bloods tomorrow. And I know what he'll say: "All right then, was it, doc? I wasn't down long, was I?" And he'll die within months.'

'What's the official line?' asked Dominic, after a pause.

'His wife doesn't want him to know, but I expect they'll have to tell him if he asks. Nobody tells *us* what to say, you know, they just assume we'll pick it up somehow, on the way. It's rather more difficult than sticking needles in though.'

'Perhaps he won't ask. He probably knows already.'

'I'm not so sure. He kept talking about gallstones before the op.'

'You'll just have to follow the lines the others take then.'

'I know. But I can't keep from thinking about him and I know that's wrong. I should be able to put it behind me when I leave the hospital.'

'I daresay yours is a pretty common reaction at first. Quite normal, I would have thought.'

'Do you really think so, Dommy?'

'I do. Haven't you asked any of the others?'

'I told Eileen about this man and she said: "Oh, isn't that awful?" But not with the same conviction, somehow.'

'Why don't you have a word with your tutor?'

'Oh, Dommy, I couldn't!'

'That's what he's there for, surely?' Dear Dommy! He was always so much more mature and sensible than I. 'I don't think you've really any need to worry about it, though. I think you've got to give it time.'

'I'm sorry I've spoilt your birthday meal.'

'Nonsense. It's a relief it was nothing worse.'

Much later on, lying in bed in the dark, comforted by his arms, I said: 'Dommy, I haven't told you the truth.'

'No?'

'There's much more to it than that. Everything I said about Malcolm Smith was true. And there's plenty of others . . . like that girl last term with MS who was only my age. But that's not all. I get upset by cases like that, probably too easily, but I expect I can get over it eventually. They don't go away if you ignore them, after all. But I can't be the one who copes with it all, Dommy, I really can't. Casualty's the worst. Everyone else seems to enjoy it! But I sit there paralysed with fear, wondering what's going to come in next. Half the time it's something trivial anyway. But, when we do get something dramatic like a cardiac arrest or a really bad RTA, I freeze. I panic, Dominic, I really panic! It doesn't matter much now. I'm just meant to watch the others and not get in the way. But what happens when it is my turn? I always assumed that, if you knew at least theoretically, what to do, it'd be all right. But now I know and I still feel the same. I'm so afraid, Dominic. I had to stitch someone's scalp the other day, to stop it bleeding. It was all quite academic and useless because the anaesthetist had already intubated her and you could see her pupils were dilated. She was dead already, really. It was horrible. I can't do that again. And I'm frightened I'll break down.'

There was a long silence.

'I know it's despicable,' I said, in tears, 'but please don't despise me.'

He held me tight and stroked my hair. 'Hell, I don't

despise you, Jenny. I'd be utterly useless in that kind of situation, I can tell you! It's just a matter of personality . . . No, I was just thinking . . . You're a pretty capable person *really* you know.'

'But I'm not. That's what I'm trying to tell you!'

'Perhaps it's just lack of experience. It must come gradually, after all. I'm sure most people feel like that to start off with.'

'Some of the others appear so much more confident.'

'Oh, I don't think that means anything. It's like exams, surely . . . they're always the ones who fail.'

'Dommy, promise me you won't go on telling me things you think I want to hear, if you come to feel they're not true!'

'Of course I wouldn't. That would be cruel.'

'Then do you really think I should carry on?'

'Yes, I do. Until you're farther into the course. You might feel entirely different about it then. Learn to suppress your panic.'

'But, if I wanted to change course, it would be so much easier to do it now.'

'You could still do it later. You'd be a bit older, that's all. It wouldn't matter.'

'Wouldn't it?'

'No, of course not.'

'What will you do next year, Dommy?' (For it was his final year.)

'Well, providing I don't cock the exams up altogether, I'd like to stay on. Become an academic, I suppose.'

'I thought you wanted to write?'

'Well, I do. But it's too soon. I'll have to earn some money anyway. And I'd rather lecture than teach, I think, in the end. Seeing as it's home truths night, I don't mind telling you I don't want to leave the university cloisters for the real world just yet, thanks.'

'I can't see you as a don!'

'Well, no.' He yawned and I buried my head in his neck, breathing in his being. 'Maybe not. I expect I'll be more anxious to move on when you've finished too.'

'Dominic, that's wrong!'

'What is?'

'To let me influence you, like that!'

'Oh, rubbish! It isn't just that anyway. And I've got plenty of time. So have you, though you don't appear to think so.'

My fingers traced the line of his jaw, then slid down over his Adam's apple to the root of his throat.

'I'm glad you're not going. I should miss the Arts lot.' It was true, but I wished I hadn't put it quite like that. Lumping them all together. It sounded so casual and offhand. As if Dominic was just another one of them. He had stated his loyalties openly enough and I could have done the same, but now the moment had gone and I could only kiss him and hope he knew what I meant. Perhaps I had become slightly scared. He did scare me sometimes, with his simplistic candour and his assumption that that was the way things should be.

'What happened to Malcolm Smith?' he asked, several days later. 'Did he go home?'

'No, he dropped dead with a pulmonary embolus post-op.'

'Oh! Bit sudden, wasn't it? I thought you said months.'

'He was unlucky, or lucky, depending on how you look at it. It's a complication of surgery, especially in a debilitated patient.'

'I see.'

'His wife was distraught. She said we should never have opened him up. Just left him to die quietly at home.'

'But he might have had something more curable?'

'Well . . . just possibly, I suppose. It wasn't really likely. But you can see her point of view, can't you? I'm glad I wasn't the one who had to tell her. I couldn't have coped with that.'

'Well, no . . . not yet.'

CHAPTER EIGHT

I took Dominic home at Easter, after a carefully-worded letter to my parents in which I judiciously avoided the use of the word 'boyfriend'. It was not a great success. My mother was pleased enough to learn his father was a GP. But she didn't like the fact that the family were Roman Catholic, despite my protestations of his lapsed state. However, the real hurdle was Dominic himself, as I had known all along it would be. She did not approve of his jeans, his boots, his bomber jacket and the length of his hair. Well, that was only to be expected. But it went deeper than that. I could see that she resented his confidence and apparent maturity and she was stung to suspicion by his physical beauty. The charm was uselss on Beth. We spent a rather tedious weekend under the same roof and I am ashamed to say that I did not dare show him any of my usual affection, in case Beth noticed. My father was his normal, jovial self and friendly enough, though understandably stymied on hearing some of Dominic's views. But, on the last day, I felt I had to apologise to Dominic. His own parents had been so welcoming in contrast. They had not, of course, put us in the same room – despite the revelation – and I could see his mother was upset because he wouldn't go to Mass – but they had still been sweet to me.

'I'm sorry, Dominic,' I said miserably. 'I knew it would be like this. That's why I haven't asked you before.'

'Oh, don't worry!' he said with a smile, completely unabashed. 'It's early days. They have to get used to me first.' And he insisted on kissing me boldly, in full view of the bay windows of 'Lorelei'. 'Roll on the new term!' Then he got into the yellow Beetle, waved cheerily and drove away.

I waved too, feeling unutterably lost and lonely. (Why hadn't I told them I loved him to distraction?) I wished I was going back to Southport with him. But he was calling in to see one of the masters at his old school first and I had no part in that earlier life of cold, echoing halls and corridors where boys in black blazers trooped forever up and down and Jesuit fathers kept the sacred flame burning before the tabernacle in the chapel. After that, he was going to see Giles at his theological college and I would be even more at sea there.

Beth eyed me with suspicion when I re-entered the house. 'Well dear,' she said. 'He's a charming friend.'

'I thought you didn't like him.'

'Oh yes, he's a very nice boy really, though he should get his hair cut and wear some decent clothes. You wouldn't think a doctor's son would go about looking like that.'

'Actually, his father looks as if he's put the first thing on he came to when he opened the drawer in the morning,' I said, rather rudely. 'His socks don't even match each other, never mind his tie and shirt. But he's a dear, kind man and he was lovely to me. I do think you could have been more welcoming to Dominic.'

Beth's mouth had dropped open, but she shut it with a snap. 'Well, really darling, he's had our hospitality for the best part of three days! Practically eaten us out of house and home as well!'

'That's not the same thing at all.'

She went on, determinedly: 'I can see you're rather smitten by him.' I coloured at this. 'You know you really can't afford to get serious about anyone at this stage in your career. Are you serious?'

'No, he's just a friend.'

'He doesn't seem to have any prospects, either.'

'What do you mean?'

'Well, I'm sure his father must have been terribly disappointed he didn't take up medicine. What's a boy like that doing messing about with English?'

'Dominic's very talented. He's highly likely to get a First.'

'But what's he going to do with it?'

It was the same old chestnut. Beth couldn't see the point. As far as she was concerned, the entire artistic world was useless. I didn't dare tell her Dominic wanted to write. Nor voice my own secret fears.

'Ah, well!' Beth shrugged. But the matter wasn't quite finished. A few days later, she happened to be 'tidying my drawers' when the inevitable happened. She found my current packet of pills.

'Jennifer Sugden! I want a word with you.'

With a sinking heart, I climbed the stairs. 'Yes?'

'Not serious, eh?' She waved the pack at me furiously. 'Not serious! I knew straightaway he was that sort of boy! Well, in my day, this would have meant it was very serious.' She plunged on, without even drawing breath. 'Of course I realise it's all very different now. No doubt your father and I are old-fashioned fogies who don't understand? I suppose you keep these handy because you never know when it might happen or who with?'

'That's a horrid thing to say!' I was stung to retort. 'I've never been with anyone but Dominic. I love him very much. We've done nothing wrong.'

Beth put her hands to her head and wailed: 'Oh, Jennifer! How could you put your career at risk?'

'What on earth's going on?' Ken had appeared in the doorway and Beth threw the pills at his feet. I had never seen her so angry.

'Just look what your daughter's brought home and hidden away. After all we've done!'

All the clichés were coming out. But it wasn't even remotely funny and I felt a good deal less sure of myself than I sounded. If only Dominic had been there! As it was, I could only manage: 'You shouldn't have been looking in my drawers!' with considerable bitterness, as if that solved the whole problem.

'Now, Jennifer,' said Ken, sternly. 'Don't talk to your mother like that.' He had gone rather pale too for he had only, just that moment, realised his little girl was a woman.

The ensuing fracas went on for hours. In vain did I attempt to point out that my actions had been responsible and designed specifically *not* to affect my career. Paradoxically, that seemed to make matter worse. I was forbidden ever to see Dominic again. Beth wanted to ring up his parents but Ken managed to divert her from that, thank heavens. I was threatened with all manner of privation and punishment. The pills went in the wastebin and then were hastily retrieved some time later, when Beth realised there might be an outside chance of pregnancy if I didn't complete the course. Somewhere amongst it all, my brother Peter sloped in and out again, making shocked noises and grinning all the way down the other side of his face. I remembered thinking his girlfriend had probably been on the Pill for years. But he didn't have to hide them round the house. They wouldn't have been so shocked over him anyway. It was all so unfair. I cursed myself for forgetting to claim the pills were a treatment for painful periods. Not that Beth would ever have believed me.

Gradually the storm settled, although it showed disturbing signs of resurrection for days afterwards. I returned to university in disgrace, with a promise I had no intention of keeping and long faces all round. There had been no chance to talk about medicine and my growing anxieties at all.

Dominic was characteristically unalarmed. In fact, he was pleased the secret was out. 'Oh, they just need time to get used to the idea,' he said, airily.

'But, Dommy, they are not like your parents,' I insisted.

Then he said something I found amazing: 'Well, of course they are. They're people, aren't they? What you should be wondering is why your mother reacted in that manner. Try to understand her.

'Understand her? Well, that's easy enough. She's afraid I'll get pregnant and give up medicine.'

'But you won't if you're on the Pill.'

'Oh, she still thinks there's a possibility. I might forget to take it or something.'

Dominic shook his head. 'Not good enough. No, it's me she sees as the threat. She doesn't want you involved in any kind of loving relationship. I wonder why?'

'Well, it comes down to the same thing, doesn't it? She's still afraid I'll give up medicine because of you.'

'But why should you? Why is it so important? There's something more there than the simple desire for a daughter to do well . . .' Then Dominic shrugged and spread his hands. 'Well, is it a loving relationship or not, after all that? I haven't seen you for weeks.'

I reached over and put my arms round his neck, pulling his hair gently. 'Of course it is. I've missed you so much. It's been really hard, Dominic, especially with all the fuss. It's getting worse every time.'

'Well, I've missed you too. Are you going to stay with me then?'

'Of course I am, silly. I want to go to bed right now. And I love you so much.'

But I found I had to be more careful to keep the peace. Beth took to ringing Eileen in the flat, at all sorts of odd hours, obviously checking on my whereabouts. Although the girls did their best, it meant I had to be there some of the time. We were no longer so free. Occasionally Dominic stayed there with me but he didn't fit in and we neither of us liked it very much. So inevitably we spent more nights apart. I think he must have been very disappointed at my weakness, though he was careful not to show it and pretended to accept my excuse of 'not wanting to hurt my parents'. His finals were fast approaching, anyway. So it seemed more sensible all round. And Eileen was glad to see me at least partially back in the fold.

Dominic got his First (and Jocasta an Upper Second) so we celebrated in fine style. I can remember feeling pretty envious of them both. So thrilled for Dominic though. And I had managed fairly creditable marks in my end-of-year exams. They were never really a problem. If I just kept on going and stuck to it, I would be there at the end. So I deceived myself. Even Beth was somewhat mollified. But the long, summer break was a problem. I could no longer invite Dominic to 'Lorelei' and I couldn't visit him in Southport either, without my parents knowing. In the end, we met up in Cornwall for a month. I was supposed to be going camping with Eileen and Pauline. Shabby, I know. And Dominic hated it, though he tried not to mind. But it was worth it.

The thought of that holiday gives me a lump in my throat even now. It rained a lot and we got awfully wet. We spent most of our time in sweaters because it was unseasonably cool. Then the car kept breaking down and Dominic didn't have a clue what to do with it. I dropped my camera and broke the lens and Dominic left his wallet on the beach. Then we both ended up with filthy colds and, while Dominic couldn't stop sneezing, I coughed and spluttered all night long. We should have been yelling and screaming at each other. But we didn't. We managed to remain in love and it wasn't even an effort. There were sunnier days too, somewhere amongst all that rain. Walks along the shore and memorable sunsets down by the creek. I can remember a pale salmon sky, with blue-grey cloud banked high above it, fading each moment to a pallid white while the leaves and boughs of the trees which stirred all around us, turned black. Then the limpid light changed into a subtle violet and the sea from grey into night. I can remember watching all that with Dominic – and much more – and wishing we could stay forever. He was all mine there and I his. We made love a lot. If only we could have stayed like that. But it wasn't Dominic's fault that we didn't, because he had grown to love me more. He had also begun to worry about me, for I had suddenly become very determined to cover everything up and to display no sign of strain.

The crisis came the following winter. In the meantime, my gut feelings about medicine had not improved . . . in fact, they were considerably worse. There seemed to be a new hurdle to face every day. No one knew about it except Dominic. I had even tried to close up on him a bit because he kept urging me to see my tutor and I couldn't bear the thought of that. Instead of coming clean, I lost weight and became increasingly irritable. Then everything came to a head when I was doing Obstetrics.

I was living in, parted from Dominic, at one of the city's maternity hospitals. We had to carry out twenty normal deliveries, under the watchful eye of a midwife, and write them up as cases. At first, it was light relief. Everyone enjoyed it. It was what they called 'a slice of the happiness cake'. Like a breath of fresh air after the terminals and the geriatrics and psyche patients. Nothing beats the wonder of a successful birth. And I was learning to stitch competently at last. I was doing something worthwhile.

When it came, it came out of the blue. One of the babies I had delivered died on me. Not straight away but within a few hours. What made it worse was that it was such a precious baby. Of course, all babies are precious. But this mum had been infertile for years. She had no other children and she was getting old. It was a wonder she had got pregnant at all. I saw the child deteriorate and die for no apparent reason. We couldn't save it. The paediatrician thought it might be an intracranial haemorrhage from a tear in the brain tissue. That was something which could happen during a precipitate delivery. It could also happen during a normal delivery. But the element of doubt remained. Of course, there would be a post mortem.

I went to pieces. I couldn't stay in the hospital a moment longer and ran to Dominic. I searched through all my textbooks for everything I could find on intracranial haemorrhage and every other cause of peri-natal death. I was convinced it was my fault. In the end, I made poor Dominic almost as distraught as I was. I can remember him shaking me by the shoulders. 'Jenny, Jenny! Please don't torture yourself like this! It couldn't have been your fault. You did nothing wrong. You've got to believe it. Please don't!'

I went back because I had to. But my confidence had gone. Always a fragile, uncertain thread, it had now snapped forever. The post mortem confirmed an intracranial haemorrhage, though it laid no blame on anyone. In my mind, the doubt remained. I managed to get through the rest of the Obsterics course somehow, but the magic had gone. I was always afraid now when I was called onto the labour ward. And we had four grossly abnormal foetuses delivered in the next few weeks. Everything had gone wrong.

I tried to find a way to combat my fear. But the more I thought about it, the clearer and more harrowing the future became. All those decisions. The ever-present possibility of being wrong. The endless repercussions of every action I might take. The constant onus to perform well. The eternal coping with disease and accident and death. Of course there would be rewards. I had to remember that. Joys and satisfactions too, no doubt. And it was worthwhile, despite all the frustrations. Probably the best thing in life I could do. But it would always be jumbled up together. You had to swallow the lot. And I couldn't go on. I couldn't do it. It had all been the most dreadful mistake. A terrible delusion.

My living-in period ended and I returned to Dominic. I

slept with him every night now, regardless of the consequences. Not that those particular nights were anything but entirely innocent. He just sat and held me when I couldn't sleep and listened to the outpourings.

'You can't go on like this,' he said. 'You'll make yourself ill.'

He drove me up to Southport to see his father, one grey and windy afternoon. The rain was coming down in sheets over the distant sea and the sand-dunes. But Dr Grant was nevertheless out playing golf, though it was difficult to see how. His wife made us tea in the draughty, warm and friendly house and did her best to make me feel calmer. Then the doctor returned and Mrs Grant and Dominic left us alone together in his study.

I think I was very afraid of what he would say, but he seemed to understand and was extremely concerned about me. In the end he said what everyone said at some stage: that everyone feels like that occasionally. But I think I did convince him that this was more than that: that the horror was permanent and would not go away. He was genuinely upset. Saddened in quite a different way from Dominic and his mother. They only worried about me.

But I was glad I'd seen him. He persuaded me at last to go to my tutor and that was my next interview, which ran on similar lines. There was the added angle that the medical school was extremely loath to lose me at this late stage. Apparently, I had never given any cause for concern before and they prided themselves, I think, on knowing their students pretty well. But yes, if I was really sure, a transfer to the microbiology course could easily be arranged. Of course it was better to find out now. Though they would be equally willing to give me more time. Their desire to help was almost embarrassing.

But I had made up my mind. I had even told all my friends. They were all shocked and sad. A little shaken too, to think that one of their number should not only consider leaving, but actually do it. Pauline Parker even cried. Bonnie and Ruth were flabbergasted, the others rather embarrassed. I could see them all in ten years time, at some reunion, saying: 'Do you remember that girl who dropped out in fifth year?' 'Oh yes, Jennifer Sugden, she was a queer one . . . I wonder what happened to her?' Only Eileen was perhaps less than surprised. She had always suspected me of belonging to another world.

It was all decided. But I couldn't yet feel the relief I longed for, for I still had to tell my parents and it was really only that which had held me back so long. Unwisely, I begged Dominic to go with me.

'Please, please, Dommy. I can't face them alone.'

'I'm not sure it's such a good idea.'

'But I need you there.'

He could see that I did. I was mentally and physically exhausted. So together we set off in silence, in his patched-up, yellow car over the Pennines on that most dreadful of days.

CHAPTER NINE

The weather was fine as if to mock us, for it was one of those days in mid-March which stand out sharply against the generally drab backdrop of winter and let you know that spring is coming. Cohorts of orange conifers stood in close ranks against the wind but the hills were mainly bare, the valleys knee-deep in bracken. The grasses bent and shivered in the breeze and the bare trees held out twisted arms like beggars. But the sunlight made the patterns of green and grey and purple scrub look splendid and we sweltered behind the glass of the snub-nosed, yellow car. Dominic was very uneasy, I know. We had not told my parents of our intended visit because I could not face the telephone call. It would only be the second time he had met them and he had hardly begun on a good footing. But he did his best to cheer me up.

'Don't worry,' he said, laying a hand on my arm. 'You'll feel better when it's all out in the open. Making the decision was the worst part. It'll soon be over.'

'Thank you for coming, Dommy. I know you didn't want to.'

'Oh, I don't know. You were probably right. You could do with some moral support.'

'Lorelei's' pebbledash was bathed in the sun as we drove up through the cypresses. Its leaded casements blinked at us under the red-gabled roof but remained tight shut. My mother's new bronze Capri stood in the driveway. Beth herself was in the garden, gathering evergreen leaves for some flower arrangement. She wore gloves and carried secators like a surgeon and a neat little wicker basket hung draped over her arm. She had several moments to compose herself while we were getting out of the car and she was perfectly controlled when she came up.

'Jennifer, what a nice surprise! You should have told us, though. I could have got your room ready.' Dominic was icily ignored.

'It's just a short visit,' I mumbled.

'What a shame! I was feeling so bored too, with your father away.'

'Daddy's not here?' I darted a nervous glance toward Dominic.

'No, he's away on business. I'm expecting him back tomorrow. Come in and have some tea.'

She led the way and we sat down awkwardly in the green lounge while she made it. She looked marvellous as usual, in a cream sweater and camel skirt with an amber necklace round her throat and spotless, camel-coloured boots. Her hair and her face were both carefully 'done'. I am sure we looked out of place in her lounge. I noticed everything about it, as if I were seeing it for the first time, instead of having grown up there. It was more of a museum than a room. All in excellent taste. But perhaps there was a little too much of everything after all: too many Lladro figures, too many exquisite lamps and elegant useless tables. The carpet and the suite shouted money. So did the wallpaper and the curtains. The cherubs on the extremely well-stocked cocktail cabinet pranced around inanely. I think we both could have done with a drink, but we sipped our China tea from china cups in meek silence. Or at least I did. Dominic managed to knock his all down the sofa, which scarcely helped. Beth was perfectly prepared to be decent and sweet about it, in her automatically brittle manner, until she realised he was not quite so embarrassed as he should have been, despite the profuse apologies. Dominic was always the master of any social situation because he had long ago decided such trivia didn't really matter. I sat and crunched my shortbread biscuit in agonised silence. It seemed to turn to putty in my mouth and I thought I would never get rid of it.

'Another biscuit, Jennifer?' Beth enquired, after the mopping up operation.

'Oh no, thank you . . . I'm not really hungry.'

'We've actually come to tell you something,' Dominic said, sensing I needed a push. 'Something very important.'

Beth put down her plate carefully and wiped her hands on her napkin. She looked at us and smiled a rather pettish smile.

'I can see that. And I know what it is. The answer, of course, is no. It's out of the question.'

'But you can't possibly know what we're going to say!' I broke in.

Beth held up her hand, condescendingly. 'I wasn't born yesterday. I realise I haven't had your education, Jennifer, but I can put two and two together. It's perfectly obvious why you've come to see us. No doubt this young man is disappointed your father's not here. But it makes no difference because the answer would still be no.'

A horrible light began to dawn on us both and Dominic stirred restlessly in his seat.

'Mummy, please listen . . . '

'I can see that you have disobeyed me, Jennifer, and that the two of you are still carrying on. All right, I admit defeat though I must say I am extremely disappointed in your behaviour. But I realise times have changed since I was a girl. I'm prepared, seeing as you force me, to overlook it. What else can I do? But, if you're going to even start contemplating marriage, the answer is that it's ridiculous. You're far too young, you haven't finished your training and I very much doubt,' her eye swept Dominic deprecatingly from top to toe . . . I noticed for the first time he had a hole in his sock and mentally cursed him, so over-strung was my mind . . . 'if this young man,' she refused to mention his name, 'can keep you as you ought to be kept.'

'Mother!' I almost screamed at her to stop and she looked at me then, in some surprise. 'Please listen! It's nothing to do with that! Dominic doesn't even believe in marriage anyway.' Of course it was a stupid thing to say. Beth regarded him even more coldly.

'I see,' she said. 'One of those. Wants his shirts ironed and his meals cooked without the bother of a ring! Well, really Jennifer, I thought you had more sense.' She laughed hollowly. 'Women's Lib! You may have the Pill, but you're just an anxious as your grandmother was to serve.' I was too worked up to pay much attention to this comment. Instead, I retorted, 'You're being unfair.'

But, at this point, Dominic obviously felt things had gone far enough. He put down his cup, ran a hand through his fair mop and prepared to pontificate. I knew the denouement was about to follow and shrank back in my chair. I hated myself, I hated my mother, I even hated Dominic a tiny bit for being so sensible and open and obviously in command. Not that he had ever criticised me. He had tried his hardest to make me see I did not personally stink just because I wasn't suited to medicine and had made a mistake. Unfortunately, he hadn't succeeded.

'Mrs Sugden,' he said. 'This is all highly irrelevant. Your daughter and I do have a serious relationship. But this isn't the time or place to discuss it.'

'Then why are you here?' Beth's voice was higher and harder now. She was not going to be intimidated.

'Purely because Jenny wanted me to be. She's been under considerable strain recently.'

'Strain? What sort of strain?'

I thought Dominic was going to continue with his assessment of events, and indeed rather hoped he would, but no. 'Tell her, Jenny,' he said, gently.

'Mummy, I've decided to give up medicine.'

There was a charged silence.

'Have you taken leave of your senses?'

'I have to. I can't cope with it anymore.'

'But your exam results have been fine!'

'Yes, I know . . . it's not that. It's the actual work involved on the wards – the day to day reality of it. You don't understand. One day, I'll have to take actions and make decisions I really don't feel capable of making. It's just not me and the sooner I admit that and give it up the better. I'd like to change course to something emotionally less demanding.'

Beth stared at me for a long time. Then she said briskly: 'You're overtired, that's all. You must stay the night and we'll talk about it tomorrow, when your father gets back.'

'Mummy, I've seen my tutor several times and it's all arranged.'

'What's all arranged?'

'I can transfer to Microbiology next term if I want to.'

Beth got up and paced about the room, distractedly. She was beginning to show the first signs of fraying round the edges.

'Oh no,' she said, bitterly. 'Oh no, you don't!'

'Mrs Sugden,' Dominic tried again, 'you must realise this decision hasn't been taken lightly. Jenny's felt this way for a long time and kept it to herself. She's almost made herself ill worrying about it.' Beth told him quite rudely to shut up. He didn't. 'She's shown a great deal of courage in facing up to the problem and making this decision.'

Now Beth ignored him completely. 'What did your tutor say, Jennifer?'

'He said they would be sorry to see me go, but in the end, if I wasn't happy, that was what mattered. He suggested I wait a while longer but, you see, I've felt like this ever since starting clinical work. I can't really imagine why I ever thought I could do it. I should have stuck to painting. That's what I did best.'

'You must at least finish the course.'

'Mummy, I can't.'

We faced each other and neither of us was able to yield.

'Jenny feels the situation is best resolved now,' added Dominic. Beth rounded on him, all of a sudden. 'You, of course, would approve, wouldn't you? You have a vested interest!'

'Mummy, that's unforgivable!' I was shouting again. If only my father had been there! What a fool I had been not to ring first.

'Well, you obviously do support her, don't you? Agree with her, egg her on?' Dominic sighed and uncrossed his legs. 'Well?' Beth carried on, maliciously. 'Let's hear what you have to say, seeing as you were so bloody anxious to come!' Her veneer of drawing-room culture was slipping and her Yorkshire accent sounded stronger as her words became blunter. 'Do you think she's right?'

'I think she would make a terrific doctor,' said Dominic. I glanced at him in surprise. 'But I don't think she'd do herself much good. She's too sensitive, too hard on herself. She'd worry herself into the ground- . . . maybe even take the wrong decisions because of it. It's an unfair burden to lay on her.' He looked at me sadly (I think even then he may have realised he had lost) and took hold of my hand before he continued: 'And, seeing as yes, I do love her – very much – and want to look after her, I wouldn't be willing to take the risk of pushing her on somewhere she doesn't want to go. Not into a profession where the incidence of alcoholism and suicide is so high.'

His speech had a phenomenal effect. I was touched and the tears rolled down my cheeks. Beth went mortally pale but remained silent which lent me extra courage.

'I've made my decision, mummy. I can't go back. I know I've let you and Daddy down and school and the faculty and everyone who's ever helped me. But I just can't do it.'

Beth came and sat down, as if she had accepted it all. But she hadn't finished yet. Not by a long way. She stared hard at Dominic with intense hostility and, though he didn't drop his eyes once, he must have felt uneasy again.

'All right, Jennifer,' she said quietly. 'If that's your final word, then so be it. Though you'll surely concede that Daddy and I will want to speak to your tutor. You're obviously overwrought and you'd better stay with us for a while till you recover and regain your health. But there'll be no Microbiology course or anything else. If you leave the university, you leave for good. I don't see why Daddy and I should continue to pay for your further education under these circumstances.'

We couldn't believe it. Dominic cried out, 'That's monstrous!'

Beth turned back to him, coolly. 'I would suggest it's none of your business, young man,' she said, turning the knife. He leapt to his feet.

'You still don't understand, do you? You don't know her one little bit. She isn't out of the woods yet. She's going to feel wretched and guilty and blame herself for everything when she's only been misguided. She's going to need help and encouragement and something equally worthwhile to do so that she can regain her self-respect. If you make her leave the university altogether, she'll never recover!'

'I don't think we really need you any more,' Beth said. It was a fight between the two of them now and she had temporarily forgotten my very existence. 'Thank you very much for bringing my daughter home. It was good of you and I shall see you're reimbursed for the petrol as I expect you need the money. But we can look after Jennifer now. There's no place for you under this roof and I'd be glad if you'd kindly leave.'

It was horrible. I knew Dominic had never been so insulted in his life. His face showed shock, though he did his best to control it. But, in a way, I felt relieved that at least he now knew what I was up against.

'Jenny,' he said, struggling to keep the agitation out of his voice, 'I really don't think you ought to stay here tonight. I think you should come back to Liverpool with me.'

But Beth was a viper now. She was determined to part us. I did not understand why then, but now I think – yes, I am sure – that she felt his attraction, physical and mental, just as I did. She could see why I got into bed with him. She would even have liked to do it herself. She wasn't totally impervious to the charm . . . even if he did spill tea down her best settee and wear socks with holes in them. But he was anathema to her. He was a piece of living heresy. She saw my willingness to subjugate myself to him only too clearly. Saw it and understood why. But she could not accept that such a love would be equally returned, nor that I could ever be happy in loving him. It was against her creed and she wanted to save me from what she viewed as a grave danger. Because of this, she had to make him the scapegoat for her immense disappointment in me. She had to do him down and her only means of attack was through me. She may not have known me as well as Dominic did, but she was still my mother and knew best how to apply the pressure.

'Jennifer, if you leave home now with this man, I can promise you that neither of you will come to this house again. Ever! And I mean it.'

Of course, in a novel, I would have got up and gone and doubtless you will further despise me for not doing so. But, in real life, one rarely takes such dramatic action. I was utterly exhausted. Outside, it was getting dark. Not that that really made any difference, but in a way it was symbolic. Of course I wanted to go with Dominic. But, faced with that ultimatum, it hardly seemed prudent to do that there and then. I looked at him desperately, hoping he would understand. He must have done because he came right over to kiss me on the cheek and squeeze my hands.

'I'll go now then, Jenny. You certainly need some rest. But I'll telephone as soon as I get back. Will you be all right?'

I nodded. 'Yes. And thanks, Dommy! Thank you for coming. I'll see you soon.'

He stood back and inclined his head stiffly towards Beth. 'Mrs Sugden. Goodnight.' And then he was gone. He left his lighter on the coffee-table and I put it in my pocket later, stroking it distractedly with my fingers, turning it over and over with his image still in my mind. We heard the car start and then saw the beam of his headlights cut across the steep drive, sweep down into the road and reflect once, right across the whole room, before they too were gone. I felt terrible, as if he had deserted me, instead of the other way round.

As soon as he had left, Beth changed her approach. She sprang up to draw the curtains at once, insisted on pouring me a large brandy, and said, 'You poor lamb! What a time you've had,' and burst into violent tears. I hadn't the slightest idea why she was crying but joined in. Then she packed me off to bed with two of her sleeping pills and tucked me up with reassurances that of course I wouldn't have to go back if I really didn't want to. Not surprisingly, I slept. I didn't hear the telephone when Dominic rang nor Beth's cool reply, although she told me he had rung to ask how I was, the following morning.

My father arrived back at lunchtime, all unsuspecting into the middle of the crisis, and the whole argument started again. It seemed to go on for days, never really getting anywhere. Sometimes it would appear to reach a conclusion and everything seemed to be sorted out. Then, within half an hour, it had broken out all over again. Gradually, one fact emerged. I was not going back into medicine. But I had counted on my father to support my change of course. Now, to my horror, he actually agreed with Beth and said I shouldn't go back at all. Of course, Beth had presented very credible reasons. I had

had a minor nervous breakdown (she said) due to overwork. What was the good of exchanging one set of textbooks for another? What I needed was a complete break from academic life.

Ken saw me looking wan and underweight and strained. In his anxiety and love for me, he made the wrong decision. A holiday abroad would do me good for starters (he said). Then a spell at home. Then we could think again. In vain I protested that, if I did that, my chance of a degree was gone forever. I had shot my bolt. He had always feared I had been pushed too hard, he said (frowning meaningfully at Beth). I had all the time in the world. A complete reassessment was necessary. For my own good, he would not be willing to make up the minimum grant (which was a pittance) in the event of a change in course. I threatened to use my grandmother's money. But that was no good either. Beth was the trustee until I was twenty-five. She would block it until it was too late.

And, all this time, Dominic did not ring. When I woke and reached out for him in the night, the bed was empty. I felt so desolate. Why had he left me alone?

But, within days, his letter arrived. My mother handed it to me at the breakfast table with pursed lips. The envelope had been slit open.

'Have you read this?' I couldn't believe it, for it was clearly marked with my name – in Dominic's handwriting – and postmarked Liverpool. Ken had already left for work and I was alone with my mother.

'Of course I have.'

I coloured angrily. 'You've no right to open my personal mail.'

'I did it in your best interests. I knew, of course, it was from him. And I'm glad I read it, for it contains schemes I should be aware of and, I'm sorry to say, Jennifer, I couldn't rely on you to tell the truth.' She made it sound as if I was the one in the wrong. I pushed back my chair and got up from the table.

'Where are you going?'

'I'd rather read it for myself – alone – than have you tell me about it, if you don't mind.'

'But you haven't had your breakfast.'

'I don't want any.'

I went upstairs and locked myself into my bedroom, before taking out the letter with trembling hands. There were three sides of his scrawling hand:

Jenny, darling,

I have 'phoned repeatedly but your mother will not let me speak to you. I only hope you are allowed to receive this letter. I am so worried about you and now I feel I really shouldn't have left you alone that night. I was afraid this sort of thing would happen.

You may be sure that I was thinking about you all the way back. In the end, I decided to go home too for it is now obvious to me – beyond all shadow of a doubt – that you and I should get married as soon as possible! Naturally, I wanted to discuss it with my own parents, in view of their continuing financial support. I have to tell you that my father wasn't too keen on the idea. Nothing to do with you as a person . . .(and my mother, of course, was over the moon to think I would no longer be 'living in sin', though equally disappointed when I told her it would be a registry office wedding – which I am afraid does not 'count' in her eyes, nor those of the Catholic church) . . . but he feels I am going to be pressurising you at a difficult time, which could be disastrous. I suppose that's true. But hell, Jenny, I KNOW this is right and I just have to believe you will feel that too. I told my parents how I feel and of course they will not stand in our way.

If your mother intends to stick to her threat of not paying for you to go on with another subject and turns you out of house and home if you do (and, you know, I really think that she will – what a screwed-up woman she is! One ought to feel sorry for her really, but I am finding it very difficult at the moment) then it is clear you cannot return to the university at all. The only way to get round it would be to marry me at once. Then her power over you would be gone. As my dependant, you would be entitled to a full grant anyway. Now, please read on to the next paragraph awfully quickly!

OF COURSE THIS IS NOT PRIMARILY WHY I WANT TO MARRY YOU. It is only why I want to marry you NOW. I am not being noble or charitable. I merely want to preserve the status quo, with the one exception that you are on the Microbiology course. Getting married, I grant you, is not exactly doing that. But you can forget all that crap about not believing in it. I don't want to lose you, Jenny – I don't ever want to lose you – and so it strikes me that I must want to marry you, whatever I've said in the past. I only hope you will want to marry me too.

I really feel you should come back to Liverpool straightaway . . . after all, you can still stay with Eileen and co. though, natch, I hope you will come to me. I don't trust your family set-up one little bit – I am afraid they will take you away, do something to you, if you let them. Don't listen! Please come and discuss it with me first.

I am fully aware – as you will be too – that, in marrying me, you will be cutting yourself off from your family entirely . . . perhaps for good, though I doubt that myself. I know that's asking a hell of a lot. And that it's going to take courage. Only you can decide. If I could make it any easier, I would. But that doesn't seem to be possible right now. Please say yes, Jenny! At least think about it. I love you very much. Dommy.

Nobody else used the rather childish diminutive. To the world at large, he was Dominic or Nic. I'm sure he never thought of himself by that name. In signing it for me, he was making his strongest appeal, his most confident claim upon my heart.

I read the letter over slowly three times and cried quite a bit. Beth had certainly got more than she bargained for when she had opened it. Everyone's cards were on the table now. Except mine. I know it was crazy, but I had no real idea what I would do.

After a while, I got dressed and went downstairs.

CHAPTER TEN

My mother was sitting in the sun-lounge. For the first time ever, I noticed she was beginning to look old. She wasn't even as smartly dressed as usual. Her shoulders were slightly hunched over the morning newspaper, although she wasn't really reading it.

'There's coffee still in the pot,' she said, indicating the percolator. 'Help yourself while it's still hot.' I poured it out and sat down. She had obviously taken the letter pretty hard.

'Well,' she said, 'when are you going to see him?'

'I don't know.'

'Oh, really? I thought your case would be packed by now! Pour me another cup too, would you?' She took out her cigarette-case and offered me one. The action was unprecedented. In a daze, I took one and let her light it for me.

'Somebody had to be pinching them when you were home,' she said. 'I'm not daft, you know.'

I blushed and bent my head. 'I'm sorry. Of course I should have asked.'

'Well, have you decided what to do?'

'Not really. But I must go and see him. Tomorrow, if possible.'

She did not protest. In fact she said, 'Yes, I should do that. It was an urgent sort of letter.'

Her casual manner disturbed me. But then she put down the newspaper and said: 'There's something I haven't told you, Jennifer.' My heart sank even before I knew what it was. 'It's about your father. He's had some pains in his chest recently and the doctor thinks it angina. He's supposed to lose weight but of course he can't. Take things easier at work, too, but of course he won't do that either.' She paused and sipped her coffee. The truth was that the business led a precarious existence these days. Ken and Beth lived from month to month. Everything had to be done on the side and my father dared not retire. 'Your giving up medicine has upset him dreadfully. He thinks it's made you ill and we're to blame. Now, if you go and marry someone we feel is totally unsuitable, think what the worry of that will do to him.'

Now I saw what she was trying to do and I didn't like it. But I loved my father very much. 'I rather thought Daddy and Dominic got on well together.'

'But that was when he believed him to be a casual boyfriend.' I remained stubbornly silent but Beth went on: 'I may be a screwed-up woman, Jennifer. But I'm just asking you to think!'

This direct approach was disconcerting to say the least. My mother had never spoken to me like this before. For the first time, she sounded as if she was prepared to view me as a person. The morning sun made the room warm and pleasant despite the wintry weather outside. Like everything my mother touched, it was exquisitely decked out. The table and chairs were of light woven cane and the window-seat an attractive chintzy print, which matched the cushions on our chairs. Thriving green plants spilled tropical leaves out of their terracotta holders. It was the new look – straight out of a high class women's magazine – cottagey and cosy and twee, in a way no old villager's cottage (and certainly not my grandparents') had ever been. My bones ached for rest and I closed my eyes in the chair, drawing on my cigarette.

'You are listening, aren't you?'

'Yes.'

'I know you love this boy. I daresay he loves you too, in

his way. But are you really right for each other? Just consider. You come from quite different backgrounds. He's a Roman Catholic. A doctor's son and a public school boy.'

'I would have thought you'd have approved of the last two.'

'I might have, had he not dropped out of all that. He's now a total atheist, an aspiring writer so you tell me, with no plans for the future. He hasn't a penny to his name and his opinions are alarming. I shan't ask you if he takes drugs, but I wouldn't be surprised.'

I groaned and let my head fall back in my chair. 'He doesn't take drugs.'

'But he is a bit of a drop-out.'

'I suppose so . . . in your way of looking at things.'

'Have you thought once about what marriage to him would really be like? In the real world? Oh, it's all very well now, shacking up together in a student flat. Yes, I know the slang too! You needn't be so surprised. I can see why you like him. He's quite good-looking in an unusual sort of way. I'm sure he's great in bed. And he's a charmer. Very sure of himself. A real artist too, no doubt. But, imagine it all ten years from now! You're still in a flat with the paper peeling off the walls. Oh, it may be a bit bigger than the one you're in now, but only because you have four children and there's another on the way. Say what you like, these Catholics breed like rabbits. And there's no spare money to enjoy yourself because he never did make much of a living.'

'There's more things to life than money', I said.

'Money is very important,' said Beth, 'and don't you forget it! Have I ever really told you what life was like for your grandmother?'

'Frequently.'

'Then how can you doubt it?'

'But I'm not Chloe and he's not Willie.'

'But you are in love and so was Chloe . . . at least at first.'

'It's entirely different.'

'I wonder. He'll be the one who's out charming people while you stay at home with the kids.'

'Not if I do Microbiology,' I said, slyly now.

'Oh, fiddlesticks!' I had made her impatient. 'You know perfectly well you'd always put his needs first.' There was a lot of truth in that.

'But he does care about me too. You read the letter.'

'He certainly thinks he does. But his father's absolutely right. He is pressurising you monstrously. What a time to pick to propose!'

I had to admit this worried me too. But it was so like Dominic, of course. The whole letter had been typical. I was staunch in his defence.

'He feels it's right that's all. He feels things very strongly . . . and so do I. We understand each other.'

Beth snorted. 'And how many more of his gut feelings – or shall we say 'whims' – will you have to kowtow to during your married life together?'

'Oh, do stop it.' I said, irritably. 'I love him and that's that. I shall marry him because I need him.'

'You only think that because you're young. How difficult it is to explain to someone of your age that your views will change when you grow older! I don't like to say: 'I know better', Jennifer, I really don't. But it's true. You're not thinking far enough ahead. Why, you haven't even thought about the wedding! Do you really want to get married in some scruffy little registry office in Liverpool, with nobody there except the witnesses?'

'You really wouldn't come then?'

'Certainly not.'

'And you wouldn't ever see me again?'

'Not with him in tow.'

'Well, that just shows how much you care about me, doesn't it?' I ground my cigarette to ash bitterly while Beth tried again.

'I'm merely trying to stop you from making a big mistake. You're mixed up now . . . upset. This business about medical school has been a strain. I can see that now. But all your father and I really ask is that you wait a while before you rush into anything too hastily. Give it time. Is that so unreasonable? If he loves you, surely he can wait? Personally, I don't think he will, but he ought too, if he really loves you.'

'You'd never accept him anyway,' I said, sourly. 'You've been set against him from the start.'

'I don't think he's good enough for you, no.'

I tried to drink my coffee but it had gone cold. 'Would you let me do Microbiology, if I promised to delay any decision until completing the course?' But she was not to be bamboozled this way.

'We've been through all that before and the answer is no. But we'll look after you, Jenny, don't you worry. We'll fix you up with a good job and see that you're comfortable and secure. Don't turn that down because you know it's important. You could have a flat too, like Peter, if you wanted. Anything.' The carrots were coming out now.

'But not the Microbiology course?'

'No.'

'Well, I shall just have to marry Dominic then, won't I? I'd better go and pack.'

'Please don't tell your father just yet,' was her parting shot.

Of course, I didn't believe a single word of her argument, far less agree with it. But the substance of it kept on echoing in my ears, all the way to Liverpool on the train.

I sat on the wall outside the Arts Reading Room in the afternoon sun and waited for Dominic. He came out at last, swinging confidently through the doors, and the sight of his cornfield hair flipped my heart over as usual.

'Jenny! Why didn't you tell me you were coming?'

'I thought it was all right just to come.'

'Well, of course it is. But you might have missed me.'

'I knew where you'd be.'

'Did you get my letter?'

'Yes.'

'Then let's walk.'

He put his arm around my shoulders and we walked back towards Abercromby Square. The Easter break was late that year and it would soon be blossom time. The forsythia and flowering currant were already out and new green leaves were starting to unfurl in the breeze which rumpled his hair.

'How are you?'

'All right.'

'Really?'

'Well no, not really.'

'Are you ready to talk?'

'Yes.'

'Shall we go back to my flat?'

'No. Let's have a drink first.' I couldn't say what I had to in the flat. I would only want to go to bed with him there and then and that wouldn't do at all, for it might make me change my mind. We went to the pub across the road. It was quiet enough as the usual lunchtime crowd had already been and gone and we managed to find a private corner. One of our favourite records was playing on the juke-box. Another Moody Blues. Ironic really. I always cried when I heard it on the radio afterwards.

'What are you going to do?' Dominic asked when he had got the drinks and given me a cigarette. He wasn't in the least bit nervous.

'I don't think I can marry you, Dominic. Not now, under these circumstances. I do love you, awfully, and I would like to marry you. But I can't do it now.

He nodded, reasonably cheerful. 'I thought you might say that. Well, of course you don't have to. You don't ever have to if you don't want. We can go on as we are now . . . or perhaps I should say were? Things will just be more difficult for a while, that's all.'

'Yes, I know. There's no way I can do Microbiology or

anything else.'

He put down his pint. 'Jenny, what are you saying? You must! There'll be another way.'

'I have no money, Dominic.'

'I thought of asking Dad for a loan . . . '

'Don't be silly, Dominic. I can't do that.'

He stared at me and I could see that he didn't understand.

'It wouldn't work, Dommy! I'd still have to cut my ties with home just the same, if I came back to the university. They would know I was defying them.'

'Aren't you prepared to do that?'

'I can't. My father's not well.'

'Jenny, I want you back!' He was really alarmed now and he transmitted his panic to me.

'I can't go against them.'

He took a deep breath and I hated to see the look on his face. Why had I chosen the pub? It wasn't fair. He had deserved better than this.

'You realise what you're saying? About us, I mean? It's all over isn't it? Finished . . . period!'

'Can't you wait for me?' I faltered. Even as I said it, I knew it was puerile. He grabbed both my hands in his.

'Think, will you! What are you going to do and where are you going to live?'

'I don't know, Dommy! I'll get a job somewhere.'

'Back in Kingley, I suppose?'

'I suppose so.'

'You suppose so! Then how can I see you?'

'Oh, but I shan't live at home. I can still get a flat. I do want to see you again, Dominic – you know that!' We looked at each other in horror at the way that the quarrel had blown up, but couldn't do anything to stop it. Dominic released my hands in despair.

'But your mother will never sanction us being together . . . '

'No.'

'Then in the end you'll have to choose between her and

me! So why can't you do it now?'

'Please don't push me, Dominic! No more! I've told you why. Please understand.'

'Oh, but I do! I understand that you've chosen her instead.'

'No, it's not like that!'

'But it is. It's true!'

'You can still come and see me if you want to.'

He shook his head despairingly and I was shocked to see that his eyes were slightly moist. It frightened me, but not enough. I couldn't believe he meant what he said next.

'No, I don't think so, Jenny. Isn't it better to accept the truth now? You said that yourself once. Oh God, why did you have to bring us here?'

The words of the song pounded into our brains:-

'It's not the way that you say it when you do those things to me,
It's more the way you really mean it when you tell me what will be . . .

And when you stop and think about it,
You won't believe it's true,
That all the love you've been giving
Has all been meant for you . . . '

I began to cry.

'But I do love you, Dommy.'

Then he really hurt me. 'No, you don't Jenny. You're not capable of loving anyone at the moment. You have to become a proper person first.' And he stood up and left, without saying another word.

'You all right, lovey?' said the barmaid, clearing the glasses sometime later. She must have noticed my heavily tear-stained face, not to mention the number of empties and stub ends in front of me. I gulped an nodded.

'You don't want to worry about it, chuck,' she said.

'They're like the buses . . . always another one along in a minute. Men! Only trouble is they're all the same.'

''Spect you're right.'

'Have to turn you out now. Three o'clock, you know. Mind how you go, now. Had a bit too much, haven't you?'

I stumbled through the door, from dingy tap-room gloom (all Liverpool pubs are awful) into brilliant sunshine, blinking in an alcoholic blur. The wonder is I didn't throw myself under a bus then and there. I felt pretty sick actually, but managed to control it. Inside my pocket was Dominic's lighter, which I had brought with me intending to give back and had forgotten about. I kept it for years. It was a strong, contributing factor to my not giving up smoking earlier than I eventually did.

I didn't go back to Dominic's flat and wait for him like I should have done. I just walked around aimlessly for a bit to sober up and then went to my flat to collect a few things. Peter or Dad would come for my trunk later. No one was there and I was glad. I couldn't have faced Eileen. I never saw her again but I never really wanted to. I was sick in the sink and had to clear it up. But at least it settled my stomach for the train.

Clickety clack. Over the points. Out of Lime Street for the last time. Past all the familiar place names. Edge Hill, St Helen's Junction, Manchester Victoria, Stalybridge, Huddersfield . . . I kept my face turned to the window the whole way. So many tears. In my innocence, the only thing I could think of was that my mother had been right. Dominic hadn't really loved me after all. But then I never knew whether or not he had been crying too when he walked out.

Nobody said much when I got back home.

'You're back then?' Beth managed and that was all. But she knew from my face she had won.

Nobody said much for days. In fact, I don't remember anyone saying anything really serious ever again for years. Not till Suzanne was born and shocked us all out of our complacency.

'What on earth is that great pile of paper?' asked Beth, pointing to it.

'The doctor asked me to write down some thoughts,' said Jenny. 'To help her understand me better, I suppose . . . and maybe to help me understand myself.'

Beth sniffed. 'They have a strange way of doing things in here.'

She had come tripping, nosily staccato, down the ward in her mink jacket and high-heeled shoes.

'I saw your consultant, you know, Dr Mahler. What an impudent man! Most blunt. And, you won't believe this, but his flies were open too.'

Jennifer smiled. 'I'm sure it was entirely an oversight,' she said. She had smartened herself up for her mother and was getting through the session pretty well. Writing everything down about Dominic had helped somehow, although she had wept buckets towards the end. Perhaps that was Dr Jowett's idea. To clear her system out, like a self-induced catharsis.

'Well, you don't look too bad to me,' said Beth. 'Why on earth did you give us all such a fright? You must have had too much to drink and taken those pills accidentally.'

'Yes, I believe I did.' It was so much simpler to let Beth think that.

'Then why won't they let you out?'

'Oh, they think I need a rest, I suppose.'

'Then what have you been writing about?'

Jenny looked at her coolly. 'Actually, I've been writing about Dominic,' she said. 'Every single thing I can remember.'

Beth started. It was like a bad dream come true. 'Whatever for?'

'Because I felt depressed, I suppose. I've been trying to reassess it all.'

'How silly to re-hash all of that. He was just an old

flame.' Jennifer remained silent. 'And what conclusion did you come to?'

'Oh, that you were wrong of course, mother, as always.' Beth flushed painfully. 'But then so was I. I was the one who really hurt him and deserted him. You just aided and abetted me. In fact, you were downright evil, mother. But it was really my fault. Always my fault. I wouldn't do any of it now. None of it the same. I must have been mad to let him go.'

'Well!' said Beth. 'Well! I see!' The wind had gone right out of her sails. 'Those drugs have done something to you. You're not the same girl at all.' But was that really true? She remembered the day when Jennifer and Dominic had driven over to see her from university. The day Jennifer gave up medicine. They had come to see Ken as well, of course. But he hadn't been there. She had had to cope with it all alone. The worst day of her life . . . until the 'phone had rung to say her daughter was in a psychiatric ward. From the moment they had stepped out of the car, she had known something was wrong, Jennifer looked so desperate, so thin and waif-like and tired. It was the first time she had ever realised her daughter might be anything less than perfect, that she could ever really be in trouble. And there *he* was beside her, with his hair all bright and yellow in the sun. Was it any wonder that she had assumed he was responsible, that he had been sucking Jennifer's blood? And now, after all this time, after Mike and Sarah and when she was in the middle of her divorce, to have he affrontery to bring him up. Still Beth found she couldn't shrug off her guilt. But it had all seemed for the best. And even Jennifer in the end admitted it had been her decision.

'You were quite right, doctor,' said Beth to Annabelle Jowett, whom she happened to pass in the corridor on her way out. 'My daughter does need to be in here. I hope you can do something with her. May I compliment you on the ward, by the way? So bright and cheerful, isn't it?'

CHAPTER ELEVEN

'And did you ever see Dominic again?' asked Annabelle, after reading the whole of Jennifer's script.

'No, not once. Awful, isn't it? After we'd shared so much. I wrote to him of course, after a while, to let him know what I was doing. But he'd moved out of his flat by then, left the university altogether it seemed, for I tried the English department as well. I assumed his donnish aspirations hadn't lasted very long, for I couldn't believe he wouldn't have answered my letters. Then I sent a brief note to Southport when I moved into my flat – you know, one of those cards you use when changing address. He must have got that. But he never got in touch. It hurt me of course, though I could hardly blame him.'

'But you got over it.'

'Sometimes I wonder. It's a world away, of course. Nine years. A very old wound. How can you really tell, after all?'

'You built yourself a completely new life.'

Jennifer grimaced. 'Oh, yes.'

Annabelle doodled on the case-sheet, then crossed it out guiltily. 'I think that is a good sign. You must have been shattered then, but you managed to get yourself a job and a flat. And you married someone else within – what? – three years? I know that didn't work out in the end, but you did it all, just the same. Don't you think that's encouraging?'

'No,' said Jennifer, 'I don't. I didn't do those

things . . . they just happened to me. I drifted along and allowed other people to make the decisions.'

'Oh, but surely not in getting married!'

'That was largely panic.'

'I don't understand. Tell me about it.'

'Well, in the beginning, I was merely shell-shocked. I couldn't believe I wouldn't see Dominic again. My parents took me away on holiday as they'd promised. Somewhere in Greece. I sat in the sun and got drunk on ouzo and cheap wine every day. Not obviously so, and certainly not happily so. But I needed the blur it gave me and I made sure it was there most of the time. For the first time, I was using alcohol as something more than a slight social prop. My parents didn't bother about it too much, though I expect they must have been worried about me.

'When we got back, my father fixed up a place on a secretarial course at Kingley 'Tec. That started in the autumn and, by then, I was glad of something to do. And it was all right in its way . . . quite useful and a complete change. I think my father had some idea of taking me into the firm when that year finished, and letting me work my way up from the bottom, like Peter. I suppose it would have been a soft number providing the business survived. But I didn't want that. I got a job with a firm of solicitors in Bradford instead and moved into my own flat off Manningham Lane.

'Still shell-shocked?'

'Coming round to harsh realities. The area was awful. I only chose it because it was near the park. But it wasn't Liverpool and it wasn't like being a student. I was entirely alone. Dominic was right about the need for readjustment. Leaving the university in itself was an immense, cultural shock. The 'Tec had cushioned it slightly for a year, though everyone there was just passing through and I hadn't really made any friends. But now, here at last was the real world and I felt isolated in it. It was so difficult to relax after work, for I no longer had the company of my kind. I could hardly go out. There was only the television and gin. The one thing I really do envy men for is their freedom of movement. Even today, it is difficult for a woman to socialise alone. I joined a social club for post-graduates but felt I was there under false pretences. It didn't work anyway. I didn't particularly want to meet a man, you understand, just make new friends. But everyone had gone for the same reason and no one really wanted to be there. They would have avoided its artificiality if they could. In the end, I couldn't bear its falseness any more and stopped going. Perhaps that was a mistake. I don't know.

'Then I went out with a German fellow once or twice. He lived in the same block of flats and was doing a year as an assistant at a local school. But I really only did it because he had blond hair. But he wasn't a Dominic and that didn't last very long.'

'What about the people at work? There must have been other girls in the office.'

'Yes, of course there were and that's what kept me going. But I didn't really get close to them. They all seemed to be either school leavers or much older than myself. And, although I never told anyone I'd been to medical school, somehow it got out and they thought I was a bit of an odd-ball (which of course I was). I suppose I knew the senior secretary best, Miss Bryant. She was a spindly, grey lady who used far too much perfume and wore blouses with frills down the front like a Scottish dancer. But she was an intellectual in her way. In her youth, she had given up the chance of further education in order to nurse two elderly parents. Well, you can imagine how guilty that made me feel! But she sought me out as a possible kindred spirit. We went to a series of concerts together that winter, and very glad I was of them, too. Occasionally, she would invite me back to her flat for cocoa. It was remarkably similar to mine, except that it was outstandingly clean, but I could see myself developing the same fussy habits in time. Miss Bryant was due for retirement in a couple of years and, one day, I realised she was grooming me to take her place in the office. It chilled me to the core for I knew I should become just like her. I wouldn't be able to help myself as the years slipped away. I wouldn't even have the solace of the Church to revolve my life around, as she did. I could only fret about the price of marmalade and start making my own.

'And that is really why I married Mike. That and the inevitable camaraderie which springs up between any two people who are working closely together, providing they get on at all. It is surprising how intimate and deep that can become. Mike was my boss, you see. He was a junior partner then, not a typical professional perhaps. He was a little too dark and dapper for that, too thrusting and forceful. Actually, I believe he must have missed his way as well. He should have been a criminal lawyer or maybe even in big business. Instead, he had settled for conveyancing and matimonial work for a quick return.

'The younger girls, without exception, were in love with him, for he was textbook handsome. But they didn't like doing his typing because he could be a bit of a sod. That's unfair, really, he was merely a perfectionist. I didn't mind, so I ended up doing all of it. The work there never bothered me. I can't claim it fascinated me either, but there was a certain satisfaction in doing it well. Of course it didn't really matter. No one was going to die if I made a mistake. In fact I hardly ever did. So, not only did I do all his typing, but gradually I made all his arrangements as well, chased up all and sundry and became, apparently, indispensable.

'Jennifer, my love,' he would say, in that easy manner which is possible when you don't really mean it; "You're a marvel. What would I do without you?" Of course it was a mistake to try and extend the relationship. But it so happened that Michael Warrender had been systematically and determinedly hunting for a wife for some time. I suspect he may have had a list of desirable qualities to tick off: mid-twenties, white, C of E, a good cook, capable of child-bearing, and child-rearing, intelligent but not too clever, looks of secondary importance though must be slim and presentable. I'm only guessing now, you understand. A bit of brass in the background might have come in handy, as well.

'He made his first move one evening when he had kept me very late at work. Claiming an attack of contrition, he took me to eat at the steak bar around the corner. We sat in a crimson glow under heavy-fringed lamps and peered at the menu: he in his three-piece pin-stripe and me in my plain black dress, relieved only by a blue metal pendant he had given me at Christmas. There was nothing significant in such a present, it was the custom for all of the secretaries to receive some such token.

'Perhaps the red light brought out the better colours in my hair. Perhaps it was too dark to be anything other than flattering. At any rate, his kindling interest must have been refuelled. He talked for hours and I listened. Come to think of it, that's a pretty good summary of all our time together. Does that sound very bitter? It isn't meant to be, because it wasn't really his fault. I should have had a warning notice attached to my forehead explaining that I was touchy and sensitive and thought quite different thoughts.

'He ran me home and I considered asking him in for a night-cap, but ducked the issue. I knew he only drank scotch anyway and I had nothing but the gin-bottle. I just thanked him profusely instead. But, after the weekend, he slipped me a note in the middle of some papers on a house search: "Isn't this boring question mark, Will you come to the theatre with me tomorrow night comma, open brackets Chekhov or some such close brackets, question-mark stop." The warning lights should have been flashing by then but I really wanted to go. It never occured to me then that he didn't really like that sort of thing at all. When he went to sleep in the middle of "The Cherry Orchard", I assumed that he'd had a hard day. I thought we had something else in common, not that it was just a ploy. It also restored my self-respect to be seen out again with such an obviously desirable man. I'm not very proud of that, but I have to be honest now.

'After that, we dated regularly and I was forever buying bottles of scotch. In no time I was cooking him the odd meal in his flat which, I might add, was definitely upmarket from mine. Then of course sex reared its head. Honesty again. Of course I wanted it, him, the whole damn thing. I wanted to lay the past too. And he was undeniably attractive. Though he failed to move me in the way Dominic had. My heart never turned over when he entered a room. There was only the vaguest stirring of emotion now and then, during an embrace, and it settled back down again afterwards as if it had never been, so that I couldn't be sure if it had really existed at all. I reckon now it's best to judge that kind of thing out of bed, anyway. I never really agonised with Mike nor fussed over him nor failed to be objective about his shortcomings. I had done all of those things with Dominic. But did that mean anything? My relationship with Mike appeared to proceed pleasantly enough. It was easy, so very easy to become engaged, to allow myself to be swept along.

'Beth was over the moon. I forgot to tell you that Mike's parents originally lived in Kingley, so she knew the family well. It was the kind of set she had long yearned to break into, for they were pillars of the Round Table, the Rugby Club, the Golf Club and the right church. They held bridge parties and lived higher up the hill. She found Mike so suitable, I should have been alarmed.

'It had to be the wedding of the year, with Beth in charge. Everything was classily done: discreetly plain invitation cards, old parish church with choir and bells, bride in the whitest of white with the colours of her bouquet toning exactly with all the other flowers and fifty-nine bridesmaids (or so it seemed to me at the time) in shaded shades of blue. Morning suits for the men, naturally, Rolls-Royce cars, the best photographer and, to cap it all, an immense blow-out at the most stylish local place that year. I'm surprised my poor father didn't have his coronary then and there. It hurts me so much to think how proud he was that day. Even the sun shone, for it was that gloriously hot summer of '76, when the reservoirs dried up and no one was allowed to use a hose.

'It had all snowballed once the huge rollercoaster got going. Unthinkable to call it off. Though I have to admit I didn't want to. I was almost as carried away as Beth. There was only one nasty moment when I arrived in church on my father's arm and spotted a head of cornfield hair. I gripped Ken more tightly, but he misunderstood and patted my hand. When the yellow head turned round to look at me, it was actually a girl. Some cousin of Mike's I hadn't met before and haven't since. That was the only time I felt like running. And the feeling had passed by the time I reached the end of the aisle.

'Afterwards, I smiled happily enough at the world. I rustled across a green lawn in my mediaeval dress and Juliet cap with its frothing veil. The picture the photographer captured wasn't entirely false. I have it still to torment me. The bridegroom is tall, dark and handsome as if tailor made, like the suits from Moss Bros. But, when I had been carefully manoeuvred into that vast car (how on earth did mediaeval ladies manage to get about?) and he had joined me on the seat, I did realise fleetingly that I really didn't know this man at all.'

'Mike was moved to the Leeds office and we bought a double-fronted detached house in a residential suburb. I was fond of that house. It reminded me of 'Lorelei' and a lot of hope went into it. It had plenty of character and was waiting for us cheerfully enough. We were the ones who let it down.

'Like my grandmother before me, I threw myself into my new role with vigour. But, of course, unlike her, I continued to work. No problem, with today's labour-saving devices. Or so I thought. The reality was rather different. Cleaning, cooking and commuting don't mix that well, even with the best organisation. They make you tired. And, although the automatic does the shirts, someone has to put them in and take them out and iron them. Not as bad as scrubbing with a brush at a collar, I'm sure, but bad enough, after the ringing of a 'phone and pounding a typewriter all day, not to mention crawling in low gear most of the way home. I didn't envisage working for long, however, for I had decided I wanted a baby. Motherhood was the next logical step, although I hadn't really given it a great deal of thought. But here, at last, seemed to be something anyone could succeed at. I prayed I wouldn't turn out to be infertile. Mike was more cautious. He thought we should wait until we had everything we wanted for the house.

'I had hardly unpacked the wedding presents before I realised I did not like Mike's friends very much. I still had none of my own for I never saw the neighbours, being out all day. For the life of me, I can't explain why. They couldn't all have been the same. It must have been my jaundiced eye. But they all lived in the same houses with the same sort of furniture and had fondue sets. They all drove the same kind of car and they definitely held the same opinions. We fell into a round of dinner parties and they became the bane of my life. I am not a bad cook when the creative mood takes me, but the dinner parties had to be all the same as well, though ideally a little better than the last, and under the pressure, my soufflés flopped and my meringues went brown and cracked with depressing regularity. Mike used to set the table and pour out the wine. He wasn't into sharing the housework.

'We never went to the theatre or a concert any more and I soon discovered Mike's real love was sport. That was another reason why I didn't fit in with his friends. Whatever it was, I couldn't do it. And there was quite a range: golf, squash, badminton, tennis. Then there was the rugby . . . although at least I was only expected to jump up and down on the touchlines for that. I still didn't enjoy it very much, but I didn't dare sit at home with a book as I should have liked to. Mixed doubles in the summer inflicted my greatest suffering. It was like school all over again.

'The first year trickled slowly by. We got over the 'toothpaste being squeezed at the wrong end' stage. If I had been honest, I would have admitted it was all a dreadful mistake. But I couldn't give up so easily. Anyway, didn't everyone say that 'opposites attract' and that's what most happily married couples are? I no longer believe that over-simplification.

'The enjoyment of sex had soon gone. We were both working pretty hard, of course, no longer together for I had stayed in the Bradford office, and were tired and snappy when we got home. Mike was desperate 'to get on', while I still thought I wanted a baby. And weekends were crammed full with the relentless expenditure of energy, followed by an equally relentless consumption of food and drink.

'You're just a wet blanket,' Mike said, when I complained.

'And you're just a crashing bore,' I retorted. So much for camaraderie. But I kidded myself that everyone's marriage was like this. Perhaps it is, but I do hope not. You wouldn't have known anything was wrong in public. It was 'darling' every two minutes then. Always a bad sign, I think. But I only occasionally remembered Dominic. Whenever I did I used a kind of 'double think' . . . I wouldn't have dared otherwise.

'Then at last Mike agreed I could come off the Pill and after a short time, to my surprise and delight, I became pregnant. That put a different complexion on everything. When the time came, I gave up work, not to mention tennis and badminton, with a sigh of relief and settled down cosily to wait. Mike missed the money but enjoyed having me home. The house actually looked clean and tidy and his dinner was on time. We had achieved our fitted kitchen with its dishwasher and split-level, the new carpets and the dining-room and lounge suites. Now we kitted out a beautiful nursery. All that we, this less than perfect couple, needed in this perfect house was the perfect baby to go with it.

'I shall never forget the night Suzanne was born. Sometimes I dream – not exactly about it – but that I have to give birth and the same thing is going to happen again. People said: 'Didn't you know?' or 'Didn't you guess?' But I didn't. I was on top of the world all the way through that pregnancy, apart from a little sickness at the beginning. I had never felt better. Having Sarah was much worse. I had no feelings, no intuition or ESP – nothing like that.

'I even went into labour at the right time. Mike drove me in, in the early hours. Of course I was nervous. Who isn't? But everything seemed to be under control. The pains were not exactly as I had imagined them. It all seemed to be going on in the back, but they were building up steadily enough. The pethidine made me sick, but the monitor which kept on galloping through the night was reassuring. So was Mike, although he didn't want to be with me for the actual delivery. I didn't mind that; I could understand it. When I was ready, just as I was beginning to think I couldn't take much more of it, he left.

'Then the room and I collected the usual green drapes and suddenly I was terrified. I hadn't been in sight or sound of a hospital since being 'on the other side', remember. All the memories came flooding back: the peculiar smell of placentas, the blood on the wellies, the heat of the lamp, the clatter of forceps in dishes and bowls. Inevitably, *that* baby. So many things which could go wrong in so many different ways. I began to panic.

'Now look, lovey,' shouted the midwife. 'Don't tense up on us. You've been to your classes. You know what to do.' She showed me the mask. 'Make this gas and air work for you, don't just shout and scream. And push into your bottom with the next pain, not your throat. We'll have this baby out in no time, if you do as you're told.'

'I had heard it all before. The vast majority of deliveries are normal. Normal labour is a retrospective term. I still needed to shout and the head kept on slipping back. The episiotomy was inevitable. But, by that time, I wasn't thinking of what might go wrong. I was too busy clinging on to the mask as if my life depended on it. But everything comes to an end and, once the head was out, the body slipped out afterwards like a dream.

'A little girl,' they said.

'Is she all right?' I asked.

'She's fine,' the said. 'A bit mucousy. We're just clearing her out.'

'I wept with relief when I heard the thin, whimpering cry. The room had gone very quiet and they hadn't given her to me yet – she was still on the rescusitaire although it didn't sound as if she needed to be now. For all my experience, I didn't realise the silence was an awkward one. Somebody asked which paediatrician was on call.

'Have you got a name for her?'

'Suzanne.' I raised myself on one elbow, all pain forgotten. 'Can I see her now?'

'They handed her to me then, wrapped up in a little bundle. Now you will think me really stupid, in view of my training. But I didn't immediately know. Not in those first few minutes. I even said: 'Isn't she pretty?' And in a way she was. She had lots of silky thin auburn hair which never really changed, although it was a bit plastered down and messy then. I have read a lot about women having to struggle to identify with their newly-born. Even seen it happen. But for me it was never a problem. The animal instinct always responded. Instant wonderment and love. Bang! Like imprinting in reverse. It was there at that moment. Maybe that is why I didn't realise. Or perhaps it was because they soon whisked her away again for a bath. They don't bother so much about that kind of thing now. But, even as recently as that, it was all different. I could hardly remember what she looked like at all. And it seemed hours before she was returned all clean and pink and labelled. In fact it *was* hours, because they were busy. I had already been stitched and washed and vomited back my cup of tea. I had even been moved into a side-room on my own, away from the other mothers. Even that didn't make me suspicious.

'But then, when she did come back, and I looked properly at my poor, skinny-bottomed, ugly-beautiful baby with her freckled and flat features and those obliquely set eyes, I realised. She was an obvious Down's Syndrome. Not that we were so carefully correct in those days either. The term in common usage was still 'a mongol'.

CHAPTER TWELVE

Even now, I find it very difficult to explain how I felt. Of course it was a catastrophe. Naturally the possibility had always been there, right at the back of my mind as it is with any pregnant woman. But I hadn't really believed I would have an abnormal baby. Why us, I kept on thinking, when what I really meant was: why me? I wasn't even very old. What had I done wrong? Of course, the answer was nothing. Then, why me? Why not? came back the only possible reply. Why should you escape and go swanning through life scot-free?

'I didn't cry. Well, only on the third day, when everyone does. But I thought about it all fairly clearly, what it really meant without any whitewash. I wondered if anything else was wrong. I felt horror in my heart and a dread of the years to come. I felt repulsion and shame. Shame at having an imperfect child and shame for feeling ashamed. Then I picked her up when she cried and fed her just the same. It wasn't an automatic response at first but the contact broke the barriers down. Then I wondered if we could possibly be mistaken, despite all the signs. I longed for the paediatrician to come and for the results of the tests. I couldn't rest at all for I wouldn't leave her wet for a second then, so anxious was I to do my best.

'Don't handle her so much,' said the nurses. 'Leave her be when she isn't crying.' But I had to keep on looking and touching to make sure. Perhaps I would have done that anyway. But I had no other girls to talk to in my splendid isolation. So there was only Suzanne to see to and plenty of time to think.

'Mike was devastated and, at first, I felt sorrier for him than I did for myself. After all, he had been the one with the endless, awkard phone-calls.

'Yes, it's a girl. And they're both all right but . . . ' It must have been hard for him. He wasn't as used to failure, as I was.

'The first time he came in to see us – after that night – he brought the conventional long-stemmed, red roses and was very sweet. 'How are you? Are you feeling all right? I'm sorry I couldn't stay. You must be worn out.' 'You haven't looked at the baby yet.' 'But are you all right?' 'Yes, but you haven't looked at the baby yet.' His eyes flickered briefly over the cot.

'She's very auburn isn't she?'

'But her feet are just like yours.' He looked at me as if I'd said something obscene.

'Have you seen the paediatrician yet?'

'No. Have you?'

'Yes.'

'Tell me what he said.'

'Oh, he'll tell you much better than I can.' I thought I understood his reluctance and did not press him, although I was anxious to know. There were so many things we hadn't discussed before our marriage (not least whether I was in any way physically capable of returning a service ball in a tennis match). Our reactions to a handicapped child certainly hadn't been included. We didn't even discuss it now. I suppose that we both assumed we would react in the same way.

'My interview with the paediatrician took place later that day. It was all much as I had expected, although Suzanne did have a heart murmur. He thought it was a small VSD (a hole in the heart) and it might require surgery later. But, for the moment, she was in no danger. There were no decisions to take. She had no other abnormalities. She was just there, as she was going to stay, and I had to wait for the numbness to wear off and get used to it all.

'Miss Bryant sent me a card from the office and, rather to my surprise, wrote me a letter. It was full of spiritual counsel and God's mysterious ways. Not much help to a godless mother. But I appreciated it all the same, for there were precious few other congratulation cards.'

'Of course, you won't be keeping her, will you?' said Beth. 'I mean, not actually at home?' She fussed about with the magnificent bouquet of flowers she had brought and eyed her daughter carefully. Jennifer looked pale and washed out in her dressing gown on top of the hospital bed. She seemed more tired now than she had done initially. The breastfeeding wasn't going too well. She wanted, with a desperate irrationality, to go home. The slightest little thing made her weep. Beth understood all of that of course. But the time had come to find out what Jennifer intended to do.

'Don't be silly, mother. She's our child. Of course we'll be keeping her at home.'

Beth prodded the stem of an errant carnation firmly into place. 'You can't have thought what that means,' she said. 'You've got to remember Mike as well.'

'I know I have. It won't be easy. But we have to get used to it.'

'Mike won't.' Beth spoke quite sharply and Jennifer turned her head in surprise.

'Has he been speaking to you about it?' she asked.

'A little.'

'I see. I know he's shattered, of course. It was such a shock. It's bound to take time . . . '

'He doesn't want her, Jenny.'

'Oh no, that's not true! That's not true at all.'

Beth sat down and crossed her legs. 'It's about time you two talked, isn't it? I think you should listen to him too, Jennifer. He's got a point. You're not thinking straight at the moment. You can't when you're post-natal, I know. See what I mean?' Jennifer's eyes had filled up again and she stared desperately at the ceiling.

'You don't believe I can think at all. That's the trouble.'

'Oh, really, Jennifer . . . what a silly thing to say! But you don't want this to come between you, do you?'

'Her name is Suzanne.'

'I know it is. Don't be so sensitive! But having a child like her is a terrible strain on anyone's marriage, you know. I've seen it happen.'

Jennifer fought for control. 'Mother, if you say, 'I know', one more time, I'll scream! She's here. She's been born. It's unfortunate, but there it is. We can't undo what's happened.'

'But there are places for children like this, you know.'

'There is no reason why a straightforward Down's can't stay at home. Especially at this stage.'

Beth shrugged. 'Of course it's up to you . . . and Mike. But, if I were you, I wouldn't be so silly. I'd put her in a home and have another one straight away. One that's all right, I mean.'

'We can't keep her, of course,' said Mike that same evening, standing with his back to the cot and looking away out of the hospital window. 'Not actually at home.' Jennifer raised her head.

'I gather you've been talking to my mother,' she said. 'Don't you think you should have discussed it with me first?'

Mike turned round. 'I'm sorry. I didn't mean to. Beth and I get on well. We understand each other and it seemed natural enough.'

'You should have married her,' said Jennifer wryly. 'She would have like that.'

'Don't be mean, Jenny. It's time to face facts.'

'I know that. But are we going to?'

Mike sat down beside her, not unkindly, and took her hand. 'Jenny, listen to me please. I've had a talk with the paediatrician. It can all be arranged. Of course he wasn't too keen. Gave me a long lecture about the family environment being far and away the best. But I think I managed to convince him it wasn't on. You only have to say yes and it'll all be sorted out.' Suzanne woke up and began to yell and Jennifer got up distractedly. 'You can go to see her . . . if you like. My guess is you won't want to much, after a while. Can't you see, Jenny? It's all for the best. We can have another one.'

'She's our child. Our responsibility.'

'Of course she is. I intend to pay for her. Through the nose, more than likely. But we can't have her home. You haven't thought about it.'

Jennifer paced up and down, nursing and shushing her baby. 'I've thought of nothing else.'

'Then why can't you see? It must be the hormones. But you'll agree with me later.'

Suzanne was not to be placated. She kept up a furious racket, despite Jenny's silent prayers for her to stop.

'I'll have to feed her, Mike. She's hungry.'

'We've got to get this straightened out now. Can't you get a nurse to do it?'

'You know I'm breastfeeding . . . '

'Like hell you are!' He rang the bell imperiously and, after an interval, a nervous junior scuttled in.

'My wife's decided she doesn't want to go on breastfeeding,' Mike said bluntly. 'Please take the baby away and give it a bottle.' The girl looked a bit shocked and darted a glance at Jennifer, who nodded despairingly. Suzanne was put back into her crib, which made her bawl more urgently than ever. Her fists fought the air and her little screwed-up face grew redder and redder. Then the nurse wheeled her away, clucking, and silence was restored.

Jennifer sat down, feeling desperate. 'You've no right to do that. I shall feed her later on tonight.'

'What's the point?'

'You can't just get someone to come and take her off our hands forever, because she doesn't exactly fit in with the golf club and the solicitor's office and your sporty friends, you know!'

'Look, Jenny! You can paint me as black as you like. But someone has to have the courage to make this decision. I'm thinking of you too, you know. How are you going to feel when she's thirty and still has the mind of a child?'

'I'll meet that when I come to it.'

'Are you really strong enough to face it all?'

'What do you mean by that?'

'Beth told me why you left medical school. All about your breakdown. We don't think you could cope with a handicapped child.'

'Now wait a minute! I gave up medicine because I'd made a mistake. I was pretty cut up about it at the time, of course. But I did not have a breakdown. And it had absolutely nothing to do with this. This is entirely different. I'm not a complete emotional cripple, you know!'

'I didn't say you were. But looking after this child will be a big strain.'

'Can't you at least let me try?'

'I can see I shall have to be the ogre after all, for your own good.'

Jennifer raised her hands to her head in despair and blinked back the tears. 'I don't believe this is happening to me,' she said.

Mike turned away again to the window. 'I'm not having her home,' he said. 'It's out of the question. I couldn't stand it and it wouldn't work. You can visit her if you like, but don't ask me to go with you.'

Jennifer stared at him in horror. That was it then. The real reason was out. It was Mike who couldn't cope – not her. She supposed she should have understood. Perhaps it was similar to her decision to pack in medicine after all. He could not tolerate handicapped children. That was all there was to it. But, unfortunately, acknowledging one's own foibles and shortcomings does not necessarily help in understanding others'. They were divided by a gulf which could not be crossed. If Mike couldn't change, she would have to give in. She didn't breastfeed at ten. There was no point any more. But she spent a wretchedly sleepless night, staring into the dark with eyes that were continually full.

'It's disgusting!' complained Sister Delaney, banging about the office of the post-natal ward. She shifted her glasses on her nose and peered fiercely at the auxiliary, who was of her vintage and an old friend, despite the fact they were positioned at opposite ends of the nursing hierarchy.

'What is, Maud?'

'The way that girl's been got at.'

'You mean Mrs Warrender?'

'I do. Left to her own devices, she'd still be breastfeeding. Not talking about putting her own flesh and blood into a home. I don't know what the world's coming to! That husband's such a smart alec. They haven't been married very long, you know. Plenty of money. Too much, if you ask me. Ducking their responsibilities like that. You mark my words, Doris! One day they'll be swopping them if their eyes don't match the colour of the fitted carpets!'

The auxiliary sighed. 'Poor Mrs Warrender!' she said. 'You can see it's breaking her heart.'

'She wants to stand up for herself a bit more then.'

'It must be very difficult though, don't you think? If your husband's as definite as that.' Doris had put up with her own husband bashing her about for years when the children had been little. But Sister Delaney belonged to the old school. She was indomitable, uncompromising and unmarried. She pursed her lips grimly and said:

'We make our own beds to lie on, Doris. It's no good moaning about it. Mind you, I must say the mother's poison. I've seen her type before . . . ' She clamped her mouth shut as the junior nurse walked in. It wouldn't do to be caught sounding off like this about the patients with

Doris. But, for once, she had really had to let off steam.

'Shall I take Baby Warrender to mum's room to be fed?' asked the junior, looking at her watch.

'No, leave her in the nursery unless she asks,' said the sister. 'Looks like Mrs Warrender's going home with an empty carry-cot.'

'And the worst of it was,' Jennifer said to Annabelle, 'that all Mike's friends said we'd done the right thing. Can you imagine how that felt? It was appalling to be so alone. Surrounded by people but forever lonely. Sometimes I think that's how it's always been. My father didn't really approve perhaps, but he ended up by protecting me as usual and keeping quiet. Everyone was on Mike's side. And Beth's, of course. All I had to hold on to was the idea that Dominic would never have done it. Even if he had felt like Mike, when faced with the reality, he would never have *made* me do it. I'm convinced of that.'

Annabelle thought for a long time before her next comment. It had the ring of Mahler about it which pleased her, but she wasn't sure whether she should actually say it or not, nor how Jennifer would respond.

'No one *makes* people do what they really don't want to, surely? Don't we just use that as an excuse?'

Jennifer smiled sadly. 'I don't know,' she said. 'I wonder. There are so many indirect ways of piling on the pressure, aren't there? So many reasons and motives and different strands making cause and effect come together. I can see it all now. Of course, you're right in your way. I should have done more instead of being so wet. And the ridiculous thing was that I ended up losing Mike anyway. I didn't even really want him any more.'

'But you did stay married for another four years and have another baby.'

'Yes. But he had killed stone dead any love there might have been.'

'What did you do?'

'I shut the nursery door and went back to work.

Everyone said, 'have another baby', but I didn't want to just then. I used to visit Suzanne regularly at weekends but it all became very traumatic. Mike was right. After a while I didn't want to go. I still loved that baby but I thought it might be better all round if I could imagine she was dead. I think that may be when I really began to hate myself. Mike too. But chiefly myself. I used to get pretty depressed. Beth is right, you know. The divorce wasn't all Mike's fault. I wasn't much fun to be with. I refused to entertain any more and didn't go out. I just withdrew into a private hell.'

'When did you move down here?'

'Very shortly afterwards, thank goodness. Mike got a new job, which meant I had to give up mine, but at least it was a fresh start. I did begin to try again a little. Though at the back of my mind, the guilt of leaving Suzanne behind always festered.

'The move gave me something to think about, anyway. Nothing spiritual, of course. Just new kitchen units and the pattern of the curtains. One day I woke up sick of it all. But for the moment it absorbed me, just as it does my mother. It's frightening how materialistic you can become without realising it, when you haven't got enough to do and you're unhappy.'

'And when did you have Sarah?'

'She's nearly two. She was born two years after Suzanne.'

'You didn't wait too long then?'

'Well, no.' Jennifer shifted uncomfortably in her chair. 'I have to admit she was a mistake. I already knew Mike had been having an affair. It was the last thing we wanted. He suggested a termination, of course. But I'd had enough. We decided to try again for the sake of the baby. Misguided, I know. But I thought he meant it. I had tests of course, to make sure she wasn't another Down's. But when they seemed OK I went on with it, just the same.'

'And Mike's affair continued too?'

'Yes. I believe there was a short interlude, after the baby was born. But it didn't last long. Mike loves Sarah and is very concerned about her in his way. But he doesn't actually like babies and toddlers. He will prefer her when she's ten.

'It's all a terrible mess, I know. I'm sure you wonder how I could ever have become pregnant again. But we were on holiday, you see, and I felt very unhappy, because I knew about Maeve – that was the girl involved – and I didn't know what was going to happen or even what I wanted to happen. I drank too much as usual and forgot several pills. And we did . . . well, what we did. How difficult it is to find a suitable word without being coarse! More than sleeping together obviously. But certainly not making love. Making a baby, in this case, anyway. I couldn't even tell you how I felt. I'm sure I was much too drunk.'

'And are you an alcoholic, Jennifer?'

'Aren't you supposed to tell me that?'

'I'd like to know what you think.'

Jennifer considered the question seriously.

'No,' she said. 'Not yet.'

CHAPTER THIRTEEN

'So you don't really mind getting divorced?' asked Annabelle innocently. A little flurry of icy rain hit the window like a shower of stones.'

'Like hell I do!' Jennifer snapped back. This prissy girl was beginning to annoy her. Annabelle raised her eyebrows. Jennifer Warrender was getting rattled at last. Strange it should be over this, despite all the protestations.

'But you seem to want your marriage to end, from what you've said.'

'Do I? How can I tell? It's just happened to me. From the outside, like everything else. How can I be sure what I really feel?'

'You seem to have left your husband in no doubt.'

'Yes, I know. But that's something else. It's part of the hurt. You have no idea – how could you – what it feels like to be on the wrong end of adultery. No matter how much you try to accept it philosophically, you can't run away from the facts. Someone else has been preferred and you are discarded. Second-rate and second-best. There's no place to hide and no way to get back the self-respect. Maybe there never will be.'

'Was that really why you took the tablets, then?'

'It had an awful lot to do with it. I can't pretend otherwise.'

'Then you really want your husband back?'

Jennifer shook her head slowly. 'Oh no, not now. It's over and gone. Of course I still feel something for him, though I never really loved him properly. But it can't be salvaged now. There are too many nails in the coffin.'

'Then you're ready to start a new life without him?'

'I haven't much choice, have I, seeing as your colleagues pumped me and dripped me and got my heart-rate under control?'

'Would you do that, again?'

'For God's sake! Look, I know you're supposed to ask, but what the hell is the point? Do you really think I would tell you anyway?'

Annabelle looked uncomfortable.

'I haven't the slightest idea what will happen to me but I did discover after all that I wanted to live . . . and not just for Sarah . . . although she's the one who'll keep me going. Satisfied?'

Annabelle had no idea what to write in the case-sheets when Jennifer had gone. Today was Thursday and it was Dr Mahler's ward-round tomorrow. What could she say about Jennifer? Had there been any progress? Any healing value in all those tears? She sighed. What was the point in patching up all these people anyway when they didn't want to be helped? Her fiancéwas right. There was no way she should stay in Psychiatry.

Dr Mahler settled himself behind his desk, tucking in his tummy and winking broadly at Annabelle. Then he cast his eye quickly down the list of patients.

'Well, shall we deal with the easy ones first? What about Jennifer Warrender? Ready for discharge?'

Annabelle shuffled her feet despairingly.

'Come on, Annabelle-on-a-bike, what do you think? I hear you've spent oodles of time with her.'

'Have you seen the notes, sir?'

'Briefly. I'd rather know what conclusions you came to and why.'

'Well, quite frankly, sir, I just don't see how she's going to manage if we let her go home today.'

Dr Mahler pressed his fingertips together and chuckled. 'Would it surprise you, Annabelle, to know that the impression the outside world receives of such people is quite different from ours?'

'Well no, but surely ours is the truer version?'

'I wonder. We're just a stage along the road, you know – a temporary refuge. We're not really all that important. You sit here and listen to the sorry tale and wonder how on earth they managed to get as far as they did, without invoking our help. Am I right?'

Annabelle nodded in fascination.

'And you certainly can't see how they're going to manage when they go out. But they will. They'll go on . . . possibly making the same mistakes over and over again of course, but getting by. Yes, getting by. And that's what it's all about! Naturally I'm not talking about your true depressive or your schizophrenic now. They do need our help. I'm probably not talking about your true inadequate either. Not Helen anyway. But basically normal people like Jennifer Warrender. You make the odd mistake, of course. But you can't keep them all under lock and key. Is she still suicidal?' He spread his hands, as if to say: who knows?

'I don't think so,' admitted Annabelle. 'At the beginning of the week, I would have said yes. She just sat and cried and had an incredibly low opinion of herself. But that seems to be over now. I just don't know.'

Dr Mahler smiled and pointed to Annabelle's notes. 'I agree with you that there is a tremendous potential for depression here. Her suicide attempt was serious enough. But you have to remember she's going through a crisis right now and she'd been drinking heavily. I hope you impressed on her the need to cut back on that, by the way. I think she'll feel better when this divorce is through. It may be just what she needs: the chance to make her own decisions at last. She's not very good at that, of course, because she hadn't had much practise. Her upbringing is to blame. We've both met Mrs Sugden. Classic. But Jennifer has got some initiative. I think she will make out . . . Well, I don't want to spend all day on this girl. Can we have her in now please, Sister?'

When Jennifer came into the room, her hair was brushed, her clothes attractive and her make-up was on. Dr Mahler gave Annabelle a significant look.

'Sit down, Jennifer,' he said. 'Nice to see you looking better. How would you feel about the idea of going home soon?'

'Soon?' Jennifer appeared to be disappointed. 'Actually, I had arranged with my mother-in-law that I would pick my little girl up tomorrow. Dr Jowett hinted there might be a possibility . . . '

'Excellent. Then our views concur. You may go whenever you wish.'

'There's only one thing . . . I'm not sleeping very well and I did wonder if I might have a small supply of sleeping tablets.'

'I don't think that would be advisable,' said Dr Mahler. 'Of course, you are perfectly free to go to your own GP if the problem persists and ask him; but I hope you won't. It's not because I think you'll scoff the lot, but because it would be preferable not to start that habit.'

'I understand.'

'And you're not going to let yourself be wheeled back into our ITU, are you?'

'I shall try not to.'

'Excellent. You must forgive my apparent flippancy. There's no point in beating about the bush.'

Jennifer smiled to show that she appreciated that and the effect was remarkable. Sitting there with the sunlight on her hair, she was managing to look completely self-possessed and Annabelle was amazed.

'I can see you're in no mood to bare your all this morning,' Dr Mahler continued. 'So it's just as well that Dr Jowett has filled me in with all the details. One thing which strikes me is that this renunciation of your handicapped child could be remedied, you know. Perhaps you could start going to see her again? Then taking her out. She'll be four now, won't she? Maybe build up to the idea of having her home for short periods. Not all of a sudden, of course. Do it gradually and only when you feel you can cope with it. I could be wrong, but I think that might go some way towards assuaging your guilt feelings. Oh yes, and you won't let your mother continue to blackmail you emotionally, will you?'

Jennifer nodded. 'I think I've come to very similar conclusions myself,' she said. 'Rather belatedly. I just wish I could relive it all and get it right second time round.'

'Oh no,' said Dr Mahler. 'You wouldn't want to do that. Don't even think about it. You'd cock it up worse than before!'

Annabelle gasped and Jennifer raised an eyebrow.

'My worthy house officer is shocked . . . but I think you will be able to see what I'm driving at. It's no good wishing that sort of thing. Life will never be perfect. There's no such place as a Garden of Eden. Instead, we've got one holy muddle. You have to get by as best you can. Given the mistakes, the wrong turnings and your own failings. You can't just say: if I only knew then what I know now. That's not allowed. You have to get on with it. And you'd never get it all right, you know. People always think they would, but they wouldn't.'

The sunshine flooded into the room. Outside, the trees were trying to creep sneakily into leaf and the birds were singing. In another week or so, the leaves would appear in their newest, freshest lime and apple green and the gardens would all be in flower.

'Lecture over,' said Dr Mahler. 'Keep off the booze. How would an out-patients' appointment in six weeks suit you? I shall be away unfortunately, but Dr Jowett could check you out.'

'That reminds me,' said Jennifer. 'I think I was rather rude to Dr Jowett last time we talked and I wanted apologise.'

'Oh, don't worry about that!' said Dr Mahler, blithely. 'She's used to it and, if she isn't by now, she jolly well ought to be.'

Well thought Annabelle crossly, if that doesn't just about take the biscuit! But she was rather glad to hear what Jennifer had said, all the same.

She found herself feeling quite curious six weeks later, on seeing Jennifer's name on her clinic list. The woman who walked into her room didn't look any different. She was still smartly, though more casually dressed. Her voice, when she spoke, held the same intonations . . . that Yorkshire accent, with its edges knocked off. But she did have a two-year-old with her.

'I had to bring Sarah. I hope you don't mind.'

'No, of course not.' She watched Jennifer taking some toys out of a bag for the child who studiously ignored them and set off straight for the trolley which held all the equipment for taking blood.

'Hello, what's your name?'

That produced an immediate scurrying back to her mother's skirts to hide, with a solemn face. Rapport, thought Annabelle, was a strange thing. Children were far more predictable than adults. Despite their intensive conversation, she and Jennifer Warrender didn't really have it. They would have to start all over again. And yet Mahler, for all his bluntness and lack of time, had homed straight in on the right target.

'How are you getting on?'

'Not too badly.'

'Are you sleeping any better?'

'Oh, yes! I'm always tired now.'

Not perhaps the good sign it appeared to be. Annabelle tried again. 'And your general health?'

'Oh [illegible] all right. I do forget to eat or can't be [illegible] I haven't really lost much weight.'

[illegible]ade any plans for the future?'

[illegible]e house is virtually sold. So I'll be

putting them into action soon. I'm going to move back to Yorkshire. Not, I hasten to add, to be near my mother, but to make it easier to see Suzanne. I couldn't possibly take her away from where she's settled. Unfortunately, the two things do rather go together – but I told Beth quite plainly I didn't expect to see much of her. We had a row of course. It's impossible to do anything else when you cross my mother. But I've got a house, although the contract's not quite through yet. It's empty though, so I'm reasonably hopeful. It's about eight miles from Kingley . . . a tiny cottage someone's recently done up. Thank goodness the differential in house prices has worked in my favour for once . . . I couldn't have afforded anything decent down here.'

'Have you seen Suzanne?'

'Yes! I was very worried about it. But it went reasonably well. Of course I'm sure she's not aware I'm really her mother . . . just an aunty who's turned up out of the blue, with nice things. I can never give back the time she should have had. Or expect her to respond as well as she might have done. But I think it's going to work out.'

'You really have been very busy, then!'

'Yes, that's good, isn't it? I suppose I'll fall flat on my face after the move. There are still some bad days when I can't stop thinking about the past. But, generally . . . it's getting better.'

'Do you know anyone in Yorkshire, now?'

'Not really. I've been away some time.'

'You might find a single parent group, like Gingerbread, useful.'

Jennifer shook her head, with a wry smile.

'I don't think so. I've been through all that before – that sort of thing, anyway, and it didn't really work for me. I guess I'm a bit of a loner.'

'And never lonely?'

'Of course I am. But I'm not as afraid of it as I used

to be. I shan't become Miss Bryant now.'

'Because of the children?'

'I suppose so. I'm not loveless now, you see. Just sexless. Which is of lesser importance. I think I can be reasonably content.'

'They'll grow.'

'Suzy won't, that much . . . but I take your point. We all have that problem in the end though.'

'Are you drinking as much now?'

'No. It's still a prop, I'll admit that. But it's under control. I shan't become an alcoholic.'

Of course they always said that and Annabelle wondered. But the time had come to discharge Jennifer Warrender and they both knew it.

'Would you like to continue seeing a psychiatrist up north?'

'Oh no, I don't think so.'

Dr Jowett nodded. 'Fine. Well, I'm sure Dr Mahler needn't see you again. It only remains for me to wish you all the best with your move.'

'Thank you very much.'

At the door, Jennifer turned. 'Tell me, are you going to stay in Psychiatry? I know it's a bit of a personal question but I'd like to know.'

'That's all right . . . I don't mind. Yes, as a matter of fact I am.'

Jennifer nodded.

'Good for you . . . I'm glad. I'm sure you'll do very well. I found you were very easy to talk to and I'd like to thank you for that.'

Well, what do you know, thought Annabelle Jowett! She felt considerably cheered up. But why on earth had she said she was going to stay in Psychiatry? Because she had only decided in the last five minutes. She knew it was what she wanted, after all. And that was important. Her fiancé wouldn't be entirely pleased, she suspected. But it mattered and she had to remain faithful to that.

Somewhere in the long cream plastic corridors with their glass windows and hospital smell, Jenny met Pauline Parker on her way out. Of all people in the world! She was bustling along in a white coat, with her hair scraped back under a theatre cap and her flat, black nursing shoes squeaked and flapped over the endless miles of lino. It was really due to Sarah that they met at all because she had been determined to toddle in the opposite direction from her mother. When Jennifer had tried to coax, she sat down on some stairs and shrieked 'no' in an ear-splitting yell. Exasperated, Jenny walked away waving but that didn't work either. It was on her way back that she bumped into Pauline: a ghost from the past who had hardly changed at all.

'Ooops! Sorry! I say, it's Jenny, isn't it? Jennifer Sugden!'

'Yes, it is. Hello, Pauline. How are you? Are you working here?'

'Yes! In anaesthetics. Registrar, still, of course. But hoping! I'm fine.' Heavens, she must have improved! 'How are you?'

'Oh, I'm fine, too. I've just been to an outpatient's clinic, that's all.'

'You look marvellous.'

Bound to, thought Jennifer wryly. It just shows you.

'Are you living near here then?'

'Yes. Quite near.'

'Really? I say, do come and see me sometime.'

'Well, actually Pauline, I'm about to move back to Yorkshire.'

'Oh, drat! Never mind. Has your husband got a new job then?'

'No,' Jennifer hesitated. There was no point in prevarication. 'In fact, I'm divorced. It's just me and Sarah going back.'

'Oh, Jenny! I'm so sorry. Trust me to put my foot in it.'

'Of course you haven't! It's all right. I've had a bit of a rough time but it's all over now. It just didn't work out.' How easy it was to sound so glib! Perhaps if she said it often enough, she could start to believe it herself.

'And this is your little girl? Isn't she pretty?'

'Yes, that's Sarah. Excuse me.' Jennifer darted away to rescue some plant pots from the window. 'No, Sarah – that's naughty, don't!' The baby giggled and clapped her hands, then ran away at a cracking pace only to trip over her own two feet and fall flat on her face. But, after an indignant wail, she picked herself up and carried on.

'Heavens, she's off! I'll have to go, Pauline, I'm sorry! Its nice to see you again though. I'm glad you're doing well . . . I must say I admire you for it. Perhaps I'll see you again. 'Bye!'

They carried on their separate ways with separate thoughts. Pauline Parker – soon-to-be consultant anaesthetist, no doubt. And here am I, chasing a child I can hardly cope with down a hospital corridor, after visiting a psychiatric clinic. But Pauline felt downcast too. She had always liked Jenny and she would have really liked to see her again. Pauline was a great one for keeping in touch. She had a Christmas card list as long as your arm, possibly to disguise the fact that she still had no real friends. That year she was able to add a little gossip to the one she sent Jocasta . . . 'met Jenny Sugden briefly this Spring . . . she had just got divorced and was going to move back to Yorkshire. Poor Jenny! She doesn't seem to have much luck, does she?'

In the car-park, Jennifer struggled to strap Sarah into her safety seat. They were both cross and tired. In the end, she managed it despite a rigid body and screams of protest. Then she drove off as it started to rain, while Sarah mercifully began to suck her blanket and her thumb. Within minutes, she was asleep and peace had returned. Jenny relaxed to the rhythm of the windscreen wipers and the swish of the tyres over a wet road. She didn't care how long it took to drive home now, although the traffic would be appalling as usual. Sarah wouldn't sleep again today, so she might as well make the most of it. Why had she ever imagined being a mother was easy? She was glad she had her, though, just the same. Sometimes it was fun. And there was still nothing else.

The sky grew dark and the trees seemed greener while the wet blossoms made splashes and patches of colour through the rain. For mile upon mile, wet roofs shone like snail-shells and Jennifer drove on, feeling absurdly hopeful.

CODA

O! Never say that I was false of heart,
Though absence seemed my flame to qualify.
As easy might I from myself depart
As from my soul, which in they breast both lie:
That is my home of love; if I have ranged,
Like him that travels, I return again,
Just to the time, not with the time exchanged,
So that myself bring water for my stain.
Never believe, though in my nature reigned
All frailties that besiege all kinds of blood,
That it could so preposterously be stained,
To leave for nothing all thy sum of good;
For nothing this wide universe I call
Save thou, my rose; in it thou art my all.'

WILLIAM SHAKESPEARE

'Would you do me a favour, Jennifer?'

Jennifer bit back the automatic urge, sprung out of years of excessive politeness, to say: 'Why, of course!' Instead she hesitated and immediately thought of all the feminist meetings she had attended with Sue, the nuclear disarmament meetings, the conservationist pressure groups and the favourite Third World charity. She remembered how uncomfortable she had felt at all of them and said, rather warily, 'Well, that rather depends on what it is.'

This time she promised herself to be honest. She was getting better at it, though not quickly enough. She was aware of growing tired of instant classification from people she hardly knew at all. Still she poured out the coffee for her friend and employer and pushed it across the table with a rueful smile.

'Not another meeting, Sue. I've too much on.'

'Oh no,' said Sue. 'It's nothing like that.'

It was three years later and a warm afternoon sun was finding its way somehow into the darker recesses of the second-hand bookshop which Sue ran in this now fashionable little Yorkshire town on the edge of the Dales. It was an autumn sun. The rowan berries had been out for some time and the day was still and peaceful and already well advanced. There was something convincing about its quietude which stated quite plainly that summer had gone, despite any evidence to the contrary. The shop was deserted and the two women, with time on their hands, were cataloguing new stock.

'Tell me, then,' said Jennifer.

Sue sighed and pushed large lenses back up her nose. She was rather a pretty person but the enormity of her glasses magnified her in a manner which tended to startle.

'It is a bit of a trial', she admitted. 'It's to do with the Literature Festival next week.'

'Oh yes. Do you want me to do extra hours at the Book Fair? I don't mind that so much.'

'No.' Sue sipped her coffee. 'But you know I've got to entertain a visiting author . . . dinner and all that? Well, I could do with some help . . . with the social chit-chat, I mean.'

Jennifer was relieved. 'You mean that you're asking me to dinner? That doesn't sound too unpleasant! A week Friday, isn't it? Peter Donaldson? I expect I can come.'

Sue grimaced. 'A week Friday, yes. But Peter Donaldson, no. He can't come now because his wife's seriously ill. There's been a panic on. They've managed to get Dominic Grant to speak the same evening instead. You won't have heard of him. And now I'm lumbered!'

The door of the shop opened and the tinkling of its bell sounded very loud to Jennifer in her silence. Both women listened and waited until they heard the contented footsteps of a browser and then they relaxed again. Jennifer pretended to study the index she had been completing earlier.

'Actually, I have!' she said brightly. 'Heard of him, I mean.'

'Sorry! I didn't mean to be condescending . . . he's just not that well-known. I should have realised I could rely on you. You haven't actually read his books, have you?'

'I've read two of them.'

'And the third one's only just come out! How marvellous . . . Jennifer, you really are a gem! Now you really have to come along and help me.'

'I don't know . . . Friday night is rather difficult. I'd forgotten about Suzy coming home and that complicates the babysitting arrangements. I'd probably have to ask my mother which I don't like doing . . .'

'Oh Jennifer, please! I know it isn't easy for you and I can't even promise you such a good evening now. Peter Donaldson would have been great, I was really looking forward to him. But do please try, Jennifer . . . you can't leave Phil and me to cope alone.'

Jennifer felt ruffled. 'Why ever not?' she asked. 'What's wrong with . . . Grant?' She imagined the surname sounded awkwardly on her lips when Donaldson would have been just fine.

'Oh well, nothing really,' Sue pulled distractedly at her very short hair, 'but you know the type.'

'No, I don't.'

'Well, goodness knows I've learnt over the years I've helped with the Festival that writers are not necessarily the most entertaining creatures when they open their mouths, but this guy's a real pain.'

'You've already met him, then?'

'Oh yes, a couple of times. He's been before, though not recently. He's a Roman Catholic of course and very right-wing, which naturally doesn't go down too well with me but it's not just that . . . '

'He used to be very left-wing and he's not a practising Catholic anyway, you know.'

'Oh yes he is! Dyed in the wool, I would have said.' Sue stopped short, suddenly suspicious: 'How do you know?' she asked.

Jennifer laid down her pen with great care. 'He graduated from Liverpool.'

It took a while for the significance to sink in. Then Sue remembered. 'Of course! You were there too for a while. Did you know him as a student then? That's interesting! How well did you know him?'

Jennifer decided there was no point in prevaricating, but no need to tell the whole story either.

'He asked me to marry him once.'

Sue gasped. 'No! An old flame then?'

'I suppose so . . . yes.'

'Heavens! Obviously you said no. How extremely intelligent of you!'

'I wasn't convinced of that at the time.'

'No? Well, I can imagine he *might* have been a spectacular sort of student. But nobody else said yes either, so you must have been right.'

'You mean he's still unmarried?'

'Confirmed bachelor, I believe.'

'Oh dear, that doesn't sound like Dominic at all.'

'I say, you don't still . . . well, feel anything for him, do you?' Sue asked awkwardly.

'Well, of course not . . . it was just a slight shock to hear his name again.'

'Yes . . . sorry! Silly question really. Will you be embarrassed?'

Jennifer considered. 'No, I don't think so. But do tell me why you don't like him.'

'Did I say that?'

'You implied he was a pain in the arse. In fact, you said so.'

'Yes, well, I'm sorry, but he is.' Sue looked at her friend warily but, seeing that she appeared to be amused, began to laugh too. 'He must be one of the most arrogant men I've come across. Talks all the time but it's always about himself and his bloody boring books. I hesitate to use the word chauvinist . . . '

'Naturally!'

' . . . but really I have to say he's done the world a service by remaining single. Though actually I'm quite surprised he hasn't found some doe-like home-loving creature to plod round after him from pillar to post, picking up his socks and generally being there to provide.'

'You're very cutting,' said Jennifer. 'Don't you think you could be being a teeny bit unfair?'

'Nope,' Sue shook her head firmly. 'Not with this one. Of course he's superficially charming. But that doesn't cut any ice with me. Attractive, possibly . . . but of course he knows it. No, I'm convinced you had a very narrow escape!'

'I'm not convinced we're talking about the same person!' laughed Jennifer. 'Though of course people change, don't they?' She couldn't in truth feel sure of that but tried not to sound too doubtful. 'Anyway, I'll see next Friday.'

The customer in the shop had started to cough and shuffle his feet and she got up, glad of the diversion.

'You are coming then?'

Jennifer nodded. 'I have to, now. You've fired my curiosity.'

'Jolly good.'

'But he ought to know I'm going to be there. In advance, I mean. We had rather a stormy parting twelve years ago. I don't suppose it means much to him now but he ought to know. Is he speaking before or after dinner?'

'Before.'

'That's something then. But he has to know and you must have some other guests as well. It wouldn't be fair otherwise.'

'Yes, Jennifer. I am trying!'

Jennifer drove along the Grove in her blue Mini. It was still an amazingly beautiful afternoon though the days were shortening perceptibly. The late summer flowers had all gone long since in the brevity of the northern summer. The contents of the hanging baskets on the lamp-posts were withering daily and the only splashes of colour in the fields now came from scarlet berries and amber-turning leaves. The stubble from the corn had been burned or ploughed back the month before and the only bales left out now were getting sodden.

She had forgotten so much about the ambience of this area once: how high and green the hills were, how up and down each road, how wide and open the moors and even how much grey stone there was built into each wall and house and outbuilding, each oddly rural mill-chimney. It was only since coming back that she had realised how deeply its atmosphere was impregnated in her bones. She wouldn't want to leave it now.

She picked Sarah up from infant school and drove on, another eight miles, up past the big reservoir and down into the next deep valley where Beth still lived on the outskirts of Kingley. This place still seemed more confined. Normally they would have gone straight home. But, this week, a visit had been promised. Initially, after moving back into Yorkshire, Jennifer had assiduously avoided her mother. But Beth was aging and alone. It was also clear that, not only did Beth enjoy Sarah, but Sarah enjoyed Beth. Even Suzy was welcome now. Jennifer had gradually come to realise that she had no right to keep her children from their grandmother. It was bad enough that they never saw their father (which was Mike's decision, not hers). It made life easier in a way but she worried constantly about the effect it would have on them. So she had made her peace with her mother.

Beth had moved out of 'Lorelei' long since but her new bungalow in no way resembled a pensioner's. Jennifer reflected that there was something intrinsically Beth-like in its perfectly laid out garden, its fabulous fully-fitted kitchen complete with microwave and its pin-clean, heavily-ornamented lounge. Of course she still had help. Ironically, Ken's insurance policies had left her better off now than if he had been alive. She was strangely touched and yet untouched by his death. Jennifer thought of her father with indulgent but critical fondness as she got out of the car.

Her mother received them with exclamations of delight and too many cakes for tea. She wore russet like autumn itself and looked as neatly manicured as ever. They both tried to find out what Sarah had been doing at school for it was still all very new, but they weren't successful.

Jennifer could see that her child was on a high and yet, underneath it all, exhausted as well. She wondered if she could skip her bath when they got home . . . there was so little time in the morning though. Her job at the bookshop, which had started quite casually as another favour to Sue, was involving more of her time now Sarah had started school. Of course that was welcome. Like many women, Jennifer was aware that she was working beneath her capabilities, but she didn't really care. There was at last something else. Over the last three years at her cottage by the beck, she had started to paint again. She didn't expect to make her living from it. But it was very important. A separate 'me' had a last emerged from the children and it was her art which gave that expression. She still felt inadequate because the family survived on Mike's alimony and social security. She didn't earn much at the bookshop. But things were settled and sorted and working out after a fashion. Life was not so bad alone after all. She felt herself growing older and more balanced with the increasing maturity. To her surprise, she could even feel content. At least, she had done until today.

'I've got some sweeties for you,' Beth told Sarah, getting up rather stiffly from her chair.

'She's eaten hardly any tea,' Jennifer complained, noting the stiffness, as usual, with surprise. Her mother was shrinking, continually shrinking . . .

But Sarah was already jumping up and down.

'Ooh yes! Yes, yes!'

'We'll keep them until tomorrow.'

'Oh, don't be so strict! Grannies are allowed to spoil.'

Jennifer watched Sarah relentlessly work her way through the bag of sticky sweets and drop bits on the floor. She couldn't believe she had ever been allowed to do that. How times changed! Were they all role-playing, all of the time, then? Had Beth only done what she had out of misguided motherly love? The thought appalled her because she knew now that she might unintentionally do the same. Then she looked across the room straight into the shy eyes of a very young Chloe in a very old photograph, dandling a baby on her knee. Doubtless Sue would have described Chloe as 'doe-like and home-loving'. And she, Jennifer, was far more like Chloe than Beth. She twisted the thin band of gold she now wore on her right hand. But not, she told herself firmly, to that extent. Not in the least. She had thrown off the chains of an earlier unsatisfactory marriage and struck out on her own. In particular, she had nothing to fear from seeing Dominic again. Though suddenly the very idea of it scared her half to death.

'Are you all right, dear?' asked Beth. 'You seem a bit low today.'

Beth was often surprised at how well her daughter had coped alone. With her illusions finally shattered, she had adopted the more common attitude of deprecation toward her daughter. Any achievement now was a source of mild astonishment. And the spectre of the psychiatric ward still on occasion, rose to haunt her.

'I'm fine, absolutely fine,' insisted Jennifer. 'Just a bit tired. I expect it's the time of the month. Can I ask you to babysit for me a week Friday?'

Beth tried not to look too pleased. 'But of course, dear!'

'Suzy as well.'

'Now you know I love her too. You don't have to say that every time.'

The criticism was justified and Jennifer felt slightly ashamed. 'I'm sorry. Would you like to stay the night? I could be late.'

'Couldn't I have them here? There's so much more room and it would be a great treat.'

Jennifer hesitated but once again Sarah jumped up and down. 'Ooh! Yes please, mummy!'

'Don't bounce on Granny's sofa! Are you sure that's all right?'

'Well, of course it is! You go out and enjoy yourself. Have a lie-in in the morning too, for a change. You know I don't think you go out enough. Those nightclasses don't count.'

'There's not actually anywhere much to go, for someone in my position. I tend to rely on a few good friends.'

'Haven't you ever thought of a singles' club or computer dating?' Beth asked brightly.

Jennifer groaned. 'You don't know what you're talking about,' she said. 'I'm not that desperate.'

'But you're not going to stay unmarried for the rest of your life, I hope?'

'Why not? I rather like it.'

'It's not normal.'

Jennifer was exasperated. 'Don't be silly, mother,' she said. 'The world has changed, thank goodness. I don't need a man . . . certainly not a computerised one. I'm not lonely. I've made some good friends.'

'Your arty crowd in Bickley?'

'If you like.'

'You always have been attracted to that sort of person.'

'Well, I am an artist.'

'But not a proper one . . . I mean professional. Where are you going on Friday?'

'To Sue's . . . for dinner.' Because she was still smarting over her mother's last remark, devilment drove her on. 'Actually, someone you know will be there.'

'Someone I know?'

'Yes. Dominic Grant.'

Beth's eyes registered all manner of emotions. 'Don't fall for an old flame,' was all she said finally. 'It's never a good idea.'

Jennifer laughed. 'I'm inclined to agree with you. But you've nothing to worry about. He's only visiting and he's supposed to be much changed. Sue doesn't like him one bit.'

'Oh dear, do you really think you should go?' Beth had begun to panic.

Jennifer chose to ignore this. 'Sue says he's become

positively right-wing . . . mind you, that doesn't mean much, coming from her. But he's also gone back to the Church.'

Beth was frankly relieved. 'Well, he won't be able to marry you now then, will he?' she said. 'Not if he's become a proper Catholic. They don't agree with divorce.'

'Still hate him, mother?' asked Jennifer, softly. 'After all these years? Don't worry! I'm only going to lay a ghost and help Sue out.'

'Mummy, what's 'puter dating?' asked Sarah out of the blue, when they had got home.

'Something you can do with computers,' said Jennifer, warily. She didn't like to be misleading but she wasn't ready for this one. 'Hurry up with those clothes.'

'Granny said you should have one.'

'*I* don't think so. It's time you were in bed!'

But when she was, and instantly asleep despite all protests, Jennifer rather wished she wasn't. She lit the lamps and drew the curtains and poured herself a large drink. That was unusual now. Normally it was coffee, to revive herself before painting for most of the evening. Not the ideal time of day to work but it was almost the only time she had to herself. But she couldn't do it tonight. She put a record on . . . Albinoni's 'Adagio' . . . but that wasn't a wise choice with its wistful, regret-laden strains and she ended up by turning it off sharply and going outside into the garden instead, in search of fresh air.

It was already dark. The beck which ran on the far side of her fence was full of its own song in the night. The moon was up too, a giant orange harvest moon, over-blown and surrealisitic. Soon the leaves would start to drop more thickly. She stood and listened to the silence which was only accentuated by the silver tongue of the stream, the rustling of the black leaves and the modest lights of her neighbours' houses. Somewhere close at hand, an owl screeched and she had the strange and awful feeling that her fate was approaching relentlessly on wings through the night.

But that was such rubbish! She mustn't fall into that trap. So Domi was coming back and she had behaved impeccably at e news. It was only to be expected that her inner feelings were far from impeccable. Confused. Uncertain. Unwilling to believe he could still hold the same magical quality for her. But wondering . . .

At first, she had found it hard to accept the picture Sue painted. She had first suggested they were talking about different people, then that Dominic had changed. But of course he hadn't, given the not uncommon swing in political and religious views which occurs between youth and early middle age. Of course it was Dominic. It was Dominic all over. It was just that she, in her own youth, had never seen him like that. Beth had been right all along and she had been wrong. I never made my own mind up about anything, Jennifer thought. And if I had thrown off my mother's tyranny, it would only have been to accept Dominic's. She swallowed hard. People didn't really change. Where did that leave her then?

But things *were* different now. Of course it was a mistake to say she had divorced Mike. He had decided to leave her and the resultant hurt left her no choice. But it had turned out pretty well, hadn't it? She was doing things now she would never have done, had she stayed with Mike. She had a modest job, a place of her own, she had started to paint, she was re-educating herself slowly. She thought about what Beth had said about marriage. It was true that she no longer wanted to marry. There had been two or three men at Sue's meetings and even at the nightclasses who had shown an obvious interest. One of them had really been very pleasant. She had shied away, keeping herself private and untouchable. Over the last three years, she had painted a lot of the pain out of herself . . . in dark colours and weird shapes and disturbing scenes. But it was still there, raw and untouchable underneath.

The confident, self-appreciating identity that had emerged was mainly veneer. She didn't think she was bitter about men but she didn't want another relationship with all its hazards, thank you very much. She was aware that some of the men believed, because she was so close to Sue and they were often together and because of the feminist meetings, that they had lesbian tendencies. But she didn't even care very much if it kept them away.

But Dominic was different. He had breached the defences a long time ago. Unless she was to be disillusioned, he would provide a serious challenge. He had even inconveniently remained unmarried. She worried about that. Had she marked him in some way then? But no, surely not! That was a colossal conceit. She could not have been that important. And as her mother had rather triumphantly pointed out, the divorce would provide a barrier if he was really serious about his return to Catholicism.

But why had she said she would go? Because there was no alternative once Sue had told her of the opportunity. She didn't know what she expected or even what she wanted. But she had to go. Wasn't that her all over? It was entirely wrong. She did not have to go.

'Sue . . . I know this is very silly of me and I do hate to let you down . . . but I've decided not to go after all.'

Yes. That was what she would say. She rehearsed it a little before she got to the shop.

'He knows you're coming,' said Sue briskly.

'Oh no! Sue, he doesn't!'

'I'm afraid he does. You did say, Jennifer . . . in fact you were most insistent about it.'

'I know. I was, wasn't I?'

'What's the matter?' Sue's voice sounded gentle. 'Cold feet syndrome?'

'Yes . . . very much so.'

'Don't worry, darling. We'll take good care to protect you!'

'I'm not sure that you can.'

'Well, if you feel like that about it, you really must come and prepare yourself for disillusionment.'

'What did he say about me?'

'How nice it would be to see you again.' Sue thought about it. 'There was a slight gap when I told him . . . four seconds' worth, I guess. He may have been temporarily floored. But he made a good recovery. Of course I didn't tell him you were divorced, though I did speak of you as Jennifer Warrender.'

'Of course. Have you found anyone else?'

Sue mentioned the names of two other friends. 'And my sister's coming. They're not exactly literary, though. I still need you.'

'I'm not exactly literary.'

'You've read his books. Are you planning on going to the talk first?'

'Yes, of course.'

'Good. Then you can collect him and drive him back to us.'

'Oh no!'

'Well, I shan't have time. And it seems a bit impersonal to send Philip. Anyway, I think it's a jolly good idea. You can say anything you have to in the car on the way over, instead of storing it up all through dinner. I say, can you remember if he likes curry? I forgot to ask on the phone.'

'He didn't use to. Not very much anyway.'

'Bloody hell! I just knew he was going to be awkward.'

It was not a bad turn-out but Jennifer could hear people saying what a shame Peter Donaldson was unable to make it. She took her seat at the back with vicarious nerves. There were her own to contend with as well. Of course she had had her hair done and was wearing new clothes and make-up. Twelve years was a long time. No matter how much she might dislike him now, she couldn't allow herself to feel unattractive.

He was late, which was totally in character, and the room was noisy with uncontrolled conversation. It was also very hot and Jennifer removed her jacket. She felt that the lights were harsh and bright when they could have been dimmed quite easily, for the venue was a small theatre above a hall. Only the front seats were really full. A table, with two chairs behind it and two glasses of water on it, waited against the black backdrop of the stage. Outside it was raining and you could hear large drops spatter the window-panes occasionally. All day there had been that unearthly glowing light which comes from the co-existence of dark black clouds and sunshine. Jennifer's legs had taken root and her palms were clammy.

There wasn't an instant hush when he arrived. In fact it took a while for the babble of conversation to die down . . . it abated temporarily but rose up again so that Sue, who had brought him in, had to hold up her hands. Jennifer would have been irritated normally but could only feel the shock. She thought she had forgotten what he looked like but it wasn't true. Her recognition was instant although there were several changes.

She tried to take them all in as Sue introduced him and his female interviewer before discreetly disappearing. (It was felt unwise to let an author spout without any guidance at all.) He had put on a little weight and he looked older. He was not, after all, the type of person who never changed. Naturally his hair was shorter. It was very unusual to see a man with long hair now. It seemed to have lost something of its cornfield brightness with the cut, although it was still very blond. A somewhat faded flaxen yellow perhaps. She realised suddenly that he would go white rather than grey. It was still very thick hair which tended to fall onto his forehead, despite being cropped, and he still had the ineffectual mannerism of brushing it back with his hand. He was wearing glasses and that was a surprise. She couldn't remember that he had ever been short-sighted and she couldn't imagine him old enough yet to have problems with longsight. Perhaps they both were. The frames of his glasses must have been very pale and thin and neutral in colour because, unlike Sue's, they hardly obtruded at all. He wore a collar and tie which was also entirely new. His shirt was a garish burgundy stripe, his trousers and tie black, but his jacket a definite chestnut shade of brown and she found herself suspecting that the resultant clash was entirely intentional.

It was difficult to concentrate but she must pay attention if she was later to make comments which were not inane. He was reading a passage from his new novel at present to illustrate some point or other, as requested by the interviewer. He did not appear to be nervous but then she wouldn't have expected all that old confidence to evaporate without any trace. Nevertheless, when he had finished, he slouched back in his chair with his hands in his pockets and his attitude held more than a touch of defiance. Sue had said that his first novel had won a prize. She had rather glossed over the second which had drawn critical reviews. ('Pretentious', 'unnecessarily complex', 'savage in places but ultimately weak', and, inevitably, 'disappointing after "Roads to Hell" and such a long gap'.) Jennifer had enjoyed it, though she thought she had detected several layers of un-Dominic like uncertainties.

Something had definitely happened to him since 'Roads to Hell'. That had been the kind of book she had expected him to write, with its fierce indictment of religion in general and Roman Catholicism in particular. Whatever had produced his change of heart? The interviewer was obviously equally intrigued.

'With the publication of your new book, Mr Grant, and despite your earlier novel, "Roads to Hell", you could now be classed as a leading Catholic writer. Have you any comment?'

He had, and he took lengthy issue about being a Catholic and being a writer separately but not a Catholic writer at all, which seemed unnecessarily pedantic. Jennifer found it very difficult to follow what he was saying. She had sat at the back deliberately to avoid putting him off his stride, but his voice carried and it wasn't that. Nor was she uninterested. On the contrary. But she did feel numb, as if temporarily frozen and suspended in space. The important thing was to get through the evening in as normal a way as possible.

When it was all over, there were a few questions from the floor which were limited in nature. You couldn't say it had been a resounding success. Jennifer wanted to get up herself, idiotically, to keep things going, but the idea of presenting herself to Dominic's eye in that manner, for the first time, was intolerable and she kept her seat. She continued to do this when people began to file out. At least a small knot of fans had gathered around the table to have copies of their books signed as the room slowly emptied. At last Jennifer got up to hover on the edge of the group. It gradually thinned until there were only two or three people left, hell-bent on collaring him for further discussion and argument. He must have seen her now but he gave no sign. It must have been difficult for him, standing there, trying to argue cogently and be generally impressive when he could see out of the corner of one eye a ghost from the past waiting for him. But he seemed to manage it and she thought he would never get away. Her nervousness was mounting again and she wanted to get the initial encounter over and done with. At last he held up his hands with a bland smile, indicated Jennifer and said: 'This lady is waiting to bear me off.'

There was an immediate rash of apologies then, countered by suitable disclaimers from Dominic and the last people filtered out with a few backward glances of curiosity at Jennifer.

'Jennifer! How are you?' It was said warmly enough and she was glad that she had placed herself at the opposite side of the table, to avoid any demonstrable greeting.

'I'm fine. How are you?'

That left him with the more awkward response and he smiled ruefully, knowing it. 'Very well.'

'I enjoyed your talk.'

'Oh, did you? I thought it was a bit of a disaster myself.'

'Of course it wasn't! It was good.' She wished she could have made her praise sound less hollow.

'Thank you.'

He busied himself gathering up his books and papers from the table. One sheet slipped off and curled down to the floor and Jennifer, desperate for something to say or do, knelt to retrieve it, then wished she hadn't because she felt rather ridiculous kneeling at his feet. She couldn't help noticing his shoes needed cleaning. Couldn't avoid touching his fingers briefly as she handed the paper back.

'Sue is expecting us shortly after nine, so we'd better go. I have a car outside.'

'Fine. I'm desperate for a drink. You could have rescued me earlier!'

'I wasn't sure if you wanted to be.'

'Hell, yes! I thought they'd never go. Is that your coat?'

Jennifer realised he wanted to help her put it on. 'Oh, I'm too hot,' she said hastily. 'I'll carry it for the moment.' They both knew it was a rebuff.

'Yes . . . it is hot. Those lights were appalling. I felt as if I was being grilled. Shall we go then?'

They left and she found she had forgotten how quickly he walked. He seemed to be perfectly at ease now and she was rather glad a few people she knew called goodnight to her as they passed through the hall downstairs, then ashamed of feeling that way. It had stopped raining outside but there was a chilly breeze.

'Are you sure you don't want your coat on?'

'Yes. The car's up here . . . it's not far.'

When they reached it, she had to stop in her tracks to pull him up, as you do with a companion who has no idea where he is going. She noticed, for the first time, that in her agitation to get to the hall, she had parked a good two feet from the kerb and hoped he wouldn't notice too.

'It's a Mini,' she said unnecessarily. 'Bit of a squash. I hope you don't mind.'

'Not at all.'

It was all so embarrassing and she fiddled with the keys to cover her confusion, inevitably dropping them on the floor, not once but twice, for heaven's sake. She made quite sure that she picked them up herself though. She was not in the mood for his good manners.

Inside, the car had never seemed so small. It meant he had to be unbearably close and Jennifer felt vaguely threatened, especially when he turned to fix his seat-belt. It was even worse when she tried her own.

'You've put it in the wrong thing,' she said lamely, feeling the beginnings of a blush. 'That's mine.'

'I'm sorry!' He had to bend over again to remedy the situation and, as he did so the top of his hair brushed against her briefly, electrifying her numbness and threatening to shatter it. Close up, she noticed his face had grown pleasantly lined. For a moment, madness began to prevail. She wanted to shout and scream at him, and his perfect behaviour: 'For God's sake, it's me, Jennifer! Do something, won't you? Grab me and kiss me, slap my face, try ripping my clothes off . . . anything which isn't cautious and polite!'

But rationality took over as she turned the key in the ignition and the wipers sprang shockingly into life. Somehow they had to achieve some kind of balanced conversation to break the ice before they reached Sue's. She let in the clutch and pulled out.

'Have you been to Bickley before?'

'Oh yes, though not recently. Have you lived here long?'

'Nearly three years.'

'Do you like it?'

'Very much.'

'I must say it was a bit of a shock when Sue rang and told me you would be coming to dinner.'

Jennifer felt more confident now because driving had given her something to do. How wise Sue had been!

'Yes . . . I thought it was best for Sue to warn you.'

'Oh well, that was kind but quite unnecessary. You must have known I'd love to see you again.'

'I didn't, really.'

She was aware that he was looking at her intently now, taking her to pieces, but it didn't matter because she had to watch the road and wasn't required to look back.

'You look just the same.'

'I'm sure I don't!'

'Better, actually. More lovely by far.'

'Oh, go on with you!'

They had achieved it then. The perfect balance. She didn't need to be so determinedly bright any more. He was just an old flame putting in a few compliments for form's sake. And she was the one who demonstrated, by playfully rebuffing them, that she knew they weren't intended to be serious. They could both relax.

'I have two little girls now . . . though we don't live with their father any more, as we divorced.' Casually said and casually received.

'I know,' said Dominic.

'You know!'

They had stopped at traffic-lights and she risked a glance, but Dominic looked away.

'How on earth could you know?'

'Well, not about the girls, but about the divorce. Remember Jocasta?'

'Could I ever forget?'

'She always get a Christmas card from Pauline Parker, though I doubt if she ever sends one back.'

'Heavens! Yes, I see. Goodness, that's very tenuous. More than you know.'

But Dominic was thinking how it had crossed his mind even then to look Jennifer up. But he had never done it because it had seemed so inappropriate.

'How is Jocasta? I'd love to see her again.'

'Oh, she's in the States now. In publishing. I haven't seen her for two years myself. But she doesn't seem to change. Still mildly outrageous, I suppose.'

'Lovely! And what about your parents and sisters? How are they?'

'Well, my mother died a few years ago.'

'Oh, Dominic, no! I'm sorry! She wasn't very old.'

'No . . . she had breast cancer I'm afraid. She had rather a bad time of it.'

'Oh dear, and she was such a lovely person! What about your father? How has he coped with it all?'

'Oh, he's all right, I suppose. He's retired now, of course, but I don't think he was too sorry about that. He's got his golf and his friends and the Church of course.'

'Yes.' She wanted to ask about the Church with its capital C but wasn't sure if this was the right time. They were already turning into Sue's road. Instead she said:

'And what about you, Dominic? Do you write all of the time?'

'Heavens, no! I'd starve if I did! I do all sorts of things . . . quite a bit of supply teaching, believe it or not, which I actually enjoy. Literary reviews, freelance articles . . . the Catholic press are quite good to me these days of course.'

'We're here.' Jennifer braked and turned into Sue's drive. 'A bit late but Sue must have known the discussion might run over.'

'Not as long as with Peter Donaldson, I imagine.'

He was still worrying then. Or was he fishing for compliments, perhaps?

'Oh, rubbish,' she said. 'I'm sure you were just as good. It wasn't your fault you were a stand-in.' Tactless but too late now.

Jennifer approached Sue's door with some relief and rang the bell once, then stepped inside.

Dominic felt terrible. He wished she would take his

hand or at least an arm. He wanted to explain he didn't know these people and they didn't really know him. He was tired and depressed and fed up with being in a fish-tank. He wanted her unequivocal support and he sensed it wasn't forthcoming. Initially she had been nervous but now she seemed relaxed and self-assured, positively brimming over with self-confidence and self-containment, in fact. She obviously didn't need him or anyone else. This wasn't the girl who had cried on his shoulder for endless, terrible nights and he had been rather a fool to assume she would be. She had grown up entirely, just as he, in his cruelty, had once suggested she should. Despite the hints of a stormy divorce, she had not only survived but positively blossomed into maturity. She looked marvellous in a boldly colourful dress which somehow managed to avoid eccentricity, despite being intensely individual. Her hair too had a wonderful sheen on it. He approved and yet disliked the metamorphosis at the same time. He was acutely aware he might not have weathered half so well and that Jennifer would be bound to notice. That was if she intended to take any further notice of him at all, which he doubted. He could tell by the way she entered the house, marching straight in like that, speaking to the dog and scooping up the cat, then calling out to him to come straight in too, while she poked her head round the kitchen door to say hello to Sue, that she was at home here, amongst what he immediately recognised as the hand-made Third World paraphernalia of rugs and hessian, jute and cane and a certain rampant, hanging greenery; and that she was accepted and valued, maybe even loved, for herself. He was the outsider and he began to resent it.

'Dominic . . . this is Phil, Sue's husband. Frances and Derek. Sue's sister, Marge. Dominic Grant, everyone. I'll just see if Sue needs any help in the kitchen while Phil fixes you a drink.'

Thus intimidated and then deserted, Dominic mentally shook himself and began to rise to the occasion.

'How's it going?' hissed Sue, giving the casserole a stir.

'All right, now. But it was a bit sticky at first. That looks nice.

'I told you it was best to pick him up, didn't I? God, the soup's boiling over! Can you rescue it, Jen? You do see what I mean, don't you . . . about him?'

'Well, not really,' said Jennifer. 'At least not yet.'

'You will,' said Sue grimly.

By the end of the evening she had to admit that she did. There seemed to be something about the assembled company which brought out the very worst in Dominic. She could have sworn that even the public school accent became more pronounced. Why did he have to do that? He lost his diffidence with the first drink and increased in confidence with each one thereafter. Before dinner, Jennifer sat quietly opposite and secretly admired the flow of urbanity and charm, though she could see Sue looking reprovingly at her whenever she laughed at his jokes. He was still the most charming man she had ever met, when he wanted to be. She was fully aware that his eyes were on hers all the time and his performance was at least partly for her benefit.

But then, when they had sat down, his attitude seemed to change and he appeared to virtually ignore her. He continued to talk and became increasingly assertive as his wineglass emptied . . . far more quickly, Jennifer noticed, than anyone else's . . . she was sensitive to such things, having once done the same. But it hurt to see it in Dominic. Sue need not have worried about having Jennifer to supply feeder questions. Dominic talked all the time now. In fact, he was slowly becoming obnoxious, just as Sue had said he would.

'And what do you do?' he asked Jennifer eventually, after Marge had managed to get in something about her social work and Frances had revealed that she was a teacher. (Derek and Phil had long since struck up a private conversation about climbing)

'Oh . . . lots of things,' Jennifer said quietly, toying with her food.

'Such as?'

You pig, she thought. Not to pick up the vibes. You, of all people, should know I didn't realise my full potential and am not particularly proud of it. But she was determined not to be browbeaten.

'Well, I bring up two girls for a start.' She wanted to explain about Suzy's handicap but it hardly seemed fair when she only had her at the weekends anyway. They were mother and daughter again, despite the odds and she was proud of that, but could hardly broadcast it to the dinner-table.

'And I help Sue with the shop.'

Under the pressure of his masculinity, she imagined it did sound rather pathetic.

'And I paint.'

He didn't pursue the topic and Jennifer felt put down until Sue broke in.

'Hardly a harmless hobby, I might add. Jennifer has three paintings in this year's exhibition of local artists. Have you seen them?'

'No, I haven't.'

'Well, you should. They're quite exceptional. No, Jennifer, don't mumble self-deprecatingly, you're far too modest. They're amazing.'

'I'll go and see them first thing tomorrow morning,' he promised.

'Do!' Sue stabbed with her fork triumphantly and grinned at Jennifer. She had been determined not to let that one pass.

But Jennifer continued to look rather miserable. Sue was worried about her. She was far too quiet and had hardly eaten a thing. Surely she couldn't still be affected by this dreadful man? Naturally Sue had seated them together, but now she began to see that it might all be the most dreadful mistake. Jenny was, after all, a bit of a mystery. She had always surprised Sue. When they had first met at a play-group, drawn together by the compulsory baby-minding activities, she had been shy and quiet. No, that wasn't right . . . reserved and private were more accurate words. Then Sue had discovered Jennifer's artistic talent and done all she could to help and encourage her, drawn even more by Jennifer's domestic circumstances. It was a long time before she had found out the story behind Jennifer's obvious medical knowledge which she normally took pains to hide. She was certainly a remarkable person and Sue felt perennially guilty that she let her 'help in the shop'. But, on the other hand, she had helped get those paintings into the exhibition, which Jennifer was thrilled about on the quiet. And she was very fond of Jenny. Enough to worry now.

It was not that Jennifer hung on his every word nor failed to challenge him occasionally. She was too intelligent for that. But there was something . . . Take the way she had mopped up the mess when he had knocked her glass of wine all over the tablecloth, telling him not to worry and claiming it was really her fault anyway, when everyone could see that it definitely was not. It seemed to Sue that they looked into each other's eyes a little too directly at that point and Jennifer smiled rather too tenderly, with Dominic the first to look away. Sue was so worried that she allowed herself to become embroiled in a political argument with Dominic afterwards, which was stupid, because she knew that Jennifer didn't agree with all her views and would therefore sympathise with him. But she felt compelled to show him up somehow. The heat was almost tangible as they both became increasingly bitter. Marge weighed in on Sue's side while Jennifer and Frances strove unsuccessfully to change the subject and keep the peace.

By the time they got round to coffee, Jennifer was feeling exhausted. 'I shall have to go,' she said, when she had gulped down the hot liquid. 'It's five to twelve.'

'Oh, must you?' said Dominic, airily. 'Like Cinderella?

How wonderfully dramatic and terribly boring!' He had recovered some of his composure since the argument, but appeared to have a certain amount of difficulty in standing up.

'Babysitting problems, you know,' said Jennifer firmly.

Of course he wouldn't know and could therefore be relied upon also not to know what a wonderful excuse it could be.

'I'm sorry . . . I really must go. But it was lovely to see you again and I wish you every success with the new book.'

She stuck her hand out a little awkwardly and he bowed his head over it in an exaggerated fashion, which alarmed her, because she thought for a moment he was going to kiss her fingers, though he stopped short of that.

'Sue . . . a lovely dinner! Thank you so much. No, don't get up, Phil, I can see myself out, I don't want to break things up. Goodnight everyone!'

But Sue followed her onto the doorstep and out into the drive.

'Thanks, Jennifer.'

'It was a pleasure.'

Jennifer got in her car and fumbled with the keys.

'No, it wasn't! It was a bit of an ordeal and I'm sorry.'

'Nothing to be sorry about. It was a good evening and a super dinner though I didn't do it justice.'

'Be honest, Jen! It was a bloody disaster and I'm not talking about the food!'

Jennifer grimaced. 'Yes, well . . . never mind. We've done our duty. Both of us. I hope you don't mind me not taking him back to his hotel. I'm not sure I could cope with that.'

'I wouldn't let you do it, don't worry! No, we'll get him a taxi shortly and shovel him into it somehow. Are you very upset?'

'A bit.'

'He could have come to the door at least.'

'I don't think he would have made it, do you? Anyway,

why should he? What there was between us is ancient history now. We've both changed.'

'You ought to talk about it, you know. Why don't you come back when he's gone?'

'Oh, Sue! I really couldn't! I'm awfully tired. You're ever so kind but I don't really need that. I'm not that upset.' And she started her car, then backed carefully into the road, pausing to wave cheerfully before driving off.

'Why don't I believe you?' Sue wondered aloud.

When Jennifer got home, her cottage was silent and empty. Through force of habit she visited the girls' room before her own, although she knew the beds were empty. Only toy animals returned her gaze and mobiles swung in the dark. She felt strange, as if she had lost a limb and regretted her decision to send them to Beth's.

In her own room, she sat down heavily in front of the dressing-table mirror. It was over then. Just as she had hoped it would be. With no repercussions and no alarming discoveries or revelations. Just a nasty flat feeling because she was unlikely to see Dominic ever again and hadn't it all been an illusion anyway? Oh, but how she had loved him! She couldn't ever love so uncritically again. Not a man, at any rate. Not even Dominic. Only a child. Their affair had been part of her youth, that was all, and Beth had been so right. But she should have let me find out the hard way, Jennifer told herself. Because the chemistry's still there. He still makes me feel slightly breathless and my heart definitely did something abnormal when he came into the room, even though it mainly felt like fear. He wasn't entirely unaffected either . . . I could tell that by his eyes. If only he hadn't been so incredibly awful at dinner . . . If only. But that, she told herself firmly, was precisely what Sue wanted to demonstrate and very effective it had been. It had opened her eyes and he would never deceive her again. Still, she didn't feel very good about it. Was that how you were supposed to feel when you laid a ghost?

At first she thought the telephone had to be a child crying, though the sound wasn't right. It was still very dark and the bedroom furniture blended into the background, not even a collection of humps. It was cold too and she wished she had thought to put on her dressing-gown before stumbling downstairs. It must be Beth. One of the children . . .

'Jennifer? It's Dominic.'

She was instantly relieved. 'Dominic! But what time is it?'

'About half past four.'

'What? In the morning? Whatever's the matter? Are you ill?'

'No, of course not. I just had to speak to you. I'm sorry . . . I know it's awful. I hoped you had a bedside phone.'

'Erm . . . well, no I don't. I'm not even properly awake yet. Good grief, Dominic! Do you always make your phone-calls in the middle of the night?'

'I'm sorry. I know it's unforgivable. But I couldn't sleep and I couldn't leave things as they were.'

'You couldn't sleep? I would have thought the alcohol would have seen you through till lunchtime at least!'

'It wears off quickly with me. Jenny, I want to apologise.'

'That's all right.' Jennifer pushed her hair out of her eyes sleepily. 'You don't have to ask me how much you can drink at a dinner party. If you want to get pickled . . . '

'I didn't mean about the booze . . . I'm talking about being a pompous ass.'

Jennifer smiled into the phone, fully awake now. 'Ah! You were aware of it, then?'

'I want you to understand why. First there was the talk. I hate those things, I really do. Especially as a stand-in as you so neatly put it. I bet there weren't more than three or four people in that room who'd actually read any of the damn books. They'd just come along to gawp at a writer and hear him making a fool of himself.'

'You're far too sensitive!'

' . . . and then there was you. It was a bit of a shock you know, to put it mildly. Seeing you again. You felt it too, I know . . . at least you did at first. And then you suddenly became so bloody self-assured and contained and handled it all so well . . . not to mention looking marvellous into the bargain. You kept me on the end of a barge-pole and I couldn't bear that.'

'I didn't!'

'You did, you know!'

'Well, I didn't feel that self-assured, I can tell you!'

'It didn't show. Then there was your ghastly feminist friend with her tame husband and clone sister and those other awful people . . . '

'Dominic! You're supposed to be apologising . . . '

'I am, but to you, not to them.'

'Well, just be careful, will you? I'm very fond of Sue!'

'I'm just trying to explain why I behaved as I did. I know I talked too much, I know I went over the top about everything. I always do when I'm nervous.'

'And sometimes when you're not!'

There was a silence at the other end of the phone.

'Dommy,' Jennifer said more gently, 'are you still there?'

'Yes. Why did you call me that?'

'Oh, I don't know,' Jennifer smoothed her nightie over her knees. 'It just came out. Old habits die hard, I suppose.'

'Am I an old habit?'

'Can I go back to bed now? It was nice of you to apologise.'

'Can I come and see you? I hate the telephone. We haven't said that much to each other after twelve years.'

'Oh, I don't know, Dominic . . . I'm busy tomorrow. I have to pick the children up from Beth's for a start . . . '

'I didn't mean tomorrow. I meant now.'

'Are you mad or still drunk? It's the middle of the night!'

'Please, Jenny! I have to get the early morning train back to London tomorrow . . . today, I mean. So I shan't stay long. And we are both awake. I can't go back without seeing you again.'

'Oh, all right then. I don't suppose I could go back to sleep again now, anyway.'

'Where do you live?'

She told him, then hung up and immediately panicked. What a fool thing to do! Better by far to have left matters as they were . . . unsatisfactory and blighted by disillusionment. At least he had apologised. Now he would turn on the old charm. Glancing wildly into a mirror, she decided he should not find her in a nightie and dashed upstairs to put something else on. She found she was shivering and chose a track-suit for warmth and convenience. She combed her hair and cleaned her teeth because she felt sluttish. No make-up though. Let him see her as she really was.

When she let him in, she had the absurd impression he was about to step forward and kiss her, so much so that she actually put her hand on his chest to stop him.

'Be careful! That barge-pole is still there. I don't trust you.'

He raised his hands in desperation as if to show they were clean. Perhaps he had only meant to touch her arm or her shoulder instead. He had always done that. It didn't mean that much.

'Come in and sit down. Would you like some coffee?'

'Please.'

She noticed that, despite the hour and the after-effects of drink, he was wearing a clean shirt and a pair of bright yellow trousers and generally looked much fresher than before, as if he had showered and shaved.

'How do you like your coffee these days?'

He grimaced.

'Well, at the moment I'll have it strong and black with about three sugars in.'

'Ugh! Sure you wouldn't like a can of treacle instead?

Oh, all right then, I don't feel that brilliant myself, so heavens knows what you feel like. I'm still surprised you're not out cold.'

'Please don't moralise.'

'I'm not.'

The ground floor of Jennifer's cottage was open plan and so she could see him easily through the divider between kitchen and lounge as she made the coffee. He didn't sit down but walked around restlessly, looking at pictures and books and turning down the gas-fire which she had on full blast.

'Hey!' she remonstrated. 'I was cold.'

'But not now, surely?'

'No. But I'm not at all sure I like you walking into my life rearranging the cushions and the heating system all of a sudden. I'm a bachelor now as well, you know.'

He came through to the kitchen with a smile. 'I never touched the cushions.'

'You know very well what I mean. Here's your coffee.'

'Thanks . . . it's too hot . . . I'll leave it on the side for a bit.'

Jennifer added some milk to hers and drank it gratefully. Where did they go from here? Dominic was looking at the easel she had left out to dry by the utility sink, with her latest painting upon it. He stared at it so long she became nervous.

'Well, tell me what you think. I commented on your books.'

'It's good.'

'You don't have to be *that* polite. *I* wasn't.'

'All right. It's bloody good! Your feminist friend actually knew what she was talking about.'

'Please don't call her that!'

'Fashionable to deny it now, isn' it? But of course she is . . . it sticks out a mile and I'm certainly not talking about her tits.'

'I told you,' said Jennifer, coldly. 'I like Sue very much. Which is more than I can say for you at the moment.'

'Would you sell someone you disliked one of your paintings?'

Jennifer looked at her picture. Her imagined title was 'Tunnel of Trees' for that is what it was. An empty ribbon of road stretched back into the distance and was covered by an archway of trees. It was far less surrealistic than her earlier paintings and the lighting and the detail of the green leaves was true to life. But the tree-trunks and the branches were incredibly gnarled and knotted and there was a definite and disturbing element of menace about it. As you looked you became uneasy and looked again.

'I'd like this one,' Dominic said.

'It's not quite finished,' Jennifer said. 'But of course you can have it when it is. As a present. Something to remember me by.'

Dominic pulled a tall stool up to Jennifer's breakfast bar and tried his coffee again.

'That sounds terribly final.'

'Well, you did say you had to go back to London.'

'Yes . . . but I may come back. I like this area. I wouldn't mind a cottage here, to write in during the summer. Maybe winter weekends as well. I'm not really tied to London you know. Would you help me find one, Jenny?'

She stared at him crossly. 'What on earth are you playing at, Dominic? You don't belong here.'

'It was an innocent enough remark. I don't see why you're so hostile.'

'Don't you?'

'No. Can't we be friends?'

'Not if we see each other at half past four in the morning we can't!'

'It's after five now and this is an exceptional case.'

'Why did you have to come, Dominic?'

'I told you.'

'And?'

'All right!' He stared moodily into space. 'If you must have utter honesty . . . I felt like hell and I wanted you badly, needed to have you with me. Can't you understand that? I suppose I wanted to sleep with you too, if you let me. Can I have some more coffee now, please?'

Jennifer took his mug and filled it.

'That's better,' she said. 'Honest if incredibly presumptuous.'

'I said if you let me.'

'But what on earth are you doing, Dominic? You know I'm divorced . . . Like the lady said, you are a leading Catholic writer now, aren't you? So exactly what are you playing at?'

Dominic took off the glasses she found so disconcerting and rubbed the bridge of his nose with one hand. He looked desperately tired and she felt a sudden rush of sympathy for him.

'I haven't the slightest idea,' he said, more quietly. 'For the first . . . no, the second time in my life, I know exactly what I want and I still can't have it.'

Jennifer turned away to the sink with her coffee cup, so she no longer had to look at him.

'You can't still love me, Dominic. You really can't! Not after all this time.' She was dimly aware that she still loved him, but that was different.

'Why not? I didn't marry anyone else.'

'There must have been others.'

'There were. Quite a few. I behaved abominably to most of them, so of course they left me in the end. Too bloody selfish, I suppose. You were the only one who got behind that.'

'But you don't know me now,' Jennifer pointed out. 'A lot's happened in twelve years. I've done some terrible things. My first daughter was born handicapped and I left her in the hospital, although I look after her now. I gave up on my marriage, long before the divorce. I even tried to kill myself once, and that's the biggest sin of all in your church, isn't it?'

'Thank God you didn't die!'

'I haven't altered my agnostic views, either. I really couldn't feel very sympathetic towards your Catholic point of view. Take the divorce question . . . it's just ridiculous, to my mind!'

'I still love you.'

'Have you listened to a word I've been saying?'

'Yes . . . to all of them. But we don't always feel as we should.'

Jennifer finished rinsing her mug and put it on the draining-board. She turned round with a sigh and was surprised to find Dominic standing right behind her.

'I realise I haven't come out of this very well,' he said. 'In any way you care to name. If you want me to, I'll go now for that train.'

Jennifer raised her hands and put them on his shoulders.

'You're a fool, Dominic,' she said gently. 'And you used to be so confident and sure about everything. But I do still love you, if it's any consolation. I don't want you to go at all. She ran a hand through his soft yellow hair, which she had been longing to do, ever since the episode in the Mini. He kissed her and they held onto each other tightly, till Jennifer levered herself away.

'You can stay,' she said. 'It's your decision this time. Always a flaw in the relationship, isn't there? But this time there needn't be. It's up to you. Don't expect me to feel guilty about your principles when they're not mine.'

But of course it wasn't so simple as that. Fragments of their conversation kept on recurring to Jennifer during the following week, after Dominic had gone back to London. He had missed more than one train as they had spent the morning in bed together with an inevitable renewal of passion. Joy was there somewhere, in the middle of a frantic lust, but it was buried deep in the end by too many layers of intensity and longing. The abandon of the old days was gone. It was almost too meaningful now. Dominic seemed half-crazy for her while Jennifer couldn't believe her earlier pretence at indifference. She would now jump out of the window with informed consent. But they weren't in Liverpool any more and in the grey but lightening dawn, lying there clasping each other's hands, they were both alternately cruel and noble.

'Why did you have to marry him?' Dominic had asked.

'Why did you never come back?'

'I did. After some time, I know. Your landlady told me you were moving out at the weekend and engaged to be married. It hadn't taken you very long. That hurt.'

'Over two years, Dominic! And you never answered my letters. Not once. One word would have been enough to stop me. But you were much too proud, weren't you?'

'Did you love him?'

'I don't know. Not like us.'

'You don't know!'

'I thought I did, then I knew I didn't, then later on I wasn't sure any more. You won't understand . . . you've never been married. Anyway, it wasn't at all like us. But I can't regret it, Dominic. I couldn't ever regret the children. Tell me why you hate Sue so much? A lot of the things she's into are very laudable, you know.'

'Oh, Jennifer, I know they are! Don't think I don't. She's probably a much better person than I am. I can't explain it. It's just a feeling I get that that sort of person is altogether too obvious and smug, as if they'd solved all the world's problems already, or would have, if it wasn't for reactionary old sods like me. I don't want to talk about Sue . . . I want to talk about us.'

'It was important. And so is the Church, of course. I was wrong when I said I wouldn't feel guilty. I shall, of course. Because I love you, your guilt will become mine. So I have to at least try to understand. Tell me why you went back to the Church. You were so cutting once . . . about all the relics and the rosaries and the endless saints. I can't believe you've gone back to believing in all *that*!'

'No, of course I haven't! But those things don't really matter, you know . . . they're just peripheral aids . . . they're not important. It was about the time my mother died . . .'

'I thought it might have been.'

'Not because I hoped she would go to heaven. Not at all. Not to comfort myself. I should hate you to think that. No. But I became aware of a spirituality and a goodness in her which gave her strength through all the horrible things she had to go through. And I didn't have that. Or at least, I might have had it once but I had deliberately turned away and denied it. Now I wanted it again.'

'Isn't wanting it rather different to really believing in it? We'd all quite like it to be true. I'm sorry . . . go on.'

'No, I'm not sure that it is. How can you believe if you don't lay yourself open to spiritual possibilities? That's what faith really is, you know, not being 100 per cent damn sure you're right and the others are wrong.'

'Hmm . . . well, some other Catholics wouldn't agree with you there, would they? Look at the Pope, for heaven's sake! Anyway I don't think you need to go to church to believe a spiritual existence of some kind is important.'

'There I have to disagree . . . you can't be serious about it otherwise. It wouldn't be the same.'

'Does it *have* to be Catholicism?'

'It does for me. Not for everyone of course. I suppose the 'J's at school left their mark after all. Or maybe it's the power of my mother's prayers for her wayward son. I don't know. But it is important to me, Jennifer. I'm not a very good Catholic, nor very orthodox, I know. But it matters.'

'I can see that. Everything always was important to you anyway. Do you have to obey all the silly rules?'

'You know that I do. I shall have to tell you all of it. When I became aware I was unlikely to get married, I thought about becoming a priest for a while. So I went into the doctrine pretty thoroughly. I didn't really have a vocation though. Not at all like Giles. I'm far too intolerant. So I gave that idea up.'

'I wouldn't have thought tolerance a terribly important qualification for a Catholic priest!' Jennifer's tone was contemptuous and he folded her in his arms again at that, stroking her hair as it lay against his bare body.

'Don't be angry! You wouldn't love me so much if I wasn't a Catholic now. There might only be the bit left you don't like.'

She knew it was true. She had loved him back in Liverpool in the days when she had hung onto his every word without question and he had continually shocked and delighted her. But this was different. They were both older and he was unimaginably quieter and more serious behind the affectations than he appeared to be. Altogether more fallible and aware of his fallibility. It was not that it gave her a sense of power, but she felt she understood him better. Understood? How could she say that when his religion was anathema to her?

'I can see that you could never publicly marry me,' she said. 'But you've done nothing wrong. You came first. You even asked me to marry you first. Couldn't we just live together, as we did before?'

He shook his head. 'But I didn't marry you first. It would still be technical adultery. You are another man's wife.'

'That's rubbish!' She pushed him away and sat up in bed, with a flaming face. 'That's a positively unChristian thing to believe and you know it. How can you be so harsh when Mike left me for somebody else? That's adultery . . . you don't know a bloody thing about it, but I do!' She was trembling with her emotion.

'It was you who said you gave up long before . . . you didn't want him to want you,' Dominic said quietly.

Jennifer caught her breath sharply 'All right, I admitted it! Is that so very wrong? Do I have to have it round my neck for the rest of my life? Don't preach to me, Dominic, with your bloody high ideals! I had to survive.'

'I don't mean to preach . . . I'm just trying to put the Catholic point of view.'

'Which you do most eloquently!' Jennifer couldn't stop the spiral of sarcasm and bitterness now. 'Most of them would probably go ahead and not confess it anyway, but not you, of course, oh no . . . you're much too high-minded for that, aren't you? Except you couldn't quite manage to stay out of my bed.'

'Jennifer, please don't!'

'Why not? You're doing your damnedest to break *my* heart! I don't seem to count for very much at all in any of this. I was doing very nicely without you, thanks, but you were determined to push your way back into my life. Now I've told you that I love you still and it doesn't seem to count for anything.'

'Of course it does!'

'How do I know? How do I know this isn't just your bloody way of taking your revenge on me because I let you down all those years ago?'

'Because . . . ' his voice sounded strangled, ' . . . because you *do* know.'

He got out of bed suddenly and reached for his clothes.

'Where are you going?'

'To get dressed . . . in the bathroom.'

Jennifer sat with the duvet hunched round her knees and tried to stop shaking. By the time he came back, she was calmer.

'I'm sorry I had to hurt you . . . again,' she said.

'It's all right. You were perfectly justified.' He took the hand she held out and squeezed it.

'Nevertheless, I shan't say any of those things again. Strangely enough, I do respect you, Dominic. I just wish I didn't always have to fall for men who don't share my own views and that it didn't always have to be so crucial! If you weaken, Dominic, and God knows I want you to, I shall feel guilty after all . . . and grateful. I should love you and care for you, all right . . . it would be a little like Willie and Chloe all over again. Do you know what I'm talking about?'

'Vaguely.'

'My grandparents. And my mother. And being a failure. I thought I'd got rid of all that guilt for good. But now here you are landing me with another load.'

'No!' Dominic touched her cheek. 'It isn't your fault. You were quite right the first time. It's my problem'.

'And what are you going to do?'

'Go back to London. Think. Maybe see Giles.'

'That won't do any good,' said Jennifer quickly. She longed to snatch him out of their grasp, although she knew it was wrong.

'I know what he'll say, if that's what you mean.'

'Shall I see you again?'

'Oh yes, whatever happens. I can't go away and forget you exist like before. It was bad enough the last time.'

'I can't be your friend, Dommy.'

'No.'

She pulled on her track-suit and they went downstairs together.

'I didn't mean it,' she said, as they held onto each other tightly at the door. 'I didn't mean it when I said I couldn't be your friend . . . Of course I would be, if that's what you wanted. I know I'm weakening my case now, but don't forget.'

'Jennifer! Phone-call for you.'

It was mid-week in the shop.

'Who is it?'

'Dominic Grant.'

'Oh!'

Sue watched disapprovingly as Jennifer leapt up as if stung and dashed to the phone. 'Dominic! How are you?'

'I'm fine. How are you?'

'Dreadfully worried about you.'

'You mustn't be. Listen, Jenny . . . I've got hold of the details of a cottage from an estate agent, up in the Dales . . . ' and he named a place some distance from

Bickley. 'I thought I'd come up at the weekend and take a look. Would you come with me? I need your advice.'

Jennifer took a deep breath. 'Is it a cottage for one?' she asked brightly.

'Probably, yes. I'm sorry, Jennifer. It's not that I don't love you . . . I'll never love anyone else more . . .'

She cut him off midstream, not wanting to hear the 'but'.

'I understand . . . sort of. It's what I expected anyway. But you don't really need my advice then, do you?' She said it with what she hoped was a deliberate lack of malice. Dominic sounded relieved.

'Oh, but I do! You know what an impractical fellow I am.'

Jennifer laughed.

'That's true,' she said. Paradoxically, it was one of the reasons she loved him the most. 'All right, then. But, if it's the weekend, I shall have both girls. The ambience will be entirely different!'

'That's OK. I'd like to meet them. Shall I pick you up Saturday morning then?'

'Yes, I'll look forward to it.'

'Bye, then.'

'Bye.'

She returned from the phone with an amused smile on her face. Of course she should be devastated by his decision but you couldn't embrace suffering all of the time. Finality hadn't sunk in yet. After all, he was coming back . . .

Sue gave her a frosty look.

'What's the matter?'

'Nothing.'

'Yes, there is . . . have I made some kind of mistake?'

'Huh!' Sue raised her eyebrows. 'You said it!'

'What?'

'You're seeing him again, aren't you? Dominic Grant. Not only that, but you've fallen for him again, too.'

'Oh! I thought you were talking about something in the

shop! Yes, I am seeing him again.'

'I can't tell you how much I regret asking you to that dinner party.'

'Oh, Sue! It isn't your fault. I would have gone to his talk anyway and then had to stay and make myself known. If anything, the dinner party rather slowed things down.'

'Is it serious?'

'It's not exactly lighthearted.'

'But you're not really in love with him?'

'Oh, I've always been in love with Dominic. Somehow our lives seem to have been welded together.'

'But that was all in the past! You were both so young . . . you can't possibly hold on to that sort of thing now. You can't recapture it.'

'No, I know. It is different now. More complicated. But better.'

Sue groaned. 'But you saw the way he behaved at dinner! He was arrogant and pompous and boorish and drank too much and . . .'

'Yes, I know. Like you said, I was there too.'

'Well then?'

'He didn't mean to be like that. It was rather a consequence of playing the great writer, you know.'

'Don't tell me he isn't really like that. I couldn't bear it!'

'No. Well, of course he is sometimes. But I understand why.'

'He'll swallow you up. You'll never get a painting into the Royal Academy now! And anyway, there's the Catholic business, isn't there?'

'Indeed there is,' Jennifer said wearily.

'He won't be able to marry you in his sodding church. What's he going to do?'

'I don't think even he really knows.'

'He'll keep you on a string for years.'

'Possibly.'

'How can you be content to be his doormat?'

'I wouldn't have put it like that, but I did tell you . . . I love him.' Jennifer began to feel annoyed.

But Sue became even more acid. 'I had a motto in a Christmas cracker last year I thought was very apt. It said: 'Love is like a dew-drop in the morning sun.' Sounds pretty, doesn't it?'

'But it dries up awfully quickly?'

'Quite.'

'This has been going on a good few years.'

'But not really, Jennifer! Unfortunately, you never did marry him. Otherwise the whole thing would have degenerated as it's bound to do. You never really got him out of your system.'

'Yes, that's probably very true.'

'Then why are you being so blinkered?'

'Oh Sue, I don't know! Why did you marry Phil?'

'Philip is quite a different sort of man.'

Jennifer sighed. 'No disrespect Sue, but I wouldn't be attracted to a man like Phil. We're all different.'

'Can't you see my relationship with Phil has thrown off the old sexual shackles and that's a good thing?'

'Frankly, no.'

'I don't understand you, Jennifer. I really thought you had more sense! I felt sorry for you when we first met, then admired you, even envied you a little . . .'

'Oh, you did, did you? You don't really know much about my kind of life at all!'

'I know some women never learn. They're their own worst enemies, despite what the womens' movement has done for them. And now you start acting in the same crazy way.'

Jennifer seethed. She had to remind herself very firmly that Sue had been kind.

'I don't suppose I can count on you in the shop any more now,' said Sue. 'You might as well not bother coming in.'

Jennifer couldn't believe it. 'You mean you're giving me the sack?' she said. 'Because of Dominic? That's ridiculous!'

'There's no need to make a scene.'

'I see. Would you like me to go now, then?'

'The end of the morning will do.'

It was absurd. Jennifer told herself that all morning. Unreasonable. Spiteful even. She kept expecting Sue to apologise and retract her ultimatum but nothing happened. Sue closeted herself in the back room instead. Finally Jennifer chose a quiet moment and plonked herself in front of the desk.

'You've no right to call Dominic arrogant,' she said. 'That's sheer hypocrisy at the moment.' No answer. 'Of course I can see your point. It is difficult . . . perhaps impossible, to equate two people's needs in a relationship. If there is any love at all, someone probably ends up giving in a little more.'

'They do with that sort of man.'

'In your own case,' said Jennifer coldly, 'Philip seems to have rather a lot of giving in to do.' She had done it now. Sue looked up and glowered. 'I'm not saying that's wrong. But your line about sexual shackles is bull. You haven't thrown them off, Sue . . . you've just tried to transfer them.'

'I'm very busy, Jennifer. If you want your cards now, you can have them. I've only been trying to warn you . . . advise you against making a mistake. You'll regret it, I know.'

'I wonder. It doesn't really matter. I've stood on the sidelines far too long, you know. Letting other people make decisions for me. It's time to accept the apple now, rotten or not.' For some reason, she thought of the statue which had always horrified her on the wall of the church in Liverpool – the one with the straining metal innards – and added: 'It's time to leap off the wall.'

'You're better off as you are.'

'Indubitably. But I'm not sure that comes into it, either. It's not necessarily what life's about.'

'It seems to be about repeating mistakes in your case.'

'Or perhaps realising why you have to.'

'You can stay till the end of the month if you like.'
'Thank you.'
But five minutes later, Jennifer was back. 'No,' she said. 'I'd rather go now. If it's all the same to you.'
'Please yourself,' Sue said sourly.

'Do you like it?' asked Dominic.
Jennifer smiled.
'I can see why you do,' she said.
It was yet another glorious autumn day. Still, sunny and peaceful. The kind of day when little boys all over the country would throw up sticks into chestnut trees to bring spiky green conkershells tumbling down. But there weren't many trees up here. The wind was whispering over the moor now but in the winter it would howl and moan.
'It does have something,' Dominic said, 'and the view is terrific.'
Jennifer looked down at the small, stone-built cottage, so uncompromisingly off the beaten track.
'Dominic,' she said firmly. 'The roof is falling in. There's no central heating and the yard is full of hen-muck. The rooms are tiny and I couldn't begin to tell you what's wrong with the kitchen.'
'But could you live here?'
She drew in her breath sharply. 'I could clout you, I really could! You don't mean that.'
He took her hand. 'Oh, but I do. I don't think I can give you up.'
'You wouldn't be able to receive communion ever again.'
'No.'
'Your God would excommunicate you.'
'Perhaps. I'd still go to Mass.'
'When did you decide this?'
'When I saw the house.'
'Oh! Then you'll change your mind fifty times before tomorrow.'

'Maybe.'

'But you'll never go away entirely?'

'No. But you haven't answered my question. Could you live here, if I asked you to?'

'I suppose if I had a Land Rover and a pair of skis to get down to the village in winter, I could,' she said, facetiously.

'You must like something about it.'

'Oh, but I do,' she said more softly. 'I could paint the sky. On a canvas as big as a wall. The clouds going back over the hill . . . I've always wanted to do that.'

'I'll buy you the most enormous canvas.'

'But it wouldn't go in the house!'

She took his arm and they walked back down to the cottage for one last look.

'Promise me you'll get a survey done,' she said.

'Whatever for? We know it's falling down already.'

'Dominic!'

'All right, I'm only joking! But I'm sure you could transform it. You're taste is better than mine.'

'That's true.' She grinned and looked down at his trousers. They were purple today and they had a zip just below the knee with a motif which said: 'Open me, please,' and she couldn't believe that he could be so intelligent and yet so puerile at the same time.

'The girls like it,' Dominic went on. 'Look!'

Jennifer watched them running round and screaming excitedly, up and down the bumpy grassland in front of the house . . . you could hardly call it a garden. Dominic had been an instant hit. She had seen that straightaway with considerable relief. He wasn't the type of man to resent them. He had insisted they all call him 'Dommy' when he had realised Suzy couldn't get her toungue round 'Dom-in-ic'. To everyone else the diminutive was 'Nic' but they were allowed the old pet-name. Then he had carried Suzy all the way up the hill to the cottage. Her heart condition had turned out to be more complicated than the doctors had originally thought and she became tired and breathless fairly easily. Jennifer could see that Suzy, with her unreserved and open little personality, had immediately fallen in love. Dammit! She could even begin to see Dominic in a domestic role, despite his professed bachelorhood. Funnily enough, the agonies of family life would suit him very well. He might claim to be intolerant with adults but would let children crawl all over him. She could picture him, still in a pair of ghastly trousers no doubt, long-suffering but happy on the beach. For a moment she wondered if that new family could ever take their adoptive father's guilt away.

'It isn't so bad,' said Dominic. 'It's only the roof. The girls could have animals . . . freedom, space . . .'

'However would you cut all that grass? You'd need a tractor,' said Jennifer. 'And anyway, two artists should never live together. We wouldn't speak for days.'

'Would that matter?'

'Don't you think you should look at something else first?'

'But I like this one!'

'Of course it's up to you.' She squeezed his hand. 'Dominic, I've lost my job.'

'Because of me?'

'I think so. It was all rather silly because I believe I could have got it back, if I'd tried a bit harder. We had quite an argument.'

'I'm sorry. I told you she was awful.'

'No, she isn't. She just sees things differently that's all. Everything in black and white. I still rather admire her, though I could never be like that myself.'

'What will you do?'

'I'm not sure. I was going to have Suzy home every day soon, too. I may have to put that off for a while now, if I manage to get a new job. Perhaps I shan't.'

'Hmm . . . I don't suppose living up here would help that either. Getting a job, I mean, not Suzy, she's a poppet.'

'You really are thinking seriously about it, then?'

'Would you come?'

'Yes, you know I would . . . if you really wanted me to . . . even if it was only to type your manuscripts. I'm rather good at that sort of thing, you know. I shouldn't have told you, should I?'

He shook his head. 'I've made you very uncertain, haven't I? About my intentions. That must be awful and I'm sorry.' He looked as if he was about to go on, but she stopped him.

'You shouldn't decide today. Wait and think some more. I want to be convinced you really mean it, when you do decide.'

'But I can't expect you to wait indefinitely.'

'I'm not going anywhere. I'll still be here. Whenever you want me.'

They called the girls and wandered back to the car, slowly, with their arms linked together.

'It's a beautiful day,' said Dominic. 'Tonight will be crisp and clear with plenty of stars. Like the first night we met. Remember? At that awful party which Jocasta had dragged you to? With the Moody Blues music? That lovely song?'

'You always remember the right things, don't you?'

It crossed her mind that way down in the next valley, Bickley would also be basking in the sunshine, with a little colour still in the hanging-baskets down the main street. There would be life and civilisation of a sort in its wine-bars, its antique shops, its coffee-places and its expensive boutiques. Down there somewhere was Sue's bookshop and all her 'arty', friends as Beth had called them, not to mention her own hard-won cottage which she loved. But up here, in this place he had so obviously set his heart on, there was only Dominic and solitude and the sky. Could she really stand that, despite the love he had only half-promised to give her? Supposing they didn't get on that well? What if he wanted a child of his own, eventually? Was she really prepared to go through all that again? Yet she knew, if he asked her, she would.

'What are you thinking about?'

She smiled and patted his cheek playfully.

'Nothing much. Perhaps how very much I love you.'

'Only perhaps?'

'But of course. The estate agent's waiting . . .' She indicated the two cars at the bottom of the hill, Dominic's grey coupe and a blue BMW. 'Are you going to make him an offer?'

'But you said it was too hasty.'

'Never mind that. You'll never be anything other than impulsive, I hope.'

Still discussing the cottage, they wended their way down the hill, with the girls straggling a little way behind, and the grey stone house under the massive sky waited expectantly, with blank windows which alternately lightened and darkened as the clouds passed slowly overhead. They had left the gate to the garden open and it swung slightly to and fro, creaking a little in the wind.

We shall not cease from exploration
And the end of all our exploring
Will be to arrive where we started
And know the place for the first time,
Through the unknown, remembered gate . . .
T. S. Eliot

LITTLE GIDDING

INSTEAD OF EDEN

For Chloe there never seemed any means of escape from the emotional poverty and parochialism of a Yorkshire village. But Chloe is a victim of her own weak personality as well as the times in which she lives. Her daughter, Beth, is so determined not to repeat the pattern that she comes to deny the existence of love altogether. Her personal road to Eden is a cold and barren one. She pins her dreams on her daughter, Jennifer, who outwardly has all the advantages of a child in the prosperous and permissive sixties. But Beth watches in horror and disbelief as Jennifer plunges from one disaster to the next, oblivious to her daughter's confusion . . .

INSTEAD OF EDEN is a novel of almost painful sensitivity portraying the eternal struggle facing women held back by tradition but who yearn to be individuals.

ISBN 0-352-31846-5

9 780352 318466

UK: £3.50
CANADA: $8.75
NZ: $15.99
General Fiction